"If it comes to it, Longarm, do you think you could take on Ki?"

"It ain't *going* to come to it. There's no way that Ki would ever do anything to harm Jessie."

"I'm just asking 'what if,' Longarm," Stills replied.

"You ever handle dynamite?" Longarm asked. "It's funny stuff. Stable as all get-out, but when it gets warm, those familiar old sticks you've taken for granted can go up in your face..."

"In other words, you don't know the answer to my 'what if' question."

"In other words, I don't take dynamite for granted..."

Also in the LONGARM series
from Jove

LONGARM
LONGARM AND THE DRAGON
   HUNTERS
LONGARM AND THE RURALES
LONGARM ON THE HUMBOLDT
LONGARM IN NORTHFIELD
LONGARM AND THE GOLDEN LADY
LONGARM AND THE BOOT HILLERS
LONGARM AND THE BLUE NORTHER
LONGARM ON THE SANTA FE
LONGARM AND THE STALKING
   CORPSE
LONGARM AND THE COMANCHEROS
LONGARM AND THE DEVIL'S
   RAILROAD
LONGARM IN SILVER CITY
LONGARM ON THE BARBARY COAST
LONGARM AND THE MOONSHINERS
LONGARM IN YUMA
LONGARM IN BOULDER CANYON
LONGARM IN DEADWOOD
LONGARM AND THE GREAT TRAIN
   ROBBERY
LONGARM AND THE LONE STAR
   LEGEND
LONGARM IN THE BADLANDS
LONGARM IN THE BIG THICKET
LONGARM AND THE EASTERN
   DUDES
LONGARM IN THE BIG BEND
LONGARM AND THE SNAKE
   DANCERS
LONGARM ON THE GREAT DIVIDE
LONGARM AND THE BUCKSKIN
   ROGUE
LONGARM AND THE CALICO KID
LONGARM AND THE FRENCH
   ACTRESS
LONGARM AND THE OUTLAW
   LAWMAN

LONGARM AND THE LONE STAR
   VENGEANCE
LONGARM AND THE BOUNTY
   HUNTERS
LONGARM IN NO MAN'S LAND
LONGARM AND THE BIG OUTFIT
LONGARM AND SANTA ANNA'S
   GOLD
LONGARM AND THE CUSTER
   COUNTY WAR
LONGARM IN VIRGINIA CITY
LONGARM AND THE LONE STAR
   BOUNTY
LONGARM AND THE JAMES COUNTY
   WAR
LONGARM AND THE CATTLE BARON
LONGARM AND THE STEER
   SWINDLERS
LONGARM AND THE HANGMAN'S
   NOOSE
LONGARM AND THE OMAHA
   TINHORNS
LONGARM AND THE DESERT
   DUCHESS
LONGARM ON THE PAINTED DESERT
LONGARM ON THE OGALLALA
   TRAIL
LONGARM ON THE ARKANSAS
   DIVIDE
LONGARM AND THE BLIND MAN'S
   VENGEANCE
LONGARM AT FORT RENO
LONGARM AND THE DURANGO
   PAYROLL
LONGARM WEST OF THE PECOS
LONGARM ON THE NEVADA LINE
LONGARM AND THE BLACKFOOT
   GUNS
LONGARM ON THE SANTA CRUZ

TABOR EVANS

LONGARM

AND THE
LONE STAR RESCUE

A JOVE BOOK

LONGARM AND THE LONE STAR RESCUE

A Jove Book/published by arrangement with
the author

PRINTING HISTORY
Jove edition/June 1985

ISBN: 0-515-08250-3

PRINTED IN THE UNITED STATES OF AMERICA

Chapter 1

It was springtime in Texas, and the way the cowboys told it on the Lone Star State's north central plains, the site of the sprawling Circle Star spread, spring hereabouts had a way of coming around rip-roaringly, grassy green, as bountifully lush as the perfumed cleavage of a bona fide three-dollar whore. At this time of the year the cowboys boasted that the wildflowers dusting the Texas prairie were pretty enough to make the testiest of bulls frolic like a kitten, and the woodlots of pecan, walnut, and hickory set a fellow to using his gun butt for nothing worse than cracking those shells for the sweet nutmeats within, a welcome change of pace from range cook's grub.

And if that wasn't enough to gladden a cowboy's heart, there was this: although lately a drover's job had been hard to come by, with the advent of spring and roundup time, a wandering cowhand down on his luck could find a good-paying albeit temporary job cutting and branding cows prior to taking the beeves on the ever-shorter drive to the nearest railroad holding pen.

As acting ramrod for the Circle Star during spring roundup, Ki had heard all of the cowboys' laments: the stories of bobwire cutting and scarring the land, shackling the prairie's free-roving spirit like a lawman's handcuffs might shackle a rambunctious drover on a hell-raising, cowtown Saturday night. Ki had listened to the worried mutterings about the future. The old Texas cattle trails—the Chisholm, the Shawnee, the Goodnight-Loving—were falling into disuse as cattlemen saw little sense in walking the profits off their cattle, when their beeves could arrive fat and tender, the way Eastern steak-eaters liked them, via the railroad. What could they do about it? the men had wondered out loud during their early-morning and late-evening gatherings around the chuckwagon campfire. There was little point in a Texas cowboy heading north of the Red River, into that fierce, strange land of scowling Utah Mormons and Wyoming wranglers who scoffed at tried-and-true sons of Texas, just because they favored calling their headgear a sombrero instead of a hat, or said "lasso" instead of "rope"...

Ki had no answer for these disgruntled men, except that in 1880, as in the years before, a cowboy's life might be considered many things, but never easy.

Now, on this sunny April afternoon, three days into the roundup, Ki let the reins of his mount go slack, granting his sturdy cowpony the freedom to do its job. His horse was the product of much mixed breeding: it had the brash, ebullient soul of an untamed mustang, and the buckskin coloring—mustard tan, with black mane and tail—of the aristocratic Andalusian Arab stock. What the cowpony had most of all was intelligence; as with dogs, Ki believed that it was the mongrel that usually proved to be the cleverest of creatures, but of course, since Ki had had a Japanese mother and an American father, he would always have a warm place in his heart for creatures of mixed ancestry...

The samurai gently guided his mount with knee pressure alone, practicing *bajutsu,* the Japanese warrior's art of horsemanship that left one's hands free to handle weapons. Here on the Circle Star spread, during roundup, it amused Ki to see a home-grown variant of *bajutsu* being practiced by almost all of the cowboys. Any experienced hand knew enough to let his horse do most of the work, knew that the art of cutting a calf out of the herd for branding was an almost mystical duel, or dance, between pony and cow. The thing for a cowboy to do was go along quietly for the ride, the better to admire the awesome concentration shown by his horse.

Ki's buckskin, a veteran of previous roundups, was trem-

2

bling, and its ears were twitching as it intently closed on the oblivious calf trotting alongside its mother. Horse and rider moved as swiftly and silently through the vast, bawling Circle Star herd as a shark might glide through a turbulent sea. Swift, silent movement was the samurai's way, taught to Ki during his childhood in Japan, along with all of the other *bugei*, or techniques of the martial arts, by the master warrior Hirata, prior to the great man's death. Ki's samurai training aside, there was another reason, and to Western minds, likely a far more pragmatic one for swift, silent movement during roundup time.

It would not do to spook these cows, Ki and the other hands knew. Roundup could be dangerous indeed. As with people brought together into a mob, a transformation often occurred when cows were massed together into one large herd. They became prone to stampedes. The slightest disturbance—a snapped twig, a bird darting across the sky, a flaring match—could set them off on an often suicidal rampage.

As Ki's mount singled out the calf and began to urge it gently toward the edge of the herd, the samurai got his lasso ready. The calf broke free of the herd and began to run; then, suddenly realizing that it was all by its lonesome, it tried to wheel around the buckskin and back to the safety of the herd. Ki's mount swerved to block the calf, and then the little cowpony showed why it was worth its weight in gold during roundup time: the horse dipped its head and gave the mewling calf a nip on its hindquarters, sending it racing madly toward the branding fire. When the calf had come close enough to the work station, Ki set his lasso's loop twirling, and then used a side-armed, underhanded cast to slip the rope under the calf's hind legs. A soft twitch of his mount's reins, and his horse came to a stop. Meanwhile, Ki had taken up the lasso's slack with a few quick dallies of the excess around his saddlehorn, so that the calf quickly toppled over onto its side, no more than ten feet from where the branding irons were heating. Ki hopped down from his saddle, and quickly used a short length of rope jammed into

3

the back pocket of his jeans to hogtie the wild-eyed calf, totally immobilizing it. Then he watched as a cowboy approached, a branding iron in his gloved hand.

Usually Ki wore cloth slippers with rope soles, or else he went barefoot, for his feet were callused and tough from his years of martial-arts training. During the roundup, however, he wore boots because he often had to dig in his heels to reel tight a big, ornery, roped steer. Except for his boots, his garb was his usual working outfit: a pair of snug-fitting, well-broken-in denim jeans, a blousy pullover collarless shirt of cotton twill, and a loose, many-pocketed black leather vest. Ki went hatless, using a thin rawhide thong to keep his thick, shiny, blue-black hair out of his eyes during the dirty work of roundup. He wore no gun, but cached away in that innocent-seeming vest were all the weapons he usually required.

Ki glowered, his hands on his hips, as the cowboy began to bring the iron's business end to bear on the writhing calf's hindquarters. "Hold it," he ordered, and the cowboy froze without touching the calf. "That iron is white-hot!"

Rusty glanced at the iron, and then regarded Ki. "Sure it's hot—white hot—but ain't it supposed to be? I mean, it's a branding iron, ain't it?" He blinked uncomprehendingly. "I mean, how's it gonna sear the cow if it ain't white-hot?" Rusty insisted. "Hotter the better, I'd guess—"

Ki took a deep breath to gain control of his temper. "Guessing is exactly what you've been doing these last few days," he replied, doing his best to temper his gruff tone, realizing it wasn't Rusty's fault that he didn't know what he was doing.

The young man was the son of a Starbuck executive back East. The boy had begged his father for a taste of the cowboy's life before finishing his schooling, and the executive had relayed the request to Jessie, who had obligingly invited Rusty to come out West for the roundup. Ki had been against it. A stampede-prone herd was no place to break in a tenderfoot, and there were many experienced cowboys looking for work, but Jessie had been adamant, and when Jessie

4

Starbuck set her mind on something, it inevitably happened. So here Rusty was, ready to set this poor calf's hide aflame with a white-hot iron.

"We're looking to brand the calf, not barbecue it," Ki explained. "If we burn too deeply, infection could result. A red-hot iron will burn through only the top layer of skin, and heal quickly."

The tenderfoot nodded in admiration. "Ain't that something! You sure do know your cows, Mister Ki! I ain't never—"

"Rusty, do you intend to continue spouting 'ain'ts' once you return to Chicago to resume your university studies?"

"Um, uh, well..."

Ki fought hard against his smile. "Rusty, your face has gone red, as has the iron you've been holding all this time. Shall we get on with the branding?"

Ki grabbed a fistful of skin on the calf's topside hind leg and pulled it taut to form a smooth site for the iron. As Rusty pressed the brand home, the calf's skin sizzled, the animal let out a bawl of anguish, and then it was over. Seared into the calf's hide was the five-pointed star within a circle that was the Starbuck brand.

"Gee, Mr. Ki, I'm sure learning a lot," Rusty said. "Do you think that I'll ever get the hang of being a cowboy?"

Ki looked the tenderfoot over. Poor Rusty was decked out in a sugarloaf sombrero and woolly chaps, covered in shaggy, grizzly-bear-like fur. Such chaps were appropriate in the winter, but were totally out of place on the warm, grassy plains in this part of Texas. Rusty had been wearing a pair of Mexican spurs, wicked-looking things that the boss wrangler had confiscated, not wanting his horses torn up. Ki had confiscated Rusty's nickel-plated, pearl-handled, likely never-fired Colt, worried that the ribbing he was taking from the other hands might get out of control if the tenderfoot were armed.

"Rusty, I think you'll become a seasoned cowboy long before that outfit of yours gets broken in."

"I guess that ain't—I mean isn't—too bad, then, Mister

Ki." Rusty nodded gratefully, and then tottered off as best he could in his brand-new, impossibly stiff, ridiculously high-heeled Justin boots.

Ki untied the calf, to send it scurrying back to its mother and the rest of the herd. He coiled up his lasso and mounted the buckskin, riding over to the tally man, who told him that two hundred and sixty-four calves had so far been branded that day. It was going well, Ki thought, but then it ought to, for a Circle Star roundup was somewhat easier than the roundups on other ranches. For one thing, the cowboys didn't have to worry about separating Starbuck cows from animals belonging to other spreads as the Starbuck range was so vast. It had to be; it took thirty gallons of water a day, and ten acres of prime grass a season, to sustain just one cow, and the Starbuck herd numbered in the hundreds of thousands. This roundup was concerned with only a fraction of the entire herd. Several days ago the roundup had begun at the far end of the ranch; they were now about dead-center of the Starbuck holdings, and they were still several days' ride from the main house and outbuildings.

Each dawn Ki and his twenty riders would stow their bedrolls and saddlebags inside the chuckwagon, and saddle up the horses assigned to them by the boss wrangler out of his remuda, kept in a portable rope corral. Ki would map out, by drawing in the dirt with a stick, the day's ground to be covered. The men would have their breakfast and then ride out to gather the herd. The chuckwagon, carrying the branding equipment, would follow. By midday the riders would have gathered and driven the cattle—both the main herd of branded cows and the loosely bunched heifers with unmarked calves—to a prearranged spot. The chuckwagon and the wrangler with his remuda were already there. The boss wrangler's helpers had already gathered deadwood along the way to fuel the cook's fire, and heat the branding irons. The branding stations would be set up, and the cutting and branding would begin, with the men working the irons well stocked with bottles of liniment to kill the screw worms breeding in the cows' sores, and long-handled clippers to dehorn the steers. By the end of the day, as the acrid stink of singed hair permeated the air, the chuckwagon would have established the hub of the night camp. Those men who were not assigned the night watch over the herd could bed down for the evening, after eighteen hours in the saddle.

But sunset was still hours away, Ki knew. There was a lot more cutting and branding to be done before Cook's supper bell would clang. For Ki, it was time to patrol.

The samurai turned his mount in the direction of the wrangler's remuda and rode at an easy lope back to the rope corral for a fresh horse. He exchanged the winded buckskin for a roan gelding. The cowponies were smart, and needed a minimum of water and feed, but also required a good deal of rest in order to thrive. The men made it a point to change their mounts several times during the workday.

Ki's saddle, complete with its boot specially designed to carry his Japanese bow and a quiver of arrows, was transferred to the roan by one of the wrangler's young assistants, and then Ki rode off to travel the herd's perimeter. He was carrying his bow in case he came across coyotes out to prey on the vulnerable calves. A well-placed arrow would make short work of a coyote, and do it quietly. Ki had issued strict orders to the men not to use their guns against predators, as he was worried that a gunshot might provoke a stampede.

But coyotes were not the only would-be predators of the herd to concern Ki. Roundup time drew cattle thieves the way honey draws flies ...

As Ki rode, the flat pastures gave way to granite outcroppings, the land broken by shallow creeks, arroyos that would soon flood, and knolls covered with scraggly clumps of post oak and blackjack. The men who worked these rough draws and pockets, spooking every last cow from the patches of brush or trenchlike ravines, truly earned their pay.

Here the men wore chaps—not Rusty's ludicrous woollies, but sturdy rawhide step-in shotguns, or buckle-on batwings—out of necessity. A cowboy after a maverick cow might find himself riding through brambles that would leave him studded with thorny prickers.

Ki concentrated on his riding, coaxing his roan to run along the narrow spine of a ridge, to climb a steep, rocky foothill, and then slide skittering on its haunches down the far side. There was a lot of country to cover if Ki was to check on all of his widely scattered men.

He pulled a bright red bandanna from his pocket and knotted it across his face against the choking clouds of dust raised by both cattle and horses. Often he stopped to lend a hand to a frustrated cowboy chasing after a bolting steer. It was no fun running down a steer after you'd done the same maneuver a hundred times in less than a week. The tedium and exhaustion turned some men mean, turned them into steer-busters.

Ki did not condone the practice of busting a herd-quitter by roping the steer's horns, slinking the rope across its hind legs, and then abruptly angling one's horse away, wrenching back the steer's head, and flipping the entire animal into the air in a violent somersault. The cowboys claimed that it taught the steer a lesson. Maybe so, but Ki had seen too many steers injured or even killed by the practice. As ramrod, he had warned his men that any rider caught steer-busting would be drawing his pay within the hour.

Cattle thieves and steer-busting; animals lost, or injured—to most of the men, such things were just part of the job, and certainly nothing to be concerned about. So what if a few Circle Star cows were lost? Jessie Starbuck had plenty more. To Ki, however, the question of whether Jessie might miss a few cows was irrelevant. He had long ago sworn an oath to the late Alex Starbuck, Jessie's father, to protect Starbuck life and property. He would fight for one cow as if it were a thousand, if need be, risking his life in the process. To do anything less would betray his samurai tradition; to do anything less would not be honorable.

"Cap'n? Yo! Cap'n!"

Ki reined in the roan gelding, twisting around in his saddle to see who was hailing him. A rider broke through a clump of stunted hickory. The cowboy looked like a ghost, or maybe a statue carved from stone come to life, for he and his lathered horse were covered with dust.

"Cap'n, I got something to talk to you about," the rider muttered, removing his face kerchief in order to spit.

"Teddy, I didn't recognize you," Ki said. Teddy Rolling-Rock was a half-breed Indian—from what tribe Ki didn't know, and hadn't asked. He didn't like people prying into his past, and so he respected others' desires to keep their histories to themselves. Nevertheless, Ki suspected that Teddy was part Ute, for the half-breed drover had that tribe's short, stocky build and swarthy coloring. Teddy kept his dark hair cut short. He wore cracked, worn chaps, ancient canvas trousers, and a dark green flannel shirt patched in a dozen places. His flat-crowned black Stetson was battered, brim-broken, and stained with sweat. His Colt Peacemaker had had its blueing rubbed pretty much off, and its black rubber grips were being held in place with several dingy twists of sticky tape. All of that was obvious about Teddy Rolling-Rock's gun because the half-breed had no holster. He kept the pistol wedged through his belt, high on his right hip.

"Got some water?" Teddy asked.

Ki handed over a canteen. "You shouldn't be out here without water."

Teddy grinned, his teeth startlingly white against his dusky, dirt-caked complexion. "Had a canteen once," he said, "but I traded it for some beans a while back." He rinsed out his mouth, coughed, spat, then took a long drink, sighed in contentment, and passed the canteen back to Ki. "Reckon I'll buy me a new canteen come the end of this job. Or maybe not, 'cause jobs for the likes of me are few and far between."

Ki nodded, understanding what Teddy was driving at. Few ranchers would hire a half-breed drover, claiming that the other cowboys would shun him, or that there'd be fights in the bunkhouse. During this roundup Ki had seen the other men ignoring Teddy. A half-breed himself, and not always welcome either in Japan or America, Ki sympathized with

9

Teddy's plight. "You said that you wanted to talk to me," Ki reminded the drover. "What about?"

Teddy dipped his head, a look of discomfort on his fleshy features. "Guess I've been holding back on that 'cause I haven't decided that telling you what I discovered is the smart thing to do..." He shrugged, his moon face once again splitting into that easy grin. "I spotted some cow thieves, Cap'n. Four of them, I reckon; leastways I counted that many, but only one horse. I figure the rest of them would be riding in that covered wagon they got with them. They've set up a chute. I watched them venting the Circle Star brand and marking their own road brand."

"Show me," Ki said.

"This way, Cap'n, but keep it quiet. They got guns."

Ki nudged his horse into a slow walk, following Teddy's chestnut gelding back through the hickory grove. They were heading up a slight rise of crumbly sandstone.

"Let's leave the horses, here, Cap'n, the better for us to creep up on them jaspers."

Ki nodded, dismounting, drawing his bow from its saddle boot, and strapping his leather quiver of arrows around his waist so that it rested high on his right hip, like a sixgun. Teddy Rolling-Rock eyed the unusual weaponry, but said nothing. He turned and began scrambling up the sandstone incline on all fours.

Ki followed, not worrying about their horses. Like all Starbuck mounts, the cowponies had been trained not to wander when their reins trailed on the ground.

The climb took several minutes. At first nothing seemed out of the ordinary. It seemed a typical warm Texas afternoon, with everything still and the only sounds those of the birds and insects. Gradually, however, the warblers' songs and the sawtoothed fiddling of the grasshoppers gave way to the bawling of calves. Teddy motioned to Ki to keep back, crawled to the top of the ledge, and peeked over. Then he gestured to Ki to come ahead.

Ki crept forward until he could look down on the action.

10

He and Teddy were at the closed end of a small box canyon, approximately thirty feet above what was a natural stone corral, just twenty yards across, and maybe twice that in length. Blocking what appeared to be the only entrance into the canyon, at the far end from where Ki and Teddy were situated, was a rickety-looking Conestoga, badly in need of a fresh coat of paint. Its wooden wheels were warped, and its canvas top was in tatters. The two mangy mules hitched to the wagon looked gaunt enough to slip right through the spaces in a picket fence.

The four thieves were busy at work, running about fifty head of Circle Star cattle through their chute. The contraption was scarcely six feet long, and formed of two parallel rows of heavy stakes, hammered into the earth about a foot apart at the bottom, angling out to a yard across at the top, to form a V. A pair of tall, hinged stakes stood at one end of the chute. As Ki and Teddy watched, the only man on horseback—he was riding what looked to be a plowhorse bareback—drove a cow into the chute. Once in, the cow could not turn around, and when it got to the far end, the second and third men working the hinged stakes locked the cow's neck in a firm, pincerlike grasp. The fourth cow thief, standing by his branding tools, easily "vented" or marked out the Circle Star brand, then picked up a second iron from the fire, to mark the cow with a brand that an independent trail boss might use to signify the transfer of ownership of cattle from the ranch to himself. The entire process took no more than ten seconds, by Ki's count. Then a new cow was started down the chute by the man riding bareback.

"I'll bet those four have got bogus bills of sale to go with their irons and other equipment," Teddy whispered.

"It seems a smooth operation," Ki said glumly. "There are still a number of small, independent trail operations around, buying up cattle from those ranchers who don't want to bother with a roundup and market drive of their own."

"Nobody would pay them folks any mind," Teddy agreed.

11

"And it'd only take them a few minutes to knock down that chute, load it and their irons into that wagon, and move on to the next out-of-the-way spot on the range."

"Unfortunately for them, I'm going to put a stop to their rustling operation before they can enjoy the fruits of their illicit labors . . ."

"Cap'n, there's something that you'd ought to know—"

"Later, Teddy," Ki interrupted. "There's no time now. I must put a stop to this and then get back to the herd. I'll circle around over the rocks to the canyon's entrance. You stay here and—"

"Cap'n, before you set off, you'd better listen—"

"What?" Ki demanded impatiently. "What do I have to know that is so all-fired important?"

"*That,* Cap'n," Teddy muttered, pointing toward the cow thief working the branding irons.

Ki looked down in time to see the rustler remove his hat to wipe the sweat from his brow, releasing a shoulder-length mane of brown hair, streaked through with gray. "A woman?" he said incredulously.

"More than that, Cap'n," the half-breed remarked. "It's a *mother.*" He pointed at the man on horseback. "That there's the daddy, and them two working the 'snapping turtle' at the chute's end are their young'uns."

"They seem grown up, Teddy," Ki murmured, peering down.

"Maybe they's growed, Cap'n, but they's young'uns just the same," Teddy replied stubbornly. "You'll notice that Papa is wearing a handgun, as is his two boys, but Mama ain't packing . . ."

"Well, she's a lady," Ki said wryly, and then shrugged. "Teddy, they are cow thieves. The fact that they are a *family* of cow thieves doesn't matter."

"Cap'n, they ain't desperadoes, that's a *fact!* I know what happens to cow thieves in Texas, and it don't seem right that lynching should apply to them. Look at their wagon, their damned nag, their *clothes!* It's clear to me that they

12

don't even have the price of a saddle for that plowhorse." Teddy scowled. "They're stealing 'cause they're hungry, not out of greed."

"Teddy, is that why you were hesitant about telling me that you'd discovered them?"

The half-breed looked away. "Reckon so," he muttered. "Guess I know what it is to be hungry. Except that I ain't never taken nothing on charity, and I ain't never stolen!" he elaborated hotly, his dark eyes flashing. "That's the truth!"

"I believe you, Teddy," Ki declared flatly. "But I want you to know that there is no lynching—not even for cow thieves—on Starbuck land."

"That's a relief," Teddy smiled. "So we can forget we saw this?" he added hopefully.

Ki shook his head. "I can't forget it, Teddy. I can't let them steal Starbuck property."

"What's the answer then, Cap'n?" Teddy asked worried. "If we rush them, they're sure to panic and use their guns. Somebody could get hurt, and the shots would carry, maybe spook the main herd into stampeding."

Ki nodded. "My original plan still seems to be the best. I will circle around, to come through the entrance of the canyon." He clasped the half-breed's shoulder. "If you will help, we can take them without a shot being fired."

Teddy looked doubtful. "How do you figure to pull that off?"

Ki shrugged off the bow strung diagonally across his back and shoulder, and unstrapped the quiver of arrows from around his waist. "Can you use these?"

Something seemed to die in Teddy's eyes. "You mean can I do a war dance, or make it rain?" His mouth compressed into a thin line. "What else you interested in, Cap'n? If I can carve a totem pole, or maybe scalp a paleface?"

"You misunderstand, Teddy," Ki replied quietly. "I meant no disrespect. The bow is part of my heritage, just as it is a part of yours. I merely asked because—"

"Sorry, Cap'n, I shouldn't have flown off the handle like that," Teddy apologized. "Guess I've been ribbed so many

13

times about being a half-breed, I got carried away."

"Yes," Ki said. "I understand."

Their eyes met, and then Teddy grinned. "Reckon you do, Cap'n. I heard some of the other boys jawing about how you were part red man. I didn't say anything, because those white fellas don't take kindly to me butting in on their conversations, but I know Injun blood when I see it, and you ain't got any, Cap'n. That's a fact! The thing is, you got a white man's face, except for your eyes. I don't reckon I've ever seen eyes shaped like your'n in any tribe I've ever come across—"

"Teddy," Ki sighed. "My mother was Japanese..."

"Let's see now..." Teddy scratched his brow. "I had me a lick of education back when I was a young'un. Learned me a spot of geography to go along with my three R's... Japanese, you say? Ain't that kinda like Chinese, Cap'n?"

"The way that Apache is kind of like Crow," Ki countered in good humor, chuckling at the way Teddy winced.

"Ouch! Point well made, Cap'n. My mother was *Ho*—the tribe called Ute in your—I mean, the white man's language. Now about that bow of your'n, Cap'n."

"My name is Ki, Teddy."

Teddy was silent for an instant, and then he nodded, saying softly, "I ain't been invited to call a soul anything but 'sir' or 'ma'am' or 'cap'n' since I been with my own people." He laughed bitterly. "Not that I *got* my own people. The curse of being a mixed blood is that a jasper ain't at home *nowhere*..."

"That is the curse, Teddy," Ki agreed. "But being alone can also make one strong."

"Amen, Ki," Teddy muttered quietly, and then said roughly, "'Bout that damned bow! I've shot a few in my time, but never one like that. Why, it's all crooked!"

"This is a Japanese bow," Ki explained, handing it over to Teddy for examination. The bow was five feet long, and curved asymmetrically. It was formed from three sandwiched layers of fire-tempered bamboo that had been glued

14

together and then wound around at several stress points with red thread.

"It sure looks funny," Teddy drawled. "But not nearly as funny as those arrows. Why, they've all got different heads! Some of them I can figure out, but some of the others..."

"A Japanese quiver holds twenty-four arrows, each of which serves a unique purpose." Ki glanced down into the canyon, where the family of rustlers looked to be wrapping up their branding operation. "There are only a few head of cattle left. There's no time for me to explain further. We must act quickly if we wish to take them without bloodshed! The two young men operating the 'snapping turtle' will be the most dangerous. Both have guns, and youth has a tendency to be hot-headed. Once I disarm them, I suspect that their mother and father will surrender meekly enough..."

Teddy shrugged. "How do you figure to get the drop on those two boys? You'll be out of sight until you enter the canyon, but then you'll have to get from the wagon to those two young jaspers. It ain't much of a run, but you'll have no cover, and Pop there, on his plowhorse, will be facing in your direction all the while."

"You must divert their attention at the crucial moment," Ki said.

"But how? I can't fire my pistol, unless you've changed your mind about risking a stampede—?"

"No, we can't risk a gunshot, but there is another sort of noise..." The samurai selected an arrow from the quiver and handed it to Teddy. "You see that clay bulb fitted just behind the arrowhead? It has holes in it to catch the wind when the shaft is fired. This arrow sings quite a song as it flies—a 'death song,' actually..." Ki grinned wolfishly. "But today we intend the song to surprise, and in that way avoid bringing about deaths. Teddy, when you see me crouched by the wagon, fire the arrow into the sky so that it soars across the canyon. It will land harmlessly against the stone wall on the far side."

"Good luck," Teddy said. "If I have to, Ki, I'll use one

15

of these other arrows to stop that jasper on horseback. You're risking your skin to give those folks a chance. I don't intend to let you suffer for it."

Ki nodded, and then shucked off his boots. "Mind these for me," he said, and then he started off, effortlessly and silently scrambling over the rocks.

It took Ki only a few minutes to travel the horseshoe-shaped spine of rock to the far side of the canyon. He slid down the short but steep incline to the entrance of the canyon, doing his best not to dislodge any pebbles that might rattle a warning to the cow thieves working within. He had little to worry about. Between the sizzle of the branding irons and the raucous bawling of the milling cattle, a cavalry troop could have moved into position outside the canyon without the rustlers becoming wise. The hard part was next.

Crouching low, Ki slipped into the canyon past the two sleepy-eyed, stuporous mules, their heads lowered in the warm sun. The samurai kept himself pressed against the wagon's side to avoid casting a shadow or attracting the rider's attention. The two young men working the "snapping turtle" were twenty feet away. They were standing with their backs to Ki, and were bracing themselves in preparation for immobilizing the cow their father was just now driving toward the chute.

Ki patted the pockets of his leather vest. He had with him an assortment of *shuriken*—glitteringly sharp throwing blades—but now that he was close to these people, he knew that he could not seriously harm them without tarnishing his own honor in the process. As a samurai, a warrior, Ki would only use lethal force against a worthy opponent. These "rustlers" were, as Teddy had already surmised, merely a poor ranching family down on its luck.

The only problem was that the two young men who were doing the hard work of operating the "snapping turtle" were very large. Ki guessed that they were twin brothers, perhaps nineteen years old. They stood about six feet four inches tall, and looked to weigh about two hundred and twenty-five pounds each. They were wearing low-crowned plainsman's hats, denims, scuffed boots, and chambray shirts with the sleeves torn off to reveal sloping shoulders and thick, powerful arms. Each man wore a revolver dangling from his right hip—thankfully, the gun butts were facing toward Ki. Getting those guns out of the way would be crucial to a relatively peaceful resolution to this incident...

Ki glanced up toward the rocky ledge where Teddy was situated, in time to see the "death's song" arrow hurtle into the sky. Instantly the rocky canyon's walls reverberated with a shrill keening sound that made the mules bray and kick and the cattle press together, rolling their big eyes. The four would-be cow thieves froze into frightened poses.

"Matthew? the woman working the branding irons cried out. "Matt? What is it?"

Ki, already moving toward the woman's brace of sons, doubted that her husband had heard her query above the arrow's ear-piercing wail. The man named Matthew was too distracted. He was craning his neck to stare, squinting, into the sun.

Ki had a bad moment when a terrorized heifer blundered into his path, threatening to disrupt the samurai's concentration and foil his plan.

Ki's wiry thigh muscles uncoiled, and then he was bounding over the alarmed cow's ginger-colored back, to land mere inches behind the two men. The samurai deftly plucked both of their revolvers from their holsters and tossed them over his shoulder.

The two men whirled. Ki, standing with his hands on his hips, nodded politely. At that moment the "death's song" arrow slammed into the craggy stone face of the canyon's far wall. A tense silence descended upon the scene as the mules' agitated bleatings subsided, and even the cattle began to settle down, to chew on their cuds as if engrossed by the drama that was about to be played out before them.

"Paw? What should we do?" one of the young men called out.

"He took our guns, Paw!" the other man added. There was anger in his voice.

The samurai turned slightly toward the man who'd spoken last. This was the bolder of the two, the one who would attack first, if violence was fated to erupt.

"Draw your gun, Paw," the first one insisted.

"But he's not armed, son," Matthew stammered, nudging his barebacked plowhorse into a plodding walk over to where Ki and his two sons were squaring off. "I can't throw down on no fella not wearing a gun, Cal."

Ki smiled inwardly, satisfied that Teddy's and his own instincts about these people had been correct. Hardened criminals were not so fussy about who they shot. He noticed that the father and mother were dressed in the same modest garb as their sons; the worn work clothing attested to the fact that these people had once earned their keep by the honest sweat of their brows. If it was at all possible, Ki intended to set them back on the right path. He thought he knew just how to accomplish that good deed...

"Listen, mister," the father began, "we don't want to hurt nobody. We're takin' these cows and—"

"I can't allow you to take them, but—"

"Cal, Keith! Grab him!" the father shouted.

"Matthew! You promised no trouble!" the woman called out, causing her two sons to hesitate.

Ki glimpsed her standing with her fist pressed against her mouth, her eyes looking huge and care-worn. "Matt," she implored, "it's not worth it. Let's give up."

"If you will let me finish—" Ki tried to interrupt, but Matthew waved him quiet.

"You done said what mattered, mister. You ain't gonna let us take these cows, but we *need* to take them!"

"I didn't raise my boys to be murderers!" the woman wailed.

"There ain't gonna be no murdering, Abigail," the woman's husband said, shocked. "How could you even think such a thing? All I'm gonna do is have the boys tie this fella up so that we can ride out of here in peace." He turned to his sons. "All right, boys. Get it done!"

As Ki had surmised, it was the one named Keith who

18

proved to be the bolder of the two brothers. He lumbered forward, grinning confidently, his callused hands extended, blunt fingers spread wide, to grab at his smaller adversary. The samurai sidestepped away, at the same time executing a *chudan-uchi-uke,* the inside, middle-area block from which were derived so many other movements in *te,* the empty-handed combat system. Ki's block caught Keith's left fore-arm with a sound like that of bulls butting their heads to-gether. Keith staggered back, cradling his bruised forearm, moaning that it was broken.

Cal had come around from behind, locking Ki in a bear hug which lifted the samurai up off of the ground.

"I got 'im, Paw!" Cal crowed, but his triumphant shout turned into a panicked cry as Ki locked his bare feet around the bigger man's calves, and then drew up his knees. Cal's boot soles skittered across the hard rock, and then his feet were out from under him. He crashed down hard, flat on his back, the wind knocked out of him both by the fall and because Ki had landed on top of him, squeezing the last bit of air out of his lungs.

The samurai hopped to his feet, brushing himself off. He was unhurt, as Cal's body had totally cushioned the impact of their interlocked tumble. Ki was well satisfied with the results of the tussle. Both young men were on the ground, and no longer seemed interested in fighting, and yet neither one was seriously hurt. Keith was still cradling his injured arm, but from the way his fingers were waggling, Ki knew that the man's arm was not broken—it only *hurt* like it had been. In all, Ki felt that he had managed to maintain his honor during this highly undignified scuffle with these two bear cubs.

He moved aside politely as the boys' mother ran to her injured sons. "Now perhaps you will all listen to me," Ki began.

"I guess it's you who'll do the listening, mister," Matthew cut in, still on horseback, drawing his battered-looking Colt .45.

"Teddy! Don't kill him!" Ki shouted.

Matthew smiled uneasily. "You can't fool me with that old ploy. You'd never have come down here by your lonesome if—"

"Who do you suppose fired the arrow that made that noise a little while ago?" Ki asked.

"He's right, Matt," Abigail said as she knelt by her boys. "*Somebody* did it!"

"Well..." Matthew said, his jaw tight as he twisted around to scan the surrounding cliffs. He turned back to his wife. "Are the boys all right?" When she nodded, he told Ki, "I guess you're gonna be our hostage outta here, mister..." and thumbed back the hammer of his Colt.

"Stop it!" the samurai demanded. "I'm running out of patience with all of you." He extended his hand. "Matthew, hand over that gun, or else I'll take it from you."

Matthew mulled it over. "You ain't gonna be our hostage, eh?" he asked glumly.

"Certainly not!"

He nodded, lowered the hammer on the Colt, and tossed it to Ki. "I surrender," he said, swinging down off his tranquil-looking plowhorse. "I can't bring myself to shoot a man over a few head of cattle." He glanced at his open-mouthed, frightened-looking sons. "Truth is," he proclaimed loudly, "I ain't never shot a man nohow, and hope to keep things that way. You can hang me for cow thievery," he continued, addressing Ki. "But let my wife and sons go. They didn't do nothing that I didn't make them do—"

Ki fought back his smile. Whatever had brought this family so low was nothing to smirk at. "Your name?"

"O'Connell. My name's Matthew O'Connell."

"Mr. O'Connell, there was never a possibility of any of you being hanged. You can thank your good fortune that you chose to rustle Circle Star cattle. There are other spreads in this part of Texas where cow thieves are treated in a far harsher manner. Whatever made you think that you could get away with this?"

O'Connell looked dejected. "I guess we was hoping for

beginner's luck, mister, 'cause we surely didn't have it when it came to ranching. We have us a little spread up in Kansas. Had maybe two hundred head of beeves, and fine Kansas stock they were, too, but I guess we were located just a mite too close to Texas, and to the big Texas cattle trails. Last fall, just a few weeks after the big eastward market drive, our own cows took sick with Texas fever. They caught it off of those Texas cows passing through. Before I hardly knew what was happening, I was using the last of my cash money to buy rifle slugs to put them cows of mine out of their misery. That was that, mister. In one afternoon, everything my family and I had was lying out there in my pasture. Our future, just swelling up and stinking in the sun."

"Told you so," Teddy Rolling-Rock remarked softly, coming up behind Ki. He had the samurai's bow balanced across his shoulders, the quiver loosely strapped about his waist, and Ki's boots tucked under his arm.

"All through last winter I brooded," O'Connell continued. "I reckon I got so crazy bitter I came to believe that you Texans were to blame for what happened to me. I got to thinking that maybe it was more like getting even than stealing to come down here and help myself to a few Texas cows. This here Circle Star spread is one of the biggest. I figured it'd be easy to grab a few cows and get away unnoticed back across the Red."

"In other words, you were not planning to steal again?" Ki asked. "It was this one time, and that was to be the end of it?"

"That's the truth, mister," O'Connell said plaintively. "I just wanted to get back enough to have a seed herd. I ain't asking you to forgive *me*, understand, only to let my family go."

"You have about fifty head here, correct?" Ki asked.

"Fifty-three, to be exact," O'Connell replied. "Thirty heifers, twenty calves, and three yearling bulls."

"That is three too many," Ki frowned. "I must take back three head—heifers with no calves. The remaining fifty

21

head are now your cattle."

O'Connell gaped. "Mister," he whispered, "tell me I ain't dreaming..."

"I cannot tell you *that,*" Ki replied, allowing himself a ghost of a smile. "I can only assure you that the cattle are really yours. They should make an adequate seed herd, one immune to the ravages of Texas fever. If you'll fetch me paper and pen, I'll write up your bill of sale in case you need to prove ownership during your trip home." As one of the O'Connell sons hurried to the wagon to do Ki's bidding, the samurai continued, "I intended from the very first to give you the cattle, but you and your boys never let me get a word in edgewise."

"Mister, we'll never be able to thank you," Mrs. O'Connell said. "You don't know what this means to us."

"You can thank me by going straight back to Kansas," Ki declared. "You and your husband go back to raising your boys to be ranchers, not cow thieves."

Teddy Rolling-Rock went to fetch their horses while Ki remained in the canyon to draw up the paperwork for the O'Connells. It was coming on late afternoon, so the family asked Ki's permission to camp where they were for the night, and start on the first leg of their journey back to Kansas come sunup.

A short while later, Ki and Teddy were back in the saddle, herding the three reclaimed heifers back toward the round-up's night camp. The sun was beginning to set, streaking the Texas sky with blood-red bands of color.

"I got some questions," Teddy finally muttered as the two riders poked along, the three cows between them. "First off, what was all that palaver about honor and protecting Starbuck property and so on? I mean, if you was gonna let them steal those cows anyway—"

"First of all, it has ended up not with the O'Connells *stealing,* but with my *giving* them the cattle. The first instance would have been dishonorable," Ki explained. "The latter instance is not. Secondly, I did not give them Starbuck property."

22

"No? Then who's damned beeves were they?" Teddy demanded.

"Mine," Ki replied. "A few weeks ago Miss Starbuck presented me with some cattle as a gift."

"You gave that family your own cows?"

"I am a samurai," Ki told the half-breed cowboy. "I have my weapons, I have my honor, I have my duty to uphold. Anything more is a burden to me, Teddy. Miss Starbuck and I have been a team for many years. There is much that she understands about me—" He paused, then went on, "And much that she does not. I accepted the generosity of spirit *behind* the gift, while burdened by the gift itself. Now I am no longer burdened."

"Well, I'll be damned," Teddy muttered, shaking his head. "I tell you, brother," he added, lapsing into the Ute's mode of address between friends, "I never *ever* met your like. One thing still confounds me: why take back these three cows? We could've made much better time without them, and—" He stopped, his dark eyes growing wide, and then crinkling with amusement. "Say, brother, just how many cows did Miss Starbuck give you?"

Ki smiled back. "How many do you think, brother?"

"I think fifty is the number."

"No more, no less," Ki agreed.

"So now you got nothing?"

Ki did not reply. Who was he to lecture another? Each soul learned life's lessons in its own time.

Soon the three heifers ceased their balking, catching the scent of the main herd on the wind, and anxious to rejoin it against the gathering darkness. Ki and Teddy were able to make better time. As they approached night camp, a lone rider came streaking across the prairie to meet them.

"Who'd that be?" Teddy wondered out loud. "Whoever it is, he sure can ride!"

Ki peered. "That 'he' is a 'she,'" he said at last. "You are about to meet Jessie Starbuck."

"Hot damn! Always wanted to lay eyes on that filly. Heard she was a mighty fine piece—" Ki's hard look si-

23

lenced the cowboy. "I say the wrong thing, brother?" Teddy asked meekly.

Ki nodded stiffly. "Indeed."

"Sorry. I didn't mean to get out of line. Didn't know you had your brand on her, Ki—"

"I don't, Teddy," Ki replied. "I've sworn an oath—a warrior's oath—to serve and protect her. I could never allow personal feelings to intrude upon that oath. Emotion could cause me to waver in my duty."

"Whatever you say," Teddy replied doubtfully. "I got my own thoughts about what might be locked up inside a fellow who reacts the way you just did to my comments about Miss Starbuck, but I ain't figuring on calling you a liar, not the way you mopped up them two O'Connell boys. What kind of wrassling was that you pulled on them?"

"Something I learned as a boy in the Japans," Ki said. "But you have overestimated the O'Connell boys. They were nothing."

"They was big!"

"They had the strength that comes from hard work, not from a warrior's training, and the two are quite different, Teddy. The ox is big and strong, yet it must fear the panther."

"Ki!" Jessie called to him, and Ki spurred his horse forward to meet her.

After all their time together, Jessie's beauty still had the power to startle and mesmerize the usually cool and aloof samurai. She was in her twenties, and as long-legged as a colt, with high, full breasts, a slender waist, and generous hips. None of her curves were in the least hidden by her tight denim jeans and wrangler's jacket, or her white silk blouse. The clothes were her range outfit, and fit her like a second skin.

"What's brought you to the roundup, Jessie?" Ki asked, wheeling his roan cowpony to trot along beside the tall, dapple-gray Virginia Walker that Jessie was riding.

Jessie's tan Stetson was dangling on her back, held in place by its rawhide chin thong. She shook her head to allow her tawny mane of copper-blonde hair to ruffle in the first cool breeze of the coming evening.

"Maybe I got lonely back at the ranch, with you gone these past few days," she drawled, fixing her magnificent eyes, as green as the finest jade ever plundered from the Orient, upon her old friend. She smiled bewitchingly. "Or maybe I came out to give you the news..."

She paused as Teddy Rolling-Rock rode up to them. Ki introduced them, and then quickly filled Jessie in on what had taken place with the O'Connells.

"So!" Jessie pretended to scold him. "I knew you'd figure out a way to get rid of those cattle I gave you!" Her expression softened as she turned her attention to Teddy. "I'm very grateful to you for assisting Ki."

Teddy blushed as crimson as the sun, which was just then sinking fast below the horizon. "Shucks, ma'am, I'd like to think that Ki and I are kinda like two peas in a pod, 'cause of our mixed blood." He gestured toward Ki's bow. "Now we're brothers, he and I—'brothers of the bow,' as my people like to say."

"I wish I could reward you by offering a permanent place on the Circle Star," Jessie sighed, "but there isn't a vacant spot, and I can't turn out a hand for no good reason just to be able to sign you on."

"Wouldn't want that on my conscience at all, ma'am," Teddy assured her, smiling. "Can't say as I wouldn't have taken the job if it was available, but..." He shrugged. "I'll be taking these heifers back to the main herd."

As Teddy rode off, Ki thought that the half-breed drover had been very wrong when he'd suggested that by giving away his cattle, Ki had been left with nothing. The samurai had the majestic beauty of the sunset to ponder, and he had Jessie's company.

He considered himself a rich man indeed.

★

Chapter 2

After spending a night out under the stars and watching the sun rise, turning the world as pink as a newborn baby's bottom, Jessica Starbuck wouldn't have traded places with anyone in the world. Still, there were times when being who she was caused a whole passel of problems. It was a distinct disadvantage to be a woman when trying to run a rough-and-ready outfit like the Circle Star.

Jessie had her own opinions about a lot of things—especially about a female being her own person, and speaking her mind when need be. Just the same, it was hard to argue with those who held with the notion that cattle-ranching was a man's affair.

Jessie often wondered how she might have ended up if things had gone differently. Would she right now be some cattleman's pampered wife? There was just no telling what might have happened if her father hadn't died—murdered by assassins working for a shadowy group of ruthless men who would stop at nothing to gain their own desires.

Alex Starbuck had first encountered the minions of the deadly European cartel many years ago, when he was not much older than Jessie was now. In those days, Starbuck ships were busy carrying trade goods between East and West. It was this import-export business, based in San Francisco, that had formed the foundation of the Starbuck fortune. Members of the cartel had initially approached Alex with a proposition to use his clipper ships to transport slave labor and opium to the West. When Alex refused, the cartel had used force—violent force—in their attempt to get him to submit to their wishes. But a Starbuck submits to no one. Frustrated, the cartel tried to assassinate Jessie's father, but they failed, accidentally killing Jessie's mother, Sarah Starbuck, in the botched attack. A grieving, rage-filled Alex Starbuck struck back, killing the son of the Prussian ringleader. Things became quiet, and had remained so until fairly recently, when a cartel ambush finally brought down Alex Starbuck.

Since then, Jessie had divided her time between running the far-flung Starbuck business empire, managing the Circle Star spread, and fighting that damnable cartel. With Ki's help, Jessie had so far managed to foil the cartel's numerous attempts to infiltrate America.

Jessie ran her hairbrush through her spun-gold tresses, kissed with coppery highlights from time spent beneath the strong Texas sun. She hauled on her boots, and then she packed away her personal things in her saddlebags, to carry them, along with her bedroll, over to the chuckwagon.

As she hoisted her burdens, a number of wranglers offered to carry the stuff for her. Jessie politely but steadfastly refused their help. She didn't want to encourage these men to ponder the fact that there was a female in their midst.

Now, Jessie liked men as much as they liked her, and that was a fact. She believed that the fun a man and woman could have together was one of the greatest pleasures of being alive. But there was a time and place for everything, and a cattle roundup was serious, dangerous business. The drovers already had plenty to think about, and she didn't want to distract them. She took pleasure in the way men looked at her, just as she liked to look at a handsome male, but she thought that any female who enjoyed getting men randy just for the sake of it deserved a bottom-blistering trip to the nearest woodshed.

Normally, for instance, Jessie would have worn a sturdy tweed skirt and matching jacket, her usual outfit when traveling or going out riding. A skirt and jacket were flattering, but didn't reveal quite as much of her charms as did her

28

denims. Unfortunately, this country was just too rough for anything but her sturdy jeans and wrangler's jacket.

At least Jessie could be thankful that there was no need to wear her gun. It seemed that nothing riled some men more than seeing a female with a six-shooter strapped about her waist. Jessie's revolver and gunbelt were stashed in her saddlebags. She knew how to shoot; her father had taught her just as soon as she was big enough to hold a gun, and now she could outdo most of the gunslicks who thought they were something. Her gun had been a gift from her father for her eighteenth birthday; he'd had it commissioned at the Colt factory during one of his Eastern business trips. It was a .38, but built on a double-action .44 frame to diminish recoil in Jessie's slender hand. The Colt was finished in slate gray and had grips of polished peachwood.

Just because the Colt was packed away didn't mean that Jessie was going about defenseless. Her ivory-gripped, double-barreled .38-caliber derringer was just now tucked discreetly out of sight in her boot top. When she was wearing a skirt, Jessie kept the little gun in a garter-belt holster, high up on her thigh.

Jessie wouldn't have ridden out to the roundup at all if it hadn't been absolutely necessary. She'd come to tell Ki to remain in Sarah Township after the market drive. During Ki's absence, Jessie had arranged for their next business trip to inspect Starbuck holdings. They were returning to Nettle Grove, Wyoming, an up-and-coming cattle town where she had earlier invested seed money in a number of small ranches and, in the process, ruined the Prussian cartel's plans to bankrupt those ranchers. The Prussians had gotten a greedy cattle baron to act as their front; the deal was for the cattle baron to buy up the bankrupt ranchers' land with cartel funds, in exchange for allowing the Prussians to lay foreign claim to the property's valuable below-ground mineral rights.

Jessie and Ki, with the assistance of some brave Nettle Grove townsfolk, had put an end to all of that double-dealing. The cattle baron had died trying to outrun justice, while the cartel land-grabbers were once again forced to accept defeat at Jessie Starbuck's hands...

All reports had it that Nettle Grove had grown fat and sassy since that adventure. Jessie was looking forward to seeing how much progress had been made in the town she had worked so hard to save.

She and Ki would be leaving from Sarah's rail depot, and since Jessie could bring their baggage along with her in the buckboard, there was no point in having Ki ride all the way back to the ranch only to have him accompany her right back to Sarah the very next morning. After the exhausting roundup and market drive, the samurai could better use that day resting in town for the trip to come.

Last night Jessie had delivered her message to Ki. This morning she would have started to the Starbuck spread, but the dawn's first sun had quickly given way to a gray, overcast sky. The air had grown humid and still. A thunderstorm was in the making, and when a storm was brewing, cattle had a way of growing restless and finicky.

Now that the roundup was almost over, the herd had grown large, maybe even too large for the number of men that Ki was ramrodding. There was a real question as to whether there were enough drovers to control the herd under adverse conditions. After a quick discussion with Ki during breakfast, the samurai had agreed that it would be helpful if Jessie remained a little while in order to lend a hand. She was an accomplished rider, and could lasso and hogtie a steer as well as any man.

As Jessie set to work that morning, the herd stretched out like a huge, mottled brown-and-white blanket across the green prairie. She rode hard, helping to maintain the cut of perhaps five hundred heifers and calves separate from the main herd. The process reminded her of whittling; that smaller herd of five hundred was just a shaving of bark off the tree trunk that was the main herd.

At first the other drovers were flabbergasted by Jessie riding herd with them. Then they were appalled, then surprised, but finally hugely entertained by the sight of a woman wrestling down a stubborn maverick yearling steer five times her size, and holding it down for branding by twisting its horns.

Jessie could tell that Ki was pleased by the way things had turned out; when cows get restless, cowboys get ill-tempered and edgy from trying to control them. Jessie's decision to stick around, and her ability to do the dirty work and do it well, had cheered the men. A woman drover was just the sort of novelty that they'd needed to make it through this rough morning.

Only Rusty, the tenderfoot from back East, seemed to remain moody. Jessie tried to tease him out of his funk, but when that failed, she came straight out and asked him what was wrong.

"It just isn't fair, Miss Starbuck!" the tenderfoot finally exclaimed. "None of the other fellows will so much as talk to me, unless it's to yell that I'm doing things wrong. They've accepted you right off. I know that you're their boss and all, but you're a female, for gosh sakes." Rusty looked away. "No offense meant, ma'am, but it is awfully hard to swallow that a tenderfoot ranks even lower out on the range than a *woman!*"

By midday the storm's imminent threat had begun to abate. Jessie, dog-tired but pleased with herself for the amount of work that she had so far done, found Ki riding herd on yet another bunch of mavericks that had just been brought in.

"It looks like we can keep things under control," Ki said, obviously relieved as he gazed at the gradually brightening sky.

"If I'm no longer needed, I'll start back for the ranch," Jessie said. "With your permission, of *course*, Mister Ramrod." She winked playfully.

"Permission granted. You have worked very hard. I even forgive you for saddling me with that tenderfoot."

"Poor Rusty," Jessie pouted. "I feel so sorry for him. He's so lonesome—"

31

"What did you expect? He's here for a lark, an adventure. He's not one of them, and the men sense it." Ki's expression turned sour. "So far I've kept him pretty much out of trouble. He hasn't strangled any of our cows with his lasso, nor has he nipped off any of his own fingers while twisting his rope around his saddlehorn. Earlier today, Teddy Rolling-Rock had to reprimand him; Rusty had been riding drag on a herd of strays that he and Teddy were bringing in. Just as they reached the main herd, Rusty decided to have himself a smoke . . ."

"Oh no!" Jessie paled. "Maybe I was wrong to force that tenderfoot on you."

Ki shrugged. "Fortunately, Teddy saw what Rusty was about to do, and stopped him. With the way the weather was a few hours ago, a struck match, or the smell of burning tobacco, might have spooked the herd."

"Teddy certainly deserves a bonus," Jessie remarked.

"I've already offered him one, but he will not accept it," Ki replied. "He doesn't see why he should be paid more, merely for doing the job he was hired to do."

"Maybe I should take Rusty back with me to the ranch . . ."

Ki frowned. "Would you feel safe traveling with him all alone?"

Jessie laughed once again. "Feel safe? With Rusty? I should think so! If he ever tried anything, I'd hogtie him belly-down across his horse for the rest of the ride, and *then* I'd tell his father on him!"

"Take him!" Ki implored. "The way things are now, I would rather lose a man than have the other nineteen wasting time keeping an eye on him—" Ki suddenly pointed toward where the herd was milling, still treacherously excitable due to the swiftly changing weather. "There Rusty is now. You can tell him—"

"What's he doing?" Jessie wondered, watching the tenderfoot dig something out of the breast pocket of his gingham shirt. "I hope he's not going to try to light up another smoke."

"Worse than that," Ki exclaimed. He kneed his horse into a run towards Rusty. *"Put that away!"* he began to shout. *"Stop!"*

Totally oblivious, the tenderfoot began tooting an off-key tune on a harmonica. A nearby steer tossed its head and began to trot away from the disturbing sound...

Another followed. And another...

In scant seconds, like a flock of sparrows taking wing, the herd stampeded.

"Dammit!" Teddy Rolling-Rock swore from amid a swirling cloud of dust. "They're heading for that deep arroyo! We got to turn them, boys! We'll lose hundreds if they go busting their fool necks tumbling down the steep banks of that dried-up river!"

As Rusty looked on, astounded at what damage he'd done with his innocent-seeming mouth harp, Jessie, Ki and the other drovers spurred their mounts in a desperate attempt to turn a half-mile-wide mass of lumbering fury away from a route that would lead to self-destruction of the herd on a massive scale.

Jessie rode full out, leaning far forward to cut wind resistance, becoming an extension of her valiant little pinto cowpony, racing along the stampeding herd's flank, angling in so close that she could reach out to ruffle the shaggy hides of the panicked longhorns.

The noise had grown unbelievable. First the cowboys at point position and then the men along the herd's swing points let loose with blood-chilling shouts, firing their handguns into the air. The only chance now was to scare the lead cows into slowing or turning, or else divide the herd, and in that way lessen its momentum. In addition to the racket the men were making, there were the thundering hooves and sonorous bellowing of the cows themselves, everything echoing in the ear until the sense of hearing faded away into blessed numbness.

Gradually the fury of the stampede began to dwindle; the lead cows began to tire, to slow. The men riding swing

33

nearest Jessie angled in on the main body of the herd. As the cows along the outside edge faltered, they acted as a brake upon the entire herd.

Suddenly a renegade bull bolted past the surprised drovers, sending the men's cowponies bucking and rearing in terror as perhaps two hundred animals followed the bull, overwhelming the cowboys in a flood torrent of pounding hooves and tossing horns.

Two hundred prime head had begun a second, flat-out sprint to their own deaths at the clifflike edge of the arroyo!

Jessie twisted the pinto around and lit out after that renegade splinter herd. As she rode, the dust almost blinding her, she cursed the fact that her Colt was back at the chuckwagon. All she had were the two shots in her derringer.

She leaned sideways, tugging the ludicrously tiny pistol out of her boot. She intended to sacrifice the lead bull, to shoot him, and in that way cause the herd to turn. Once it did, it would inevitably slow. By then, the danger of the arroyo would be past, and some of the other drovers would have caught up to take over.

She was at the rear of the herd now. Digging her spurs into the horse's ribs to get a last bit of speed, Jessie angled in on the lead bull.

Two shots. Jessie forced herself to wait until the last moment; the derringer had little accuracy beyond a few feet.

She was riding parallel with the lead bull now. She was so close to the rampaging brute that if it chose that instant to toss its head, its foot-long horns could easily gouge Jessie's pony.

She rose up in the saddle, her weight resting on the soles of her boots shoved into the stirrups. She extended her arm to shove the derringer into the careening bull's ear, and fired once, twice . . .

The .38-caliber derringer's twin reports were lost in the general roar of sound all around Jessie. The only way she could tell that the gun had gone off was from its recoil.

At first she thought she'd failed, that the two shots hadn't been enough. But then the bull tottered sideways, *toward her!* Jessie hauled on the pinto's reins to veer clear of the beast. She looked back in time to see blood streaming from both wide black nostrils of the bull, spraying the cattle immediately behind. They bellowed in fear as the blood of their own kind soaked their snouts. Meanwhile, the mortally wounded bull's front legs collapsed. It slid forward for twenty more yards, carried along by its own momentum, before lying still and dead on the grass. Confused, frightened, leaderless, the herd began to turn.

But their turning had not come soon enough. The arroyo now loomed dead ahead. The herd's momentum would still take them over the edge if Jessie didn't manage to bring them to a complete halt.

There was no time to think, to consider the consequences of her action. Jessie rammed her pony across the path of the stumbling herd. The very breath of the herd seemed to scald her body, and once her pony screamed in outraged terror as a steer's horn hooked upward to draw a red, jagged line across its trembling, sweat-matted haunch. Jessie hung on for dear life. If she fell from the saddle now, those hooves would have her; there'd be nothing left for the drovers to find . . .

But the cattle held back as Jessie rode an invisible straight line along the face of the herd. To the rear, some of the cattle turned to head back toward the main herd. Those in the middle and in front began to dip their heads to graze. Mothers began to bawl for their calves.

It was over. The little piece of hell that was the stampede had vanished as quickly as it had come. The murderous herd was once again just a bunch of placid cows. *Thank the Lord,* Jessie thought, wiping the sweat and grit from her eyes.

"Jessie! Are you all right?" It was Ki, riding with several of the drovers.

"I'm fine, and you men take it slow!" she ordered as the drovers took charge of the herd. "I don't want any more profits run off these cows," she muttered, and then asked Ki, "Anyone hurt?"

35

"No, everyone is fine. Thanks to Rusty," he added.

"Rusty!" Jessie exclaimed. "I can't countenance thanking him!"

"He risked his life to rescue Teddy," Ki explained. "Teddy's mount went down in the path of the main stampede. Rusty saw it happen, and rode to Teddy, letting him ride double to get him out of the herd's way."

"I see." Jessie nodded, and then shrugged. "All right, then, I suppose I'll forgive him. After all, there was no real harm done, except to that bull," she added, shrugging wistfully. "One thing puzzles me, though, Ki. Teddy went down well in front of the stampede, right?" Ki nodded. "Then he was in no real danger! Even *stampeding* cows will make a path around a man or horse if they've got the time to maneuver."

"You know that, we all know that, but Rusty didn't!" Ki said, his almond-shaped eyes glinting with humor. "The tenderfoot showed great courage in riding into what he *thought* was a dangerous situation. The fact that the situation was *not* dangerous in no way lessens that act of bravery."

"What about the other men?" Jessie asked. "You mean they're going along with it?"

"Indeed," Ki smiled. "Cowboys can be a sentimental lot. I suspect Rusty's actions touched their hearts, as has the boy's modesty concerning his 'heroism.'"

"Still want me to take him back to the Circle Star?" Jessie asked.

Ki shook his head. "The men wouldn't have it, I'm afraid. They've announced their intention of holding Rusty accountable for terrorizing both man and beast with tin-ear harmonica playing. There is to be a 'kangaroo court' tonight, after supper."

"Poor Rusty!" Jessie laughed. "That almost makes up for my losing that bull..."

"The men will find him guilty, and probably toss him in a stream as punishment, but they're already calling him 'old Rusty,'" Ki said. "It doesn't matter what a cowboy calls you; as long as he prefaces it with 'old,' he means it fondly."

"It sounds like Rusty is going to have a vacation to remember, after all!" Jessie said. "And I guess I'll be starting back home. I'll be in Sarah, with our luggage, the day after you arrive."

Ki nodded. "And then on to Nettle Grove."

Chapter 3

Denver was a pretty town. The gold dome of the Colorado State Capitol building glittered in the sun, competing in majesty with the Front Range of the Rockies, a scant fifteen miles to the west. Denver was also an expensive town, no matter which side of the little sandy wash of Cherry Creek a man called home. A United States deputy marshal only got paid once a month, and that stipend didn't amount to more than a mouse fart's worth of pocket change anyhow. Was it any wonder that Custis Long got a mite ticked off when he was told that he couldn't cash his pay chit?

"You can't go in," said the man loitering in the doorway of the First National Bank, one of Denver's largest, located at the foot of Capitol Hill.

"What do you mean, I can't?" Longarm demanded. He dug his Ingersoll pocket watch out of his vest to check the time. "It's well after nine, old son. Something wrong in there?"

"Nope. She's closed, is all," the jasper said. He was wearing a tan corduroy suit and a dark green derby hat. Longarm spotted the telltale bulge of a big-bore piece of iron riding underneath the man's suit coat in a shoulder rig. "Bank examiner is in there combing through their books. I guess they like to do that sort of thing in private," the man added, shrugging. "Sorry, but you'll have to move along." He showed Longarm the badge pinned underneath his lapel. "I'm with the Ace Private Security Company, and it's my job to keep this area clear."

Longarm frowned. He'd never heard of that particular

gumshoe outfit, but there were lots of them coming and going all the time in Denver. "Any idea when they're going to be opening up?"

"None at all. Now move along!" Green Derby insisted, his voice taking on a threatening edge.

Longarm nodded evenly, not taking offense at the man's brusque tone. The security guard didn't know that he was a fellow lawman, after all. Longarm kept his silver badge pinned inside his wallet, only transferring it to his lapel when it was necessary to advertise his status.

He looked past the glowering guard, trying to see into the bank, but the shades were drawn on the glass doors as well as on the big picture windows to either side of it.

"Damned inconvenient," Longarm muttered to no one in particular, and then moved on, past a hitching post where half a dozen mounts were tethered, to the end of the block, where he stood on the corner and wondered what to do.

He had just come from Billy Vail's office in the Federal Courthouse. As Chief United States Marshal, First District Court of Colorado, Longarm's boss had himself a pimply-faced clerk who handled all the office's paperwork. It had been that clerk whom Longarm had gone to see, passing through the oak door with its gilt lettering and into Vail's outer office, in order to collect his pay chit.

"Where are you going, deputy?" the youngster had demanded as Longarm headed back out, his chit in hand. "Don't you remember? You've got an appointment with Marshal Vail at nine-thirty."

Longarm glanced uneasily at the frosted glass door that led to Vail's inner sanctum, and then put his finger to his lips, hushing the clerk. "I'll be back in plenty of time, Henry. I just want to run down and cash this before the bank gets busy."

"He'll skin you alive if you're late again," the clerk warned, sounding like he was looking forward to it.

"Quiet down, will you?" Longarm asked. "He'll hear you."

"The marshal's got a new assignment for you. I've been

40

typing up your travel vouchers, Deputy—"

"Shush!"

The clerk swiveled his desk chair toward Vail's door. "—Deputy Long!" he finished loudly.

"One of these days..." Longarm muttered at the twittering clerk.

"Longarm?" Vail called.

"Guess you'd better go in—" the clerk began, gloating triumphantly.

"Tell him I'll be *right* back," Longarm cut the twerp off, and hurried out of the office.

And Longarm had meant to go right back, he surely had, but now here he was, standing on the corner, waiting for the First National—the only bank that would cash the consarned federal payroll chits—to open up for business.

He checked his pocket watch again. Nine-fifteen. He'd wait another few minutes, and then he'd have to start back up Capitol Hill if he wanted to be on time to see Billy Vail.

Longarm angled his way across the street, to sit down on the bench in front of a barbershop. As he did, he caught a glimpse of himself reflected in the tonsorial parlor's mirrored windows.

What he saw was a sun-bronzed, rangy jasper who looked like he'd spent most of his thirty-odd years in the saddle, a jasper with close-cropped, tobacco-brown hair, a longhorn mustache, and blue-gray eyes. Longarm was wearing brown tweed trousers that fit like a second skin over his lean hips, and a gray flannel shirt, gussied up with the black shoestring tie that regulations now decreed a federal lawman had to wear. Over the shirt went a vest cut from the same brown tweed as his trousers. Completing his outfit was a brown frock coat and a snuff-colored, flat-crowned Stetson positioned dead center on his head.

Longarm settled his rawboned, six-feet-four-inch frame down on the bench. What with his polished, low-heeled cordovan boots, the folks walking by might have taken him for a prosperous cattleman, although if they did, the joke would have been on them.

Right now, Longarm didn't have the coins in his pocket to buy himself a cup of coffee. Hell, he'd been without one of his two-for-a-nickel cheroots since early yesterday afternoon! He was dying for a smoke, which was why he'd been so all-fired anxious to cash his pay chit. He'd wanted to be able to light up if he was going to settle in opposite Vail's desk for a lengthy palaver...

Well, it looked as if he was going to have to go without one of the cheroots he was presently craving. Last night he'd spent his last money buying a handful of .44-40 cartridges for the double-action Colt Model T—its barrel cut down to five inches—riding butt forward, high on his left hip. He'd been down to his last five rounds, a full load, as Longarm always kept the hammer resting on an empty chamber. It had been a tough choice—a few spare rounds, or some smokes? Longarm had decided on the ammunition. It made no sense for a lawman to be down to his last five cartridges. It was better to be dying for a smoke than to *actually* die for want of a spare round...

Longarm checked his watch for the third time. *Damn!* It was now or never to start back if he wanted to be punctual. He tucked the Ingersoll back into the left-hand pocket of his vest, adjusting the watch's chain as he did so. Linked to the chain's opposite end, and nestled in his right vest pocket, was a brass .44 derringer. The glittering, gold-washed chain draped between the watch and the pocket shooter like a cardshark's leering grin.

Longarm stood up and began to trudge back towards Capitol Hill, thinking it was just his luck that Vail's clerk was too young to smoke, and that the Marshal himself favored a pipe...

The gunshot was muffled, but it froze Longarm in his tracks. The shot had come from within the bank, he was sure of that. He'd been in that main branch a hundred times. Once he'd even shot it out with desperadoes in there while on undercover stake-out duty. The bank had a cavernous, marbled interior that would cause a gun's report to reverberate in just that softened, dreamlike manner.

42

Longarm kept his eye on the security guard as he extracted his wallet from the inside pocket of his frock coat, removed his silver badge from its fold of leather, and pinned it to his lapel. Mr. Green Derby had drawn his revolver, all right, but instead of rushing inside the bank, he was still standing with his back to the door, keeping his eye on those six horses tethered a few paces away.

"Son of a bitch," Longarm swore softly. "I've been sitting out here watching a bank robbery in progress!"

Green Derby saw Longarm approaching. His eyes flicked towards Longarm's lapel, and then widened.

"Yep, mine's real, old son," Longarm told him. "I reckon your badge isn't. Now drop the gun—"

A female bystander began to scream as Green Derby snapped a panicked shot in Longarm's general direction.

"One chance is all you get," Longarm warned, brushing back the left side of his frock coat as he spoke.

Green Derby gripped his revolver in both hands to try again. Longarm reached across his belt buckle with his right hand, drawing his own Colt from its waxed, heat-hardened holster in a whip-fast motion. Green Derby was still aiming when Longarm shot him in the stomach. The man doubled over, dropping his gun as he crumpled across the bank's threshold.

At that instant the bank's twin doors were kicked open. Longarm glimpsed five men, dressed like saddle tramps, elbowing each other to get out of the bank. The first man, his gun drawn and a set of saddlebags thrown over his shoulder, was so anxious to get away that he actually tripped over the corpse of the man Longarm had just shot. The outlaw went sprawling, losing his gun. His saddlebags' flaps came open, spilling paper money into the street.

Longarm ignored him, closing in on the remaining four. "Federal marsh—" was all he got to say before one of the men took a shot at him.

Longarm crabbed sideways as the slug whistled past his ear. He fired twice, not wanting to, not liking the circumstances of this shootout at all. The phrase "shooting fish in a barrel" sprang into Longarm's mind, for that's what he was doing—shooting four gun-toting but very trapped fish in the narrow barrel that was the bank's vestibule.

Longarm's first round caught the outlaw who'd shot at him square in the chest. He went down on his knees, head lolling, and then pitched forward. Longarm's second shot hit a third outlaw low on his left side. The man's gun and saddlebags fell forgotten as he danced on rubbery legs out of the bank, to tumble across the sandstone sidewalk.

The remaining two outlaws disappeared back into the shadowy interior of the bank, but not before Longarm managed to get a good look at their faces. The smaller man was unknown to him, but the larger, fair-skinned and blue-eyed, with blond hair and muttonchop sidewhiskers, was a familiar face to most lawmen, as were the man's firearms: a pair of sawed-off, double-barreled twelve-gauge shotguns fitted with pistol grips and toted in a brace of custom-designed waist holsters.

Longarm caught movement out of the corner of his eye, and looked down to see the outlaw who'd tripped slithering like a snake to reach his gun. Longarm took several quick steps toward the man, at the same time thumbing back the hammer of his Colt. The crisp, metallic click froze the outlaw in mid-slither. He looked back over his shoulder to see Longarm pointing the .44 at his head. The tip of the Colt just touched the tip of the man's nose.

The outlaw swallowed hard and tried his best to smile. He did a credible job of it, too, considering. "How about I give up, Marshal?"

"That's a deal, old son," Longarm murmured absently, his mind already working on the tricky situation inside the bank, where two well-armed, desperate men were holed up with an undetermined number of hostages.

A passel of Denver's uniformed police had arrived on the scene. They busied themselves pushing back the curious as they cordoned off the area immediately in front of the bank. A mule-drawn paddy wagon was pulled into place a few yards behind where Longarm was standing. A white-

44

haired constable with hash marks running up his sleeve ambled over.

"Morning, Longarm."

"Morning, Sergeant Moorcock," Longarm greeted the cop.

"The chief's put me in charge of this one," Moorcock said. He glanced down at Longarm's prisoner, and then eyed the three bodies littering the bank's sidewalks, turning the sandstone crimson. "Looks like we're left with cleaning up your mess again, deputy," Moorcock added wearily.

"Maybe not, Sarge." Longarm gestured with his Colt toward the bank. "Two more in there. Likely with hostages."

"You must be slowing down, Longarm," Moorcock snickered. "Not like you to leave any loose ends—"

Longarm ignored the sarcasm. "One of them is Clem Kirby."

"Kirby?" The sergeant flinched. "What the hell are we standing here for? Grab your prisoner and let's get to cover behind that wagon! Kirby could start blasting away with those cannons of his at any moment!" He pointed at the saddlebags of money lying in the street just outside the bank's entrance. "Longarm, fetch that cash, would you?"

"*You* fetch it!"

"Screw it, then," Moorcock decided. "It ain't going nowhere. Let's get to cover."

One of Moorcock's constables handcuffed the prisoner securely to the paddy wagon, and then Longarm and the police sergeant interrogated the man.

"Can't say for sure how many were in the bank when we went in," the prisoner replied to Longarm's first question. "A bunch, anyway. We stationed Ben—the fellow all decked out to be the security agent—at the front door, and then herded all them customers and tellers and whatnot against one wall. We had them lie belly-down on the floor with their hands on top their heads."

"Who got shot?" Longarm asked.

The prisoner looked down at his boots. "A bank officer, some dumb turd, gave Kirby some backtalk. Tim Slate—

45

he's that little fellow in there with Kirby—he drew his pistol and, just as cool as you please, shot the poor jasper in the back."

"Shot him dead?" Moorcock demanded.

The prisoner nodded.

"I was hoping it was Kirby that did the shooting," Longarm mused. "That way we could have appealed to this Slate, tried to get him to surrender. Kirby's already wanted for murder. Now that Slate has committed a hanging offense, they'll stick together." He shook his head. "They'll want to go out tough, I reckon." He began to reload his Colt. "Looks like I made the right purchase last night when I bought these extra rounds." Longarm turned back to the prisoner. "Is Kirby as bad as usual?"

Moorcock scowled. "What's that supposed to mean?"

"He's worse," the prisoner told Longarm. "Last few weeks, he's turned plumb loco. Never know what he's going to pull next. And when he gets to drinking..."

A shotgun blast blew out one of the bank's plate-glass windows, shredding, but more or less leaving intact, the drawn shade.

"I'm king!" Clem Kirby began roaring. *"I'm king of Denver!"*

"It's the inside of that there bank what set him off on that 'king' stuff," the prisoner said. "It's all gilded ceilings and tan marble, right? Kirby said it looked like a palace, and—"

"I'm king!"

"You boys take up positions covering those windows and the door," Sergeant Moorcock ordered his men, drawing his own revolver.

"Who killed—who killed the king's soldiers?" Kirby was shouting. "Who dared to fire upon my soldiers?"

Moorcock gestured toward the bank with his short-barreled, bulldog-shaped revolver. "What do you think we should do about that madman and his accomplice, deputy?"

Just then Kirby appeared in the bank's doorway, holding a pale, quietly weeping young woman in front of him, one of his sawed-off shotguns pressed against her ear.

"The king is waiting for his answer!" Kirby roared. The outlaw's blue eyes were wild and bloodshot. Spittle dribbled down his chin. The woman, trembling, clasping her shawl about her shoulders with white-knuckled hands, was silently moving her lips; Longarm guessed she was saying her prayers.

Kirby pulled back the twin hammers on his pistol-gripped shotgun. His female hostage began to weep at the death-knell sound of those clicking hammers.

Longarm, his Colt holstered, stepped out from behind the paddy wagon. "Reckon you're looking for me, old son."

"King!" Kirby screamed in outrage. "I'm the king! Of Denver, damn your eyes!"

"Pardon the mistake, sire," Longarm smiled. He kept his hands in plain view as he took a couple of steps toward the crazed bank robber. Kirby's shotgun had been cut down to a twelve-inch barrel length. The weapon's blast would cut a man in two at five yards, but likely never touch him at twenty. While Longarm stood where he was, he was relatively safe.

"Who is it, there?" Kirby asked. "Come forward, knave."

Longarm stayed where he was, but knelt, going down on one knee, hoping to amuse the crazed outlaw and make him forget the order he'd just given. "Reckon we've met before, Clem. It's Custis Long."

"Longarm?" Kirby squinted as if the sunlight hurt his eyes. "Is it really you?"

"It is, and you'd be doing me a real favor, Clem—"

"I am the king!"

"Excuse me, sire. You'd be doing me a real favor if you took that scattergun away from that girl's head."

A face appeared over Kirby's shoulder. It was Tim Slate. Now that Longarm could get a good look at the fellow, the little shit reminded him of Marshal Vail's young clerk, gone bad. Like the clerk, this young outlaw had an angry red, pockmarked complexion. He was wearing a black Stetson with a hatband of silver conchos. From the way he was

47

waving around his nickel-plated, ivory-gripped Colt, he was either very drunk or he just didn't care who he killed.

"We need more liquor!" Slate yelled out. "I want liquor, or I'll shoot me another of these fine townsfolk!"

"The prince requires drink," Kirby observed pleasantly.

"Right away," Longarm smiled. "We'll fetch it right away, but first, sire, won't you take that shotgun away from that girl's head? You don't want to hurt any more of your subjects, sire."

"Hurt them? Of course not, Longarm," Kirby said thickly. "With this, my scepter, I merely release their souls to soar heavenward, thusly."

Kirby's shotgun went *thump!*, and the girl's head dissolved in a spray of crimson mist. There were screams from the surrounding crowd as the woman's decapitated body folded at the knees, to lie twitching across the corpses of the outlaws shot by Longarm. Before the shocked police sharpshooters could have at him, the grinning, blood-splattered killer stepped back into the shadows of the bank.

Longarm had retreated to the relative safety of the paddy wagon. He felt sick to his stomach, and fought back an urge to vomit.

"God, oh God," Sergeant Moorcock was murmuring to himself over and over. "Oh God . . ."

"Here are the king's demands," Kirby intoned from somewhere inside the bank, while Tim Slate's high-pitched giggle formed a horrible counterpoint. "First we want liquor. Second, I desire my queen. Send me Big Lil—only she will do!"

Longarm looked at Moorcock. "Big Lil?"

"He just shot that girl's head off," Moorcock was mumbling. "Oh God . . ."

"Snap out of it, Sergeant!" Longarm ordered. "She's dead! We can't help her! We've got to think of the other hostages in the bank. Now what about this Big Lil?"

"A prostitute," Moorcock said wearily. "She runs a house in the red-light district off Larimer, near the railroad yards. She's a big woman—over six feet tall. Full-figured, you

48

know?" Moorcock blushed. "I guess Kirby did business with her and liked what she had to offer..."

"Send a couple of men to bring her here," Longarm instructed. "Put handcuffs on her if you have to, but get her here!"

Moorcock hurried to do Longarm's bidding.

"Kirby!" Longarm shouted. "Lil's on her way. Your queen is coming, sire! She'll have liquor with her."

"My men are on their way," Moorcock said quietly, returning to Longarm's side.

"Then I guess we wait," Longarm sighed. "There's no other way in or out of the bank but that front door. The rear windows all have bars across them. Not that Kirby and Slate have any desire to sneak away..."

"What do you think they've got in mind for a getaway?"

"I don't reckon they've thought it out that far," Longarm answered. "But I don't mean to let them live long enough to consider it."

It was a few minutes later that Moorcock's men returned. There was no doubt that the woman they brought with them was Big Lil.

She was big all right—one of the tallest, widest-hipped, biggest-busted women Longarm had ever seen. He estimated her to be close to his own height, and her snug-fitting, red velvet dress showed without a doubt that her lush hourglass shape had nothing to do with her being fat. Big Lil was just... *big!* And pretty, too, with pouty, bee-stung lips, a small upturned nose, and big violet eyes. A few tendrils of auburn hair peeked out from beneath the "Little Bo-Peep" bonnet she had knotted beneath her chin.

"What the hell is the meaning of this, Moorcock?" Lil demanded. "Get these little shrimps away from me!"

Longarm had to grin. Moorcock's two uniformed constables were both of average height, which put them about a head shorter than the woman they were escorting. Lil looked like a grizzly about to shake off two pesky terriers.

"My name's Custis Long, but folks call me Longarm. I'm a deputy U.S. marshal, and I need your help, ma'am."

"Good-looking, and polite to boot," Lil drawled, winking lasciviously. "What can I do for you, big boy?"

Longarm filled her in on everything that had happened, including Kirby's coldblooded murder of the young woman, and his last demand that his "queen" be brought to him.

"No chance," Lil declared. "I ain't going in there. You don't know Kirby! He's crazy! He's—"

"We *do* know about him," Longarm cut her off. "And I have no intention of sending you in there. All we want you to do is show yourself to him, and say that you're going to a saloon to fetch his liquor. You say that you'll be right back—"

"And then what?" Lil demanded suspiciously.

Longarm told her.

"Sonofabitch, that might just work," Moorcock said, awestruck. "Kirby's so filled with booze already, he might not notice the difference until it's too late."

"I'm not taking off my clothes, and that's final!" Lil announced.

"I just told you that one innocent girl has already been killed," Longarm said firmly. "You're going to take that dress off, all right, or else I'll do it *for* you!"

"Now you're talking, big boy..." she said with a leer.

"Just do as he tells you, Lil," Moorcock said.

"We'll take you over to that barbershop across the street," Longarm added. "It's got mirrored windows, so you'll have privacy getting undressed."

"That'll be a novelty," Lil chuckled. "All right, let's get it done."

"Come with me," Longarm said.

"I'd love to," she replied bawdily as he led her out from around the paddy wagon, so that Kirby could see her.

"Here's Lil," Longarm called out to the bank robber. "Here's your queen, sire!"

"Huh?" Lil asked, puzzled.

"Just play along," Longarm whispered.

"Lil? My queen?" Kirby called, his voice thick and hoarse. "Is it you?"

50

"Yeah, honey. It's me. Can you see me?"

"Lil, my head hurts," Kirby bawled piteously. "It hurts!"

"I'll make it feel better," Lil soothed.

"I'm the king," Kirby muttered. "The . . . king . . ."

"Where's the liquor?" Tim Slate shouted. "Don't see no liquor—"

"I'm going to fetch it now," Lil said in response to Longarm's quiet coaching. "I'll fetch it and be right back."

"Right back . . ." Kirby echoed vaguely. "I'm the king . . ."

Back behind the paddy wagon, Moorcock was sighing with relief. "Good thing Kirby ain't thinking too clear."

Longarm nodded in agreement. "Okay, Lil, let's head on over to the barbershop. Moorcock, get me a paper sack from the general store over yonder. I'll need it to seem like I'm carrying a couple of bottles of drink when I go in there."

Moorcock nodded, saying, "I already had the barbershop vacated. It's all yours, deputy."

Longarm escorted Lil across the street, past the red-and-white striped barber's pole, into the darkened, shades-drawn shop.

"How do I look?" Longarm asked Moorcock when he returned to the cop's side a few minutes later.

"Like celibacy is the answer, after all," Moorcock smirked. "What you got stuffed in there, anyhow?"

"Some of the barber's towels," Longarm replied.

"It'll never fool Kirby."

"It will if I don't let him get fresh," Longarm said.

Lil had helped him pull together his disguise. Longarm was bare-chested, but wearing his own trousers, gunbelt and boots beneath the big woman's dress. A few balled-up towels stuffed into the dress's gaping bodice was the best they could do to approximate Lil's top-heavy figure. The madam's bonnet covered up Longarm's lack of womanly tresses and—he hoped—most of his face.

The disguise was a piss-poor one, of course, and wouldn't have fooled a child in broad daylight, but Longarm was staking everything on the fact that Kirby and Slate, in their

51

liquor-induced stupors, would not immediately recognize him when he passed through the dimly lit vestibule of the bank.

After that, it wouldn't matter who they thought he was . . .

"How's Lil?" Moorcock asked.

"She got a bunch of those barber cloths to keep her warm. She'll be fine. Did you fetch the paper sack?"

"Yeah, what are you planning to do with it? Put it over your head?" Moorcock snorted.

Longarm lifted the dress's hem and drew his Colt. He'd already slid an extra round into the gun to give him a full six shots.

He unfolded the paper sack that Moorcock handed him and tore a slit in one side of it. He inserted his right hand, holding his Colt, through the slit, and cradled the sack against his bogus bosom with his left hand, as if he were a woman carefully cradling fragile glass bottles against breakage.

"All right, then." Longarm nodded to the sergeant. "Let them know I'm coming."

"Kirby, Slate!" Moorcock called. "Kirby!"

"Yeah, we hear you."

It was Slate answering them. Longarm and Moorcock exchanged a look. "Maybe Kirby's passed out?" Moorcock asked hopefully. Longarm shrugged. "If so, I'll take him alive."

"Slate!" Moorcock shouted. "Lil's come back with the liquor!"

"It's about time," Slate snarled. "I was about ready to shoot me another hostage, just to—"

"Where is my queen!" came Kirby's roar.

"Get her in here fast," Slate twittered, "before the two of us turn this here bank into a morgue!"

Longarm, his bonneted head tucked low, stepped away from the paddy wagon and did his best to approximate a woman's mincing steps as he hurried toward the bank's entrance. Behind him he could sense the concern of Moorcock and his squad as they watched and waited tensely to see if this desperate charade would succeed. Longarm understood their anxiety; if he failed, Kirby and Slate would not only kill him, but, in their rage at having been tricked, likely kill all of their hostages as well.

Longarm picked his way through the grisly, fly-blown remains littering the vestibule. Inside the bank his heels clicked ominously upon the polished floors, the sound echoing against the gilded cathedral ceilings of the tomblike, gaslit interior. Longarm saw Tim Slate, his gaudy pistol drawn, hurrying toward him. He had only seconds to survey the crazy scene. Paper money lay scattered everywhere, and the gates of all the vacant tellers' cages were swung wide. The slain bank officer was still lying where Slate had shot him. The dead man's blood had pooled beneath his corpse on the tan marble floor. Longarm saw twenty or more hostages clustered against the wall at the far end of the bank. Some of them were quietly sobbing. About fifteen feet away from where Longarm stood was an area fenced with a waist-high oak railing. This was where the middle-level bank officers had their desks, but the furniture had all been piled together in a jumble about ten feet high, and lounging on top of this, as if in some kind of crazy throne, his brace of twelve-gauge scepters on his lap, was the self-proclaimed "King of Denver," Clem Kirby.

Kirby's black-and-tan, checkerboard-patterned shirt was sweat-soaked, and splattered with the dried blood of the girl he'd murdered. His eyes were half closed, and his dirty-blond curls hung in greasy ringlets on his forehead. He was muttering to himself unintelligibly while his left hand twirled the hairs of his muttonchop whiskers and his right hand alternately fondled his crotch and his sawed-off shotguns.

Longarm kept his head down as Slate reached him. The pimply-faced killer smiled, showing his mossy teeth. He holstered his revolver in order to reach out for the paper sack.

Longarm looked up at Slate. "You didn't say a thing

53

about my new dress," he scolded. As Slate was frantically clawing for his gun, Longarm, his Colt still inside the paper sack, shot him in the face.

Slate's hat went flying as he fell. Longarm was tearing the smoldering paper from his .44 when Kirby, screaming incoherently, let loose a charge from one of his shotguns. Kirby was fast, and an accurate shot, despite his condition; his shotgun blast just missed Longarm, some of the pellets shredding the skirt of Lil's dress. In his haste to backpedal out of range, Longarm's leather soles slipped on the polished marble floor. He fell flat on his ass, but the fall saved his life, for Kirby chose that moment to fire again, this time placing an awesome, fifteen-inch-wide shot pattern into the wall at about the height where Longarm's head would have been if he'd remained on his feet.

Kirby, giggling, was bringing his second shotgun to bear when Longarm fired three times, riding the potent .44's recoil as he stitched bloody holes up Kirby's chest. The shotguns went clattering to the floor as the self-proclaimed king, howling in agony, was knocked from his perch.

Longarm got to his feet and walked over to where Kirby lay still, his pale blue eyes staring up sightlessly. The hostages were all moaning and crying in a frenzied panic. Longarm pulled off Lil's bonnet, telling them, "It's over. You're safe. I'm a federal marshal."

One of the bank's officers approached timidly, his tellers bunched warily behind him. Moorcock and his men, their guns drawn, were streaming into the bank.

"Longarm, you in there?"

It was Marshal Billy Vail's gruff voice hailing him. Longarm glanced at the bank's big pendulum clock. It was almost noon.

Longarm rolled his eyes heavenward. He could probably use busting up the bank heist and hostage situation as an excuse for being late for his appointment with Vail, but the finicky, deskbound marshal was sure to raise hell over the fact that Longarm had done it all without wearing his necktie!

The bank officer was a stout, baldheaded little jasper. He and his employees were all clustered around Longarm in a show of gratitude.

"You saved our lives!" proclaimed the bank officer.

One statuesque, redheaded lady teller with a comely figure caught Longarm's eye. He favored her with an easy grin and a wink.

"Wasn't much," he drawled. "I just came in here to cash my pay chit..."

Chapter 4

Marshal Vail had taken one look at Longarm decked out in Lil's dress, and had then hurried back to the relative sanity of the Federal Courthouse building, muttering that he'd read about it all in Longarm's report. A half hour after the shoot-out, Longarm, wearing his own clothes, his pay chit cashed and a fresh supply of cartridges and cheroots stashed in the pockets of his frock coat, was comfortably settled in the red morocco leather chair in Vail's office. The deputy was contentedly puffing on a smoke while the baldheaded, big-bellied chief marshal glared at him from across his mahogany desk.

"One o'clock in the afternoon," Vail grumbled, glancing at the banjo clock ticking away on the oak-paneled wall.

"I wasn't exactly sleeping late, chief," Longarm reminded the gruff old buzzard. "Clem Kirby was at the top of our wanted list."

"I know that, damn you," Vail fairly snarled.

"It took Moorcock a while to locate Lil, and—"

Vail quickly put his hands over his ears. "Don't tell me nothing about it!" he winced. "I'll read your report. Damn! Just thinking about how you looked in women's clothes gives me the willies! Likely put me off my feed for a month!"

Longarm looked up at the thirty-eight stars of the red, white, and blue flag on the wall behind Vail's desk, and waited for his boss to finish up his fussing and fuming and get on with business.

"I suppose the Justice Department is supposed to pay for that whore's dress?"

"She's a good woman, Billy," Longarm replied evenly. "She helped us save a bunch of innocent citizens' lives. Reckon for that good deed alone, she deserves to be called better than a whore, no matter how she earns her keep."

Scowling, Vail looked away. "Reckon so," he admitted. He busied himself pawing through the litter of files on his desk. "I got something fairly routine for you this time around, Longarm. I'm sending you out to assist in tracking Will Sayre—"

Longarm almost choked on his cheroot as he began laughing. "Hell, Billy! While I'm at it, why don't I put the cuffs on Paul Bunyan and Good Saint Nick!"

"You don't believe Sayre exists, is that it?"

Longarm shrugged, wiping the smile from his face when he realized that Vail was dead serious about his going out after Sayre. "Well, I know that there hasn't been an eyewitness report of Sayre being involved in a job for years."

"That doesn't prove a thing," Vail replied. "Who knows what Sayre looks like after all this time?" The marshal tapped his file. "Start from the beginning, Longarm, tell me what you know."

Longarm settled back in his chair, puffing blue smoke rings as he collected his thoughts. "Well, now, first I heard of Sayre was sometime after the War. Lawmen in Utah and Wyoming began receiving complaints from some of the larger cattle spreads about cow thievery. In every incident a branding iron was found left behind—*purposely* left behind, as a calling card. A circled four and five..."

Longarm picked up a pencil from Vail's desk, and wrote the number 45 on a piece of scrap paper, drawing a circle around it.

"The way I heard it, that brand was supposed to stand for Sayre's .45-caliber Colt," Vail said, glancing at Longarm's drawing.

Shrugging, Longarm leaned back in his chair. "Reckon that explanation is as good as any," he said. "Nobody has ever seen a cow carrying that brand. Those trademark irons weren't meant to be used for anything but aggravating

58

cattlemen and lawmen, and creating a legend around Will Sayre. Anyway, pretty soon those irons were popping up in Colorado, Arizona, Nebraska, and Kansas. Will Sayre left them behind during bank robberies as well as cattle thefts. Pretty soon it became clear that Sayre himself couldn't possibly be in so many different locations at once; the law figured Sayre had himself a gang that numbered maybe fifty men."

Vail nodded. "Nobody knew for sure if Sayre was riding with his men at all, or just sending them out on jobs from some hideout. The law has tried to bring Sayre to justice, but the honest citizenry has never been at all interested in lending a hand. Folks would just out-and-out refuse to be part of any posse that aimed to track a Sayre gang."

"Sayre is smart, all right," Longarm said. "I don't know if it's true or not, but folks sure do *believe* that every now and then a church, a down-and-out farmer or rancher, or a widow lady with kids to feed finds a tow sack of money on the doorstep, with that .45-caliber brand burnt into the burlap."

"I've heard tell that when a bunch of robbers would barge into a bank and show that Sayre running iron, the damned bank tellers themselves would cheer fit to bust!"

"You can't blame them, chief. Those tellers weren't losing a dime of their own money when they handed over the cash. Sayre has been careful to rob only the bigger cattlemen's association and mining banks. He's never robbed the general stores that serve as the banks for the common folk. And he's never pulled a job where anybody got killed." Longarm smiled. "Reckon you could say that Will Sayre was just like Robin Hood."

"Who?" Vail sharply asked.

"Robin Hood, chief," Longarm replied.

"What part of the country does he operate in?"

Longarm had worked for Billy Vail a long time. He knew that Vail had once rode with the Texas Rangers, a mean bunch if ever there was one, and Billy's temper hadn't exactly mellowed with age. He was very careful not to smile when he said, "Sherwood Forest, chief, but you see, Robin Hood isn't—"

"Isn't in my jurisdiction," Vail interrupted as he peered at the map hanging on the wall. "So I don't give a damn about this Hood. Let's get back to Will Sayre."

"Yes sir," Longarm said, relieved. "Come to think of it, I'm a mite surprised that the Justice Department is concerned with Sayre. Like I said, nobody has claimed to have seen him for years. What makes him a big number all of a sudden?"

Vail smiled thinly. "He's made himself a bad mistake, Longarm. A Sayre gang robbed a railroad mail car, leaving two clerks dead."

"A *Sayre* gang did that?" Longarm asked doubtfully.

"They left behind a 'forty-five' branding iron," Vail said with a shrug. "I don't see how a maverick gang would dare commit a crime in Sayre's name if they weren't really working for him."

"You're right, Billy. They'd be signing their own death warrants if they tried that." Longarm stubbed out the remains of his cheroot in Vail's ashtray. "You know, it's kind of a damn shame, after all these years, for Sayre to start preying on little folks."

"I know what you're saying, Longarm, but those are the facts of the matter," Vail replied.

"You said that I'd be *assisting* on this case?"

"That's right. As you know, the Post Office has its own agents to handle mail thefts. There's a man already en route to take charge of the case from the local law. His name is"—Vail riffled through the typewritten pages in his file—"Broadwick. Postal Inspector Lloyd Broadwick."

"Never heard of him," Longarm mused.

"Don't reckon that you would have. My understanding is that Inspector Broadwick has made his reputation back East."

Longarm frowned. "They're sending out a tenderfoot to track Will Sayre?"

"Hell, no!" Vail grinned maliciously. "They're sending

the good inspector out to *arrest* Sayre. I'm sending *you* out to *track* the owlhoot."

"But Billy—"

"I know, I know," Vail cut him off. "You like to work alone. You don't like taking orders." Vail shrugged. "I don't care. We work for Justice, and my orders are to send one of my best men to assist this Broadwick in his task. So that's what I'm going to do. You've got your orders, Longarm. Pick up your travel vouchers on the way out."

Longarm nodded. His saddlebags, bedroll, and possibles were all packed and ready to go, stacked alongside his .44-40 Winchester in the closet of his digs at his rooming house on the far side of Cherry Creek. It would take no time at all to head over and gather up his stuff, inform his landlady that he'd be away for a while, and then swing by the livery stable to pull his saddle and bridle out of storage. The federal government would cover the expense of renting a horse whenever he got to where Vail was sending him.

"I reckon I'm heading for Utah, right, Billy?" Longarm glanced at the clock. "Looks like I missed the last of the trains west until tomorrow."

"I know that!" Vail snapped. "Inspector Broadwick is likely already there, waiting on you. Anyway, you're meeting him in Wyoming, in a town close to the scene of the mail-car robbery, and not far from the rough country in Utah where we believe Sayre's hideout is located."

"Where exactly, Billy?" Longarm asked, getting to his feet.

"A place called Nettle Grove," Vail grumbled, waving him out. "My clerk will send Inspector Broadwick a telegram confirming your arrival. And, Longarm . . ." Vail added, "try to keep out of trouble until you're on that train!"

Chapter 5

After the miserable drudgery of the cattle roundup and the drive to market, Ki was hugely enjoying this peaceful trip to Nettle Grove. He and Jessie had arrived a few days ago, via the Union Pacific. The last time they were here, Nettle Grove had been an honest but rather shabby little township...

The samurai smiled to himself. It appeared that, thanks to Starbuck magic, the dreary caterpillar had been transformed into a radiant butterfly!

During the past week, while Jessie was occupied with business matters, Ki had spent most of his time exploring the town. There were new residential neighborhoods where the gleaming white clapboard cottages marched along in rows, like the crops in a carefully cultivated garden. A new wing had been added to the grammar school, and the railroad warehouses and cattle pens near the tracks were now all freshly painted and constantly bustling as Nettle Grove claimed its place as a center for shipping cattle to more heavily populated areas of the nation.

On their last visit, Nettle Grove's main thoroughfare had been rutted and dusty, and its bordering sidewalks had had cracked and missing boards. Now the street was regularly raked and sprinkled, and the raised wooden sidewalks were all in first-class condition. Most of the once-vacant storefronts were now all rented, and the townsfolk were proudly boasting that Nettle Grove's array of stores, cafes, saloons, and other businesses had begun to rival those in Cough Creek, the county seat.

Ki was appropriately attired for his tour of the town. Usually he disliked dressing up, but after living in his denim jeans and leather vest through the roundup, his blue-gray tweed suit, light blue flannel shirt, and black shoestring tie were a pleasant change. A gray Stetson and low-cut, black Wellington boots completed his outfit.

Ki did not wear a gun. He had nothing against firearms; after all, the Japanese had been using them since the sixteenth century. It was merely that Ki, like any samurai, considered guns clumsy, inelegant, and untrustworthy. Let others trust to their Colts or Smith & Wessons; he would rely on other weapons, and mostly on his razor-sharp warrior's wits.

Ki continued on his walk, often returning the friendly greeting of a passerby who recognized him as Jessie's companion. Miss Jessica Starbuck and her friends were quite popular in Nettle Grove these days, but that had not always been the case.

Not at all, the samurai thought as he paused at the corner where Main Street intersected with a narrow avenue dubbed Schiff Street.

Ki frowned, his memory casting back to those days when Tom Schiff, the arrogant owner of the largest cattle spread in these parts, boasted that he owned Nettle Grove, and had no use for Jessie Starbuck or anyone else who might try to come to the aid of those smaller ranchers who dared defy his rule. Schiff had made a devil's pact with Jessie's sworn enemies, the Prussian cartel; they would help him force the ranchers off their land, and in exchange he would grant the cartel the area's mineral rights.

Defeating the land grabbers hadn't been easy, Ki now remembered as he wandered down Schiff Street. Schiff's gunslicks, masquerading as cattle rustlers, had murdered Hiram Tang, the leader of the struggling confederation of small ranchers. While attempting to protect Tang, Ki himself had suffered a head wound from a ricocheting bullet that had left him temporarily blinded. Hiram's young son Danny, determined to avenge his father's murder, had stood by the

64

disabled samurai, as had a spunky—and passionate—female storekeeper named Mary Hudson. Jessie, for her part, had managed to persuade an honest deputy town marshal named Hank Stills to investigate the land grabbers' schemes, and so they were foiled . . .

Now Hank Stills was Nettle Grove's town marshal, with a deputy of his own to command. He and Mary Hudson had married, adopting the orphaned Danny. The three were making a go of it running the Triple D spread left to Danny by his father. The reunion with their friends had been a joyous one, and Ki's reunion with young Danny had been especially satisfying. Ki had forged a close bond with Danny; like himself, the boy had been orphaned at an early age, but had shown a warrior's mettle in confronting his enemies. It had been Danny himself, then barely fourteen years of age, who had killed Tom Schiff, the cattle baron who had been responsible for the murder of Danny's father.

Danny had grown a head taller since Ki last saw him. Hank and Mary Stills had confided to the samurai that Danny was as happy and boisterous as any adolescent approaching manhood. Ki had been told that Danny's greatest desire was one day to journey to the Japans, in order to learn Ki's style of "wrassling."

Ki turned right at the end of Schiff Street, to wander along Market Lane. This backstreet looked more like it belonged to the *old* Nettle Grove. Ki passed pawn shops, used furniture and clothing emporiums, and dreary saloons selling watered-down whiskey to down-and-outers who didn't have enough money to buy their fill of the real thing in the better part of town.

The street was curving around, back towards Main. Ki decided to follow it back to the town's center and then head over to the hotel for a cool drink and a nap on the shaded front porch. There wasn't much else for him to do. Jessie would be busy meeting with the town's chamber of commerce for a while longer; it was a six-hour ride, round trip, to visit his friends at the Triple D spread; and Hank Stills was just now involved in town marshal's business, out riding with a newly arrived postal inspector, here to investigate a mail-car robbery that had taken place on the Union Pacific line, just outside of town.

He was just coming to the end of Market Lane, passing a laundry on the opposite side of the street, when he saw a young woman step out of the laundry's doorway in order to struggle with several large wicker baskets of soiled clothing.

She was strikingly pretty. Ki guessed that she was in her early twenties. Ash-blonde hair fell in soft waves about her shoulders. She had brown eyes and a scattering of freckles across her wide cheeks and the bridge of her upturned nose. The freckles, combined with the supple-looking, firm tone of her lithe, agile body, made her seem something of a tomboy. Her lack of cosmetics or frilly adornments of any kind added to the tomboy effect: she was barefoot and wore a plain, short-sleeved dress of sky-blue, lightweight cotton. Her capable-looking, sinewy, but somewhat water-reddened hands testified to her strenuous washerwoman's work, as did her backside, as firmly round as an apple. This latter fact was clearly discernible from the way the thin fabric of her dress was stretched as she bent to pick up a laundry basket.

She must have sensed Ki's eyes upon her. As she straightened with her burden in hand, she turned in his direction and smiled shyly.

"I know you," she called to him across the narrow street. "That is, I know who you are!"

Even from this distance Ki could make out the outlines of her smallish breasts, the nipples all but poking through her taut cotton bodice.

"You seem to have the advantage of me," he said.

"I doubt that," the young laundress laughed. "From what folks hereabouts say, Jessica Starbuck's friend Ki is a regular fighting rooster who calls no one his better. Of course, I don't *know* that for gospel. We only moved here a short while ago."

"You said 'we'?" Ki asked, feeling a pang of disappointment and instantly scolding himself for it. Of course she would be married! How could he ever have thought that such a diamond in the rough would have gone unnoticed among the eligible males of Nettle Grove?

"My mother and I," the young woman replied. "We moved here long after you and Miss Starbuck straightened out all of that cattle ranch trouble." She set down her basket. "My name's Dorsey Smith, by the way." She gestured behind her. "I run this place all by myself."

"Your mother?"

"Oh, she's an invalid. Stuck in a wheelchair with rheumatism. She pretty much keeps to her cottage, around back behind the laundry. We've got a little yard between the two buildings. Mother likes to set out there and let the sun warm her bones." She nervously shifted her bare feet in the dust, and then shrugged. "Well, nice to meet you, Mr. Ki—I mean, having heard so much about you..." She bent to pick up her laundry basket.

"Let me help you," Ki said, crossing the street toward her.

"Oh, no!" she said, appearing to be genuinely shocked. "I couldn't! I mean, you're so important, Mr. Ki—"

"It isn't 'mister,'" the samurai chuckled. "Ki will do. And you must not be ashamed of having to work very hard." He scooped up a pair of baskets and carried them into the laundry.

"That's easy for you to say," Dorsey replied, lugging along the last basket as she followed him inside. "I've heard that kind of hypocritical preaching before. It always comes from folks who don't have to do the hard work they're so fond of praising."

Ki, stung by her harsh tones, set down the baskets just inside the door and turned to face her. "It is easy for me to say because I am familiar with hard work, Dorsey. I believe that hard work is the shortest path to honor. It's easy for me to say because I believe it is true." He smiled. "Now stop that pouting. You're far too pretty to pout."

Dorsey placed her basket on the laundry's front counter.

"I *could* have been pretty, if things had turned out different."

"What do you mean?" Ki asked, puzzled.

"Nothing," Dorsey said quickly. "I only meant that hard work has worn me out, taken away my shine..."

"That isn't true," Ki replied softly. "It's hard work that has made you so lovely."

"Oh, you go on..."

"Your beauty is such that it held me transfixed."

Dorsey anxiously brushed back her blonde hair. "Please, Ki...don't fib," she pleaded. "I mean, we're not friends, so you don't have to fib."

"I think you're beautiful," Ki declared. "And I would like to be your friend."

"Lord," Dorsey breathed. "Those dark eyes of yours are kind of burning me all over. Why do I think you can see right through my dress?" As she spoke, she slid her work-roughened hands behind her back, as if to hide them from view.

Ki boldly reached around behind her, making her jump as his fingers brushed her hips. He captured her hands and tugged them forward. "You should not be ashamed of your hands," he said.

"No!" Dorsey blurted. "It's not true. Don't lie—"

Ki silenced her by raising her reddened fingers to his lips and kissing them. Dorsey looked on, mesmerized.

"Lord, it's gotten warm in here," she mused, and then laughed throatily. "Warmer than usual, and in a laundry, that's saying something!" A mischievous glint appeared in her brown eyes. "Well, if you're so all-fired fond of hard work, would you mind hauling those two baskets around back, to where my washtubs are?"

She swung around the counter, grabbed her basket, and disappeared through a curtained doorway. Ki pondered the situation for an instant, and then, a smile tugging at the corners of his lips, picked up the two baskets and quickly followed.

The back area of the laundry was a single, large, window-less room, lit by kerosene lamps. A huge wood-burning stove took up one side wall. It was a warm spring day outside, but the woodstove was nevertheless fired up, both to heat buckets of water and to dry some of the damp clothing hanging nearby from crisscrossed, pulley-strung lines. There was a back door, and Ki guessed that through it one would find more clothing drying on outdoor lines strung in the yard that Dorsey had mentioned. The rest of the laundry's wall space was taken up with shelving piled high with neatly folded and tagged bundles of clean clothing, but there was also a shelved area devoted to scrub brushes, boxes of soap, and other assorted tools of the young woman's trade. A hand pump above a soapstone sink stood in one corner, near some ironing boards. In the room's center, on a raised wooden grate to allow for drainage, stood an enormous wooden washtub five feet in diameter and perhaps thirty inches deep. It was filled with steaming water.

There was more steam rising from the buckets of water heating on the stove, which itself was throwing off a good deal of warmth. The close, humid atmosphere was not unpleasant; in fact, it reminded Ki of the noblemen's bathhouses of his own homeland, where highly skilled geishas catered to a man's every whim and fancy as he relaxed in a tub of hot water.

Dorsey picked up a scrub brush and began nervously fidgeting with it as she watched Ki roam about the laundry. "That water is clean. I just filled the tub," she announced as Ki curiously peered into the enormous scrubbing basin. Suddenly she tossed the brush she was holding into the water, causing a splattering splash that soaked the front of Ki's trousers.

"Oh! How clumsy of me!"

"Indeed," Ki muttered wryly. "Dorsey, it seems you have made me wet..."

She blushed as cherry-red as one of the grates on her wood stove. "I—I didn't do it on purpose..."

Ki smiled. "No? Then I *am* disappointed."

Dorsey swallowed hard. "Well, if you'll take them off, I'll dry and press them for you."

Ki's almond eyes narrowed. He had engaged in some lighthearted flirtation with this attractive young woman in order to bolster her flagging spirits. Now the flirtation was taking a new and serious turn. He presumed that Dorsey was a virgin; it would not be honorable to take advantage of an innocent young woman made vulnerable by her lack of self-confidence.

"Well?" Dorsey demanded. "Aren't you going to—"

"I think it would be better if I kept my trousers on."

"What's wrong?" she interrupted him. "Don't think that I've never seen a man nude before, because I have! I was engaged to be married, and my fiancé and I—" She paused. "What I'm trying to say is that I've seen what men have, and a lot more than just *seen* it, if you get my drift . . ." she added meaningfully.

"If you were engaged, why did you not marry?" Ki asked.

Dorsey shrugged. "We had a fight, and in the heat of it he said that I should consider myself lucky that he was willing to marry a washerwoman in the first place; I told him that I never wanted to see him again. He tried to apologize, but, well . . . he'd already *said* it, understand, Ki? Some things you just can't take back."

"He was a fool," Ki said. "He lost himself a treasure."

Dorsey came around the tub toward him. Ki gently tilted up her chin and kissed her.

"Mmmm . . ." Dorsey swooned against him. "Let's both undress and get in the tub together!" she breathed. "I've often thought about how that would be. Do you think me scandalous?"

Ki shook his head. "As a matter of fact, I was thinking exactly the same thing." He quickly explained about the Japanese bath houses.

"These geishas . . . they're of lower station than the men they give their favors to, right?" Dorsey asked.

Why are you so obsessed with matters of social station? Ki wanted to ask in turn, but the question flitted from his mind as Dorsey began to stroke the swelling between his legs. He quickly shucked his boots, then his clothing, draping his damp trousers over one of the racks near the stove, to dry. As Dorsey pulled her dress up over her head, Ki palmed one of his *shuriken* throwing blades—a four-inch knife without hilt or handle—from its leather sheath inside his suit jacket.

Dorsey had turned to gaze at him. "Lord, you are the most handsome man!" She approached tentatively, to run her fingers along Ki's sloping shoulders, the wiry muscles of his arms, and the cords of his calves and thighs. She giggled as she patted his rippling stomach muscles. "Your belly has got more ridges than my best washboard!"

Ki feasted his eyes upon her tantalizing curves. Dorsey was so thin that her ribs showed, but that only made her adorable breasts, with their splendid, nut-brown aureoles and nipples, the more breathtaking. Her legs were long and well turned, and her skin possessed a tawny sheen; her high, plump, deeply clefted bottom was as smooth as satin, and her belly curved seductively to the moist juncture of her thighs beneath ash-blonde pubic fur as fine as spun gold.

Dorsey, trembling in anticipation, quickly twisted her long hair into a topknot, to pin it up. Then she stepped into the tub. As she did, Ki pressed the needle-sharp point of the palmed *shuriken* into the soft wood of the platform upon which the tub rested. The weapon would now be within easy reach if need be. Ki had no reason to expect that there would be trouble during this pleasurable interlude, but one of the first lessons a warrior learned was never to be unprepared to confront an enemy.

"Come on in, the water's just right!" Dorsey grinned happily. The steam had brought a pink flush to her face, and a few tendrils of her hair had escaped to stick to her forehead. She looked altogether irresistible, and Ki did not hesitate to join her.

The water was just warm enough to be soothing. Ki settled himself, and was reaching out for Dorsey when she suddenly shook her head.

"Wait! I forgot something!" She hopped out of the tub, her breasts bouncing and her luscious backside spraying droplets as her hips wagged. She pranced over to the shelf where her supplies were kept, rummaged through her boxes, and then returned, to scamper into the tub with a pink cake of fragrant soap.

"This soap is very gentle," she told Ki as she lathered the cake beneath the surface of the water. "It's what I use to wash the most fragile lacework."

The suds turned the water into a flowery, foamy bubble bath. Ki pulled Dorsey toward him. They enjoyed a long, wet kiss as the tips of Dorsey's breasts rubbed against Ki's chest. He leaned back against the tub's side, sighing in contentment as he palmed the curves of Dorsey's twitching bottom. Her nipples had swelled so brazenly that he couldn't resist giving them both a teasing nibble.

Dorsey squealed as she stroked Ki's hardness, bobbing in the silky water. "Before, when you told me my hands were lovely, it was the most thoughtful thing that anyone had said to me in a long time," she whispered. "What you didn't realize was how strong and nimble a washerwoman's fingers can become!" She smiled, catlike, as her fingers lightly danced along the entire throbbing, swollen length of him. "For instance, when I wash lace, I must be careful not to tear the fragile material, and yet I still must make sure to get it clean. *This* is how I do it..."

Ki gasped as Dorsey's fingers enveloped him, giving him almost unendurable pleasure. Her nails gently teased and pinched, while her deft squeezes contained him. Squirming uncontrollably, Ki leaned forward to press his face against Dorsey's moist, sudsy cleavage. He inhaled her musky scent, intoxicating on its own, but when mixed with the perfume of the soap, enough to make the giddy samurai's head spin.

"I want you inside me!" Dorsey crooned. A delightful pout appeared on her pretty face. "But how? I mean, if we do it the usual way, I'll be underwater." She eyed Ki's marblelike hardness and licked her lips. "And something tells me that you can last a hell of a lot longer than I can hold my breath!"

Ki laughed. "I think I have the answer." He rose up to

his knees, at the same time easily lifting Dorsey. He spun her around so that she was also on her knees, her back to him. "Now lean forward and hold on to the edge of the tub to support yourself," he instructed her.

Dorsey did as she was told. Now her splayed, curvaceous rump, made rose-pink by the warm water, was jutting out at him. Ki stroked the satiny softness of her soapy bottom as he reached between her legs to press a finger against the core of her sex. Dorsey moaned, arching her supple spine to present more of her hindquarters to him.

"Take me now!" she begged. "I can't stand it another moment!"

Ki entered her from behind. As delightful as the warm, soapy water had been, it was nothing compared to the buttery softness of Dorsey as her silken furnace gripped and stroked his shaft.

"Oh, oh, I'm coming already!" Dorsey cried out. Her hands formed small fists that beat upon the tub's rim. What she was experiencing must have been overpowering, for as Ki pressed ever deeper she attempted to pull away, rocking her hips and tilting her pelvis until just the tip of him was inside her. Chuckling, he patted her soapy haunches.

Dorsey couldn't decide whether to laugh or howl, so she did both, the sound a cross between birdsong and a spanked brat's yelp. Her hips began to churn the water, and in her haste to envelop every inch of Ki, she lost her grip on the tub, sinking below the surface, and getting her hair wet, after all. The samurai hauled her up, sputtering and on the brink of orgasm, and then reached around with his free hand to fondle her nipples—by spreading his fingers, he could just span the distance between both crinkly-hard nuggets of delectable flesh.

Dorsey was coming continuously now; her hips bobbed and her head lolled as she emitted a series of guttural moans. Ki felt her powerful internal muscles convulse uncontrollably.

He began to pump within her like a steam piston, all the while stroking and massaging her lithe torso. She wiggled like a snake. It was all Ki could do to hang on for the ride.

He shuddered as he came. Dorsey laughed in delight as he threw back his head to howl like a wolf.

After a few moments Ki pulled free of Dorsey's molten center and fell back, sliding completely under the water. He popped up like a seal, shaking his head, sending droplets flying everywhere as his long, raven-black hair whipped around his head.

Dorsey was floating. "Oh, but that was lovely," she sighed, still flushed with sexual abandon. "Wouldn't it be nice to stay in this tub forever?"

Ki nodded. "It would indeed be a wonderful way to spend eternity," he sighed.

"More wonderful than spending it with Miss Starbuck?" she asked, and then smiled.

Ki was shocked, and more than a little unsettled by Dorsey's obvious envy. "What does she have to do with anything?" he asked.

"Answer my question!" she commanded. "Was I or wasn't I better at loving than Miss Starbuck?"

Ki fought back his own angry impulse to dry off this silly female's backside with the palm of his hand. "It is really none of your business, but considering what we have just shared together, I will tell you that I have never made love to Jessica Starbuck. Nor will I ever do so."

Dorsey's triumphant laugh rescued Ki from having to confide anything more about his relationship with Jessie.

"Well, it's satisfying to know that there's at least *one* thing I've had that Jessie hasn't," the woman gloated.

Ki was now totally mystified. "Why are you so concerned about Jessie? What possible connection could a wash er—" He stopped, cursing himself for not thinking, but it was too late. The damage had been done.

"There is no connection between a washerwoman like myself and a beautiful, wealthy young woman like Jessica Starbuck," Dorsey replied evenly. "How could there be?"

"Dorsey, you do not understand what I was trying to say—"

She shrugged, smiling faintly. "You gave no offense by merely speaking the truth. You are a very nice man, but it's getting late. Perhaps you'd better go."

She climbed out of the tub and went to a shelf to fetch them both towels. Sighing, Ki stepped out of the tub as well, feeling very much as Adam must have felt upon his exile from the Garden of Eden.

There was an awkward silence between them as they dried themselves and dressed. It did not matter in the least whether he was able to convince the laundress that he did not look down upon her. What counted was that Dorsey—despite anything anyone might say—would continue to look down upon herself . . .

Ki was torn from his brooding reveries by the blast of a shotgun.

"That came from the backyard!" Dorsey exclaimed.

Ki was already racing for the laundry's back door. As he passed the tub, he bent to pull his *shuriken* from its place in the wooden grating.

"Hurry!" Dorsey cried out. "Mother's in the cottage, all alone!"

Chapter 6

Ki wrenched open the laundry's back door and stepped out into the yard. He ducked beneath several clotheslines, the garments upon them snapping like flags in the breeze, and remained crouched. He listened, giving his eyes time to adjust to the bright sunlight after the relative darkness of the windowless laundry.

"I've got another barrel left!" a woman shouted. "So you git! Go on! Git, and don't come back!"

"Easy now, lady," a male voice warned roughly. "You watch that scattergun. We don't want to have to hurt you."

Ki could not see what was going on through the tangle of clothesline-hung clothes. Readying himself, he stepped clear.

There were three of them, in trail garb; definite hardcases, but fortunately their guns were holstered. The time it would take them to draw was the edge Ki would need.

One of the men had a full black beard mottled with patches of gray. He appeared to be the leader, from the way he waved the other two forward to advance upon the gray-haired, worn-looking old woman seated in her cart-wheeled chair on the elevated front porch of the modest cottage. Instead of steps leading up to the porch, there was a hand-railed ramp to facilitate the woman's wheelchair. Just now she sat at the top of that ramp, brandishing her smoking, double-barreled shotgun.

"What should we do, Jack?" one of the men called to the bearded man. "The law is sure to come running, after that shotgun blast."

Jack nervously stroked his beard as he scowled up at the woman. "Why can't you listen to reason, you old witch?"

"That will do," Ki said, drawing the three's attention.

The man nearest him glanced Ki's way. "Didn't know they had a Chinaman working in the laundry."

Ki noticed Jack backing away. "He ain't no Chinaman!"

The third man spat, "He's the one travels with that Starbuck bitch!" And he reached for his gun.

Ki snapped his wrist forward, letting fly the glittering *shuriken*. The little blade spun through the air, closing the distance before its target could even clear leather. The blade took the man in the throat. His gun, half out of its holster, fell to the dust as his fingers clawed at the shiny, deadly thing embedded just beneath his chin.

The man nearest Ki had his own gun out and was leveling it at the samurai. Ki measured the distance between them and then executed the sideways snap-kick called *yoko-geri-keage*. The man had time for one quick shot that went wild before the edge of Ki's boot sent his Colt spinning away.

The man backed off, rubbing his wrist, his lips pulled back in a snarl of hatred. Ki glanced around; the man with the beard was nowhere about, and the first man to have tried drawing his gun was lying dead, the *shuriken* still lodged in his throat.

"Watch out!" Dorsey cried, stepping out from the shelter of the laden clotheslines.

Ki returned his attention to the man he had just disarmed. The outlaw had drawn a long, curved, double-edge skinning knife from its belt sheath. "I'm gonna gut you, Chink!" he snarled. "I'm gonna skin you alive—"

Ki endured the insults with weary patience, waiting for the man to make his move.

The outlaw lunged forward, thrusting low but with his knife's wicked point angled up.

As his opponent attacked, Ki went into a stance that put his entire weight on his back leg, leaving his front foot lightly balanced to kick out. His *gedan-barai*, or downward block, began with him raising his right fist up against his

78

left shoulder. As his opponent's blade thrust forward, Ki's right fist swept down to catch the man's forearm. The outlaw cried out as the knife fell from his numbed fingers. An instant later, Ki's front snap-kick landed like a sledgehammer against the outlaw's chin. The man's head snapped back, his neck breaking with an audible *click!*

Ki guessed that his adversary died before he'd even had time to hit the ground...

Dorsey was stammering, "I don't believe it...I just don't—"

The old woman, still clutching her shotgun, was whimpering to herself as she sagged in her wheelchair.

The entire incident, from the moment that Ki had shown himself, had lasted less than a minute. It had all happened so quickly that it was hard to believe it had happened at all, but while Ki had moved too fast for the eye to follow, the women's gaze could now linger on the results of his actions—the two corpses lying in the yard.

"Yep, I figured it'd be you..."

Ki turned to see Hank Stills, the town marshal, enter the yard. Close behind was Jessie, her derringer at the ready, and a stranger in city-slicker garb.

"Whenever there's lots of killings, without too many shots being fired, I figure my old pal Ki is up to his tricks again," Stills observed, glumly shaking his head.

Stills's promotion from deputy to his elected position of town marshal had not changed him much. He still favored broken-down boots, scuffed jeans, and well-worn flannel shirts. Just now the good-looking marshal, in his early thirties, hitched one thumb in his gunbelt, from which a double-action Colt dangled, and with his other hand he removed his Stetson, to scratch at his tousled golden curls. "Well, who wants to tell me what's happened here? Mrs. Smith, why don't you start?" he suggested, glancing at the old woman in the wheelchair. "Reckon it was your shotgun there that fired first."

"You say your name is Smith?" Jessie interrupted, while Ki watched and listened. He'd already noticed how Jessie, since her arrival, had been staring wide-eyed at both mother and daughter.

"You heard my mother!" Dorsey snapped at Jessie. Her lips were pressed into a tight frown, and her eyes were cold. Jessie stared back at her, and suddenly Dorsey seemed to be on the brink of tears. She was nervously twisting something black and ribbonlike around her water-reddened fingers. Ki, his hand rising to his open shirt collar, realized that it was his necktie.

"I must apologize for my daughter's rudeness," Dorsey's mother told Jessie. "I'm Mrs. Barbara Smith. I'm a widow. My husband died long ago, you see."

There was a beseeching look on the old woman's face. Seeing it, Jessie nodded slowly. "Of course, Mrs. Smith."

"What's going on?" Stills demanded, his brown eyes narrowing in suspicion. He turned toward Dorsey, who was heading back into the laundry. "Hey, where do you think you're going?"

"Let her go. She's got work to do, Hank," Mrs. Smith said. "I can tell you everything that happened." She set down her shotgun and wheeled her chair down the ramp into the yard. "These two dead men, and one other who ran away, tried to break into my house."

Stills looked doubtful. "Why, Barbara? No offense meant, but it's slim pickings for holdup men in this part of town."

"I can't answer that," she said with a shrug. "Anyway, when I saw them, I got that shotgun of mine and tried to scare them off with a blast into the air. That didn't work. About that time, this gentleman appeared." She gestured toward Ki. "They recognized him as Miss Starbuck's companion. One of the men ran, as I said, but the other two stayed to fight. They drew first, or at least they *tried* to. Miss Starbuck's friend defended himself, that's all, Hank. I believe he also saved *our* lives. There's no telling what they would have done to us if he hadn't been here—"

"Excuse me, but I feel that you were in no danger," Ki interrupted. "Those three could have disarmed Mrs. Smith at any moment," he told Marshal Stills. "They chose not to, keeping their guns holstered. I think they were hesitant to harm a woman, an invalid woman, at that."

"Could be," Stills mused. "I've known some of the meanest owlhoots who wouldn't dream of hurting kids or women, or folks who have themselves a handicap."

Ki nodded. "Unfortunately they had no qualms about shooting at me."

"That accounts for the second shot we heard," Jessie observed, transferring her derringer to her skirt pocket. When Ki nodded, she continued, "We were already on our way when we heard it. It helped us pinpoint the location of the trouble."

"I am glad it was of service to you all," Ki smiled.

"I'd just finished up with my business appointment," Jessie added. "I looked for you at the hotel, and then I went to Hank's office, thinking I might find you there."

"It's lucky for you I'd returned from my ride with Inspector Broadwick," Stills told Ki. "Otherwise my deputy would have checked this out. He doesn't know you, and he might have shot first and asked questions later."

"Just a moment," Inspector Broadwick spoke up. He was a fat, barrel-chested man, a little over six feet in height. He wore a finely tailored brown wool suit, a derby hat, a peacock-blue silk waistcoat, and a matching tie. He had a pencil-thin mustache, and his high starched collar emphasized his series of double chins. "You there, fellow!" He pointed imperiously at the samurai. "What's your name?"

"Ki."

"Ki *what?*" Broadwick demanded.

Before Ki could reply, Jessie broke in, "That's his name, Inspector, and I would advise you to be polite—"

"Keep out of things that don't concern you, little lady," Broadwick said in dismissal. "Now then, *Ki,*" he snorted. "Do you expect us to believe you defeated these two gunmen without a firearm?"

"I don't expect you to do anything," Ki shrugged. "But that's what happened."

Broadwick moved closer. Ki could tell from the lumbering way the man moved that he was used to intimidating others with his size. The postal inspector's bulk almost, but not quite, concealed the shoulder holster under his left armpit.

"I'd be careful, Inspector," Hank Stills drawled.

"Stay out of this! If you can't handle this fellow's insolence in the face of the law, then I shall!" Broadwick turned to Ki. "Do you know who I am?"

"A postal inspector."

"And as such, a representative of the federal government!" the inspector proclaimed. He was now less than two feet away from Ki, his breath thudding against the samurai's face as he bellowed, "Now then, I want the truth! How did those two men meet their deaths?"

Ki smiled. "Like this," he said softly.

The samurai performed a lightning-quick roundhouse kick, never actually touching Broadwick, but neatly sweeping his derby from his head.

Broadwick stood blinking stupidly. His hand rose to touch his hat, but ended up patting his bare scalp. He was bald on top, with a horse-shoe fringe of mousy-colored hair ringing his ears.

"Warned you, didn't we?" Stills chuckled.

Jessie's exasperated expression faded, and then she too began to laugh.

Evidently Broadwick was not at all used to being laughed at. His jowled face was mottled with rage as he stared at his battered derby lying in the dust. "Pick it up!" he hissed.

Ki, smiling politely, shook his head.

"I said—"

"I heard you."

Broadwick made a move for the gun beneath his coat, but hesitated when Ki's smile abruptly faded.

"You know how close you are to dying?" the inspector blustered.

"Each of us is close to dying at any moment," Ki replied softly. "I'm prepared to face my death. Are you ready for yours?"

"What about those two men?" Broadwick asked, his tone now noticeably more agreeable.

"They took one step too many," Ki said.

"Never liked that damn derby anyway," Broadwick muttered, using the opportunity to step away from Ki. "I ought to get myself a cowboy hat, like Hank here!"

The tension broken, everyone laughed. Ki, watching the postal inspector, noticed the hard look in the man's smallish, piglike eyes. This was a man who held on to his grudges. Broadwick would not soon forget his humiliation at Ki's hands, and would brood until he could find a way to get even.

"Well now, I'm glad we're all friends again," Hank Stills said. He fingered the brass star pinned to his shirt, and pretended to scowl. "Otherwise I'd have to run the lot of you in! Isn't that how the constables talk back in St. Louis, Inspector?"

"Yes, just like that." Broadwick smiled absently. "Well, I think I'll go back to the hotel to rest until dinner. That was quite a horseback ride we took this morning." He rubbed at the wide expanse of his trousers seat. "I'm not used to horseback riding, I'm afraid." He smiled at Jessie. "Until tonight, Miss Starbuck."

"Until tonight," Jessie replied. "Ki, the inspector has invited us and Marshal Stills to dinner at the hotel's restaurant."

Broadwick looked appalled. "You mean, *he's* your traveling companion?"

"Why, yes," Jessie said ingenuously. "I couldn't ask for a better bodyguard, don't you agree, Inspector?"

"But—but how can he sit at the table with us?" Broadwick sputtered. "I mean, he's an *Oriental!*"

Stills offered Ki a wink. "Just what are you trying to say, Inspector?"

"Oh, nothing." Broadwick sighed in consternation. "I suppose the frontier *would* be a bit more, shall we say, egalitarian—"

"The cafe don't serve no eagles, but they got plenty of

beefsteak," Stills replied, keeping his expression absolutely deadpan.

"Yes, I think I'll go rest for a while," Broadwick said, and hurried off in defeat, stopping only to snatch up his derby.

Jessie, who'd been biting down on her lower lip, exploded with giggles once the inspector was out of earshot. "Oh, Ki, how *could* you? Kicking off that man's hat!"

"Hell, he deserved it," Stills broke in. "I've had to listen to that pompous ass all morning. I gotta do what he tells me, dammit; he's got total authority to investigate that mail car robbery."

"I sympathize with you," Ki said.

"We'll be getting along now, Barbara," Stills told the invalid woman. "I'll have my deputy and a couple of others come by right away to cart those two bodies out of here. I'm sorry for the trouble, but I'm glad you and Dorsey came out of it all right."

"We did, thanks to Miss Starbuck's friend," Mrs. Smith smiled. "Um, Miss Starbuck?" She hesitated. *"Jessie?"*

Jessie turned to regard the old woman. "Yes, Babs?"

"I just wanted to say . . . you look fine. *Real* fine," the old woman murmured fondly.

Jessie smiled. "So do you, Babs, and so does Dorsey."

Barbara Smith's smile faded. "Again, I can only apologize for her behavior—"

"Stop," Jessie pleaded, shaking her head, her eyes suddenly grown shiny. "I can't listen to that, I really can't."

She hurried from the yard, Marshal Stills and Ki right behind her.

"What was that all about?" Stills asked. "First you didn't know their names, and now you and Babs are carrying on like old friends."

"I don't want to discuss it right now," Jessie said.

"Did you meet them during our first visit here?" Ki persisted, but then he shook his head. "That isn't possible. Dorsey told me earlier that she and her mother settled in Nettle Grove *after* that business."

Jessie spun around at the samurai, her expression unusually fierce. "Listen, just don't ask me any questions! And I won't ask *you* any, like just when it was that you and Dorsey had your little talk? Like why both Dorsey's hair and your hair are damp?" She flicked a finger at Ki's open collar. "And *finally*, just how Dorsey ended up with your tie twisted around her fingers back there." With that, she flounced off.

"She's something when she's mad, ain't she?" Stills chuckled in admiration. He clapped Ki on the back. "Cheer up, at least there ain't no lip rouge on that collar of yours. But then, Dorsey don't *wear* lip rouge!" He winked. "Say, I didn't think you Japanese fellows ever blushed..."

"I'm part American," Ki said. "It's *that* part of me that is blushing..."

"Is that the part Dorsey enjoyed?" Stills taunted. "She runs a mighty fine laundry, don't she? Most places put the starch *in*, but I reckon that Dorsey would rather take the starch *out!*"

Ki pretended to lunge for Stills, who ran, laughing and calling over his shoulder, "Don't you be kicking *my* hat off my head! I'm the town marshal!"

Chapter 7

A few minutes before the appointed hour, Ki came downstairs from his hotel room for the dinner that was being hosted by Inspector Broadwick. The hotel's main-floor restaurant had sawdust-sprinkled floors, brass lanterns hanging from the ceiling rafters, bentwood chairs, and tables covered with red-and-white checked cloths. Ki, wearing his suit and a new black ribbon tie, hung his Stetson on a wall peg near the table where Jessie was already seated, waiting for the others to arrive.

He had not seen her since their harsh exchange earlier that afternoon. Since then, Ki had sulked in his room next door to Jessie's. He was upset and, to a degree that surprised and disturbed him, jealous over the fact that there were aspects of Jessie—her past; the way she thought—that he knew nothing about.

The control of his emotions was a goal Ki was still trying to achieve, especially his turbulent mix of feelings concerning Jessie. This afternoon's spat had made him gloomy, and he was not cheered as he approached the table to see that Jessie's expression was still dark and brooding. She was so wrapped up in her thoughts that she didn't even realize he was standing there before her!

"Is there nothing I can do?" the samurai asked softly.

Jessie started, but her eyes softened as Ki sat down across from her. "There's something *I* can do," she said. "And that's apologize for this afternoon. I behaved terribly. Just understand that my foul mood had nothing to do with you."

Ki nodded. "Clearly it was seeing Barbara Smith and her daughter that so upset you."

"Yes, and you'll understand why when you hear my story. It starts long before you came to America." Jessie paused, her gaze shifting towards the restaurant's entrance. "Here come Hank Stills and the inspector," she whispered. "I'll tell you and Hank everything later, after Broadwick's gone."

"My dear girl, you look positively ravishing!" Inspector Broadwick complimented her. "How ever did you find a skirt and jacket the same lovely emerald green as your magnificent eyes?"

"You're too kind, Inspector Broadwick," Jessie replied politely.

"Not at all, my dear, for it is *you* who are all too kind to grace us with your presence." Broadwick turned toward Hank Stills. "Isn't that right, Marshal?"

"Took the words right out of my mouth, Inspector," Stills grinned, winking at Jessie. "Ain't a prettier girl in town. I would've said the entire territory, but I've got to take my own wife, Mary, into account."

Both Stills and Broadwick hung their hats on the wall pegs. The inspector smiled grimly at Ki as he did so, saying, "No need to get up, my friend, I am quite capable of removing my hat."

Ki's smile was barely perceptible, as was the glint of self-mocking humor in Inspector Broadwick's close-set eyes. The samurai began to think that he had been unduly harsh in his initial estimation of the postal inspector. Perhaps Broadwick was willing to let today's altercation between them fade into the past. The man's present good nature certainly suggested that he was amenable to letting bygones be bygones.

The meal was served. The steaks were excellent, but Ki was too preoccupied to notice the food, so anxious was he to get through the meal, so that he and Jessie could be alone and she could finish telling him the story she'd barely begun.

"This is a real treat for me," Stills said as he dug into his steak. "Usually I have my dinner sent over from the cafe near the jail. Food's okay, but nothing like the spread they put together here! 'Sides, it's grand fun to eat with folks for a change! My deputy lives with his wife and kids in town, so he goes home for dinner. Nettle Grove's a quiet town. I ain't had a prisoner in my cell for months, but there's times I feel like going out on the prowl to find me a drunk, just so's I can bring him in and have me a dinner companion!"

"Is it far to your ranch, Marshal Stills?" Broadwick asked.

"Oh, yes sir," Stills sighed. "Six hours there and back. I'm sorry to say I only get home a couple of days a week."

"So your wife and adopted son manage the spread all on their own?" Broadwick marveled.

"Pretty much," Stills beamed proudly. "We've taken on an old retired drover to help with the chores. He's grateful for room and board and a little tobacco money. We couldn't pay him no more than that. I'm holding on to this town marshal's job because we need the money to make ends meet. By next year we hope to have ourselves a nice little herd; soon as the ranch becomes self-sustaining, I intend to turn in my badge. For now, my deputy keeps an eye on things the couple of days a week I'm home."

"Quite admirable," Broadwick sniffed. "I myself would never leave a woman and boy alone in such rugged territory, and I quite doubt that these little homesteads will ever amount to much, but I suppose the little man must struggle to raise himself up, no matter how great the odds."

"You learn a lot about ranching back in St. Louis, Inspector?" Stills snapped, obviously stung by the way Broadwick had dismissed everything the hard-working marshal was struggling to achieve. "I figure you know about as much about cows as you do about horses, and I just about had to tie you into the saddle this morning to keep you from falling off."

"Do tell us about the robbery you're investigating!" Jessie broke in, doing her best to change the subject before Stills totally lost his temper.

"Well, there's not a whole lot to tell," Broadwick demurred. "And I certainly don't want to go into the grisly details of the murders perpetrated by Sayre's men. Such things are not for feminine ears." Broadwick stroked his pencil-thin mustache in what he undoubtedly thought was a debonair manner. Ki fought to control his anger as the inspector's fat face broke into a lewd smirk. "Especially not such lovely, shell-pink ears as *yours,* my dear."

"What makes you so certain it was the Sayre gang that pulled the mail-car robbery?" Ki interrupted.

"Well, who else would have the audacity?" Broadwick shrugged, setting down his knife and fork. "There hasn't been trouble on this particular spur of the Union Pacific's line in years."

"That's true, Ki," Stills put in. "The trains haven't carried anything of interest to outlaws since the last gold strikes hereabouts petered out, a good ten years ago. Mail is the only thing traveling the tracks that's worth stealing."

"And most badmen are loath to touch the mails," Broadwick declared proudly, "lest they bring down upon themselves the wrath of the United States Post Office!"

"And yet you believe Sayre's gang did have the audacity to pull the robbery?" Ki persisted.

"I do, for several reasons," Broadwick replied. "Foremost among them, one of Sayre's trademark 'forty-five' branding irons was left behind at the scene of the crime."

"Circumstantial evidence, at best," Ki observed.

Broadwick pretended not to hear the samurai's comment. He busied himself signaling the waiter, who quickly brought their desserts of deep-dish apple pie and mugs of strong black coffee.

"There's more for me to base my suppositions on than merely that branding iron," Broadwick continued, as he attacked his dessert. "We know, for example, that Will Sayre must be getting on in years. This clearly accounts for the violence perpetrated during this mail robbery. Try to follow as best you can the indisputable logic of my deductions," the inspector pontificated, his jowly chin littered with pie-crust crumbs. "First, we know Sayre is old. Since outlaw gangs are run in the same savage manner as wolfpacks, it is obvious that due to the infirmity of age, Will Sayre has lost control of his men. Accordingly, they have begun to revert to their previously wanton nature, in the process murdering those two unarmed postal clerks aboard the plundered mail car."

"I think I'm able to follow that," Stills remarked wryly, sipping at his coffee.

"But I agree with Ki," Jessie said. "Your evidence is still circumstantial. You really have nothing beyond that branding iron to link Will Sayre to this crime."

"My dear lady," Broadwick remarked, obviously intrigued, "you almost sound as if you wished that Sayre were *not* involved! Why is that?"

"Well—I—" Jessie lowered her eyes. "It's just that—"

"Aren't women positively adorable!" Broadwick chortled. "My dear Miss Starbuck, you needn't say another word! We all know that Sayre's gang was dubbed the 'Ladykillers' because Sayre himself is rumored to be devilishly handsome. He is older now, but even weathered good looks can have their effect upon a fair maiden's heart. I detest shattering your girlish fantasies, my dear, but there is more evidence to link your handsome vagabond highwayman to this dastardly deed. The gang brazenly decided not to wear kerchief masks during the robbery. A passenger on the train was later able to identify Rube Silva—a particularly ruthless outlaw—from his wanted poster's likeness. The federal government has known for a while that Silva has been riding with the Ladykillers..."

"It's true, Jessie," Stills remarked glumly. "Broadwick here showed me the bulletin on the matter. The information circulated to federal marshals and county sheriffs months ago. 'Course, it never filtered down to the town marshals' level."

"Now, now, Hank." Broadwick smiled condescendingly. "We mustn't have you small-town boys overreaching yourselves. You could get hurt."

Stills glared at the postal inspector. "Anyway, Rube Silva is a bad apple if ever there was one. If it's true that he's taken over the Ladykiller Gang, there'll be a lot more blood-

91

shed before it's over, and it'll likely take the army to finish it."

"Stills! No talk of blood!" Broadwick admonished. "There's a lady present. And I hardly think that the army will be necessary. I expect that Deputy Marshal Long and I will prove adequate to the task—"

"Long?" Jessie gasped. "You don't mean *Custis* Long?"

"Why, yes, the very man," Broadwick replied. "Do you know him?"

"Oh, I should say I know him," Jessie said noncommittally. Ki, watching Broadwick and Stills exchanging puzzled glances, tried his best to hide his smile.

"Well, I'm sorry to say that you won't get very much time to visit with your friend," Broadwick told her. "I intend to run him ragged. He's been sent to aid *my* investigation, you know. I simply can't continue to take Marshal Stills away from the confines of Nettle Grove. The murders and mail robbery took place outside of the town's jurisdiction, after all. It is a federal matter, and as such, it should be investigated by federal lawmen. According to the telegram I received the other day, Deputy Long will arrive on to-morrow morning's train." Broadwick looked at his pocket watch. "As I want to be up bright and early to greet him at the station, I believe I shall say good night. It has been a long day. Miss Starbuck, thank you for giving me the pleasure of your company this evening. Gentlemen, I've already arranged for our meal to be placed on my hotel bill. Good night to you all."

Stills waited until Broadwick had fetched his derby and left the dining room. "You know," he said mildly, "I could almost like him, if he'd only keep his mouth shut."

"I know what you mean," Ki replied. "Anyway, if he hasn't yet forgiven me for this afternoon, he'll forget it once he has Longarm on his hands."

"Longarm?" Stills asked.

"The federal marshal that Broadwick mentioned," Jessie explained. "Longarm's sort of a nickname of his."

Stills smiled. "The 'long arm of the law,' eh?"

"I guess you could say that," Jessie replied. A silence descended on the table as Jessie's face took on a faraway expression.

Ki cleared his throat and said, "Excuse me for changing the subject, Jessie, but Broadwick's gone now, so perhaps you'd like to tell Hank and me what was behind that exchange you had with Barbara Smith this afternoon."

She blinked and looked up. "Yes, of course," she said, and sighed. "I know both of you can keep a secret. I'd like a drink, though, to help me get through this yarn."

"Sam!" Stills called to the waiter. "Can you fix us up with some of your 'special' coffee?"

When the waiter nodded with a wink, Stills confided to Jessie and Ki, "Cafes ain't supposed to serve hard drink, just saloons."

The waiter came from the kitchen carrying a coffeepot, which he set down on the table. Stills refilled their three mugs. Jessie took a sip from hers and coughed, wiping the tears from her eyes.

"That there is full-strength rye whiskey," Stills chuckled. "It's laced with as little coffee as possible. That's what makes it so special!"

"Well, I guess I've got no excuse now," Jessie remarked quietly. "The story begins a long time ago. I was just a toddler myself. My mother had just been murdered in a botched assassination attempt directed at my father by the cartel—"

"Those same Prussian fellows we licked hereabouts last time?" Stills asked, frowning.

"Yes," Jessie nodded. "The same. The war between my father and the cartel was heating up. My father brought me to our Circle Star spread, believing I would be safer there. He himself, however, was still spending a good deal of his time tending to the import-export aspects of his business empire, in San Francisco."

"Alex just left you there alone?" Ki frowned. "That doesn't sound like him."

"I had a small army of hired hands and professional

bodyguards to watch over me," Jessie said, and then smiled, lightly touching Ki's hand. "Of course, neither my father nor I truly felt safe until *you* came to us, Ki . . ."

"Indeed," Ki said gruffly, scowling fiercely, trying his best to control his emotions.

"I ask you both to try to imagine the loss and bewilderment I was experiencing," Jessie continued. "I was so young, I had just lost my mother, and now my father had taken me to a strange place and left me there—*abandoned* me there. At least, that's how it looked to me at the time."

"Hell, you were just a little girl," Stills said, sipping at his rye.

"A little girl all alone," Jessie agreed. "I don't know what I would have done if it hadn't been for the folks who owned the neighboring spread, the Lucky Seven. The 'Seven' was as large as the Circle Star, and its herd ran to ten thousand head. That may not sound like many now—"

"Hey, what I wouldn't give for ten thousand cows!" Hank Stills sighed.

Jessie grinned. "Point well taken, Hank. And in Texas, in those days, ten thousand head were a grand number of cattle to carry one man's brand."

"Whoever that one man was, he sounds mighty lucky. What was his name?" Stills asked.

Jessie took a long swallow of rye. "Tom Smith," she said at last.

Ki stared. "Smith? Do you mean to say—"

"Yes," Jessie replied. "Barbara Smith is his widow. Dorsey is his daughter. They had everything a family could want in those days. Babs was like a mother to me, and Dorsey might have been my sister; that's how close we became. I tell you both now, if it hadn't been for them, I believe I would have gone crazy with sorrow over my mother's death. Pretty soon I was spending more time at the Lucky Seven spread than at the Circle Star. My father, when he could get away from his obligations in San Francisco, soon learned to come calling for me there on his way back to the Circle Star. He and Tom Smith became fast friends.

In some ways, they were two of a kind.

"Well, my father tried to get Tom Smith to invest in something other than cattle, to spread his interests a little. But Tom wouldn't listen. The idea of becoming involved in anything other than Texas rangeland was incomprehensible to him.

"Then came the War. I was still a very little girl when it started. I don't remember too much about that awful time; I guess I don't *want* to remember too much. Tom Smith went off to fight for the Confederacy, and got captured. He spent most of the War in Fort Delaware, the Union prison."

"In other words, he spent it in hell," Stills said softly.

Jessie nodded. "Early on, Texas was cut off from the rest of the Confederacy. There was no market for beef. What little law there had been in Texas broke down completely. It was every spread for itself. My father was busy keeping his own holdings together. It was the fact that we'd diversified that allowed us to survive. There was nothing my father could do to protect the Smith holdings during that chaotic period. Suddenly Babs and Dorsey Smith were staying at the Circle Star. Dorsey and I were so young—we just didn't understand! We treated that time together as if it were a holiday, and meanwhile Babs was always crying." Jessie paused, looking pale. "I remember the tears," she said softly, "but it was years before I was old enough to understand what they were all about.

"You see, when the War ended, Tom Smith, like so many men, came home to find that his ranch had been looted, his range rights and cattle stolen by unscrupulous neighbors. New papers had been filed on the land, and his cattles' brand had been altered. After his years in that Yankee prison, Tom Smith came home to find that he'd been ruined—wiped out—and there wasn't a damn thing he could do about it."

"Well, I guess he had to try and rebuild, right?" Stills asked.

Jessie shook her head sorrowfully. "My father offered to stake Tom to a new start, but he was too proud. Dorsey and I sat huddled in each other's arms in my bedroom the night the two men quarreled, their shouts filling the house. I remember hearing my father beg Tom to consider their friendship. Tom refused to do so. He shouted that while equals could be friends, my father was now his superior. Then Tom said, 'I'll call a man a sonofabitch before I call him "sir," and I'll shoot him if he doesn't like it! Our friendship is over, Alex!'" Jessie gripped her coffee mug. "At that instant, as we listened to Tom Smith cursing, Dorsey abruptly pulled away from me—"

"Oh, damn," Hank Stills said softly. "Damn..."

Meanwhile, Ki was sitting very quietly, regulating his breathing, trying to calm his thudding pulse, trying to tame the rage inside him, the rage that made him to lash out at a world so cruel...

"There was more quarreling between the two men. It ended with Tom Smith rushing out of the house, mounting his horse, and riding into the dark night. Dorsey cried out to him to come back, but he left her and his wife, left all of us. As far as I know, he never returned to the Circle Star. I believe my father never saw him again. I know I never did.

"Everyone in the region who knew Tom knew that something was going to happen. We didn't have long to wait to find out what it was. Within one bloody fortnight, Tom gunned down five men who he held responsible for stealing all that he'd built for himself and his family. For all of that, it still could have ended well for the Smith family. The men were guilty. The *law* had been unable to punish them, but everyone knew they'd taken what had once been Tom's, and we were all willing to accept this man's version of Old Testament justice. But Tom didn't—couldn't—stop there."

Jessie shook her head. "Mind you, I'm not judging him. No one has the right to do that! Maybe those years in Fort Delaware had sapped his spirit of what a man might need to start his life over. Maybe he didn't want to let go of his violent, vengeful quest, because when he did, he would have had to face the fact that he had nothing left."

"He had his family," Stills said. "Hell, he had a wife and kid."

"As I said, I won't judge him," Jessie repeated firmly.

"You said it *could* have ended well for them," Ki spoke. "And yet it did not. What happened?"

"Tom continued his hunt for people to punish. An itinerant preacher took it upon himself to talk some sense into him. It happened in a small town near the Rio Grande. Tom was goading the brother of one of the fellows who'd robbed him into drawing. This was a man who'd never even been in our part of Texas, understand. His only crime was that he was blood-kin to one of the men who'd wronged Tom. Well, what happened that day has never been clear. Somehow that preacher ended up the one being shot dead. Some say it was Tom's doing, others that it was Tom's would-be victim who panicked, firing the stray shot that took the preacher's life. The fact of it was that Tom got the blame, and that killing turned folks against him. The War still loomed in the past. Folks had had their fill of killing. They wanted to forget, and they resented a man like Tom constantly stirring up old grudges. That preacher's killing was what put the price on Tom's head. The Texas Rangers lit out after him. Tom dropped out of sight."

"They ever catch him?" Stills asked.

"The price is still on his head," Jessie replied.

"What about Barbara Smith?" Ki asked. "What about Dorsey?"

"They stayed on with us at the Circle Star for a while, but things became uneasy. My friendship with Dorsey came unraveled. We were just kids, remember, and kids can be so cruel to one another. One afternoon we were playing together and began to quarrel. I said something like, 'Dorsey, this is my daddy's ranch, not yours!' And she screamed back, 'Why couldn't it have been your daddy who got ruined!'"

Jessie smiled wistfully. "I remember going to my father and asking him to throw Dorsey off the ranch, and getting

97

my tail tanned for it. A while later, Babs and Dorsey left the Circle Star. Clearly they were too proud to go on living on our handouts. That was the last I saw or heard of them until this afternoon." She blushed. "The thing that bothers me most, and you'll both likely think me silly for it, is that Dorsey and her mother left before we could make up our childhood quarrel. And from the icy reception she gave me this afternoon, I believe Dorsey is still angry at me."

"She still asks herself that same question," Ki mused. "Why wasn't it *your* father who was ruined?"

Jessie's eyes locked with his. "Yes, you *would* understand," she whispered. "It wasn't very long after that that you came to the Circle Star. And then my father settled on the ranch more or less permanently."

"That's quite a story," Stills remarked. "Quite a story." He looked around the hotel's dining room. All the other tables were vacant, stripped of their cloths, with their chairs turned upside down to facilitate sweeping the floors. Their waiter was off in a corner, yawning as he stood with his arms crossed and his toe tapping.

Stills checked his pocket watch. "It's almost ten. Guess we'd better clear out and let them close up."

Jessie stood. "I'm going upstairs to bed," she announced, stifling a yawn.

Stills nodded. "Ki, care to take a stroll? I'll buy you a nightcap."

"Can we find some Scotch whiskey?" the samurai asked.

"Scotch, eh? Well now, the only place in Nettle Grove that'd have anything other than rye, bourbon, or draft beer would be Braxton's. It's the biggest saloon in town."

"You boys have yourselves a good old time," Jessie drawled. "Hank, do you intend to be up and around in time to meet Marshal Long's train?"

"I surely do. I wouldn't miss getting a peek at your Longarm for anything."

"Then I'll see you at the station tomorrow morning," she laughed.

"I'll be there as well," Ki said. "Good night, Jessie."

The men retrieved their hats and escorted Jessie out of the dining room. They paused in the hotel's quiet lobby while Jessie climbed the stairs to her third-floor room. Finally Ki nodded to Stills, and started out.

"What were we waiting for?" Stills demanded.

"Until Jessie was safely in her room."

"But how could you know that?"

"I heard her lock her door."

"You *what?*" Stills scoffed. "No way! I didn't hear a thing."

Ki smiled noncommittally. "Then you weren't listening," he softly chided. "Now let's go get that Scotch."

Chapter 8

The night was cool, and most of Nettle Grove seemed tucked away in bed as Ki and Stills walked down Main Street towards Braxton's. Neither man spoke as they walked. There was no sound but the clunking of their boots on the raised wooden sidewalks as they made their way toward the pool of light cast by Braxton's entrance.

"This saloon was the town's first," Stills informed Ki as they stepped through the swinging doors. "Mike Braxton started it as a general store, but pretty soon he was making more money selling rye whiskey than rye flour. He built a two-story extension and added this separate entrance."

The saloon was doing a bang-up business. A constant drone of conversation and laughter, as well as a blue haze of tobacco smoke, rose toward the high ceiling. The long, polished oak bar was crowded with men jockeying for the three harried bartenders' attention, and most of the tables were occupied, especially the green baize card tables, where dour men dealt earnest hands of poker.

Stills pointed up to the second-floor balconies at both ends of the room. Behind the railings were narrow, curtained doorways. "Mike's idea was to make his place an inn as well as a saloon and general store. He built the staircases on the building's outside, so that folks wouldn't have to pass through the saloon to get to the rooms. Of course, he didn't figure out how folks were supposed to sleep with all this downstairs ruckus. Now that we've got a hotel and boardinghouses, those rooms aren't used much except for an occasional saddle tramp too drunk to wander far in search of lodging, or to care about the noise." Stills pointed to an archway leading into a darkened area. "That's the store, but there ain't no stock on the shelves. Braxton pretty much concentrates on his saloon business these days. This is the town's biggest and busiest. I would have taken you someplace more quiet, but this here's the only place where you'll find Scotch whiskey."

The two men elbowed a place for themselves at the bar. At first it was difficult, but when the other customers saw the brass star pinned to Stills's shirt, they backed off to give the town marshal and his companion plenty of breathing space.

The bartender nodded to Stills and Ki in turn. He was a small, thin-featured man with thick black hair brushed straight back. He wore a white shirt, a red shoestring tie, and black sleeve garters. "The usual, Hank?"

"The usual, Mike, and Scotch whiskey for my friend, if you've got it."

"We do . . . somewhere," Mike scowled, and then went to the far end of the bar to pull a bottle from one of the liquor-laden shelves. He set the bottle and a glass in front of Ki, saying, "Since you're with the marshal here, I figure I can trust you to settle up fair and square for what you drink. I got enough tallies to keep straight in my head right now." He poured a shot of sour mash and set it before Stills, and then drew a mug of draft from a tap decorated with an ornate metal spigot to keep the sour mash company.

"Was that Mike Braxton?" Ki asked, pouring himself a measure of Scotch.

"Hell, no! That's just another jasper named Mike. Old Braxton don't come in here no more. Don't have to. He just sits home and counts his money . . ." Stills knocked back the sour mash and then sipped at his beer to put out the fire. "I can't get that story that Jessie told us out of my head," he said.

"Yes." Ki took some of his Scotch, rolling it around in his mouth to savor it before swallowing.

Stills chuckled. "You look about ready to smack your

102

lips, son. You are a strange old bird; for who you are, I mean..."

"I do not understand?" Ki inquired, as a tall, red-haired man wearing a fringed, buckskin shirt and pants nudged his way into a tight space at the bar alongside Stills.

"Excuse me," the man said, and then, noticing Stills's badge, added, "Marshal," in respectful tones.

"Sure, stranger," Stills replied agreeably. "Room for all."

He turned his attention back to Ki. "Something's eating at you, old son," he said, "and since I don't figure it's likely you're going to tell me what it is, I'm going to try some of my suspicions on you. You don't have to say anything if you don't want to, or you can just tell me to butt out, but here goes.

"Since you was here last, I had the librarian at the town library order me up some books from San Francisco, and I've done a little reading up on your home country. You-all have some funny ideas about honor and suchlike, but they seem to make some sense to me. Like this business about 'karmer'..."

Ki smiled faintly. *"Karma,"* he corrected Stills gently.

"Yeah, right," Stills said. "It seems like a funny way of looking at things, but not so different from what good Christian folks believe—the Golden Rule and all."

Ki looked at him quizzically.

"You know," Stills explained. "'Do unto others as you'd have them do unto you'?" He cleared his throat. "Well, I suspicion I know what went on betwixt you and Dorsey this afternoon, and I sure won't fault you for it, but I think you figure, since Jessie told us all that about her and Dorsey, that your destiny is all tied up with Dorsey's now, and of course Jessie's too. Somehow you figure you've got to make peace betwixt the two of them, because your own honor's at stake. How'm I doing so far?"

Ki smiled. "Not bad at all," he replied.

"Well," Stills went on, "I just wanted to tell you that I'll do anything I can to help. After all, I feel kind of like family to you and Jessie—"

"Now *here's* something that sticks in my craw!" a rough voice snarled from behind Ki. "Here I am waiting to get me a drink, and who's got my place at the bar but a damned Chinaman!"

Ki sighed. "I'll handle this," Stills began.

"But then you ain't Chinese, you're a Japanese, and supposed to *be* something in a fight!"

As Ki and Stills turned around, their tormentor's arm thrust itself between them to grope for the bottle of Scotch. Ki clamped his fingers around the man's wrist. The man tried to pull free. Ki let him struggle for an instant, then released him.

As the samurai had expected, the plaid-shirted loudmouth was not alone. Three others were lurking behind him, watching intently, ready to back their friend's play. They were dusty and unshaven, all wearing that combination of denim and chambray, leather and flannel, that could have been drover or outlaw garb, and anything in between. Ki had half expected to see the man with the black beard from the laundry incident somewhere about, but he wasn't. He began to hope that this would turn out to be nothing more than a few rowdy saddle tramps thinking to have themselves a sporting time rousting a Chinaman. If so, he could make this sort of nuisance fade away rather quickly.

"You ought to know better than to lay a hand on your betters!" the man in plaid spat, rubbing his wrist. He had shoulder-length, light brown hair hanging down from beneath the brim of his tan Stetson. His eyes were pale blue, and he wore a droopy mustache. "Now, what I want you to do is hand me that bottle, and bow in apology!"

"I don't believe you, sonny!" Hank Stills was grumbling. He thumbed his badge. "See this? I'm going to lock you up until—"

Stills was cut short by the click of a revolver's hammer being thumbed back. The marshal froze as the man in buckskins who'd been standing next to him shoved a gun into his ribs.

"Marshal, I think you'd do well to sit this one out," the

104

man in buckskins cheerfully advised him. "Put up your hands, and keep them up." When Stills hesitated, the gunman's cheeerful tone vanished. "Do it, or I'll shoot you where you stand."

The saloon grew quiet as a tomb as Stills slowly raised his hands. "You won't get away with this . . ."

"Shut up," the man in buckskins ordered lazily. Next he addressed the saloon at large. "Everyone! We ride with Will Sayre! I've got a gun in your marshal's side. Nobody move, nobody interfere!"

Ki's mind worked furiously to figure a way out of this predicament. It was all so unlikely! These five men were claiming to be members of the Ladykiller Gang. Obviously they had tailed Stills and himself from the hotel. But why? What was the point of this confrontation?

"Know who I am?" the man in the plaid shirt demanded of Ki.

"Regrettably not."

"I'm Ned Tarn!" the man proclaimed loudly. "I'm fast with a gun, boy. Fast as there is." As he spoke, he chewed nervously on the ends of his scraggly mustache. "I heard you were fast too. I'm here to find out."

Ki smiled apologetically. "You are mistaken." Slowly he opened his coat. "You see? I have no gun."

"You got other stuff, though. You got knives and whatnot. I heard that you do!"

"Really? You are well informed, Mr. Tarn. Where did you learn so much about me?"

"Never mind!" Tarn, his pale blue eyes gone wild, backpedaled until eight paces separated him from Ki. "You've killed your share of men, but those days are done. You're going to fall to me!" Tarn's right hand curled, his fingers twitching toward the grips of the double-action Colt Thunderer riding high on his right hip in an elaborately tooled, black leather holster.

"For mercy's sake!" somebody yelled. "You can't draw on a man with no gun!"

"Not having a gun didn't stop him from killing two men

105

this afternoon!" Tarn snarled.

Now how did he know I did that? Ki wondered. *Did he just hear about it, or were those men at the laundry also members of Sayre's gang?*

None of it made sense, but Ki would have to puzzle it out later, if he was still alive to do so. He edged sideways, scraping his spine along the bar, to assure himself that Stills, just now standing with his hands up and a horrified look on his face, would be well out of Tarn's line of fire. The three men backing Tarn had spread out in a loose semicircle behind the gunslick.

"Get it done, Ned," the man in buckskins breathed.

Ki noticed that the man's attention was now only partly focused on keeping Stills covered as he waited for the imminent showdown to occur. He hoped Hank knew that, as well.

"Come on, boy, you're my meat," Tarn jeered—

And went for his gun.

Ki dove forward, somersaulting toward Tarn as the man fired. The gunslick *was* fast, Ki thought as he tumbled.

Tarn squeezed off two more rapid-fire shots. The sound of his Colt was like thunder as the rounds nipping after Ki tore splintery holes in the floorboards. The samurai was tumbling as fast as he could, trying desperately to stay below Tarn's angle of fire.

His third somersault put him at Tarn's boot-tips. Ki balanced himself on his hands, his back to the gunslick. Before Tarn could fire a fourth time, Ki swung his legs up and over, the way a vinegarroon will whip its tail up over its back to bring its stinger into play. The samurai's powerful ankles, locked about Tarn's neck, and then Ki twisted his hips, putting everything he had into the spin...

Yelping, Tarn was wrenched off his feet. His Colt slipped from his grasp as he hit the floor hard, his neck still caught in the vise that was Ki's scissors-hold.

Out of the corner of his eye, Ki saw Marshal Stills whirl on the man in buckskins. The two began grappling for the gun pressed between them. There was nothing Ki could do to help; Tarn was flapping like a landed fish as he tried to break loose of Ki's choke-hold around his throat, and there were still his three companions that had to be dealt with.

The man nearest Ki was just then leveling his gun at the samurai's belly. In a single smooth motion, Ki reached inside his coat for a blade and flung it.

The *shuriken* pierced the man's left eye to sink deep into his brain, killing him instantly. It was reflex action that caused the outlaw to squeeze off a shot as he fell. The bullet missed Ki, but hit Tarn squarely in the chest. The gunslick cried out. Ki loosened his ankle-grip around Tarn's neck. The dying man sagged away.

The other two outlaws had their guns out. One man was covering the saloon's patrons bunched up beneath one of the balcony overhangs. As Ki sprang to his feet to deal with the pair of badmen, he heard a muffled shot.

He glanced over his shoulder to see the man in buckskins on his knees, his hands pressed against his bloodied belly. Stills was crabbing sideways, squeezing off shots with the mortally wounded man's revolver.

Ki threw himself to the floor as one of the outlaws began shooting at Stills. There was far too much lead in the air, and the samurai wanted to stay out of its way.

Stills fired again. The man trading rounds with him clutched at his chest and toppled onto a table, which gave way underneath him with a crash.

Just one left, Ki thought, and then stared as the saloon's batwing doors swung open. Standing framed within the doorway was Inspector Broadwick!

"Get away, you fat fool!" Stills shouted, tossing aside the buckskin-clad man's empty revolver and drawing his own.

Broadwick ignored the marshal. The inspector's attention was on the last remaining outlaw. "Drop that pistol, you thug!" he commanded.

The outlaw, seeing that Broadwick had yet to draw a gun, chuckled and spun towards him.

"Damn!" Stills cursed. "Broadwick! Look out!"

The marshal's shouts were cut short by the bark of a rifle coming from the railed balcony. Hank Stills dropped his gun to slap at his left shoulder. Then he was on his ass on the floor, his legs straight out in front of him, a bitter look of disbelief twisting his features as he stared at the swiftly spreading bloodstain on his sleeve.

Ki saw a smoking rifle barrel protruding from one of the curtained doorways on the second floor. As he watched it, the rifle began to swerve in his direction.

He looked around, but there was nowhere to run for cover.

Then Broadwick went into action.

Ki watched, flabbergasted. How could such a big man be so nimble?

The gunman on the ground floor of the saloon shot twice at Broadwick, the bullets chewing holes in the doorjamb as the postal inspector dodged inside, in the process losing his derby. The speed of Broadwick's draw was astounding as he reached beneath his coat. There was a glint of steel, and then the long-barreled revolver was in the inspector's ham-hock of a fist.

There came a cannonlike *boom!* as Broadwick pegged a shot toward the balcony, spoiling the rifleman's aim, and likely saving Ki's life in the process. Then Broadwick turned on the gunman who'd shot at him. The inspector's gun spat orange fire and blue smoke, and the outlaw went down hard, and stayed down.

Then Broadwick was standing over Ki, pointing his revolver like a finger up at the rifleman's curtained doorway.

The four shots from Broadwick's revolver were like a single sustained blast. The curtain puffed inward four times. The protruding rifle barrel dipped, and then the gun clattered to the balcony floor.

As Ki and everyone else craned their necks to see, a man tottered out of the curtained doorway, hit the railing, and jackknifed over it, plummeting twenty feet to land spread-eagled on the floor.

Ki stared. One of Broadwick's rounds had torn off half

of the dead man's face, but there was still enough left of that full black beard mottled with gray for the samurai to recognize him. It was the leader of the three outlaws who'd been harassing Barbara Smith at the laundry, earlier that day.

"Well, well, what do you know?" Broadwick murmured, peering at the dead man. "I got myself old Jack Bean..."

The blue haze of gunsmoke hung in the air like a fog. The saloon stank of black powder and the sweet, coppery smell of blood.

"Somebody fetch a doctor for Marshal Stills," Broadwick called out, breaking open his hinged revolver, which automatically caused the spent shell casings to be ejected from its cylinder.

Stills had gotten to his feet. His gun was back in its holster. He was pressing one of the towels from the bar against his shoulder. "Nah, I'm okay," Stills muttered, and then managed to come up with a cockeyed grin to prove it. "Say, Inspector, that was mighty fine shooting." He watched as Broadwick thumbed fresh cartridges into his weapon. "I ain't never seen a gun like that."

"This is a Smith & Wesson Model Three, .44-caliber 'American,' with an eight-inch barrel," Broadwick said.

"Sure is big," Stills said. "Must weigh a few pounds..."

Broadwick shrugged. "I'm a big man, and I prefer a big weapon."

Stills laughed. "Lloyd, you *are* growing on me..."

Ki had gotten to his feet and was brushing himself off. "You can grow on *me,* as well, Inspector. You saved my life. I am in your debt."

Broadwick smiled. "I'll keep that in mind, Ki."

"That was excellent shooting," the samurai complimented him.

"Not bad for a fellow who got his hat knocked off, eh?" the inspector replied.

Ki walked over to where Broadwick's derby was lying and picked it up. He carried it over to the amused inspector and began to reach up to place it on Broadwick's head, but then stopped and solemnly removed his own Stetson, to set it on the beaming inspector's bald dome.

"After that wonderful show of gunplay," Ki intoned, his almond eyes glinting, "you deserve a cowboy hat."

"Much obliged," Broadwick chuckled. He looked around the saloon. Still crowded against the far wall were the patrons, and more or less scattered in the middle of the floor were the six bodies. "Too bad we couldn't have taken one of these fellows alive," the inspector brooded.

"Exactly my thoughts," Ki said. "They identified themselves as Will Sayre's men, and then that one"—Ki pointed at Ned Tarn's body—"challenged me to a duel. They went so far as to keep Marshal Stills covered. It makes no sense," Ki muttered. He went over to Stills. "Let me take a look at that wound."

"Well, I can attest to these men having been part of the Ladykiller Gang," Broadwick said. "That one with the beard is Jack Bean. He'd been with Sayre for years." The inspector stroked his thin mustache. "Jack did seem intent upon shooting you, Ki. Any reason for him to have had a grudge against you?"

"He was the third man at this afternoon's incident at the laundry," Ki said as he used one of his *shuriken* blades to cut away the blood-sodden shirting around Stills's wound.

"Is that so?" Broadwick frowned. "Wish I'd known that earlier. All right, you killed two of his cronies this afternoon. That might have caused the grudge, but why would a man like Jack Bean be interested in holding up a woman of modest means like Mrs. Smith?"

"There are more pieces to the puzzle, Inspector," Ki muttered as he gingerly examined Stills's wound. "These men here tonight knew a great deal about me." He turned toward Broadwick. "Come to think of it, so did the men this afternoon at the laundry."

"Damned strange, damned strange..." Broadwick grumbled. "How's Stills?"

"The bullet passed clean through and hit no bone or arteries," Ki said. He asked for a clean towel from the bartender, which he folded into a compress. He tore strips from Stills's ruined shirt, and used them to bind the towel bandage in place. "That will hold you until we can get you to the doctor."

"Thanks, Ki." Stills turned to the bartender. "How about a drink?"

"Might as well serve you three," the bartender scowled. "We've got no other customers now."

Ki looked around, and then laughed. "Why, everyone has gone! I didn't notice."

"Ran off, some of them without paying!" the bartender grumbled. He set a bottle of bourbon and glasses on the bar.

"Sour mash all right, Inspector?" Stills asked.

"That'll be fine."

Ki helped himself to more Scotch.

"Where's your deputy, anyway, Marshal?" Broadwick asked. "I would have thought he'd come running at the first shots."

"Oh, he lives way at the other end of town," Stills remarked. "There's no way he could have heard the shooting."

Ki glanced at Broadwick. "What were you doing out and around?" he asked. "I thought you said you were going to bed."

"Lucky for you I couldn't sleep," the inspector replied. "I went over my notes on this case for a while, and then decided to go out for a walk. I guess it's a restless night for everyone."

"What do you mean?" Ki asked.

"Well, I passed Miss Starbuck in the hotel lobby. She said she couldn't sleep either, and was also going out for a walk."

Ki frowned. "Did she say where she was going?"

Broadwick shook his head. "I asked her if she wanted to join me, but she told me that she wanted to be alone . . ."

"Hey, I wouldn't worry, Ki," Stills said. "After all, the shooting was here, right? How much trouble could there be in a sleepy little town like Nettle Grove in one night?"

The flat crack of distant gunfire shattering the evening's stillness mocked Stills in reply.

Ki was already at the saloon's doors. He stood half outside the building, cocking his head to listen to the shooting. "It's coming from around Market Lane," he said.

"Damn, you don't think Jessie is somewhere around there, do you, Ki?" Stills asked anxiously, and then shook his head in exasperation. "How am I supposed to be seeing to trouble in two places at once—"

Stills stopped short.

"Perhaps that was their strategy, Marshal," Broadwick said slowly. "Perhaps all this was nothing but a diversion to draw your attention."

"Come on!" Ki shouted, dashing from the saloon. Stills and Broadwick followed close on the samurai's heels.

"What about these bodies!" the bartender called after them. "Why dontcha clean up one mess before making another?"

"Sorry, Mike!" Stills called over his bandaged shoulder. "It looks like the cleanup, and my getting doctored, is going to have to wait! Anyway, I ain't sure all the killing is done with for the night!"

Chapter 9

After saying good night to Ki and Marshal Stills, Jessie spent a restless quarter-hour in her hotel room. She guessed that she'd gotten her second wind, for she no longer felt the least bit sleepy.

The whiskey she'd had at dinner had left her feeling fidgety, and telling that story from out of the past had stirred up turbulent emotions. Knowing that Barbara and Dorsey were just a few blocks away, and that if she only tried, she might put to rest the unresolved grudge held against her by her girlhood friend was just too much for Jessie. It was bad enough finding out that Dorsey had kept her resentment simmering all these years. Jessie couldn't live with herself if she didn't do everything possible to resolve the conflict.

And there's no time like the present, she reminded herself. It was late, but this was an important enough matter to excuse Jessie's visit at such an hour. At least she'd be sure of finding Babs and Dorsey at home. If need be, Jessie would stay until dawn, until all of it had been talked out between them.

Yes, now is the time to do it, Jessie decided as she shrugged on her green hacking jacket and slipped the leather thong of her Stetson beneath her chin. Now her heart was full of what she wanted to say. If she waited until the morning— when the rye whiskey within her had worn off—she might not have the courage to face Dorsey. Besides, Longarm would be here tomorrow, and Jessie had business appointments scheduled. Who knew if she'd have another chance before it was time for her to return home to Texas?

She paused at the room's door. Considering the lateness of the hour, should she wear her gun? She glanced at the Colt in its waxed cordovan holster hanging from the bedpost.

No, she thought. *It would make a fine impression on Babs and Dorsey to come sauntering into their home with a .38 slung across my hips!*

The derringer would do for late-night protection. Jessie hoisted up her green tweed skirt. The vanity table's gilt-framed oval mirror reflected a black elastic garter riding high upon the shapely curve of her ivory thigh. Sewn onto the garter was a tiny holster in which nestled the derringer. Jessie drew the little gun, warm from its contact with her flesh, and checked its load. She reholstered it in its special hiding place, and then smoothed down her skirt, ready to go out.

She encountered Inspector Broadwick in the hotel lobby. The inspector tipped his ridiculous little derby to her and, seeing that she was dressed to go out, aksed if she would do him the honor of accompanying him on a stroll.

Jessie thanked him, but explained that she'd prefer to be alone. She waited for the inspector to leave the hotel, giving him a few moments to build up a headstart on her, and then stepped out into the night to make her way to Market Lane.

Along Market Lane the storefront windows were all dark, and there was no one on the street. Jessie shivered involuntarily, feeling the tiniest bit apprehensive. Yes, she had her derringer, and of course she could take care of herself if she had to, but still . . .

She walked around the side of the dark laundry building, weaving her way past the clothesline barricades to the little front yard of the Smiths' cottage. There was a glowing lantern hanging from a hook on the front porch, casting a yellow light into the yard. Jessie stopped short. Beside the porch was a man on horseback, holding on to the reins of three other saddled mounts.

She began to back away, and it was then that he noticed her. "Howdy!" he called out.

"Howdy," Jessie called back. The man's horse was standing at the outer reaches of the light cast by the lantern, which put the rider's face in shadows, but he'd greeted her in a friendly enough fashion, and he'd made no move for his gun.

Jessie relaxed, scolding herself for being so suspicious.

"Go on in, if that's what you want," the man on horseback said. "I ain't gonna bite you, little lady." He eased one leg up and over the saddle and leaned back in a relaxed posture. "Me and my buddies are working on the Double Diamond spread. Ever hear of it?"

"No," Jessie said, coming closer.

"Surprised at that," the man said. "It's a big ranch. Our foreman rode in this evening, telling us we were needed." As the man chatted, he dug into the flap pocket of his shirt for a cigar and a match. "Well, we had all of our laundry here. We always have Dorsey do it for us when we're in town. It's a shame we had to come for the laundry this late at night, but we have to get our stuff and get riding if we're to be back at the Double Diamond by sunup."

Jessie came within a yard of the drover's horse. She peered up, trying to see his face. The lantern light was enough for her to see that he was wearing tan corduroy trousers, a plaid flannel shirt with the sleeves rolled up to reveal his thick wrists and well-muscled forearms, and a putty-colored Stetson. He wore his gun high on his left hip, butt forward.

The man struck his match alight with his thumbnail, brought it up to the tip of his cheroot, and puffed away. The flaring match illuminated his face, which was as long and thin as a hatchet blade. A thin white scar ran down his right cheek. His eyes were small and heavy-lidded. His nose lay flat; it looked to have been broken so many times that there wasn't much left of it.

"What brings you here, ma'am?" the man inquired politely.

"I'm a friend of the Smiths," Jessie began, but then abruptly quieted. "Listen!" she said, and a moment later, "Do you hear shots?"

"No, ma'am, can't say as I do," the man on horseback said evenly.

Jessie turned away, closing her eyes in order to concentrate on her hearing. "I'm sure there's shooting going on!" she exclaimed, turning back to the man—

Jessie had no time to think, let alone grope for her derringer. As the man dropped from his horse and came at her, she instinctively positioned herself in the neutral *te* stance that Ki had long ago drilled into her. As the man's big hands closed on her shoulders, Jessie grabbed his wrists and flung herself backwards, just as Ki had taught her. His momentum carried him up and over her as Jessie curled her spine to meet the ground, at the same time planting her boots into the man's midsection and then straightening her legs.

The cowboy—if that was what he was—flipped clear over her and landed flat on his back, the wind knocked out of him. Before he could recover, Jessie had spun around to tug his pistol from his holster. He was starting to rise when Jessie swiped hard at the side of his head with the barrel of his gun. The man grunted once, his eyes rolling up into his head, and then settled back to lay still.

The entire episode had lasted mere seconds, the only noise being the man's grunting sigh as he'd slipped into unconsciousness. Jessie, the gun in her hand, rocked back on her heels, trying to catch her breath and silence her thudding heart.

She had no idea what this man was doing here, or why he had attacked her. She figured to turn him over to Marshal Stills.

The nervous shuffling of the four horses behind her reminded Jessie that this man had come with friends. She glanced at the cottage. There were lights on inside, but she could not see inside because of the curtains across the windows. What the men who owned these horses were doing in that cottage was the real question.

Jessie rolled the unconscious man onto his belly. In her jacket pocket was a silk scarf about eighteen inches long. She used it to bind the man as Ki had taught her: she pulled his wrists behind his back and looped them tightly with the scarf. Next she bent back one of his legs at the knee, and wrapped the remaining length of twisted silk around his boot ankle. There was just enough of its length remaining to hitch a sturdy knot.

That done, Jessie sighed in relief. The man was still out cold. When he came to, the hasty job of hogtying would not hold him forever, but it would hold for a while.

From somewhere in the distance came the sound of a large-caliber pistol firing four rounds in quick succession. In the excitement, Jessie had forgotten about the shooting. Now she realized it had been going on all the while.

She listened hard, meanwhile gripping the fallen man's gun, and keeping her eyes on the porch. The shooting had stopped. Those last booming shots had ended the battle, wherever it was.

The distant gunplay slid from Jessie's thoughts as the cottage door swung open. Two men dressed in greasy trail garb came stomping out onto the porch. Dorsey—dressed for riding in a flat-topped Stetson, high boots, jeans, and an oversized work shirt belted at the waist—was between them.

The two men stared in shocked surprise at Jessie, gun in hand, kneeling over their bound, unconscious lookout.

"Kill her!" one of the men growled, as they both slapped leather.

"No!" Dorsey cried, trying to break away.

"Stay right here!" one of the men snarled, grabbing her by the wrist and holding her fast.

As Dorsey struggled, her waving arm struck the porch lantern, setting it swinging. Crazy patterns of light and shadow now suffused the porch area, making it difficult for Jessie to see what the men were doing.

One of the men's guns flashed fire, the bullet kicking up dirt a few inches in front of Jessie. She fanned a couple of shots into the air, just to panic the two owlhoots. She didn't dare seriously aim at them for fear of accidentally hitting Dorsey. Jessie would have shot out the lantern, but she figured that spattering flaming kerosene all over the wood-frame porch was not the best way to renew her friendship with the Smiths.

Instead, Jessie dove between the legs of the nearest horse. She quickly gathered up the four horses' reins, which were trailing on the ground, and knotted them together. All around her the panicked, snorting horses bucked and reared. Jessie crouched low, peering past the mounts' heaving flanks. She caught glimpses of the two men crabbing sideways, looking for a clear shot at her. Jessie fired another shot into the air to keep the living merry-go-round of whinnying, wild-eyed horseflesh moving, and to signal for help.

"Kill her! Shoot, dammit!" the man holding on to Dorsey swore. He aimed, but had to give it up as Dorsey's struggles jostled him, spoiling his aim.

"I can't get a clear shot!" the other man bawled. "I'll hit the horses!"

Jessie grinned to herself, thinking that things just might work out. "Don't give up hope, Dorsey!" she shouted. "Fight them!"

"Let me go!" Dorsey was howling. "Don't hurt her!"

Jessie was able to fire twice more before the gun she'd confiscated clicked empty. *No matter*, she thought. *Somebody must have heard all the ruckus.*

A glancing blow between her shoulder blades sent her reeling on legs suddenly turned to jelly. *Kicked by a horse*, she thought woozily, seeing stars as she tumbled to the ground.

Semiconscious, Jessie saw one of the outlaws approaching.

"Never mind her!" the one holding Dorsey said. "Get those horses untangled and help me untie Rube! We gotta get out of here!"

The derringer, Jessie thought. *Must get to it—*

It was no good. The world was spinning topsy-turvy around her, and her limbs were refusing the directives issued by her brain.

"Listen!" one of the outlaws hissed. "Footsteps! Somebody's coming!"

"Jessie! Jessie!"

"Forget Rube!" one of the men said. "Get Dorsey on horseback. We've got to ride!"

"We can't leave Rube!" the other man worried. "He'll kill us for it!"

"He'll kill us if we don't get Dorsey back to the hideout!"

"Go! Take her and go..." a third male voice ordered hoarsely. Listening, Jessie recognized it as belonging to the man she'd knocked out and bound. "Get going!" the one called Rube reiterated. "I'll meet you back at the hideout!"

Jessie heard the sound of hooves pounding away. She tried again to sit up, and this time she managed it. A few paces away, Rube was slipping free of the silk scarf and getting to his feet.

Jessie quickly hoisted her skirt and drew her derringer. "Sit quiet, Rube," she ordered. "You're not going anywhere!"

The man stared at the little gun—and at Jessie's bare legs—and grinned. "Damn, but you pack a lot of surprises!"

Jessie extended her hand with the derringer, while demurely patting down her skirt. "I said sit, and put your hands up!"

"Yes, ma'am," Rube chuckled, doing exactly as he was told.

"Jessie!" Ki burst into the yard, followed by Hank Stills and Inspector Broadwick. "Are you all right?" the samurai anxiously demanded as he helped her to her feet.

"Fine," she replied. "Just a little sore."

"This is turning out to be quite a night," Broadwick laughed, taking a pair of handcuffs out of his coat pocket and snapping them on Jessie's prisoner. "Miss Starbuck, you have captured the infamous Rube Silva!"

"The outlaw you think is Will Sayre's second-in-command?" Hank Stills scowled. "What a night, all right. Now what would *he* be doing here?"

119

"His two accomplices rode off with Dorsey," Jessie said. "They—"

"They kidnapped my daughter, Marshal!" Barbara Smith interrupted from the porch. All eyes turned toward her, sitting there in her wheelchair beneath the kerosene lantern. She looked about a thousand years old, huddled beneath a shawl, her gray hair in disarray, her face pale and drawn, her eyes swollen and red-rimmed from crying. "They kidnapped my Dorsey. She's all I have. You've got to get her back for me!"

"Easy, there, Babs," Stills soothed.

"Ki? Has Hank been shot?" Jessie asked the samurai, noticing the marshal's bandaged shoulder. "Was that part of the shooting I heard?"

"I'll explain later," Ki said.

Jessie nodded, and glanced at Broadwick. "Why is he wearing your hat?" she whispered.

"Long story," Ki replied. "Mrs. Smith," he called, "why would the Ladykiller Gang abduct Dorsey? Surely they must know you haven't the money to pay a ransom."

"Well?" Broadwick demanded of Rube Silva. "I think you can shed some light on the matter."

"I ain't saying nothing, fat man," Silva sulked. "Gloat while you got me, 'cause Will Sayre will get me out of this!" he finished defiantly.

"Jessie?" Barbara Smith called softly. "You didn't tell them—?"

Jessie shook her head. "You as much as asked me not to this afternoon, remember, Babs?"

The invalid nodded, smiling faintly. "I knew I could trust you."

"I think you've suffered enough," Jessie replied softly. "There was no reason to ruin your lives here in Nettle Grove."

"Excuse me," Stills interrupted. "Would you two ladies mind letting us gentlemen in on the conversation?"

"That story I told to you and Ki at dinner this evening was true, except for one thing," Jessie began.

120

"Wait a minute! What story?" Broadwick demanded.

Ki held up his hand to silence the man. "One moment, Inspector. Go on, Jessie."

"The owner of that ranch, the man who came back from the war to find himself ruined, his name wasn't Tom Smith—"

"His name was Will Sayre!" the elderly woman announced, a curious note of pride mixed with the misery in her voice. "I'm really Barbara Sayre. I'm Will's wife."

"Well, I'll be," Marshal Stills exclaimed. "At last things around here are beginning to make sense! Will Sayre has kidnapped his own daughter!"

★

Chapter 10

Longarm figured that his poor spine had suffered every bounce and jolt the Union Pacific's weather-warped rails could dish out to a passenger during this long, miserable trip. The chugging Baldwin six-wheeler locomotive had broken down twice while hauling the train over the hump of the Rockies, through the snow-capped Continental Divide's South Pass, and then onto the spur for the final leg of the journey to Nettle Grove. A broken-down engine was nobody's fault, but sitting still had never been Longarm's favorite pastime, and the thinly padded green plush seat of the stuffy U.P. passenger car had put a crick in his neck and cramps in his long legs.

But Longarm forgot his physical discomfort, and his soured disposition sweetened considerably, when the train pulled into Nettle Grove's depot and he caught a glimpse through the car's grimy window of Jessie Starbuck waving at him from the platform!

As the lurching train groaned to a stop, Longarm stood up, stretched, and took down his saddle, Winchester, and other gear from the overhead luggage rack. As he shouldered his burdens and made his way to the rear exit of the passenger car, he grinned in response to the hard look the conductor gave him.

The conductor had come aboard halfway through the trip, and had stopped at Longarm's seat to order the deputy marshal to transfer his gear to the baggage car. The overhead racks, the conductor had scowled, were for "refined" luggage, not saddlebags and rifles.

123

Longarm didn't like trusting the tools of his trade—his tack and firearms—to the care of others, if he could help it. He'd flashed his badge at the supercilious conductor, and reasoned with the railroad official that since the passenger car already looked and smelled like a whorehouse on a Sunday morning, his McClellan and Winchester weren't going to hurt it none. The conductor had threatened to throw him off the train. Longarm, who'd begun to get angry at this pissant's imperious style, had told the conductor to do it if he thought he could. That had ended *that* . . .

"Custis!" Jessie squealed, running to throw her arms around him as soon as Longarm appeared on the platform.

"Whoa, slow down, Jessie!" Longarm laughed. "At least let me set down this here saddle so that I can give you a proper hug!"

As he did so, Longarm eyed the two grim-faced men in Jessie's wake. One was about his own age, wore a town marshal's badge pinned to his chest, and had his left arm in a sling. The other jasper was big and fat and dressed like a city slicker, except for his hat, a nice-looking gray Stetson.

"Howdy, deputy," the town marshal said. "I'm Hank Stills."

Regretfully disengaging himself from Jessie's embrace, Longarm shook hands with the marshal, then with the other man. "I reckon that you'd be Inspector Lloyd Broadwick?"

"Yes. Please come along with me, deputy," Broadwick huffed. "There's no time to waste!"

"Inspector!" Jessie scolded. "You promised to let me fill Longarm in on what's happened!"

"Young lady, you elicited that promise from me last night, in the heat of our argument over your withholding evidence."

"But a promise is a promise!" Jessie protested.

"You're lucky I'm not holding to my promise to arrest you," Broadwick snapped back.

"Slow down, everybody!" Longarm groaned. "I just busted my rear end riding a train all the way from Denver! And I'm so hungry my belly thinks my throat's been cut."

"There's a fine cafe just around the corner," Stills said, grinning at Longarm. "I like a man who knows what's important. I wouldn't mind a plate of steak and eggs myself."

"Lead me to it!" Longarm beamed.

"Deputy, you seem to forget who is in charge here!" Broadwick thundered. "There is no time for—"

"Lloyd," Longarm cut him off. "May I call you Lloyd?"

"You may call me Inspector Broadwick!"

"Thanks, Lloyd, and you can call me Longarm. Now, Lloyd, I ain't arguing the fact that you're in charge, at least I ain't arguing it at the moment," Longarm added wryly.

"Gosh, I'm glad to see you!" Jessie blurted happily.

"Same here, sweetheart," he said with a wink. "Anyway, Lloyd, you ought to see the sense in my having something to eat if I'm going to be any good whatsoever to you, right? Anyway"—Longarm eyed Broadwick's substantial paunch— "you look like a jasper who knows how to handle a plate of steak and eggs, so what do you say?"

Broadwick inhaled a deep breath and let it out slowly. "Steak and eggs all around, by all means, *Longarm*!"

As the breakfast rush at the Railroad Cafe was almost over, there was no problem with Longarm piling his gear atop a nearby table in order to keep his eye on it. During the meal, Jessie, Marshal Stills, and Inspector Broadwick took turns filling Longarm in on the previous day's events.

After the table was cleared, Longarm sipped at his coffee and lit up a cheroot—that blessed first one of the new day. He blew a perfect smoke ring, eyeing Jessie through the blue haze. "Lloyd here is right in being peeved at you," he said. "You should have told him and Marshal Stills who Barbara and Dorsey Smith really were."

"But why ruin their lives here in Nettle Grove?" Jessie asked. "What justice would that have served? They'd been trying to make a life for themselves here. If folks hereabouts knew they were Will Sayre's kin, they would have been shunned, and their business ruined!"

125

"Miss Starbuck!" Broadwick protested hotly. "I never suggested that you make the information public, only that you confide in Marshal Stills and me!"

Jessie blushed. "I understand that *now,*" she said quietly, "but at the time it didn't occur to me that you could be trusted, Inspector." She gulped. "I mean, now I *know* you can be trusted." She looked miserable. "Anyway, I knew that if I told Hank, he'd feel duty-bound to pass the information along," she finished lamely.

Broadwick turned to Longarm. "See what I've been up against?" he appealed.

"Well, Broadwick," Stills broke in, "you must agree that no harm has been done."

"And I caught Rube Silva for you!" Jessie reminded the frazzled-looking postal inspector.

"Oh, all right," Broadwick allowed. "I never *really* intended to arrest you, Miss Starbuck."

"Call me Jessie," she said tenderly, patting his hand.

Longarm turned toward Stills. "Tell me again what Mrs. Sayre said to you all last night."

"Well, hold on, I wrote it down..."

Stills fumbled with his good right arm for a small paperbound notebook in his shirt pocket. He riffled through some pages and then began to read. "After leaving the Starbuck ranch, Barbara and her daughter Dorsey spent some time traveling around. According to Babs, they stopped over in a number of towns, sometimes for as long as a year. Babs still had the use of her legs then. She'd work as a seamstress, a store clerk, and so on, while Dorsey would be enrolled in whatever grammar school was available..."

"Must have been rough on that little girl, always moving around, always losing friends," Longarm frowned thoughtfully, puffing on his cheroot.

"Finally Babs and her daughter ended up in Cough Creek, our county seat, where she got a job teaching school," Stills resumed, reading from his notes. "This was about ten years ago. According to Babs, Dorsey taught herself to shoot and ride, just like Jessie." The marshal glanced apologetically at Jessie, and then continued, "It seems that Dorsey got it into her head that Jessie's late father was responsible for her own father's ruination. Dorsey had come to believe that Alex Starbuck let her father down by not protecting his holdings."

"I can understand her feeling that way," Jessie said. "Having somebody to blame can make terrible misfortune easier to bear. I remember how I felt when my mother was killed, and then later on, when my father was murdered." She looked at Longarm. "Remember how eager for vengeance I was?"

Longarm shrugged. "Your enemy was real, Jessie. Dorsey has only imagined that you're to blame for what's happened to her family. Marshal Stills? Did Mrs. Sayre tell you about any threats her daughter might have made toward Jessie?"

Stills seemed to hesitate, and then nodded. "She did. According to Babs, Dorsey feels Jessie had no right to happiness after her own misfortune."

"Hank! You never told me Babs said that!"

"I didn't want to upset you, Jessie," Stills replied. "Longarm, Dorsey has told her mother that she intends to even the score someday between their two families."

"But last night Dorsey begged those two kidnappers not to hurt me!" Jessie said.

"That speaks well of her," Longarm said. "She had a grudge against you, but when it looked bad for you, her old friendship with you won out."

"It was during their stay in Cough Creek that Will Sayre somehow found them, and began to visit," Stills continued. "Bab's rheumatism got worse. She ended up in her wheelchair, and had to give up her teaching job. It fell to Dorsey to make their living. Will Sayre left what money he could during his visits, but he was getting older as well, and he'd never stolen as much money as folks say, according to Babs."

"No one could have," Longarm agreed quietly. "Not even Robin Hood."

"Babs had squirreled away what money Will had given her. She decided the thing to do for Dorsey's sake was open up a business. She wanted to put down roots so that Dorsey could find herself a husband, have young'uns of her own, and put the past behind her. Cough Creek real estate was too expensive, so they came here to Nettle Grove. According to Babs, Dorsey thought it was pretty funny that they ended up in a town that owed so much to Jessie Starbuck."

"Was that the trouble with the land grabbers that was in the papers a while back, Jessie?" Longarm asked. When Jessie nodded, he said, "Go on, Marshal."

"Not much else to tell," Stills said, putting away his notebook. "Sayre's last visit to his wife and daughter was almost two years ago, while they were still living in Cough Creek. He'd tried to talk his wife into coming back with him to his hideout. Supposedly it's a regular little town hidden in the Utah canyon country. Babs refused. She didn't want Dorsey surrounded by the outlaws and whores that kind of 'robbers' roost' would attract. Babs felt that her daughter being a laundress was lowly but honorable. She felt that her daughter had too much of her father's nature. According to Babs, both of them are prideful and haughty, and believe that the world owes them something.

"That visit was the last time Babs saw her husband. Yesterday some of Sayre's outlaws showed up, led by Jack Bean and Rube Silva. They told Babs that Will wanted his daughter with him, and meant to have her, one way or the other. Yesterday afternoon Babs tried to scare them off. Last night they caused a big ruckus down at Braxton's to draw us away from what they were really after. They got away with it, although it cost them eight men, including Jack Bean, and Rube Silva is just now cooling his heels in my jail."

"Silva vowed that Will Sayre and the rest of the Lady-killers will get him out, Longarm," Broadwick said. "I think it's an idle boast."

"Maybe not, Lloyd," Longarm mused. "Sayre's been running a big, well-disciplined gang for a lot of years. Part

128

of what he offers his men is the security of knowing that he'll take care of any of his riders who get themselves pinched by the law." He grinned at Stills. "I mean no offense, Marshal, but a tough old bird like Sayre might not think twice about taking on a one- or two-man police force in an isolated town like Nettle Grove."

"I agree with you, Longarm," Stills said uneasily. "In that case, I hope you're not aiming to take on Sayre and his men here!"

"Why not?" Broadwick interrupted. "That sounds like a capital plan!"

"For the undertaker in town, maybe," Longarm said. "Think it out, old son. If we take on Sayre in Nettle Grove, who knows how many innocent folks might die?"

"Of course," Broadwick agreed. "Sorry, Marshal Stills. I suppose I'm so anxious to apprehend Will Sayre that I'm not thinking clearly." He sighed. "Last night I theorized that it was Rube Silva who was in charge of the Ladykillers, but I see now that I was wrong. It looks like that canny old wolf Will Sayre still has some teeth left!"

"What are you proposing to do, Longarm?" Stills asked.

"Just a moment, Marshal," Broadwick said. "I am still in charge."

"Well, I guess it's time for us to gnaw on that bone," Longarm said. "You're in charge of the investigation of the mail car robbery and the murders of those two clerks—"

"Absolutely correct," Broadwick began.

"But as of last night, we've got a kidnapping on our hands, and since kidnapping is outside the jurisdiction of the United States Post Office, and since the abductors have taken their captive outside the boundaries of the township of Nettle Grove, and likely the county of Cough Creek, I'd say this crime is the business of the Justice Department." Longarm grinned. "In other words, I'm in charge, as a federal deputy marshal!"

Broadwick's lower jaw dropped about a foot as he gaped at the lawman. "But—but—"

Stills and Jessie exchanged merry smiles. "What did I

tell you?" Jessie chuckled. Stills nodded and told Broadwick, "Longarm's got you, Inspector!"

"I ain't calling you wrong," Longarm said. "I'm just calling it like I see it within the limits set for me by the Justice Department's regulations."

"Then I intend to telegraph your superior in Denver to have you set straight!" Broadwick threatened.

"You can do that, Lloyd, but by the time Marshal Vail wires back, I'll be long gone on the trail, assuming that Billy doesn't back me up, which, I grant you, doesn't happen all that often, but in this situation is a real possibility. Dorsey Sayre has been kidnapped: she deserves to live her own life the way she wants. Rescuing her ought to take precedence over the mail car robbery and such."

"We still don't know what you've got in mind for a plan," Stills repeated.

"I figure to have Rube Silva lead me to Will Sayre's hideout."

"What makes you think a hardened criminal like Silva would cooperate with you?" Broadwick scoffed.

"A couple of reasons. Number one, I mean to bluff him into thinking that he's got no choice. If Marshal Stills will go along with the ruse, I think we can convince Silva that the town is so frightened of a bloody jailbreak led by Will Sayre that it's ready to lynch Silva to keep Sayre from coming around."

"That's not bad," Stills chuckled. "It won't have been the first time an outlaw with a murder warrant on him found himself the guest of honor at a necktie party."

"Yes,". Broadwick admitted. "And Silva is a cocky sort. He'll figure that once on the trail, he'll find himself an opportunity to get away from you. Yes, it'd work, all right."

"All right then, Lloyd. Let's make sure we understand each other," Longarm declared. "Dorsey's life is hanging in the balance, so I don't aim to waste time arguing. We're both after the same quarry—Will Sayre. There's no reason why we can't work together. You're a damn good investigator, Lloyd, but your home territory is back East. You're a tenderfoot out here, and that's pretty risky in itself, without trying to be a lawman at the same time."

"I'm not *trying* to be anything, Longarm!" Broadwick growled. "I *am* a lawman!"

"Maybe so, Lloyd, but what about your lawman's skills?"

"I assure you that I can shoot!" Broadwick said, opening his coat to afford Longarm a glimpse of the Smith & Wesson in its shoulder holster.

Longarm whistled. "That's some cannon, all right, but are you accurate with it? No one was ever killed by a loud noise, you know."

Before Broadwick could reply, Stills cut in, "I told you about the shootout last night at the saloon, Longarm. It was Broadwick here who saved the day. He can shoot as smooth as any man I've ever seen."

"All right," Longarm acquiesced. "So you can shoot, Lloyd. But what about riding?"

Broadwick shifted uneasily in his chair. "Uh, you might say that horseback riding is my sore spot..."

"There you have it," Longarm said. "And the ride we've got to take into Utah's rough country ain't going to be some Sunday afternoon jaunt around a St. Louis bridal path. I can make things easier for the both of us, Inspector, but only if we can work together as equals. You're welcome to tag along with me as a partner, not a boss."

"Agreed," Broadwick sighed.

"When do we leave?" Jessie asked.

"Uh, Jessie, I don't think it's a good idea for you to come," Longarm began.

"A woman coming along on such a perilous journey is utterly out of the question!" Broadwick decreed.

"Both of you gents just hush up!" Jessie scolded. "It's time for me to say a few things. Number one, Longarm and Hank can vouch for the fact that I'm an expert rider, and can handle a gun. Number two, both of you have forgotten that I *know* Will Sayre!"

"Jessie, that was a long time ago," Longarm pointed out.

"Not so long ago that he won't remember me, and the

friendship he once had with my father," Jessie argued. "With his daughter by his side, Will Sayre is going to be less anxious to start shooting. Maybe I can talk him into surrendering peacefully. If there's even a chance of my being able to do that, it'd be worth my coming along." She paused. "Or are you two men looking forward to trading lead with the entire Ladykiller Gang?"

"No, ma'am," Longarm chuckled. "Can't say as we are. Right, Lloyd?"

Broadwick looked utterly dejected. "You mean to say that she's coming with us?" he asked weakly.

"Trust me, old son. If we don't take her with us, she'll just follow on her own. And Ki has taught her to track like a bloodhound . . ."

The inspector nodded. "Very well," he sighed. "And I thought I had my hands full with Ki!"

Longarm looked at Jessie. "With all this palavering, I plumb forgot to miss that jasper! Where is Ki, anyhow?"

Chapter 11

Ki quickened his pace along Main Street as he heard the shrill steam whistle announcing the Union Pacific's arrival. That was Longarm's train arriving, Ki knew. Jessie, Broadwick, and Marshal Stills would all be at the depot to greet the lawman.

Ki would have enjoyed partaking in the reunion with his old friend, but regrettably, it could not be; the samurai had other business to attend to at the moment.

It was business that was better done while the others were occupied.

Ki entered the town marshal's office. The deputy on duty was seated behind Hank Stills's old, scarred oak desk, with his feet up. He had a scruffy, reddish beard and thinning hair, and a smoldering, evil-smelling corncob pipe was clenched between his teeth. The deputy was slender and of medium height. He was wearing black tweed trousers and a mustard-yellow flannel shirt. An army flap holster rode the deputy's right side, suspended from an old garrison belt cinched tight around his narrow waist. His brass deputy's star was pinned to the belt's cracked leather, just to the left of the buckle.

"Howdy, mister. What can I do for you?" the deputy asked.

"You're Oakley, right?"

The deputy nodded. "That's the name they gave me."

"Hank Stills has given me permission to see your prisoner," Ki said.

Oakley puffed thoughtfully on his corncob. Ki could tell

the lawman was looking him over, taking stock of his worn denims, pullover shirt, leather vest, and rope-soled black cotton slippers.

"You're that fellow who travels with Jessie Starbuck, ain't you?" Oakley said.

"I am."

"Thought I recognized you, mister—not that there's many folks passing through Nettle Grove who look like you. Well, I guess it'd be all right for you to see the prisoner, seeing as how you and Miss Starbuck and Marshal Stills are all good friends." Oakley swung his feet off the desk and sat upright. "Let me just find the keys..."

As the deputy rummaged through desk drawers, Ki took the opportunity to get the office's layout firmly fixed in his mind. A door to the rear, behind the desk, led to the jail cells. Along one wall was a rack of securely chained rifles and shotguns, and beneath the rack, facing the wall, was another desk—likely the one Oakley occupied when Stills was around, Ki thought. The wall opposite the gun rack was taken up with a collection of wanted posters.

I wonder if my name and likeness are destined to find a place upon that wall, Ki had time to muse before Oakley stood up, a jingling key ring in his hand.

"This way," Oakley said. He went to the door behind the desk and unlocked it. He glanced back at Ki and said, "You're supposed to leave your gun on the desk there, but I see you ain't got any, so come on!"

The Nettle Grove jail had not found it necessary to expand in pace with the rest of the town. The cell area was nothing more than a back room divided into two holding pens with a floor-to-ceiling partition of steel grating. General-store variety, long-shackled padlocks held both cell doors closed. Rube Silva was in one of the makeshift cells, lounging on a canvas folding cot, his hands laced behind his head. The cell adjoining his was empty.

"Who's that?" Silva demanded of the deputy, eyeing Ki.

"This fellow wants to talk to you, Rube," Oakley said.

"I suppose you want to do your jawing in private?" the deputy asked, turning to Ki.

"Yes, please—in private."

"All right, I'll be in the front office," Oakley said.

Ki waited until the deputy had left the cell area, closing the door behind him. "Do you know who I am?" he asked Silva.

The outlaw shrugged. "More or less," he muttered, sitting up on his cot. "You're the one gave old Jack and his boys a hard time yesterday afternoon at the laundry. You killed two of Will Sayre's men then, and killed yourself another pair at the saloon last night. You work for Jessica Starbuck." Silva shrugged again. "That about cover it?"

"It does," the samurai nodded. "My name is Ki."

"What do you want with me?" Silva demanded.

The samurai hesitated. "I want to make you a proposition," Ki began. "I'm willing to help you escape—"

"What?" Silva stood up and came close to the steel grating separating the two men. "Now why would you want to do a thing like that?" Silva asked curiously, his gaze as cold and flat as that of a diamondback rattler. "Don't you know that it was your boss lady, Jessica Starbuck, who put me here?"

"Yes, I do know that." Ki looked down at the floor.

"Well, then, why would you want to help the likes of me?"

"Rube, you ride with Will Sayre."

"That's a fact."

"Well, I wish to meet Sayre. I wish to join his gang."

"You expect me to believe that?" Silva spat, his lip curling disdainfully. "More likely, you want me to lead you to our hideout so that your friends can bring a posse down on us—"

"No!" Ki said. "Listen to me. Yesterday afternoon, at the laundry, I was not merely passing by when I stepped in between your men and Barbara Sayre. I was with Dorsey." Ki looked anguished. "It's difficult for me to say. It means

135

I must betray Jessica Starbuck, but I have fallen in love with Dorsey. She loves me, as well." Ki looked up hopefully into Rube Silva's reptilian eyes. "I want to join the father's gang, and marry the daughter. Do you understand?"

"So Dorsey's got a beau who wants to come calling? I warn you, Will Sayre might not take a shine to a half-breed looking to lay claim to his daughter. What if he refuses to let you marry her?" the amused outlaw asked.

Ki shrugged. "Then I will merely become another member of the Ladykiller Gang."

"You'd stay on? You'd not want to return to Starbuck's employ?" Silva asked, skeptical.

"I could not return. Miss Starbuck would not have me, and I would face a prison term for helping a wanted man to escape."

"Of course, old Will might decide to kill you and have done with it," Silva suggested, watching Ki for his reaction.

"That is a possibility, but I don't believe it to be a likely one," Ki said. "I could be a valuable gang member. I have already proved myself against four of his best men, including Ned Tarn."

"Will might be sore at you for that."

"And I believe Dorsey will plead with her father on my behalf," Ki added. "In any event, none of this should be of concern to you. I'm not asking you to guarantee my safety when I confront Will Sayre. I only ask you to take me to him, and to Dorsey. In exchange, I will have helped you regain your freedom."

Silva nodded. "All right, it's a deal, Ki. How are you planning to do it?"

Behind them, the door to the cell area burst open. In stepped Deputy Oakley, thumbing back the hammer of his Colt Peacemaker.

"I heard it all!" the deputy proclaimed hotly. "I thought you were acting powerful strange!" he told Ki. "I kept my ear pressed up against the door to listen in on what you were planning! Now I got you!" He gestured with his Colt. "Mister, you're gonna join Silva in that cell next to his."

136

Ki never even turned around. He bent forward at the waist to execute an *ushiro-geri-kekomi,* kicking out with one leg like a mule, so that his backward kick connected with Oakley's wrist, jarring loose his Colt.

The deputy stared wide-eyed, first in longing at his gun lying well out of reach on the floor, and then at Ki, looming threateningly above him.

"I'm an officer of the law!" the slender deputy announced. "I'm placing you under arrest!"

"You have done your duty in an honorable manner," Ki told him. "However, you have been beaten. Now please hand over the key ring."

Oakley clasped his hands together into a double fist and swung as hard as he could against the side of Ki's neck. The samurai hunched his powerful shoulder muscles and took the blow. There was nothing wrong with it—it might have felled an ordinary man, but Ki was not ordinary, and the smaller deputy was simply no match for him.

Oakley, out of breath and puffing, let his arms sag to his side as he stared up at Ki, waiting for the worst to befall him. Ki said, "You are indeed a good deputy," and then jabbed with stiffened fingers at the *atemi* pressure point just beneath Oakley's ear.

Oakley's eyelids fluttered. Ki caught him as he began to crumple to the floor, and eased him down. He quickly went through the unconscious deputy's pockets until he found the ring of keys. He unlocked the padlock on the empty cell and gently laid the deputy upon its canvas cot. Then he closed the cell door and locked it. Next he unlocked the cell containing Rube Silva.

The outlaw tried to reach the fallen Colt, but Ki beat him to it. "I will give this to you when I think that you can be trusted," Ki said, easing down the Colt's hammer and tucking the gun into his waistband.

The scar running the length of Silva's cheek glowed whitely as the outlaw colored with fury. As abruptly as it came, his anger faded. "All right, you can call the shots for now, Ki," Silva drawled. "But remember, you're going to need me to speak up for you with Will Sayre, as much as I now need you. What's our next move?"

"I have our horses, already loaded with supplies, around in back of the jail."

"I reckon you mean to let him live?" Silva gestured toward the unconscious deputy.

"Why kill him?" Ki asked.

"He's heard everything you told me. Stills and the others will know the how and why of you aiding in my escape..."

"By my absence, they will know that I have helped you in any event," Ki said, starting for the door. "He lives."

Silva laughed. "You're calling the shots...for now."

"Damn! I just can't believe Ki would have done such a thing!" Marshal Stills fumed, banging his fist down upon his desktop.

"It makes perfect sense to me," Inspector Broadwick grumbled.

Jessie and Longarm exchanged worried looks. "Oh, Custis!" Jessie sighed. "No matter how it looks, I just know that Ki had a good reason for doing what he did."

The four of them were all moping in Stills's office, trying to come to terms with the incredible fact that Ki had broken Rube Silva out of jail. They'd come directly from the Railroad Cafe to find Oakley just coming awake in one of the cells, while the jail that had held Silva was now empty. Between moans, the deputy had managed to stammer out what had happened. Jessie, who had some knowledge of Ki's *atemi* skills, had reassured the worried deputy that he'd continue feeling groggy and hung over for a few hours, but would soon completely recover. Stills had sent the sleepy fellow home for a nap.

"I really did try to stop him, Hank," Oakley had said sheepishly just before he left.

"I know that," Stills had replied. "Rest easy, Oakley. There ain't no shame in being beat by Ki."

That had been an hour ago. Now Stills, Jessie, Broadwick, and Longarm were trying to figure out their next move.

"You say Ki had a good reason for his actions, Jessie," Broadwick said. "I presume you have in mind a good reason *other* than the one that Oakley has recounted."

"Indeed I *do* have such a reason in mind!" Jessie said. "I just wish I could think of it . . ." she trailed off.

"Let's eat this apple one bite at a time," Longarm said, grabbing a straight-backed chair from its place against the wall, swinging it around, and straddling it to rest his forearms across its back. "We know that Ki rented horses at the livery stable. I reckon he brought his own saddle and gear along with him from Texas, right, Jessie?"

She nodded. "And the clerk at one of the general stores here in town has told us that Ki purchased canteens and supplies."

"It looks to me like he's intending to do just what he told Silva," Broadwick said. "Obviously the two of them are on their way to Sayre's hideout."

"Nobody's arguing that point," Longarm said. "We were planning on doing exactly what Ki has done, don't forget."

"But we are duly appointed representatives of the law!" Broadwick argued. "Deputy Long, I *do* hope you can remain objective, now that a personal friend of yours has become a fugitive."

"Ki is not a fugitive!" Jessie exclaimed.

"I'm afraid he is," Stills countered. "As of now, Ki is a wanted man."

Longarm could not meet Jessie's frightened gaze. "I'm sorry," he said. "But Stills is right. I'm willing to give Ki the benefit of the doubt, Jessie, but if he really *does* want to become an outlaw, the better to win Dorsey's love, he's accomplished his goal by busting Silva out of jail."

It was Broadwick who broke the room's uncomfortable silence. He'd been turning the Stetson that Ki had given him over and over in his hands, staring at it broodingly. At last he said, "I suppose we'd better rent horses of our own

139

and get after them. They only have a couple of hours lead on us."

"No rush," Longarm said. "It'll take us a while to get horses and purchase the supplies we'll need."

"But if they get too far ahead of us—" Broadwick began.

"Lloyd," Longarm cut him off, "if Ki wants us to follow him, he'll leave us a fine trail. If he doesn't, I'd rather not crowd him."

"Yes, I suppose you're right..." the postal inspector admitted.

"We know the general direction," Jessie said. "We'll just ride for the Utah hills and see what happens." She sighed. "Well, I'd best head back to the hotel and get changed into trail garb."

"I'll go along with you, Jessie," Broadwick said. "There are some things I want to take along when we go." He turned toward Longarm. "Deputy, can I rely upon you to purchase what we'll need to camp out, and to rent our horses and whatnot?"

"You can. Let's meet at the stables in two hours."

Stills took a bottle of sour mash out of his desk as Jessie and Broadwick left the office. "How about a drink?" he asked Longarm. "Sorry I ain't got glasses..."

"I'm a rye drinker myself, but I'll take bourbon in a pinch," Longarm chuckled as Stills pulled the bottle's cork with his teeth, took a long pull, and handed it across to him.

Longarm took a swallow and then set the bottle on the desk. "Hank, what's your call on all of this?" He wiped dry his longhorn mustache with the back of his hand. "I'm asking for your *real* call," he added.

Stills shrugged. "How do you know that it's any different from what I said in front of the others?"

Longarm paused, knowing full well that just as he was trying to get Stills's measure, the town marshal was doing the same with him. "Hank, we both think that Jessie Starbuck is somebody real special. Maybe the both of us are being careful what we say in front of her, so as not to upset her."

Stills fingered the bottle but did not drink. "Fair enough," he said at last. "When you planned to bluff Silva into leading you to Sayre's hideout, you intended to do it by telling him a bunch of half-truths. I think that Ki has done the same thing. I think that he got himself into this mess because he does have strong feelings for Dorsey Sayre."

Longarm frowned. "You think that he loves her?"

"Nobody can answer that but Ki," Stills replied. "If you're asking me to guess, I'd say no, he doesn't love her, but he does feel a strong personal responsibility toward her, for a couple of reasons I don't rightly feel comfortable jawing about behind his back."

"No need to say any more, Hank. We see eye to eye. But that still doesn't explain why he busted Silva out of your jail."

"Well, put yourself in his shoes, Longarm. Ki knew that you were coming here to help Broadwick catch Will Sayre, but he had no way of knowing that you'd make rescuing Dorsey a priority."

"You think he wants into Sayre's hideout to rescue Dorsey, and that he figures to bring back both Silva and Sayre, dead or alive, to square everything with us. Is that it, Hank?"

Stills nodded. "Seems to me that's exactly the deal you made with Broadwick in order to get him to cooperate."

Longarm stroked his chin. "But I made it clear to Broadwick that Dorsey was my first priority. As a lawman, I can always try for Sayre another day, if need be. Ki hasn't got that choice. He means to rescue Dorsey, but if he doesn't also bring back Silva and Sayre, he'll still have to stand for this jailbreak. He may end up paying for rescuing Dorsey by serving out a prison term."

"Or by spending the rest of his life on the run from the law," Stills finished ruefully. "Yep, this time that jasper has gotten himself into trouble neck-deep. If it wasn't for this bum arm of mine, I'd sure like to ride along with you and the others to help Ki get himself out of that hole he's in."

"I appreciate that, Hank," Longarm said, getting to his feet. "But your duty is to see to it that things stay peaceful within the boundaries of your town. I reckon I'd better get started on my shopping spree if I'm to be ready when Jessie and Broadwick arrive at the stables."

Stills stood up to shake hands. "You head on over to Simpson's general store, two blocks down on Main Street. Tell him I sent you. He'll give you fair prices on what you need."

"Much obliged, Marshal." Longarm touched the brim of his hat and headed out.

"Longarm?" Stills called, stopping him at the door.

"Yep?"

"If it comes to it, do you think you could take on Ki?"

"It ain't *going* to come to it," Longarm replied firmly. "That's why I'm doubly glad that Jessie's riding with us. There's no way that Ki would ever do anything to harm her."

"I'm just asking 'what if,' Longarm."

"Hank, you ever handle dynamite?" Longarm asked.

"Can't say as I have."

"It's funny stuff, dynamite," Longarm mused. "Stable as all get-out, most of the time, but when it gets warm, it starts to sweat little droplets of nitro, and that's when those familiar old sticks you've taken for granted can go up in your face . . ."

"In other words, you don't know the answer to my 'what if' question," Stills said.

"In other words, I don't take dynamite for granted, old son."

★

Chapter 12

Ki carefully guided his roan gelding up the incline of mossy, frost-polished granite. Silva rode ahead. Several times the samurai had to rein in his mount to keep from pulling abreast of the outlaw; Ki wanted Silva up front, where he could keep his eyes on the man.

It was the morning of their third day of travel through the remote country. Their journey so far had passed uneventfully, the two men spending the long hours on the trail locked in a never-ending give-and-take with the stern and beautiful terrain. At times their horses could lope along in a steady gait through gentle meadowlands painted with fragrant columbine, but often they had to dismount to lead their mounts through a treacherously slick, steeply graded maze that some ancient river, long since gone dry, had cut through the crimson buttes studded green with cedar. At night they made camp and watched the sunset turn the mountainous countryside vermilion red. They ate their dried beef, sipped their coffee, and watched as the scarlet sky faded like the embers of their dying campfire, first to gold shot through with streaks of indigo, and finally to starry night.

At night they slept, exhausted by the previous day. Or, rather, Silva slept soundly, while Ki dozed fitfully in a frustrating attempt to both get some rest and keep guard over Silva.

The outlaw had refused to be willingly bound, and Ki had not pressed the matter, even though he knew that in his place Longarm or Hank Stills would have manacled their prisoner. Ki was not a lawman, however. If he'd wished to do so, he could easily enough have overpowered Silva and bound his wrists and ankles with a few twists of rawhide.

Ki had not done so. He didn't want to shatter the fragile truce formed of mutual respect and need that existed between the two of them. Several times Silva had asked for the Peacemaker that Ki had taken from Deputy Oakley and now had stashed away in his saddlebags. Ki had refused to give Silva the gun; so, in a sense, his not binding Silva was a compromise gesture.

For his part, Silva had so far made no attempt to escape, but then there was no reason why he should. He was leading Ki to Will Sayre's hideout, nestled somewhere amid the canyons and cliffs of Utah. When they reached the outlaw town, their situation would automatically reverse. Silva would take control, and Ki would become dependent upon the outlaw for survival.

The inevitable change to come had troubled the samurai long before they reached Utah, following the turbulent Green River up into the high country. Silva had even brought the matter up last night . . .

"We'll be reaching our destination sometime tomorrow," Silva had begun, his face hidden by the night as he poked at their campfire with a stick. "I'm telling you now that Sayre has got some pretty foxy tricks up his sleeve, ways for the sentries ringing his town to know what's coming along the only trail in or out of the canyon." Then Silva had laughed, his teeth flashing blue-white in the shadows. "What'll happen is those sentries will get the drop on you, and will take you prisoner, stripping you of your weapons— that vest of yours, and your bow and arrows. Then we'll all ride nice and peaceful-like into Sayre's town. I'm telling you this because I know how quick you are, and it ain't going to do you any good with Sayre to kill more of his men, and get yourself killed in the process."

"I understand," Ki had said, watching Silva from his blanket on the other side of the flickering fire. "I won't struggle. We have our deal. I rescued you from the gallows.

You will give me safe conduct past the sentries to Will Sayre."

Silva had not immediately replied. "Safe conduct is what you want," he'd said at last. "But no matter what, your odds of living to see sunset tomorrow are less than even. Take my advice, Ki, you saddle up and ride away from here. Forget Dorsey Sayre."

"No."

"You that sweet on her?"

"I told you I love her," Ki had replied.

Silva had shaken his head. "Remember what I told you about those sentries we'll run into tomorrow," he'd said gruffly, and then he'd wrapped himself in his blankets and gone to sleep.

Ki had stayed awake, brooding upon the chain of false-hoods and betrayals that had begun to cinch tight around his soul. He'd sat awake watching Silva sleep, and assuring himself that he was so far doing the right thing.

He did not love Dorsey Sayre, but he did feel a bond between himself and the young woman's tortured spirit. Prior to being kidnapped, Dorsey had been balanced upon a blade's edge; the samurai feared that her abduction to her father's outlaw camp, if allowed to succeed, would put an end to any chance she might have had to live a happy, bountiful life, and thrust her headlong, with no hope of return, into a dark and hate-twisted existence.

Just such a fate could have been his, Ki now thought as he followed Silva along the slick granite trail beneath the strong noonday sun. He could have grown up with his soul stunted and gnarled, locked forever in his own bitter past, chewing endlessly on the misfortunes that had befallen him in childhood.

It had been his teacher and mentor, Hirata, who had rescued Ki from that sorry destiny. Now Ki would pass along the favor to Dorsey—pass it along the endless chain of existence that was *karma*. Hirata had given Ki his chance, and now Ki would give that chance to Dorsey. Never mind

145

that he had incriminated himself by breaking Silva out of jail, never mind that Longarm and Inspector Broadwick were likely hunting him, never mind the dishonor he had done himself by betraying Jessie...

"Look there!" Silva called back, rousing Ki from his grim thoughts.

The granite incline had brought them up to a plateau overlooking a valley. Down below, the river snaked lazily past a tumbled collection of weathered buildings.

"Sayre's outlaw town?" Ki asked, his pulse quickening.

"Hell, no!" Silva snorted disdainfully. "That's nothing but an old mining town. Folks once thought there was gold to be found in that river. They figured it flowed down from some mother lode up in the mountains. I guess they found enough of the stuff to build those shacks, and that was it. Come on, we can fill our canteens down there."

"We will go around that town," Ki said firmly.

"Can't!" Silva replied flatly. "You see?" he gestured at the timberline. "The trail winds down through those trees and right past the town. It'd cost us days to go around it. There's nothing to be afraid of. Nobody lives there anymore but one crazy old woman."

They rode down through the aspens, following the stone-studded trail to the town.

"What is this place called?" Ki asked as they rode between the riverbank and the one short, dusty street lined with a few buildings.

"Couldn't say," Silva said, shrugging. He stopped his horse and dismounted, taking his canteens from his saddle and kneeling to fill them from the river. "Town's not on any map that I've ever seen," the outlaw added. He capped his canteens and then set to work filling the ones that Ki had tossed him.

Ki listened to the wind howling eerily through the abandoned alleyways of the little town gone bust. Once he thought he saw a face peering at them from within the doorless entryway of a paint-peeling, tumbledown shack. The face ducked back into the shadows as Ki stared.

146

"You see the old lady?" Silva chuckled. "I don't know *her* name, either. Lives here all by her lonesome. Don't know what she eats. Likely whatever grows wild, and the fish in this here river." He handed over Ki's canteens and mounted up. "That way," he said, pointing toward the foothills that marked the valley's end.

"How much longer?" Ki demanded impatiently.

"Not long at all," Silva said, his voice oddly subdued.

"Then it's time for me to give you this," Ki said, reaching behind him into his saddlebags, and coming up with the Peacemaker. He tossed the pistol to the startled outlaw. "I don't want you to be humiliated in front of your friends by being unarmed," Ki said in explanation. "Soon I'll be in your keeping. Remember that I treated you honorably."

Silva was staring at the gun in his hand as if he'd never seen one before. He looked up at Ki, who said, as if he'd read Silva's mind, "It is loaded, but you can check if you wish."

Rube Silva shook his head. "I'll take your word for it," he replied, and rode off toward the foothills.

An hour later they were wending their way through pitted, craggy slopes of eroded shale. They rounded a bend in the trail to encounter three men poised on horseback, their guns drawn.

Silva smiled. "It's good to see you, Bill."

"Rube," replied a man dressed in denim pants and jacket, and riding a pinto. "What you got there?"

Silva wheeled his mount around and walked it over to Ki's horse. "Give me your bow and arrows, and hand over that vest of yours," he said.

Ki did as he was told. "How far to the hideout?" he asked.

"Along this trail, and about five miles beyond the ridge," Silva said. "But you'll never see it, my friend. You're going to die right here."

As Ki tensed, Silva drew the Peacemaker from his belt and cocked it. "I wouldn't try kicking it out of my hand, Ki. I'm a mite faster with a gun than that broken-down old

147

deputy back in Nettle Grove." Silva leaned back in the saddle. "Hey! Bill!" he shouted. "This man killed your brother Ned!"

"What?" Scowling, the man in denims kneed his horse alongside Silva's. "You telling me this Chinaman beat my brother?"

"He did."

"What are you waiting for, Rube? Shoot him!"

Silva locked eyes with Ki. "No," he said. "I'll let you do it. You and Chuck take care of it while I ride to camp. Willie, you come along with me!" he called to one of the men. "You can fill me in on what's happened since I've been gone."

Bill pointed his Colt at Ki. "I got him covered," he told Silva. "Rube, it ain't like you to pass up a chance at killing."

"Just do it the way I tell you!" Silva snarled. "Do it quick. Don't make him suffer!" He nodded to Ki. "That's the best I can do for you, friend."

"Rube?" Ki called out softly as the outlaw turned his horse. "Rube, why are you doing this?"

Silva looked back at Ki. "You say you love her, and she loves you. Maybe so, but that's no good for *me*. I'm sorry it has to be this way, Ki, but *I* intend to marry Dorsey!"

Ki watched Rube Silva and one of the other men ride off around the bend, the pounding of their horses' hooves gradually fading until there was nothing but silence amid the sun-baked shale.

"Do it, Bill," the man named Chuck demanded. He'd holstered his gun, and was now mopping his face with his bandanna.

"I'll do it, all right," Bill said, smiling coldly at Ki. "I just want to let Rube put some distance between us. You see, Chinaman, the first slug is going right in your gut. I'll let you roll around in that stinking shale for a while, thinking on the pain. The next shots will blast out your kneecaps, and the next two your elbow joints—"

"Christ, Bill," Chuck said softly, "Rube said to do it quick-like."

"Rube ain't here now!" Bill snapped. "And it weren't his kid brother got mowed down by some damned Chink!" He turned back to Ki. "After I blast your elbows, it'll take me a while to reload, but what's the hurry? You won't be going nowhere. Now get down off of that horse! Chuck! Draw that gun of your'n! We both got to keep him covered to make sure he don't get away!"

"Oh hell, Bill, where's he gonna go?" Chuck dismounted and drew his revolver, leveling it at Ki.

"Ned Tarn drew on *me,*" Ki told them. "It was a fair fight, but one that he lost."

"That's too bad for you, Chinaman," Bill Tarn spat. "Too bad *you* didn't lose, 'cause that would've been easier than what I got in store for you." He swung down off his horse, and then gestured with his gun toward the shale incline. "Start walking."

No one spoke as Ki was herded past the scrub brush and prickly grass, up into the rocks. They walked until they'd reached some granite outcroppings, where man-sized boulders lay scattered about.

"This'll do," Bill Tarn declared as Ki crested the summit of a shale mound. "Stand tall!" he ordered as Ki's knees sagged. "Look! Chuck, look! He's scared!" Bill laughed, raising his pistol. "Here comes the one that's going in your gut," he growled, squeezing the trigger—

Ki's powerful leg muscles uncoiled, his knees straightening as he did a backflip that carried him up over the mound's crest. Tarn's bullet richocheted off granite as Ki rolled down the slippery shale on the mound's far side.

Lucky, Ki told himself as he reached bottom and scrambled on all fours, kicking up slivers of shale as he dashed to the relative safety of the strewn boulders. *Lucky that the one named Chuck didn't have his gun aimed and ready to fire.* As he crouched, waiting, he could hear the two men cursing their way up the mound.

"Did you see that?" Chuck was babbling. "One minute he was there, and the next he was gone! You shot and he took off, like you was trying to swat a goddamn fly!"

"Shut up!" Bill snarled. "We gotta find him! I want him, understand?"

"He's gone! Like a goddamned fly!"

"He better not be! Find him or I'll kill *you,* understand?"

The two men appeared on the crest of the slight rise Ki had occupied earlier. He watched them searching for him, their guns held ready, as he hunkered down amid the heat-baked rocks and tried to think of a way out of his predicament. He couldn't double back to the horses; he couldn't move at all. The loose shale chips crunching underfoot would give him away. No, maneuvering was out of the question. He listened to the two gunmen coming closer. He had no weapons, and there was nothing at hand that could be *used* as a weapon—no stick to become a *jo* staff; not even a decent-sized rock to hurl at his enemies! He thumb-tested the edge on a finger-sized chip of slate. It was sharp, all right, sharp enough to cut and slash if Ki could get close to one of the men, but the chip was too light and had no balance for throwing.

Time was running out. The two gunmen were closing in!

I will rush them, no matter how slim my chances, Ki decided. *Better a warrior's death than to cower here waiting for them to discover me—*

But all thoughts left Ki as a dry, rasping, rattling sound filled the air. He froze, afraid even to blink until he knew exactly where that deadly sound was coming from.

"Rattler!" Chuck called from somewhere on the other side of the boulder behind which Ki was crouched.

"I heard it," Bill said from nearby.

Ki saw a flash of movement near his knee and looked down.

The rattler was slithering out from beneath the boulder, no more than a foot away from where he was kneeling. It looked to be about three inches thick and five feet long. Its skin was a diamond patchwork of brown and yellow.

The colors of decaying vegetation, Ki thought. *The colors of death.*

The cool earth beneath the boulder must have been its burrow, and his own shifting near the boulder must have awakened it. Now the rattler had slithered out to do battle with whatever had been foolhardy enough to invade its territory.

To do battle with *him*.

In Ki's clenched fingers was the razor-edged slate chip; as the samurai gauged his chances of successfully bringing the chip down like an ax upon the rattler, its spade-shaped head rose up off the ground, to weave and sway mere inches from Ki's ribs. Suddenly the slate chip seemed a puny weapon indeed against the rattler's venom-dripping, needle sharp, curved fangs.

The snake's forked tongue flicked out to taste the air. Watching the serpent, Ki knew that its sensitive nerve endings were picking up the ground vibrations caused by the footsteps of the approaching gunmen.

He silently willed his thoughts toward the snake as its flat black eyes gazed steadily at him. *They are your enemies, not I, snake. They will kill us both if we don't help each other.*

The approaching outlaws' boots were making crunching sounds against the shale chips. The snake rattled ominously in warning.

The crunching stopped. "Over here," Bill Tarn whispered, out of sight but close enough for Ki to hear him clearly.

The rattler had moved sideways, to coil itself like a lariat on the expanse of ground between Ki's knees. It raised its head like a battle flag. Its tongue flicked toward his groin.

Ki clenched the sharp slate fragment in his left hand. The outlaws were almost upon him.

We must live or die together, King Rattler—

His right hand shot out, the movement so fast that the cloth of his sleeve cracked like a whip. His fingers touched the rough scales behind the rattler's head as it lunged toward him.

"Help me! Help!"

151

The two outlaws turned at Ki's anguished pleas. Guns at the ready, they ran toward the sound, coming around the boulder and stopped short at what they saw.

Ki, his face contorted in agony, was sitting with his back against the boulder and his knees drawn up. One of the side seams of his denim jeans had been slit open to reveal two bloody puncture wounds on his calf. In his right hand, at arm's length, he held the rattler just behind its head.

"Holy shit!" Chuck murmured. Bill Tarn just grinned.

"It has bitten me!" Ki whimpered piteously. "Please help me!"

The two outlaws stared in awed fascination at the rattler. Its obsidian eyes seemed to take on a fiery glare of indignation as its powerful, sinewy body slashed to and fro, struggling to free itself from Ki's fist. Its rattle buzzed furiously; its jaws spread wide, the yellow-tinged venom drooled from its fangs in ropy strands.

Chuck took a step toward Ki, but Bill Tarn held him back, saying, "Leave him alone. We're going to leave him just like he is!"

"But Bill, it's a leg bite! He'll suffer for hours before the poison reaches his heart."

"That's just what I want!" the outlaw gloated. He laughed at Ki. "Sorry I can't stick around to watch, Chinaman, but I've got things to do. I bet you wish it'd been my brother who'd killed you..."

"Please, please do not leave me!" Ki begged as the men walked away towards their horses. "Please! Shoot me!" Ki wailed.

The samurai listened to the sound of them riding off, and then he laughed jubilantly. "King Rattler," he addressed the snake, "we have saved each other's life."

The rattler formed furious S-shaped curves in the air as Ki held its head fast. The samurai had been too quick for it. His fingers had closed around its throat, arresting its movement in mid-lunge toward him. With his left hand Ki had used the sharp slate chip to slit the seam of his jeans. The chip's needlelike point had also served as the "fangs" that had inflicted the "snakebite" on his calf. As Ki had hoped, Bill Tarn's desire to see him suffer had kept the outlaw from finishing him off.

The samurai got to his feet, keeping hold of the rattler's head with his right hand, while gripping its convulsing tail in his left.

The rattler had calmed in the samurai's grip. Now it merely stared straight ahead while its whip of a body methodically traced a corkscrew in the air. Ki placed the rattler gently on the ground. First he let go of the snake's tail, then its head. The samurai did not jump back, and from the snake there came nary a rattle and no attack. It just slithered away.

Ki understood. He had survived, as had the snake. And now the deal between them had ended . . .

He walked back to the trail. The outlaws had taken his horse, but that did not concern him. He did not need a horse.

Along this trail, and about five miles beyond the ridge, Silva had said.

Very well—Ki would parallel the trail, keeping to the brush, in case there were other sentries along the way. Once he'd reached the outlaw town he would infiltrate it, regain the weapons that Silva had taken from him, and find Dorsey.

They thought him dead, and would not be alert, which gave Ki the element of surprise. The samurai smiled. Surprise could prove to be a lethal weapon indeed . . .

★

Chapter 13

"Hold up, Jessie!" Longarm called out as he reined in his mount. He twisted around in the saddle to look back for the inspector.

Broadwick was bouncing along as his bay mare—one of the gentlest, most docile mounts available for rent at the Nettle Grove stable—trotted along.

"He's not doing very well, is he?" Jessie asked, a worried look on her pretty face.

Longarm shrugged. "He just can't seem to get the rhythm of it," he sighed. "You can just hear that saddle slapping his rump."

As they waited for Broadwick to catch up with them, Longarm feasted his eyes on the countryside. Behind them, the flat-topped mesas had dwindled in size. On the far side of those hills was Nettle Grove, and the lush green pastures that made Wyoming grand cattle country. During their first few hours of riding, the green grass had grown sparse, to give way entirely to patches of sere weeds and stands of scrubby cottonwood.

Longarm shook his head, not much liking how this trip had started out. He eyed Broadwick as he caught up. At least the tenderfoot—and, by now, tender-*butt*—had dressed properly for the ride. The inspector was wearing brown moleskin trousers, a tan flannel shirt, and a dark brown corduroy range coat, its bellows-style pockets bulging with spare cartridges for the Smith & Wesson riding underneath his armpit. The inspector had brought along no rifle, explaining to Longarm that he'd had little experience with

long guns, not having any call to use a rifle in his native
St. Louis.

"You going to be all right, Lloyd?" Longarm asked.

"I don't know about that, but I'll make it," Broadwick
said wryly. His jowled face was drenched with perspiration.
He removed the Stetson that Ki had given him in order to
mop at his sweat-slick bald dome with his bandanna.

"Maybe we ought to rest for a while," Jessie suggested.
She was wearing her denims, and had her Colt strapped
around her shapely hips. She'd borrowed a Winchester and
a saddle boot from the gun rack in Stills's office. "Lloyd,
you look like you're suffering something awful."

"I'm fine!" Broadwick declared, but then grimaced as
he shifted in his saddle. "I may have to sleep on my belly
tonight." He patted his considerable paunch. "But it'll make
a soft enough mattress."

Longarm grinned at the game postal inspector. "We'll
ride another hour, and then rest up. A tough old bird like
you could probably go on forever," he told Broadwick as
he shrugged off his frock coat, rolled it up, and tucked it
beneath his bedroll. "But we've got to think of the horses.
In addition to us, they're carrying all of our gear."

They made it well into the high country before stopping to
make camp for the night. There was a stand of pines to cut
the night wind whistling down from the mountains, and a
cool, still pond fed by a mountain stream for them to bathe
in and wash away the day's accumulation of dust and grit.

Longarm was scavenging in the surrounding forest for
firewood when he abruptly came to a clearing that afforded
him an unobstructed view of the pond.

Longarm froze, his arms filled with firewood. He stood
as still as a buck in the forest hearing a hunter's footfall.

Jessie, nude from the waist up, was kneeling by the
water's edge. The faded blue cloth of her skintight jeans
stretched to mold her bottom curves as she bent forward to
scoop handfuls of water over her full, lush breasts and taut
belly.

156

Longarm tried to tear his eyes away, but he couldn't. She looked like a forest nymph out of a storybook!

Droplets of water glistened in the gold-and-red tendrils of her long hair as she bathed, throwing her head back and arching her long, supple back. Her palms glided along her ribs and then back to her breasts. Her fingers began to skate around and around the dark rosettes, as drops of water, sparkling like diamonds, tipped her swelling nipples.

Longarm turned around abruptly, his heart pounding and his groin tightening with desire. He quietly walked away. He and Jessie had been together many times, seeing and exploring each other's bodies in passionate lovemaking, so his watching her had not *exactly* been like being a peeping Tom.

But to watch any woman when she was unaware struck Longarm as an ungentlemanly thing to do. He was angry at himself for giving in to temptation, and yet he was very glad that his old eyes had seen her kneeling there. He wished that he and Jessie could make love—she wished the same, he knew—but that was impossible with Broadwick around. A man and woman did their lovemaking in private or not at all, to Longarm's way of thinking.

He trudged back to camp, where he found Broadwick slicing bacon for their evening meal. He looked up as Longarm approached. "I was wondering where you'd disappeared to. I've been waiting for that firewood."

"Here it is!" Longarm snapped peevishly, dumping the wood at Broadwick's feet.

The postal inspector looked at him curiously. "Something wrong?"

Longarm took a deep breath to control his ill temper. "No," he sighed. "I'm just feeling a little out of sorts, is all. Sorry, Lloyd."

Broadwick nodded. "Then build us a fire while I finish cutting up this bacon."

Longarm knelt to pile up a small bunch of dried grass, twigs, and bark. He struck a match and set the kindling alight, puffing on it to keep it going as he fed it with gradually larger bits of wood. Finally he had quite a good fire crackling.

Broadwick set a small, covered Dutch oven into the fire. "I mixed up a batch of biscuits," he said. "I guess they'll bake all right, like that."

Longarm smiled. "Hell, Lloyd, I wouldn't have been so shy about bringing you along, if I'd known you could earn your keep by running our chuckwagon!"

Broadwick shrugged shyly. "I cooked in a restaurant to earn my living before I joined up with the Post Office. That's where I got this belly of mine."

He set a frying pan onto a smoldering log and began laying down strips of bacon to cook. "You're thinking about Jessie, aren't you?" he asked after a moment.

Longarm was startled. "Damn! How'd you figure *that* out, old son?"

"We're both lawmen, don't forget," Broadwick said, looking pleased. "We're trained to notice things. Anyway, I'm worried about her, as well. It's going to be hard on her when we arrest Ki, isn't it?"

"Yep, I reckon it will be," Longarm agreed. "I'm hoping we'll find that there was some kind of extenuating circumstance."

The bacon had begun to sizzle. Broadwick fussed at it with a fork. "I hope so too. I really do, deputy."

"I believe that, old son. I think Jessie—and Ki—know it as well."

"How are we going to know which way to ride tomorrow?"

"The same way we knew which way to ride today," Longarm chuckled.

Broadwick looked up at him in surprise. "Do you mean to say we've been *tracking* Ki and Silva? That we haven't just been wandering at random?"

"Sure, we've been tracking him. He's left us a fine trail of hoofprints in soft ground, and broken twigs, bent branches, and whatnot over hard. That's what's been giving me hope that the sly son of a gun has got something up his sleeve, other than those wicked throwing knives of his! There's no way a skilled old hand like Ki would leave such clues behind unless he wanted us to follow!"

Broadwick grinned happily. "Well, that makes me feel much better!" He returned to his cooking.

A few minutes later, Jessie returned to the camp. The sight of her damp hair reminded Longarm of the lovely scene he'd witnessed back at the pond. He flushed, and found himself unable to meet her wide, steady, emerald-green gaze.

Much later that night, while Jessie slept quietly, and Broadwick was snoring like a grizzly during the hibernation season, Longarm stared up at the starry sky, unable to keep his eyes shut. Jessie had bedded down no more than an arm's reach away from him, dammit! Of course, Broadwick wasn't much farther away, but Longarm didn't feel any temptation about reaching out to caress the postal inspector's titties!

Across the campsite, the three hobbled horses softly nickered to one another. They were town mounts, rarely out this deep into the wilderness. They'd probably picked up the scent of some woodland predator stalking about. Longarm wasn't worried. There was nothing in this neck of the woods that would come close to men, no matter how tempted it might be by a chance at horseflesh. Nevertheless, he sat up, hauled on his boots—he'd been sleeping in his trousers—and hung his gunbelt across his naked torso prior to leaving his blanket to check on the mounts. It gave him something to do, since he doubted he was going to get very much sleep this night.

As he'd expected, the horses were fine, doing a lot better than he was, wrestling with his desire for Jessie.

It was a lovely night. There was a soft wind rustling the pine boughs, releasing their clean, fresh scent into the air. There was just a sliver of bone-white moon overhead, backed up by a dusting of twinkling stars that glittered like chips of ice—glittered like the water beads on Jessie's breasts . . .

Stop it! You just stop it, old son! Longarm scolded himself. *You're out here on serious business. This is no time for you to go all randy like some gangling adolescent.*

But it did Longarm no good to lecture himself. Jessie Starbuck was somebody mighty special to him; they were mighty special to each other, and had been ever since they'd first met, back during that case when Longarm was sent to her part of Texas to ferret out the murderers of her father. A couple of times since then, Longarm and Jessie had eased around the subject of matrimony, but ease around it was all they'd done. They fit together in lovemaking the way a Colt slid into a custom-cut holster, but there were other aspects to marriage beyond lovemaking. A deputy marshal traveled a lot, and mostly to dangerous places. Longarm couldn't see taking a bride when the odds were good that she'd end up a widow before she'd even packed away her wedding dress. Anyway, Jessie had never pushed marriage at him. She had too much to do, running the Starbuck business empire and chasing after her Prussian adversaries, to get hitched up and tied down to one man...

Longarm heard footsteps behind him. He instinctively drew his Colt, spinning around into a crouch as he trained the .44 in the direction of the sound.

"It's me," Jessie called quietly, stepping out from behind the shelter of a tree.

Watching her approach, Longarm saw the outline of her own Colt in her hand, pointing down toward the ground. He smiled, proud of her, and grateful to Ki for taking such good care of her that a good deal of the samurai's wariness had rubbed off on her. It wasn't smart to go around in this part of the country unarmed, so Jessie didn't; she didn't miss a trick.

"What are you doing up?" Longarm chided her as he slid his gun back into its holster. He was relieved to see that Jessie was fully dressed in jeans and blouse. His poor, aching balls couldn't bear another peep at her naked!

"You ought to be sleeping, honey. We've got a long day ahead of us tomorrow."

"I couldn't sleep, Custis," Jessie moped, tucking her Colt

160

into her jeans at the small of her back. "I wanted to talk to you . . . about what took place at the pond this evening."

Nope, she doesn't miss a trick, Longarm thought, and then he groaned. "I'm powerful sorry about that, Jessie."

"Oh, don't be!" she cried out, softly as birdsong, throwing her arms around Longarm's neck to give him a long, lingering passionate kiss. "I've missed you so, and want you something fierce, Custis!" she hotly confided.

"I've missed you too, Jessie. I'm glad you're not peeved at me for watching you at the pond."

"I knew you were there," she giggled. "I was playing with my nipples just for your benefit! Aren't I naughty?"

"Reckon you're just right," Longarm said, giving her one final hug before letting her go and moving away.

Jessie stared at him, and even in the dark Longarm could make out the glint of puzzlement mixed with the spark of hurt in her green eyes.

"Custis Long! Are you ill or something?" she demanded, her hands on her hips.

"Nope."

"Then what's going on?" Jessie sputtered. "I mean, when a girl positively throws herself at a man—"

"I don't rightly think its proper for us to be making love with old Broadwick so close by!"

"But he's sleeping!"

"Maybe he is and maybe he ain't," Longarm replied. "What if he wakes up and comes looking to see where we are? I ain't saying he'd do it to spy on us, but out of fear of being alone in the woods, or out of worry."

"Longarm, you're stubborn as a mule!" Jessie scolded him, but then she smiled. "You're also a gentleman, more of one than I've had the privilege of meeting in the boardrooms I've visited all across this country!"

"Just have my own ideas about conduct, and I stick to 'em," he replied modestly.

"I know," Jessie whispered. "And I love you for it," she added, embracing him a second time. Her fingers strayed down to the bulge filling out the front of his tight tweed trousers. "I love you for *that* too," she giggled, giving him a mischievous squeeze.

"You get on back to bed!" Longarm ordered her, sending her laughingly on her way with a good-natured pat on her rump.

"Now I'm doubly glad that you watched me at the pond," Jessie whispered to him over her shoulder. "Knowing that your eyes were on me while I was bare is nice. Not as nice a feeling as when you're inside me, but I suppose it'll have to do until—"

"Git!"

Laughing, Jessie stuck out her tongue, and then she was gone, skipping back to her blankets at the campsite.

Longarm smiled to himself. But then his expression soured. He did a few deep knee bends, but they didn't help at all. That last little squeeze of Jessie's had turned his pecker into steel...

Well, sooner or later, Longarm meant to see to it that the girl reaped every bit of what she'd sown!

Chapter 14

Longarm awoke well before sunrise. A few hours of sleep did him fine, but he knew that others were not as resilient as he. Accordingly, he moved silently about the camp, affording Jessie, and especially Broadwick, the extra forty winks they'd need to see them through the day to come.

He used what was left of last night's firewood to build a small blaze, and then used a canteen's worth of water to fix a pot of coffee. While it brewed, he gathered up all of the canteens and his possibles bag, and went off to the pond. He stripped and dove in, letting the cool water rinse the night's cobwebs from his brain.

He let the air dry his body as he dug his razor and a small mirror out of his bag, and shaved. There was just enough light from the coming dawn to see by, and anyway, Longarm had been shaving long enough to pretty much know his way around his whiskers. When he was done, he filled the canteens and went back to camp. Jessie and Broadwick were still sleeping. The coffee was ready. He poured himself a tin cup's worth of the strong black brew and wandered off to watch the sunrise turn the sky lavender and the mountains orange.

By the time he returned to camp this second time, the sun was already burning fiercely in a clear blue sky dotted with fat, fleecy clouds. The two late sleepers were up. Jessie smiled at him over her coffee. Broadwick, his newly shaved cheeks pink, his fringe of hair still damp from his own dip in the pool, was busy rolling up his blankets.

"Well, Longarm," the inspector greeted him jovially, "I

hope you can arrange such a lovely spot for tonight's camp!"

"I'll see what I can do, Lloyd, but I wouldn't count on it. We're heading into country that has more in common with hell than heaven!"

By midday Longarm's prediction had proven true. They were gaining altitude, moving into a windswept landscape of peaks and ridges where little grew but scrub. The loose stones under their mounts' hooves made them slow their progress to a maddening snail's pace. It was crucial that they minimize as much as possible the risk of one of their horses stumbling and breaking a leg.

The sun beating down and the hot, searing wind had evaporated Broadwick's earlier high spirits. As their ride into the rugged elevations continued, the overweight postal inspector began to complain of difficulty breathing. Longarm, keeping a worried eye on the man, watched the fatigued Broadwick withdraw into himself, slumping forward and staring down at his saddlehorn, trusting to his docile, rented mount to follow along behind the other horses.

Jessie angled her horse close by Longarm's. "You still have his track?" she whispered.

"Nope. Lost it about two miles back," he muttered quietly.

"I heard that!" Broadwick exclaimed, straightening up. "You mean to say we've been wandering aimlessly?"

"Losing another man's track and being lost are two different things, Lloyd," Longarm replied. He watched Broadwick douse his shirtfront with water from his canteen in a futile attempt to cool off. "You've got to quit that, Inspector, and ration your drinking as well. If you wait until you're real thirsty, the water will taste better and do you more good."

"I'll drink as I wish!" Broadwick shouted.

"Calm down," Jessie soothed.

Broadwick looked at her, and then sheepishly eyed Longarm. He forced himself to smile. "Sorry. Of course you're right, on all counts. If you say that we're not lost—"

164

"We're not," Longarm assured him. "But we *have* lost Ki's trail. He's not trying to shake us. You can see for yourself that this is poor tracking country."

"What do you propose that we do, Longarm?" Jessie asked.

"I figure we ought to keep going until we get to Green River country."

"Is it better than this?" Broadwick implored.

"There's trees," Longarm said.

"Thank the Lord!"

Longarm nodded, figuring it would be best to keep the bit about the steep canyons and the rushing river to himself for now.

"And I suppose we'll pick up Ki's trail once we're there?" Broadwick persisted.

"Reckon we might," Longarm replied. Out of the corner of his eye he saw Jessie staring skeptically at him, but she bit her lip and said nothing. There was nothing for her to say. She knew as well as he did that their chances of blundering upon Ki's track were about as good as Broadwick's chances of blundering upon a wanted fugitive in the streets of St. Louis. Their only hope was that Ki, realizing their predicament, would find some way to leave them an obvious sign as to the direction in which he was traveling with Rube Silva. If Ki didn't leave them a sign, they would be able to do nothing but turn around and head back to Nettle Grove.

"Let's get moving," she muttered.

Longarm understood. She didn't want to return empty-handed to civilization any more than he did. The sooner they returned, the sooner both Longarm and Broadwick would have to wire their superiors about the jailbreak, and the sooner a bulletin on Ki would be going out to lawmen all across the west.

"Oh, my word..." Broadwick breathed. "Those are Indians!"

Longarm, startled out of his revery, glanced up at the ridge before them. "Utes," he muttered, squinting at the

165

five men on horseback staring down at them.

"What would Utes be doing so close to the Utah line?" Jessie wondered.

Longarm shook his head. "Up to no good, I'd wager. The Ouray reservation is a couple days' ride from here. I reckon they're renegades, out for a good time until the law escorts them back."

Broadwick began reaching for his Smith & Wesson as the Utes began riding single-file down the ridge towards them.

"You leave that hogleg right where it is!" Longarm snapped.

"But there's only five of them!"

"Five is all you can see, but I'll wager there's twice that many sighting down at us from behind the rocks, just waiting to knock you out of the saddle if you reach for a gun."

Broadwick hesitated, glancing around uneasily. "All right," he muttered, removing his hand from underneath his corduroy range jacket.

"And you let me do all the talking, Inspector," Longarm said. "These renegades, if that's what they are, are mostly hotheaded young'uns spoiling to prove themselves. Don't give them an excuse, all right?"

Broadwick nodded as the Utes brought their stocky ponies to a halt a few yards in front of them.

"You are traveling with a woman!" one of the Utes hooted derisively in English. Like most of his people, he was built like a bear, with short arms and bandy legs. This brave looked to be about twenty, Longarm thought. The Ute's moon face was pitted, likely from some childhood bout with smallpox. Like the others, he was wearing cheap government-issue clothing, and carrying a rifle. Among the five, Long-arm counted three Henry Repeaters and two brand spanking new—probably stolen—Winchesters.

Longarm nodded a greeting to the Utes, noncommittally eyeing the braves, their leader, and the rocks behind them as well, letting them draw their own inferences concerning his knowledge of Ute ambush tactics.

"You are from the Ouray?" When the brave nodded, Longarm continued, "How is my friend, Agent Caldwell?"

"Caldwell!" the brave scowled, spitting at the ground. "That is all I care about Caldwell!"

"And how is my blood brother, Hungry Calf?"

The Ute cocked his head, startled. "Who are you?" he asked in his own tongue.

Longarm understood the query, but he preferred to play dumb. Stringing the Utes along into thinking he didn't understand their lingo might later come in handy, and he figured that Broadwick could easier keep control of his short-fused temper if he could follow what was being said. When the Ute brave repeated his question in English, Longarm replied, "My name's Long, and I'm a deputy U.S. marshal on business from the Great White Father—"

"The Great White Father means nothing to us!" the Ute sneered. "He only frightens timid old men, such as Hungry Calf, but not strong young men like ourselves!"

The four riders behind him murmured their approval, as their spokesman went on, "We have ridden off the reservation to prove our courage, to gain warrior's feathers to wear in our hair. We are *Ho*, and you must pay us tribute!"

"Reckoned it was coming down to that," Longarm muttered.

"What's he talking about, Longarm?" Broadwick hissed. "What's all this 'tribute' rubbish?"

"I must parley with my friends," Longarm told the Ute brave, who nodded his permission.

"Follow me," Longarm instructed Jessie and Broadwick. He wheeled his mount around and walked it until he was out of the Utes' hearing. "The custom of paying Indians tribute started during the early cattle drives," Longarm explained to the tenderfoot. "The trail boss would cut a few head of cattle out of the herd and hand them over to the Indians blocking his path. That way, he and the rest of his drovers and cows could proceed peacefully."

"What utter poppycock!" Broadwick sputtered. "And anyway, we have no cows!"

"You've got the last part right, at least," Jessie told the postal inspector. "Longarm, what do you think they'd accept to let us pass?"

"We could try cash money," Longarm replied, "but they're wards of the government, and have got to return to the reservation eventually, so cash would do them little good. What they want is something they can show to the elders of the tribe. Something that can raise them up among the ranks of the braves."

"Like our scalps, you mean?" Broadwick asked, aghast.

"Being scalped is one thing you don't have to worry about, Lloyd," Longarm chuckled, eyeing the postal inspector's bald dome. "I think we've got to figure on handing over some weapons."

"Give guns to savages? Out of the question!" Broadwick said.

"You'll notice that they've already got guns, Lloyd," Longarm replied patiently. "What we want to do is keep them from using those guns. Jessie, how would you feel about turning over that Winchester you borrowed from Hank Stills?"

"Whatever you say, Custis."

Longarm nodded. "Buried in my saddlebags is an old Peacemaker I took off of an owlhoot a while back. That iron ought to serve as my ticket past those braves." Sighing, he turned toward Broadwick, dreading what was coming.

"I have no rifle, nor a spare gun. Surely you don't expect me to hand over my revolver?"

Longarm thought it through. "Maybe you can get by with handing over fifty or so cartridges."

"I only have fifty!"

"Well, I've got an extra box. We'll try twenty-five apiece."

"Oh, but this is infuriating! We are federal lawmen. They're merely savages—"

"Who outnumber us at least five to one," Longarm interrupted.

"No more parley!" the pockmarked Ute called out. "You come now! Pay tribute!"

"Remember what I said about those Utes likely hidden up in the rocks," Longarm said hurriedly. "Sit tight, keep quiet, and we'll live to laugh about this tonight." He rode over to the Ute braves, with Broadwick and Jessie close behind.

"You pay?" the pockmarked brave demanded.

Longarm nodded. "A fine Winchester, a revolver, and fifty cartridges."

The Ute smiled. "*Two* Winchesters, and the rest."

Longarm shook his head. "We are but two men and a woman. Do your braves wish it said about them that they deprived peaceful travelers of weapons to hunt game?"

Longarm kept his fingers crossed. He could almost hear the wheels turning in the Ute's head; how the brave replied to Longarm's offer would tell him a great deal about what this band of young hotheads had so far been up to. If the Ute was swayed by his argument, it would mean that the band fully intended to return to the reservation to boast of their exploits to their elders, and that meant they'd done nothing really very wrong. If the Ute refused his offer, if he appeared not to be concerned about his and the others' dignity, it would tell Longarm that they'd already committed a crime so serious as to make them outcasts, afraid to return to the reservation because of the punishment that awaited them.

"We are mighty braves, and it would be beneath us to argue any further with such as you," the Ute declared. "We accept your tribute."

"We thank the mighty *Ho,*" Longarm said, sighing inwardly. Clearly these young braves wanted no real trouble. It looked as if things would work out peacefully.

"Here is the rifle," Jessie called out. One of the Utes rode over to her and leaned out of the saddle to draw her Winchester out of its boot.

Meanwhile, Longarm dug the Peacemaker and a box half-filled with cartridges out of his saddlebag and handed them over to the pockmarked brave, rattling the box as he did so, to prove that it was not empty.

169

The Ute worked the Colt's action and then nodded in satisfaction.He peeked into the box of cartridges. "Good," he smiled. "Twenty-five more from the fat man, yes?"

"Dammit, why didn't you give him a full box and keep me out of it?" Broadwick complained as one of the Utes approached him.

"We've *each* got to give something, is how it works," Longarm said. "Just hand over twenty-five rounds and it'll be done."

Broadwick, the damn fool, began counting out the rounds as if they were gold coins, giving the brave ample time to view the extra ammunition bulging his coat pockets. The Ute kept his Henry repeater across his saddle, but he prodded Broadwick's chest with his hand to hurry him up. In doing so, the brave evidently felt the shoulder holster, and tried to pull Broadwick's coat open to get a view of it.

"Let go of me!" the inspector snapped, lurching away.

"Steady!" Longarm warned.

"Ugh! He stinks!" Broadwick moaned.

The Utes smelled like horse turds all right, Longarm thought, but now was not the best time to be criticizing their personal hygiene. "Lloyd, let him see the shoulder-rig, for chrissake!"

"Get away from me, you stinking Indian!" Broadwick snarled, totally out of control. The insulted Ute spat in his face. Broadwick, his features contorted in rage, swung at the brave, his fist grazing the Ute's chin.

An instant later the Ute was twisting away to bring his rifle to bear on the inspector.

"Stop it!" Longarm shouted. He whirled toward the pock-marked Ute. "Stop them!"

The Ute fighting with Broadwick was levering a round into the chamber when Broadwick grabbed the rifle's muzzle and rammed it forward, driving the stock into the Ute's midsection. The brave gasped and fell from his pony.

From up in the rocks there came a flash of fire as a shot echoed against the hills. Broadwick was spun from his saddle by a bullet in the chest.

170

Longarm and the pockmarked Ute locked eyes, sharing thoughts: what had started out as a game had just turned deadly serious. If Broadwick was dead, the renegades could not let Longarm and Jessie go free to tell what had happened here . . .

The Ute swung his rifle toward Longarm. "Do not move," he commanded. Other braves, meanwhile, were covering Jessie.

Longarm put up his hands, watching as a dozen more rifle-toting Utes came out of hiding behind rocks and trees scattered up the ridge. He silently uttered a string of dark curses as his Colt was plucked from its holster. Jessie had already been disarmed of her revolver. The Utes made no move to stop her as she swung down from her horse to go to Broadwick's aid.

"How bad?" Longarm asked her as she knelt over the moaning inspector.

"Come see," she muttered.

"Let me go to him!" Longarm addressed the pockmarked Ute, who nodded grimly. Longarm dismounted and walked over to where Broadwick was lying.

It was bad, all right. Longarm hunkered down beside the wounded man. From the bright red blood pulsing from the puckered hole in Broadwick's chest, Longarm guessed that the man was lung-shot.

"What do you think, Custis?" Jessie asked, her voice trembling, tears welling in her eyes.

Longarm didn't reply. Instead he rested his head in his hands, trying to think of a way out of this mess. Most of these Utes were too young to have seen action during the Indian Wars. They were boys more than men, and they'd wanted nothing more out of this lark of theirs than a few feathers for their headbands. Well, they were likely to get a lot more than feathers; they were likely to get a murder charge—*or three murder charges* . . .

Slowly Longarm stood up. He kept his hands clear of his pockets, well aware that, red or white, men were all the same; they tended to get a mite trigger-happy when they

171

were panicked, as these braves certainly were.

"This is bad trouble for you all," Longarm addressed the pockmarked Ute.

"It is also bad trouble for *you*," the Ute remarked.

"Give us back our guns and ride away from here!" Longarm blustered. "Hope that we forget your faces! Go! Hope that this man does not die!" Longarm doubted that the bluff would work. He was right; it didn't.

"You and the woman will come with us," the pockmarked Ute decreed. "We will bring along your wounded friend on a litter. We will blindfold you and take you to our camp. There you may tend to your friend. If he lives, you will be freed, for there will have been no murder. If he dies..." The Ute frowned. *"Hope* that he does not die."

"Custis!" Jessie called out, frightened as several of the Utes grabbed her, while another wound a greasy rag across her eyes.

"Don't fight them! And don't worry!" Longarm called out. And then it was his turn to be blindfolded.

He was led to his horse, which he mounted. This was one time he wished his McClellan had a saddlehorn. It was plumb difficult to stay mounted when you didn't know which way your horse was heading, with neither reins nor a saddlehorn to hold on to.

Longarm had plenty of time to think during the ride to the Utes' camp. He gave the pockmarked Ute credit for trying to scout his way clear of this mess as best he could.

Longarm had no doubt what would happen to Jessie and himself when Broadwick died, as the man surely would, sooner or later. If the shooting had happened in a town, the inspector would have stood a chance, but out here, with only Longarm's rough doctoring to see him through, Broadwick was doomed.

And when Broadwick died, the Utes would know that they could not leave alive any witnesses who might brand them as murderers. They'd have little choice but to kill Jessie and himself, and stash all three bodies in some out-of-the-way canyon where the corpses would never be found ...

Little choice, and nothing to lose, Longarm thought as the Utes led them to who knew where. After all, the law could only hang murderers *once*.

★

Chapter 15

Sunset was coming on by the time the Ute renegades reached their campsite hidden in the hills. Jessie's blindfold was not removed until she was inside one of their lodges. She blinked her eyes against the fading sunlight filtering through the tent flap's opening, as one of the braves used the handcuffs they'd evidently discovered in Longarm's coat pocket to lock her wrists in front of her.

Then the Ute left the tent, and Jessie was alone to ponder her circumstances.

The tent was U.S. Army surplus, as were the tattered wool blankets that carpeted the canvas floor. The Indian reservations were dumps for most of the worn-out stuff the army could no longer use, Jessie knew. She could almost feel sorry for these Ute renegades; they'd been given second-hand goods, and told to live second-hand lives as wards of the government. Deprived of their hunting grounds, and with no other means available to the young braves to prove their manhood, Jessie was surprised that there weren't more of these renegade parties exploding out of the suffocating confines of the reservations.

None of that excused them for shooting Lloyd Broadwick, of course. The shooting was a tragedy, but one the Utes had brought upon themselves; it was a crime for which they'd have to pay, as the renegades well knew...

The Utes had taken her gunbelt and boots, discovering her derringer tucked away in her boot top in the process. Since she was not about to try to escape while handcuffed, weaponless and barefoot, and without knowing Longarm and Broadwick's whereabouts, Jessie settled back against the comfortable blankets and closed her eyes. She was exhausted, and wished that Longarm were here with her. She also wished she knew how Broadwick had held up during his rough, litter-ride into camp . . .

She wasn't about to fool herself by harboring false hope. She knew that their survival now depended upon Broadwick. They would be allowed to live for only as long as the postal inspector managed to hang on.

Jessie must have dozed off, for when she next opened her eyes it was nighttime. She could hear the chirp of crickets, and the murmuring of the Utes outside her canvas walls. She sat up as two braves, one of them carrying a lighted candle, herded Longarm into the tent.

He also was missing his hat, boots, and gunbelt; he'd been stripped of his coat and vest, as well. One of the braves unlocked the cuff on Jessie's left wrist and used it to bind Longarm's right, so that they were now cuffed together, side by side. Then the Utes left the tent, leaving behind the flickering candle.

Jessie yawned, rubbing her sleepy eyes with her free hand. "Where have you been?" she asked.

"Tending to Broadwick as best I could," Longarm replied. "I didn't dare risk trying to dig that bullet out of his chest. I just bandaged him up to try and staunch the bleeding. Then Gray Hawk—"

"Who?"

"Gray Hawk—he's the one with the pitted face. While I was tending to Broadwick, a couple of braves addressed him that way in their own lingo. I'm glad I didn't let on a while back that I savvied their tongue. Now we'll be able to identify these renegades to the B.I.A. when we get back."

"You mean *if* we get back," Jessie moped.

"Chin up, Jessie," Longarm said. "We've been in tighter spots than this."

"Tighter spots than *this?*" Jessie echoed incredulously. "We're in the middle of nowhere, the prisoners of renegades, and handcuffed together. I suppose they got your derringer?"

"Yep, and my pocketknife as well, so I can't pick the locks on these irons. Did they get your derringer, too?"

"They did. Where's Broadwick?"

"They've got him in a tent across the way from this one. There's six of these old army tents for the seventeen braves I counted. Off to one side is a remuda for their ponies. They gave old Lloyd a tent of his own, as well. I reckon we smell as bad to them as they do to us. After I'd done what I could for Broadwick, I asked them to put me in with you."

"I'm glad you did," Jessie said. "But maybe you should have stayed with Lloyd."

"Like I said, I've done all I could for him. He's a tough old coot. He regained consciousness while I was working on him. He told me that he understands the situation, and he told me he blames himself for the mess we're all in." Longarm frowned. "He knows that he's dying, as well. He promised me that he'd hold on for as long as he could to give us a chance to escape."

"But there's not much chance of that, is there?"

"Cheer up, Jessie," Longarm admonished her. "As long as we're alive, we've got a chance."

"Oh, Custis, hold me!" Jessie implored, clinging against him.

"With these cuffs on us, it's kind of hard to do," he muttered.

"I have an idea," Jessie said brightly. "We'll each roll on our sides facing each other, with our cuffed hands beneath us, and then we'll each have one hand free to do this . . ." She tugged at the ends of his black shoestring tie until it came undone, and then began to unbutton his shirt.

"Just you slow down, woman!" Longarm chuckled. "There's a time and a place for everything, and—"

"Hush. Is there a guard outside?"

"Nope. Leastways I didn't see one when I was brought in. I reckon they figure we'll keep well enough without one of them sitting up all night watching us."

"There! Then you see?" She began to nibble kisses along his jaw.

"See what?" Longarm exclaimed, and tried to squirm free of Jessie's embrace.

"Hold still!" she scolded. "You can't get away. We're handcuffed together, remember? Now just listen to reason, Custis. We can't do a thing for ourselves until much later tonight, when most of the camp is asleep. So here we are in this nice cozy tent..." Jessie parted his shirt, and then slid down, to plant teasing, nibbling kisses across the broad expanse of Longarm's chest. "We're all snug and cozy on these blankets..." Her fingernails lightly raked his flat, hard belly, and then her fingers dipped lower, to tarry at the buttons on his fly. "And we even have soft, romantic candlelight to make love by..." she cooed.

"I'm not sure my heart would be in it..."

Jessie's fingers encompassed his swollen shaft, straining against his trousers buttons. "Liar," she laughed.

Longarm's free hand had meanwhile strayed to the buttons of her blouse. "If you're sure..." he mumbled thickly. Her blouse parted, allowing her magnificent breasts free rein.

"Think of it as a girl's last request," Jessie moaned as Longarm buried his face in her cleavage. "Like—like a last *smoke,* or—a last meal..."

"The angle's wrong for it to be your last meal, Jessie, but we'll see what we can do."

"I *know* what *you* can do," Jessie responded breathlessly. "I've just been waiting for you to start!"

Beneath them the handcuffs' chain links jingled merrily as Jessie lifted her hips to allow Longarm to peel down her jeans. It took him a while to do it with just one hand free, but the delay added a delicious suspense to their lovemaking, as did the imminent possibility of discovery by an insomniac Ute brave curious as to what all the heavy-breathing ruckus was all about...

At last Jessie's jeans were bunched around her knees. "Ooh! It tickles!" she whispered as she rubbed the twin hemispheres of her pink bottom against the scratchy wool. Then she rolled back onto her side, facing Longarm, and

178

began work on the buttons down the front of his trousers. Several moments and kisses later, Jessie had his pants undone. Now it was Longarm's turn to lift up, so that Jessie could tug the brown tweed down over his slim hips and lean thighs. She sighed happily, wriggling like a puppy as she caressed his hard, jutting erection. Meanwhile, Longarm pulled Jessie tight against him. He used his free hand to stroke the length of her curled body, beginning with her breasts beneath her silky blouse, and trailing his fingers down to where her shirttails left off, and it was just the palm of his hand gliding over the satin-smooth curve of her hip, buttock, and thigh.

"It's fun like this, isn't it, Custis?" she whispered. "Both of us being half undressed?" She reached between his legs to cup the weight of him in her warm, knowing fingers. "What we *can't* see makes what we *can* see more exciting!"

"I reckon you've done enough talking, young lady," Longarm growled. He once again dipped his lips toward the fragrant valley of Jessie's cleavage, the rough stubble on his jaw brushing the swollen tips of her breasts. With his free hand he began to explore the fine-spun blonde tufts of fur at Jessie's center, crooning in satisfaction at her whimpers and moans as she grew wet enough for his finger to slide right in . . .

"Oh God . . . *oh, Custis* . . ." She flipped onto her back as his finger sawed in and out, sometimes causing her to clasp her thighs in an attempt to imprison his hand, and at other times causing her to splay her legs and buck her hips in a wanton display of passion. Longarm raised himself on his elbow to afford himself a better angle, administering long, feather-light caresses to her drenched sex, watching as her back arched, her knees and elbows locked, and Jessie lifted her hips up off the sodden, musky blankets to softly moan her way through a series of orgasms that left her weak-limbed and spent.

"Hmmm," she muttered. "How wonderful"

"We aim to please," Longarm replied, pressing his lips against her rosy mouth.

Jessie suddenly rolled away to find a dry corner of blanket, but was stopped by the handcuffs. She looked down in surprised amusement at their locked wrists. "See? You made me forget my troubles," she said, and then sat up and swung around, planting her belly on Longarm's chest, forcing him to lie on his back against the cushioning blankets. "Now," she murmured, her fingers dancing along the length of his swollen, throbbing shaft, "it's time for me to make you forget *your* troubles!" She wiggled her heartshaped rump in Longarm's face, and lasciviously winked at him over her shoulder. "It looks like I can manage to give myself that last meal, after all!"

She giggled in satisfaction at Longarm's ecstatic moan as her lips engulfed him. She allowed him no respite from the intense pleasure he felt as her tongue lapped, her teeth nibbled, and her wet mouth totally encompassed him. She did not stop, not even when his breathing quickened, his hips began to buck against the blanket, and the paralyzing jolts of his climax lurched from his loins...

Longarm was still beneath Jessie, still held captive within the velvet prison of her lips, when he became aware of a low, guttural, animallike growling within the tent. It was coming from Jessie! The humming felt wonderful, causing him to swell all over again. Meanwhile, she had begun to arch her back and rock her hips, rubbing herself against his belly.

He tried to reach out to grasp her hips with his hands, remembered the cuffs, and settled for planting his free hand along the cleavage of her shimmying rump. His fingers slid down to once again enter her, and she erupted into another climax—

"Yeow!" he gasped. "Don't bite!"

She rolled off him, onto her back, knees up. Her movement drew Longarm's cuffed hand across his own abdomen. "Careful!"

"Huh? Oh, right..." she sighed languidly, gazing at the handcuffs' links glittering in the lambent candlelight suffusing the tent. She fingered Longarm's turgid member. "Talk about a last meal! I think this time my eyes were bigger than my stomach!" She sniffed. "Lord, what does this tent *smell* like!"

"Like a female in heat," Longarm chuckled.

"Oh, Custis! I'm mortified!" Jessie whispered, sitting up and using her free hand to brush her golden tresses out of her wide emerald eyes. "Do you think the Indians will realize that we've been—?"

"Jessie, they're likely going to kill us!"

"Well, I know *that,* Custis!" she pouted. "But I don't intend to let them think I'm not a lady!"

"You're lucky I've got one hand chained!" Longarm told her. "Otherwise I'd—"

"Anyway, we're not going to die," Jessie cut him off. "Hold on a second, and I'll get us out of these cuffs."

Longarm watched, flabbergasted, as Jessie reached up into her long, tawny mane to pull out a small black wire hairpin.

"You mean to say you had that all the while?" Longarm said incredulously.

"'Course I did," Jessie replied. "I haven't gone anywhere, have I?" She set to work on the cuffs, and had them unlocked within thirty seconds.

"Why didn't you tell me you had that?" Longarm scolded.

"You didn't ask," she replied sweetly, throwing her arms around his neck. "Anyway, I've been waiting for you to scratch that itch of mine for so long, I wasn't about to let you loose until I was satisfied."

"And *are* you satisfied?"

"Wel-l-l-l. . ." Jessie replied thoughtfully as she tickled his flagpole, which was just then flying at half-mast, but began to rise dramatically under her ministrations. "Why, Custis," she drawled. "Could this be the second coming?"

Longarm scooped her up and dumped her smack on her pretty bottom amid their nest of blankets. *"You* may be satisfied, Jessie, but I'll never be, where *you're* concerned!"

181

He parted her legs and slid into her honey-sweet center. Her quivering increased as he sank down to completely fill her.

"Yes, please ride me, Longarm!" she implored him, rolling and gyrating to meet his thrusts, her nails lightly raking the broad expanse of his back, her fingers urging him on as they dug into his muscular buttocks.

Before very long, Jessie was once again writhing beneath him, her eyes screwed shut and her mouth wide open as catlike noises rose from her throat.

"Custis, are we m-making too m-much noise?" she managed between strokes.

"Who cares!" he moaned, pounding hard, actually moving Jessie around the tent's canvas floor, the blankets bunched beneath her.

Jessie's eyes rolled and her mouth opened. Longarm, sensing that she was about to let loose with an ear-shattering howl, locked his lips against hers to smother her love-cry. As she came, her powerful inner muscles clutched him, the swollen lips of her sex rubbing deliciously against his groin. His climax burst forth, molten; Jessie's rippling contractions milked him of every last drop.

They stayed locked together for as long as possible. Finally he reluctantly withdrew. "We'd better get decent," he whispered. "It's been a while. They might be coming for us."

"Hmmm," Jessie replied dreamily, but then she shook herself. "Oh, I actually forgot about poor Inspector Broadwick!"

They dressed quickly, and straightened the blankets. Longarm plucked tufts of wool and stuffed them into the handcuffs' locks.

"What are you doing?" Jessie asked him.

"This way we can close these bracelets around our wrists the way the Utes had them, but the cuffs won't actually be locked. The wool will jam the mechanisms."

Jessie nodded. "You figure to try to take the braves by

surprise when they come for us?"

"I might have to," Longarm replied. "If I had my druthers, we'd wait until they all fell asleep tonight and then make our move, but if they come for us, we'll have no choice but to try our best to knock them out and get some weapons."

"One thing, Custis..." Jessie paused. "You'll probably think me silly, but we can't leave Broadwick here, not even if he is dying."

Longarm drew her toward him for a kiss. "I don't think you're silly, and I had no intention of leaving old Lloyd behind. Least we can do for him is see to it that he dies among his own kind."

"Thanks, Custis," Jessie said with relief.

"None necessary. I'm fond of that jasper, too. Now settle back and try and get some rest. You're going to need all of your strength when the time comes for us to play our hand."

Jessie nestled herself into the crook of his arm, and within seconds was sound asleep. Longarm settled back, watching the candle, which had burned down to a stub, flutter and flare before winking out in a curl of smoke. Longarm stared up at the tent's roof, letting his eyes adjust to the darkness. The Utes still had some campfires burning; their glow filtered through the tent's canvas walls.

You pissants just keep them blazes roaring, he thought. *Then, when you come in here to get us, you won't be able to see a damn thing.*

He smiled grimly into the shadows. His bravado in front of Jessie aside, they were in a bad spot, and he knew it. The *Ho* were a tough bunch of folks; Longarm figured that he knew enough tricks to lick a couple of braves in a fight, but he couldn't do it quickly and quietly, and that was a plain fact. He and Jessie had gone out of their way to keep the noise down during their love-tussle, but Longarm couldn't expect a pair of Utes to keep their traps shut while he did his best to punch out their lights. And even if he managed it and, by stretching his luck, managed to get his hands on

183

a gun, what chance would he have in a shootout with seventeen Utes, meanwhile keeping his eye on Jessie and a wounded man?

The night wore on as Longarm fussed and brooded, trying to come up with a way out for the three of them. Gradually the Utes' fires burned down, and the occasional noise outside their tent faded into nocturnal quiet.

Longarm began to grow hopeful. It was too much to hope for that they might regain their boots and horses and ride away clean, but perhaps Jessie and he could make their break, snatch a gun, and make a stand from Broadwick's tent. If they could hold the stalemate long enough, the Utes might lose patience and ride off. Of course, if he were in Gray Hawk's moccasins in such a situation, he'd simply have his braves pepper Broadwick's flimsy tent with gunfire and leave their three corpses in their canvas shroud.

Simmer down, old son, and let's eat this apple one bite at a time, Longarm thought. *We may die, but we'll die trying.*

He nudged Jessie awake, silenced her mumbled queries with a kiss, and then whispered, "Get alert. It's time for us to make our move." He grabbed the handcuffs; the steel bracelets would do some damage when swung at an adversary's head or face.

"Longarm!" Jessie whispered urgently. "I hear someone coming!"

"All right, settle back and pretend we're still locked together," he said, placing the bracelets around their wrists. *Shit,* he thought, *it looks like we're going to have to do this the hard way.*

But maybe their luck was holding after all—it was just one brave coming into their dark tent to check on them.

Longarm waited. The brave bent forward, putting himself off balance as he ducked through the tent's low flap opening. As the Ute's head and shoulders appeared inside the tent, Longarm let the handcuffs fall away from his wrist. He lunged forward to grab the Indian's shirtfront and haul him kicking into the tent's dark interior. Longarm flipped him

184

over on his back, got hold of the squirming Ute's throat, and drew back his fist to cold-cock him—

"Hold on, Cap'n! I'm a friend!"

"Huh?" Longarm stared down, peering through the shadows. "Talk fast, old son, 'cause you sure as hell *look* like an Indian, even if you don't *talk* like one."

"I'm only half Indian! My name's Teddy Rolling-Rock. Miss Jessie will vouch for me."

"I surely will!" Jessie exclaimed happily. "Teddy was one of my finest drovers during the last roundup at the Circle Star spread. Teddy, what are you doing with these renegades?"

"If you'll get this big'un off of my throat, I'll be glad to tell you."

"It's all right, Longarm, let him be," Jessie said, and he obliged, rocking back on his heels as Teddy Rolling-Rock sat up and quickly whispered his story.

"After leaving Sarah at the end of the market drive, I couldn't find more work. I wandered northward until my money ran out, and then hightailed it back to the Ouray Reservation."

"Is that where you're from?" Jessie asked.

"Yes, ma'am. Leastways that's where my mama lives. I didn't much like the idea of ending up back there as a reservation Indian. A man loses something when he does that." Teddy shrugged philosophically. "But it won't do to keep your pride if you end up starving to death in the meantime. On the Ouray I had food in my belly and a roof over my head, which was more than I had on the outside."

"So why aren't you still on the Ouray?" Longarm asked. "What put you on the renegade trail with the rest of these owlhoots?"

"I can't rightly explain it so that you'd understand, Cap'n," Teddy murmured. "After a while I just couldn't take having to beg for everything."

"Here, now, son," Longarm grumbled. "You mean to tell me that Agent Caldwell wasn't treating you right?"

Teddy took a moment to reply. "Caldwell is a good man,

185

and he was treating me, and the rest of the *Ho,* the way the law intended, but Cap'n, treating us according to the letter of the law ain't necessarily treating us *right.*"

Longarm nodded. "Reckon I can see the truth in that, Teddy," he said quietly.

"Gray Hawk came around with a few of his cousins, preaching how the reservation life was for old women," the Ute half-breed continued. "The bunch you see here rode out with Gray Hawk, and I rode with them. We whooped it up some, but we were on our way back to the Ouray, believe it or not, with not a damn crime on our consciences, until we met you on the trail. I was up in the rocks with the others, so I didn't recognize Miss Jessie here until she was blindfolded. It wouldn't have made much difference if I had recognized her earlier, though. Gray Hawk ain't about to listen to what a half-breed has to say about things."

"Who shot our friend?" Longarm asked.

"T'weren't me!" Teddy blurted.

"Never said it was," Longarm replied. "But I reckon you know who it was."

Teddy looked away. "I know—but I ain't sure I oughta tell . . ." he finished uneasily.

"Teddy, you've got to," Jessie urged.

"You know I'm the law, right, old son?" Longarm said, and when Teddy nodded, he added, "And so was that man one of you renegades shot down."

Teddy looked miserable. "I want to do the right thing," he quavered. "I wonder what Ki would do in this situation."

Jessie, swallowing hard, looked away. "I think that Ki would do the honorable thing and tell Longarm who did the shooting, no matter how painful giving that information might be."

"I suppose I could just say I was crouched behind a rock and didn't see it," Teddy theorized, glancing sheepishly at Longarm.

"You *could* say that, Teddy, but it wouldn't hardly be—"

"Honorable. You don't have to say it, deputy," Teddy

brooded. "All right, I don't favor what that itchy-fingered sonofabitch did, nohow! His name is Lean Pony. He is Gray Hawk's first cousin. The two of them had argued over who was going to lead the party. I guess Lean Pony shot your friend in order to count coup on Gray Hawk. This way, Lean Pony will be able to brag that he bested a white man in combat."

"I don't exactly call knocking a man off his horse using a rifle from a hundred feet away 'besting him in combat,'" Longarm grumbled.

"The distance will shrink in the telling, Cap'n," Teddy shrugged. "And it'll be your friend who will have fired the first shot."

"Well, I intend to tell it like it happened, and to the B.I.A.," Longarm vowed. "I'll send a wire from Nettle Grove."

"Concerning that, I aim to help you and your friends get out of here," Teddy said. "Your guns, boots, and other gear are all in Gray Hawk's tent."

"It's not been divvied up?" Longarm asked, puzzled.

Teddy shook his head. "Gray Hawk is greedy, and the others—except for Lean Pony—are so piss-pants scared over what they've gotten themselves into that they've got no stomach to argue the matter. What were you folks doing out in these parts, anyway?"

"We were looking for Ki," Jessie said. "We think he's in trouble."

"That so?" Teddy asked, concerned. "He'll *be* in trouble, all right, if he blunders near Will Sayre's hideout town."

"You *know* where the hideout is?" Longarm demanded.

"Sure, Cap'n. Most Indians do, I reckon, just from criss-crossing this territory so often."

"Then how has its location remained a secret for so long?" Jessie asked.

"Ma'am, it likely wouldn't have, if white folks usually showed as much kindness toward Indians as you have," Teddy said warmly. "But they ain't, and because of that, most Indians wouldn't go across a street to help a white, let alone reveal the location of an outlaw who's been pure vexation to the Great White Father, but never did no Indians any harm."

"Teddy, we'd appreciate it if you'd tell us where the hideout is," Jessie said.

"I'll tell you, but first let's get out of here." He pulled a battered-looking Peacemaker out of his belt and handed it to Longarm. "It's loaded and it works," he grinned in response to Longarm's dubious expression. "And it'll have to do until we can get you your own gun back. I'd take it kindly if you didn't kill any of my people with it unless you have to, and if you'd give it back to me when you get your own gun. It belonged to my daddy. It's the only thing he left me."

"You'll get it back," Longarm promised, "but I can't swear not to use it against the *Ho*—there's likely sentries watching over the camp."

"There were two, but they're sleeping now," Teddy said. "I put 'em to sleep with the butt-end of that there Peacemaker. If our luck holds, we'll be out of here long before anyone is the wiser!"

They moved out of the tent with Teddy in the lead, Jessie in the middle, and Longarm bringing up the rear. True to Teddy's word, the battered Peacemaker was held together with spit and sticky-tape, but it was functional enough to blow somebody's head off at close range.

The Ute camp was quiet. The fires had all burned down, and all the Indians seemed to be inside their tents, sleeping.

"Broadwick's over there," Longarm whispered to Jessie, pointing out the inspector's tent, inside of which a candle was burning. "Teddy, lead us to Gray Hawk. No offense to your daddy, but I'd like to get us a little more firepower before proceeding any further."

"This way." Teddy led them across the camp. "That's his tent," he said, pointing.

"Is he alone in there?" Longarm asked.

Teddy nodded. "The great Gray Hawk would never share his tent!" he spat. "He has forced the other braves to cram

188

into the remaining tents, not caring a bit that they were already overcrowded due to the pair of tents we gave over to your wounded friend and yourselves."

"Don't you fret," Longarm said. "I'm going to make Gray Hawk right sorry he's so antisocial." He handed back the Peacemaker. "Teddy, stand watch at the door." Then Longarm crawled through the entrance flap.

Gray Hawk was wrapped in a blanket and snoring soundly, his stolen plunder piled beside him. As Longarm crept toward him, Gray Hawk tossed fitfully, throwing an arm across his booty as if to give it a lover's embrace—

Then his eyes flew open.

Longarm was looming over him like an avenging angel.

"No, don't kill me!" pleaded the surprised, puffy-eyed Ute.

"Ain't being on the warpath fun?" Longarm whispered harshly as he delivered two short, hard right jabs to Gray Hawk's chin. The punches rocked the Ute's head, and then he lay still.

"Pleasant dreams," Longarm said mirthlessly. He went to the tent's entrance and waved in Jessie and Teddy.

Longarm quickly checked his Colt, then buckled on his gunbelt. Next he pulled on his boots and put on the rest of his clothing, patting his pockets to make sure all of his personal belongings were in place.

Teddy glanced down at the unconscious Gray Hawk. Even in the dark, it was obvious that the Ute's bruised face was swelling. "Cap'n, it looks to me like you broke his jaw."

"I didn't do it on purpose," Longarm said. "But I'm not saying I'm sorry it happened. The odds are already against us getting out of here alive. Most of these renegades ain't worth spit unless they've got their 'big chief' here to tell them what to do."

"That's a fact," Teddy admitted.

"Well then, number one, I reckon a broken jaw will give Gray Hawk something to think on besides our skins," Longarm shrugged. "Number two, nobody told him to become a renegade in the first place, and number three, old Broadwick is hurting a lot more than Gray Hawk. Now let's get moving. Jessie, do you have all your belongings?"

"Even my derringer!" she replied, tucking the little gun into her boot top.

"All right. We've still got to fetch Broadwick and get to our horses. Teddy, you and Jessie gather up our gear and head for the remuda. Get our mounts saddled up. I'll fetch Broadwick and meet you." He gathered Broadwick's holstered gun and some extra cartridges and left the tent.

He silently glided the few yards to the tent where they were keeping Broadwick. Once he was inside, it took only a glance for Longarm to know that Broadwick could never survive an escape.

The burning candle inside the foul-smelling tent cast a faint pool of light, but it was enough for Longarm to see the blood glistening on Broadwick's chin as it welled out of his mouth. Even worse, the bandage that Longarm had laced across the lung-shot man's chest was now soaked through with blood. Broadwick was sitting with his legs swathed in blankets, his back propped up against his own saddle. The Utes had evidently moved it in since Longarm had tended to the man.

"Deputy Long?" Broadwick called weakly. "Is it you?"

"It's me," Longarm whispered, kneeling beside Broadwick. "Talk softer, man. You'll bring the whole camp down on us."

"They brought in my saddle a few hours back. Why do you suppose they did that, deputy?"

"Couldn't say, Lloyd," Longarm fibbed. He knew exactly why the saddle had been brought in. The Utes believed that having a saddle present would allow the dying man's spirit to ride to heaven, or what passed for heaven in the *Ho* way of looking at such things. "Come on, now, Lloyd, we're getting out of here."

"Don't make me laugh, Longarm!" Broadwick proffered a bloody grin. "I couldn't ride for shit when I was well! I don't expect to make a very good time on horseback, sucking air through my chest!"

Longarm shrugged helplessly. "Lloyd, I'm right sorry about how things have worked out."

The wounded inspector smiled. "I thank you for your concern, Longarm. But I brought this on myself by being so all-fired stubborn. I should have paid you more mind." He squinted. "Is that my gun you've got there?"

"It is."

"Then hand it over!" Broadwick struggled to get to his feet. "It seems I can be of some use to you, after all!"

"Easy, Lloyd," Longarm cautioned.

"Easy, my ass!" Broadwick scoffed as he stood up, swaying uncertainly. "What's the concern? That I might get *hurt?*" He clutched at himself, his face contorting as a spasm of pain overwhelmed him. "My gun!" he rasped, extended his trembling hand toward Longarm, who handed over the holstered weapon and the extra rounds.

"Thanks, deputy." Broadwick pocketed the ammunition and drew the long-barreled revolver from its holster, tossing the shoulder rig aside. "Is it loaded?"

Longarm nodded. "All six chambers. I checked."

"Good!" Broadwick replied. "Here's what we'll do. I'll watch until you and Jessie are ready to ride. And when you mount up—" He paused, an unholy grin once again creasing his ravaged features as he hefted his revolver. "When you mount up, I'll create a diversion. These Indians were mighty quick to ambush me. Let's see how they handle themselves in some toe-to-toe shooting."

"Lloyd, do you understand what you're saying?"

Broadwick nodded firmly. "I do, deputy. No matter what, I'm going to be dead before morning." He groaned as another wave of pain washed over him. When he was able, he looked Longarm in the eye. "I might as well go out helping my friends to survive."

Longarm shook hands with the inspector. "You're a good man, Lloyd."

"You, too, deputy. Now help me out of this tent."

"Lean on me, Lloyd," Longarm said. He put his arm around Broadwick's waist and helped him lurch his way out of the tent, and then through the camp, toward the remuda. Broadwick went as quietly as he could, but he couldn't stifle all of his grunts and groans. Longarm heard stirrings in the Utes' tents as they passed.

Broadwick stopped as they approached the remuda. "I'll just hang back," he murmured to Longarm. "Jessie might raise a fuss about my decision, and anyway I look a mess. I've always been concerned with my appearance around the ladies. Seeing me would likely give Jessie a start. You give her my compliments, all right, deputy?" His painwracked gaze flicked past Longarm. "Look out!" he cried, elbowing the tall deputy aside as a Ute brave, awakened by the noise they'd made, lunged out from the shelter of a tent, his rifle at his shoulder. The Ute fired, his round going wild. Broadwick extended his gunhand, calmly sighted down his revolver's eight-inch barrel, and squeezed the trigger. The big Smith & Wesson thundered, orange flame erupting from its muzzle. The Ute cried out, falling as limp as a ragdoll.

"See you, Longarm," Broadwick said, his eyes remaining fixed on the camp, which was coming alive with Utes.

"See you, Lloyd," Longarm said, and ran for the remuda.

Jessie and Teddy were standing ready, their guns drawn. A few feet away the horses stood saddled. "What was that shooting?" Jessie demanded. "Where's Lloyd? We couldn't find his saddle, and used one of the Utes'—"

"Lloyd's staying behind," Longarm said. "Mount up!"

"We can't leave him behind," Jessie argued. "Custis, we've got to—"

"Look!" Teddy Rolling-Rock shouted. "Fire!"

Longarm and Jessie spun around. Flames were shooting up toward the night sky from the camp's center. The candle that had been left burning in Broadwick's tent had evidently tipped, setting the canvas ablaze. The Utes' camp was now bathed in eerie orange light. As the three ran to their horses, they heard shots and cries from the Utes. Sparks from the

192

blazing tent were carried aloft, only to fall on the other tents, setting them smoldering.

"There's Broadwick!" Jessie cried.

All three watched mesmerized as the inspector came backing into view from out of the smoke, a hellish, bloody apparition with a blazing gun and a wild, lurching gait.

A Ute brave was able to blind-side the dying inspector. The Ute fired from the hip, his ejected casings glittering in the firelight as he levered rounds out of his Winchester. Broadwick was hit at least twice, but he took no notice, absorbing the lead the way a valiant boxer will absorb punches, meanwhile using his deadly Smith & Wesson to hold back the main grouping of the Utes.

Longarm drew his .44 in order to drop the Ute peppering Broadwick, but before he could fire, another gun roared. The Ute dropped his Winchester to clutch at his belly before staggering out of sight.

Longarm looked over to where Teddy Rolling-Rock was steadying his rearing mount, his smoking Peacemaker still in his hand. "That was Lean Pony," the half-breed called to Longarm in explanation. "By gut-shooting him, I figure he will live long enough to suffer at least as much as your brave friend has."

Longarm nodded. "Let's ride!" he commanded.

They left the flame-ruined Ute camp behind. As they rode, the cries faded, and gradually even the gunshots diminished, but vivid in Longarm's memory was the image of Broadwick taking those Winchester rounds without flinching.

With Teddy Rolling-Rock taking the lead, they rode along a narrow, winding trail for about an hour. Finally the half-breed paused to study a fork branching up toward higher ground. He nodded, grinning.

"Us *Ho* inadvertently took you a good part of the way you'd wanted to head," Teddy told Longarm and Jessie. "This here fork will take you where you want to go. Stay with it through the rough country. Eventually you'll come to a busted-up old mining town alongside a river. Ride on by that town and you'll find what you're looking for." Teddy shrugged. "Or, more likely, Will Sayre's men will find *you*."

"Thank you, Teddy," Jessie said. "Thank you for everything."

"Glad to be of help to you, ma'am. I'm just sorry about your friend we had to leave back there."

"Listen, Teddy, if you've got nowhere to go, you might try Nettle Grove," Jessie said. "See the town marshal there; his name's Hank Stills. He's got a ranch, and I know that he's short-handed. Hank can't pay very much..."

"Miss Jessie, I'd work for just room and board!" Teddy crowed excitedly.

"Well, room and board might be the best that Hank can offer, but you'll have to find that out for yourself."

"One thing more, Teddy," Longarm interrupted. "I'm going to have to report Gray Hawk and his bunch to the B.I.A. They'll stand trial for their part in Inspector Broadwick's shooting. What's left of the renegade party will, at any rate. You steer clear of the Ouray for a while. I'm leaving you out of my report."

A blissful grin slowly stretched across Teddy's face. "I surely thank you for leaving me a free man, deputy."

"You committed no crime, as far as I can tell," Longarm said. "Anyway, it's the least I can do to repay you for saving our skins back there. Just try to stay out of trouble!"

"I will, deputy. I promise I will!" Teddy sighed. "It's grand to know that I ain't going to be wanted!"

"Good luck, Teddy," Jessie said in farewell.

"Good luck to you too," Teddy replied, before riding off. "Where you're going, you're going to need it!"

★

Chapter 16

Ki sat perched on a rock ledge. Below him, just beginning to come to life in the dawn's first rays of light, was the sprawl of the outlaw town that Will Sayre had built for the Ladykiller Gang.

The town, secreted in its high-walled canyon, reminded Ki of the austere fortress compounds of the ancient feudal warlords of Japan. There were several low-slung, single-story bunkhouses for the men, some supply shacks, and at the far end, a stable fronted by a split-log corral in which perhaps thirty horses were milling. Ki spotted a man hauling pots out of the mess hall, in order to scrub the utensils in what looked to be a natural pool formed by a rivulet of water cascading down from the wall of rock opposite the samurai's position. There was even a good-sized cottage with a fenced-in yard. From his high vantage point Ki had seen several women dressed in garish, frilly robes exit the cottage's rear door in order to use the backyard privy.

Presiding over everything, and close by the trail entrance to the canyon, was the big, two-story stone house that had to belong to Will Sayre. Ki studied the house. In his mind he charted his progress through the town to Sayre's domain; Dorsey Sayre had to be locked in one of the many rooms of that house.

The samurai instinctively pulled back from the ledge as the first yawning, stretching men exited one of the bunkhouses and made their way to the mess hall for breakfast. The men down below in the canyon were far enough away to look to Ki like scurrying insects, but despite the height,

195

Ki was able to smell the coffee brewing and bacon sizzling in the mess hall kitchen. His stomach grumbled as the tantalizing aromas reached him. He could do with a meal. He hadn't eaten since yesterday morning's sparse, saddlebag breakfast he'd shared with Rube Silva. Since his escape from the killers that Silva had ordered to execute him, the samurai had come across nothing in this inhospitable terrain that was edible, except for some hard-shelled bugs and more slithery rattlers. As yet, he wasn't hungry enough to dig into any of *those*...

In truth, Ki had many times gone a lot longer without food than a trifling twenty-four hours. It wasn't so much hunger that was making him uneasy, as *impatience* for action.

He had spent the night on this ledge, alternately dozing and listening to the goings-on in the outlaw town down below. Normally, Ki preferred to attack under cover of darkness, but this time his objective was not to kill, but to save a life—Dorsey Sayre's life, specifically. He did not wish to engage in combat unless it was absolutely necessary. The worst thing he could do would be to get into a violent confrontation with Will Sayre. True, the man was Dorsey's abductor, but he was also her father. However much Dorsey wished to return to her mother, it would not do for the young woman to witness her father's death at the hands of her rescuer. That would just add more guilt to the burden Dorsey already carried; it would add another gnarl to her already twisted, stunted soul.

All of that had precluded Ki's entering the outlaw town last night. He could not roam its shadowy alleys like a hunter, dispatching all who blocked his path. His hope had been that Dorsey would at some point show herself, making it easy for him to snatch her away. With luck, they could have been on horseback and long gone before her father knew what had happened. Ki doubted that Sayre would have pursued them once they were out of the canyon. The leader of the Ladykillers would have been more concerned that the location of his hideout had been discovered. The immediate prospect of a posse riding in would likely have over-shadowed his prior interest in his daughter.

That had been Ki's thinking as of last night, but now that it was morning, the thought of more passive waiting was unbearable. He kicked off his rope-soled slippers, stuffing them into his back pocket. He would need the use of his hands *and* his feet to clamber down the cliffs in the swift, silent, agile manner of a monkey.

His concentration was total as he began to pick his path down to the canyon floor. He dislodged no pebbles, gave no sign of himself at all as he descended, crawling over the rocks like a fly. Within a half-hour he reached bottom. Then he was sprinting away from the rock face to the shelter of one of the supply shacks.

He pressed himself against the rough clapboard siding of the shack, pausing to catch his breath. He was approximately one hundred yards from Sayre's stone house, which guarded the narrow, bottleneck entrance to the canyon. From there the trail wound upward through the high country, and eventually past the ghost town nestled by the river, where Rube Silva had yesterday suggested that they fill their canteens.

Ki peeked around the corner of the shack, glimpsing the house. It looked to be as still as death. He had not seen anyone going in or out since daylight.

The shortest route to the house would take him directly through the camp's center, past the bunkhouses, the mess hall, and even that bordello. He didn't want to risk it; he was still trying to avoid trouble. He decided to retreat to the cliffs, traveling the outlaw town's perimeter, detouring behind the stables, the rear of which backed up against the canyon's dead end. He would have a tricky time of it, slipping between that watering hole and the back porch of the grub hall, but once that gauntlet was behind him, Sayre's back door would be within reach.

It wasn't the greatest plan in the world for an unarmed man to attempt, but it was the best plan available, and one that he had to put quickly into action; the outlaw town was beginning to come alive. His chances of being discovered were steadily increasing.

He moved out, keeping low, flitting from building to building, intent upon reaching the halfway point that was the stables. About the time he reached the corrals, Ki realized his mistake. There was nothing he could do about it now, however, and there certainly was no going back the way he'd come.

From his rocky perch he'd not been able to see the blacksmith's shed attached to the rear wall of the stables. He still couldn't see it, but he could plainly hear the hiss of the bellows, the clang of hammer against iron, and the laughing banter of the men as they set to their day's work.

How many men? Ki wondered. He edged along the side wall of the stables, and peeked around the corner.

The shed wasn't a shed at all. It was a lean-to. There was no way to get around that open-walled work area without being seen by the two blacksmiths at their jobs.

Ki backed around the corner, out of sight. He slid down along the wall to rest on his heels, holding his head in his hands. He was totally at a loss. He couldn't retreat and he couldn't go forward.

There was no way that, without weapons, he could effectively take out those two. The bare-chested, sweating smiths both appeared to have been carved by the same sculptor, and whoever that sculptor had been, he had made his creations larger than life. It was not just the smiths' towering height—a good half-foot taller than Ki—or the incredible girth of their arms, chests, and flat, hard stomachs that gave Ki pause. It was also the way the two men moved in their quick and graceful fashion. One man, with sandy-colored hair swept back from his furrowed forehead, and wearing a thick, bristly mustache, was tirelessly pumping away at the thick wooden handles of the leather bellows to feed air into the fire. The other smith, dark-haired and clean-shaven, was holding a horseshoe in the flames by means of a pair of long-handled, wrought-iron tongs. Every now and then he would pull the red-hot shoe out of the fire, smack it on top of the anvil, and have at it with mighty, sweeping, one-handed blows of his huge hammer.

His best chance, Ki thought, would be to fall back into the rocks until these two titans quit the scene. With a bow or *shuriken* he could quickly and silently kill the two men. Barehanded, even with his *te* training, the best that he'd be able to manage would be a drawn-out, noisy brawl that would attract every outlaw in town.

The despondent samurai remembered a lesson that his teacher, Hirata, had long ago drummed into him: all things being equal, big warriors tended to defeat smaller ones. That went double when it was two against one. If only he had a weapon! David had prevailed against Goliath, but he'd had a sling...

A sling!

Ki got to his feet, edging forward to take another look at the two smiths; a sling would work, and he knew how to use one, if only he could find the raw materials to fabricate the primitive but effective weapon. He decided to risk searching the stable, entering through the front doors. He would find the leather for his sling in the tack room, and horseshoes would serve excellently as projectiles. He doubted that he'd run into anyone in the stable but the boss wrangler at this early hour, and unless that man was also a giant, Ki could quickly deal with him.

The important thing was that he still had the advantage of surprise, Ki thought. As long as no one knew he was here, he still had a chance to rescue Dorsey.

He glanced down as something cold and wet nudged at his ankle. A small, rather bedraggled, black and white terrier mutt was nosing at his bare feet. The little ratter was probably kept to control the rodent population in the stables. As Ki watched, the little dog began to lick his toes. The samurai smiled, reaching down to pat the little dog's head.

Startled, the terrier leaped away. It began to bark.

"Here now," one of the blacksmiths said. "What's gotten into the mutt?"

Ki heard the dull thud of a hammer being dropped to the

ground as the shrill yapping of that damned terrier continued.

"I best go see what's going on," the smith continued.

"Might have cornered himself another rattler," the other smith agreed.

Meanwhile, Ki was trying to escape, but the terrier had latched its jaws on to the cuff of his jeans. The mutt had dug its four paws into the dirt to wrestle with him. Ki didn't want to hurt the little dog, but time was running out...

"Here now," the blacksmith demanded. It was the dark-haired, clean-shaven one, standing with his hands planted on his hips as he glared at Ki. "Here now," he repeated, blinking stupidly.

Ki smiled. "Nice dog," he said soothingly. He bent to pat the terrier's head, but snatched back his hand as the snarling mutt snapped at him.

"Don't you hurt that dog!" the smith scowled, his right hand flicking out to cuff Ki.

The samurai ducked the blow and straightened up, using the momentum to add some extra spin to his corkscrew *te* thrust to the smith's midsection.

The man rocked a bit on his heels, but otherwise seemed oblivious to Ki's punch. He looked down at his belly, and then back at Ki. "Here now," he said, and, grabbing Ki by his shirtfront, lifted the samurai up and tossed him over his shoulder in the general vicinity of the smiths' work area. As Ki flew through the air, he wondered if it had been his imagination, or had that terrier been smiling?

Ki hit the dirt rolling, and was up on his feet in seconds. The sandy-haired, mustached smith left off pumping his bellows to regard the samurai. "What do we have here?" he asked his friend just now sauntering around the corner.

"This feller was hurting the mutt," the dark-haired fellow said.

"No, there is a misunderstanding here," Ki said as he smiled politely.

"Maybe you ought to pick on something your own size," the sandy-haired smith growled, wiping his hands on a rag as he stepped around the anvil and out from beneath the lean-to.

"That is good advice," Ki nodded, looking between the two giants moving in on him. "Perhaps you should follow it as well?" He began to back away, but was not able to go very far before the first of the boulders footing the rear wall of the canyon blocked his retreat. *Well, when you cannot run away, run forward!* the samurai thought, and tried to dart between the two smiths.

The sandy-haired man planted a hand on Ki's shoulder, stopping the samurai dead in his tracks. "I'll teach you to be cruel to dumb animals!" the smith muttered.

As the smith drew back his fist, Ki pivoted to face him. As the smith's punch came barreling like a freight train toward Ki's head, the samurai countered with a *jodan-age-uke,* increasing the power of his upward block by gripping his blocking arm with his other hand and pushing up against the smith's fist with everything he had.

Ki stopped the punch from knocking his head off his shoulders, but just barely. As the smith threw his weight into breaking down Ki's defense, the samurai's knees began to buckle. Ki shifted into a cat's-foot stance, putting all of his weight on his rear leg. He danced away from the smith, taking the opportunity to deliver a series of snap-kicks to the smith's belly as he did so.

The mustached man hardly grimaced as he pursued Ki. Meanwhile, the other man had come around behind the beleaguered samurai. Ki caught the clean-shaven man by surprise, landing a powerful sideways kick to the man's chin. The kick stunned the big man, and Ki used his momentary advantage to maneuver behind the smith and drive a foot at the rear of the man's knee. The smith's leg buckled, and he went down into a kneeling position. Given the chance, Ki might have been able to finish the man then and there, but the mustached smith was closing in, forcing him to give up his offensive. Then both men were back on their feet, and Ki was back where he'd begun in this unequal battle.

It was no good, the samurai realized. Sooner or later one

of these behemoths would manage to lock on to him, and then it would end with Ki lying in the dust, his skull fractured or his back broken. He had to find a way to end this, and soon, for he was beginning to tire; with fatigue he would slow down, and slowing down would prove fatal...

Ki's eyes fell on a sledgehammer lying on the ground beneath the lean-to. The two smiths followed Ki's gaze.

"Block him!" the mustached smith called to his friend.

Ki dodged and feinted, getting by the lumbering, clean-shaven smith. He ducked beneath the lean-to, and bent to lift the big hammer.

"Here now..." the clean-shaven smith muttered, backing away. Ki stayed where he was beneath the lean-to; the stable's wall protected his back, while the smiths' fire-pit, water trough, and anvil were all obstacles in his enemies' paths.

The smiths exchanged uneasy glances. Ki understood their concern. He was now backed into a corner, but he had the hammer. Like the little terrier that had gotten him into this mess, he could now deliver a nasty bite to anyone who tried to spook him out.

The two smiths were too thick-witted to realize it, but all they had to do was shout to bring armed allies rushing to their aid. Here was the stalemate that Ki had dreaded. The brawl had so far remained fairly quiet, but time—and his opportunity to rescue Dorsey—were quickly fading away.

"Rush the sonofabitch!" the mustached smith yelled in fury, rashly charging in like a bull.

Ki swung the sledgehammer at the man, missing the side of the smith's head by a fraction. The momentum of his swing carried Ki clear around, and the out-of-control hammer walloped the side of the anvil. There was an earsplitting *clang!* as steel met steel, the vibration up the hammer's handle fairly shaking the samurai's teeth. There was a splintering sound as the small wedges holding the hammerhead in place at the end of the handle gave way. The hammerhead thudded to the ground, leaving nothing but a stick in the surprised samurai's hands.

The two smiths exchanged delighted grins. "Looks like it's time for you to take your medicine, little man," the mustached blacksmith gloated.

"Leave some of him for me to stomp!" the other smith laughed.

Ki was smiling as well. What he'd been left with was a polished hardwood stick approximately forty inches long and a uniform inch and a half wide. Traditional *jo* sticks were about fifty inches long and fashioned of white oak, but this hammer handle would do just fine! With the stick, Ki could perform virtually all of the awesomely effective staff-fighting techniques; the shorter *jo* was even better than the *bo* staff for the close-in fighting in which he was about to engage.

The mustached man entered the lean-to, aiming a punch at Ki. The samurai used a *gyaku-nigiri,* or reverse hold, on his *jo,* placing his hands about shoulder-width apart, and centered along the length of the stick. He held it horizontally, his palms facing the ground, and as the smith's fist hurtled toward his chest, Ki slammed the hammer-handle against his knuckles, cracking his finger bones. The man howled, but before he could back away, Ki quickly thrust upward, the middle area of the hammer-handle smashing into the smith's Adam's apple. The mustached giant collapsed backward, falling with a huge splash into the water tub. He made no attempt to climb out of the tub, but merely wallowed in the churning water, his broken hand trailing limply over the side, while he clutched at his throat with his good hand.

"Here now!" the clean-shaven man roared in fury. He had snatched the long-handled iron tongs from out of the fire-pit. The tongs' pincer ends glowed cherry-red as he thrust them at Ki's face.

Ki used the hammer-handle to deflect the thrust, and then, holding the stick by its end, began to twirl it in a blurringly fast figure-eight pattern. The confused smith let the tongs sag toward the ground as he backed away from the whirling wood. Ki saw his opening and danced in. He rapped the stick against the side of the smith's knee. The man yelped, dropping the tongs as he tried to lumber away. Ki stepped into a *shiko-dachi* stance, his knees bent deeply, his torso erect as he stood as if he were straddling a very wide horse. He thrust the stick into the smith's lower belly, doubling the man over. Then he twirled the stick like a baton, bringing it around behind him and then up over his head in a powerful arc that finished with the business end of the hammer-handle whipping against the back of the man's skull.

The smith nose-dived to the ground, and stayed there, unconscious. His friend, meanwhile, was still lolling in the water, looking very blue as his breath rattled harshly through his swelling throat.

"Very impressive."

Ki spun around, his hammer-handle at the ready; he sighed, straightening up. There were outlaws coming around both corners of the stables. He was already covered by a half-dozen guns.

"We've been watching you," the outlaw who'd just spoken continued. "Very flashy." He gestured with his Colt. "But unless you think you can knock bullets out of the air with that ax handle, or whatever it is, you'd best let it fall to the ground."

Ki dropped the stick and put up his hands. "I want to see Will Sayre," he said.

"Shut up!" the outlaw snapped. "Start walking. Toward the house. And take it real slow, mister. You even *sneeze* and I'll shoot. I don't want to end up like these two," he finished, eyeing the stricken blacksmiths.

Ki was herded at gunpoint through the outlaw town, toward Will Sayre's house. The samurai thought he caught a glimpse of Dorsey at one of the second-floor windows, but he was uncertain; it might have been a glint of sunshine against a windowpane that he'd taken for her ash-blonde tresses.

"Inside!" the outlaw behind Ki ordered. "The door ain't locked!"

Ki pushed open the thick oak door and passed through

a dimly lit vestibule, past a staircase that led up to the second floor, and into the stone structure's main room. A slate fireplace dominated the opposite end wall, while a series of windows stretching the length of both sides of the house looked out on the bottleneck entrance of the canyon on one side, and the outlaw town of the canyon's interior on the other. The windows all had heavy wooden shutters with gun-slits carved into them. When the shutters were closed, this house would become an almost impenetrable fortress, Ki realized. A posse riding through the narrow canyon entranceway could be easily cut down by the withering gunfire that would pour from those making a stand in this room, and likely the chamber above it.

The rest of the room consisted of unadorned, whitewashed walls and a few sticks of rudely knocked-together furniture. Ki's bow and quiver, along with his vest, were heaped on a bureau near the fireplace. A door next to the vestibule doorway he'd come through led to a kitchen. In the center of the room stood a large oval table around which Rube Silva and three other men were seated, quietly talking as they pondered some papers spread before them.

Silva looked up at Ki's entrance. His battered, scarred face registered momentary surprise before his lips curled in a smile.

"Well, what do you know about this?" he chuckled. "Where'd you find him?" he asked the outlaw who'd brought Ki in.

"Over by the stables, making dog meat out of Lem and Jeff," the outlaw replied.

Silva stood up from the table, drawing his gun from a cross-draw rig as he did so. "You other boys cover him as well," he told the three who were still seated. "This one's faster than spit on a stovetop. You!" he addressed the outlaw behind Ki. "Find Bill Tarn. Don't tell him nothing but that I want to see him right away."

"Sure, Rube," the outlaw replied, and took his leave.

"Where is Will Sayre?" Ki asked.

"Out on a job," Silva replied.

"Where is Dorsey?"

"Upstairs." Silva shook his head in amazement. "You're really something, Ki. You manage to get away from Tarn, and what do you do next? Barge in here like you own the place!"

"I want to see Dorsey," Ki said.

"Well, you don't get to. I told you that *I* aim to marry that girl!"

"What does Will Sayre have to say about that?" Ki demanded.

Before Silva could reply, Bill Tarn entered the room. "What's up, Rube? I was on my way to breakfast—" The outlaw stopped in mid-sentence as he gawked at Ki.

"You told me that you'd killed him," Silva drawled, the cold glint in his eyes belying his casual tone.

"But I did! I mean, I left him snakebit! He was poisoned, I swear it!" He turned to Ki. "You were dying!" he insisted.

Ki smiled. "I got better."

"He tricked me, Rube!" Bill Tarn exclaimed.

"I *know* that." Silva smiled thinly. "I *know* that you're stupid, Bill, but what I didn't know was that you were a liar as well."

Tarn shook his head. "I ain't a liar. I ain't, Rube!"

"Sure you are, Bill!" Silva said, almost cheerfully. "First you tell me that you shot him clean, just like I told you to. But that was a lie. Now you're telling me that you left him snakebit, but here he is, standing healthy right before us! So that's two lies you told me."

Bill Tarn laughed uneasily. "Aw, hell, Rube. It's all worked out all right." He glanced at the men at the table. "Ain't that so, fellows? Ain't it worked out all right?" None of the men answered him.

"We can't have liars around here, Bill," Rube Silva declared.

"Come on, Rube . . ." Bill Tarn began to back away, his frightened eyes riveted on Silva's gun, just now trained at Ki.

"There's no place here for liars."

"No, don't!" Tarn screamed as Silva's gun swerved toward him. He didn't even try to go for his own holstered weapon, but just held out his hands beseechingly as Silva shot him in the stomach. Tarn's boots skittered on the room's hardwood floor as he sank to his knees, his face ashen, the blood welling out from between his interlaced fingers as he clutched at his belly.

"No, Rube . . . please . . ." Tarn whispered as Silva took a step forward, pressed the muzzle of his gun against Tarn's forehead, and pulled the trigger.

The three men at the table all had their guns loosely trained on Ki, but their eyes were riveted to the grisly execution. Ki took advantage of their distraction and made a break for a window, curling into a tight ball and somersaulting through the glass, sending shards flying. Shots chased after him, chewing holes in the windowframe.

"Get him!" Rube Silva screamed.

Ki hit the ground running. The canyon entrance beckoned, but to reach it he would have to expose his back to Silva and the others in the house. Instead, he ran around the side of the stone structure and, for lack of any other option, back into the center of the outlaw town. He managed to duck around the side of a bunkhouse just as a crowd of men streamed out of it and toward the stone house, perhaps to see what all the shooting was about. He began a mad sprint for the relative safety of the rocks and the cliffs beyond, but somebody spotted him, shouting out, "There he is!"

He began zigzagging as bullets kicked up dirt at his heels. The rocks were now out of the question; at any moment someone with a rifle would pick him off. He had to find cover.

He swerved behind a supply shack, wondering what to do next. He needed a place to hide until nightfall . . .

But where, in this rapidly shrinking outlaw town, could a man remain undiscovered?

Ki crabbed sideways as an outlaw came around the shack's corner, firing rapidly from the hip. "Over here!" the man yelled, putting several more bullet holes in the shack's clapboard siding as Ki ran off.

He headed for the mess hall, thinking to find himself a kitchen knife to use as a weapon, but several men cut him off. He swung around the hall's far side, running for the high fence enclosing the windowless bordello's backyard. A bullet sent splinters flying, stinging his cheek as he hauled himself up and over the fence and dropped down into the yard. He was halfway across the enclosure when the back door of the bordello opened. A brunette wearing a sky-blue lace-and-satin dressing gown waved to him.

"Come on in!" she whispered.

Ki paused. "Me?" he asked uncertainly.

Another brunette, two blondes, and a redhead popped into view behind the woman in the sky-blue gown. "Of course, you!" the brunette scolded while the other women started giggling. "Unless you'd rather take your chances with the boys!"

Ki went in. The back door led into a small kitchen. "This way," the brunette in sky-blue said, as the four other females, decked out in gowns of varying pastel shades, ushered him along. Ki found himself in a central hallway from which—understandably—bedrooms branched off. A small front parlor occupied the rest of the cottage.

"Quick, into *that* bedroom!" the brunette in sky-blue ordered Ki as someone began pounding on the front door.

"No fair, Sally!" the redhead in shocking pink scolded.

"I saw him first!" Sally argued. "Cindy, you and the others will get your chance—"

"Open up in there!" came a shout from outside.

"Let's discuss this later, shall we, ladies?" Ki nervously suggested.

"Into that bedroom!" Sally decreed, and Ki did as he was told. The other four women crowded into the small, windowless, lanternlit room along with him as Sally went to the front door.

Ki, his heart pounding, tried to hear what Sally was telling the men outside, but he couldn't because of the giggling around him. "Ladies, please!" he began, but one of the blondes pressed her fingers to his lips.

"You be quiet. *You're* going to be taking the orders around here!"

The others murmured their agreement as they closed in around the samurai.

"Is it true that you bested both Clem and Jeff in a fight?" the redhead named Cindy asked.

"If you mean the two blacksmiths, yes, I bested them," Ki replied thickly. The four women were all over him, fondling his buttocks, squeezing his groin, tickling the back of his neck. He found it difficult to tear his eyes away from their curves, so enticingly silhouetted beneath the silk and lace of their sensual dressing gowns. Their musky female scents in combination with their flowery perfume set him reeling. He gasped as one of the women behind him reached around his hips to unbutton his jeans. Cindy reached beneath his shirt to fondle his chest. He tried to stop them, but before he knew what was happening, his jeans were down around his knees, and his backside was being pinched as a girlish voice warned, "Be a good boy, or we'll tell . . ."

Cindy, meanwhile, had firm hold of his throbbing erection. The redhead eyed it hungrily, licking her lips and murmuring, "Oh, he's going to be *good,* all right. I can tell!"

As if to reward the samurai for his perceived goodness, the redhead let the bodice of her pink gown gape open to reveal her magnificent alabaster breasts, lightly dusted with a scattering of freckles . . .

Sally appeared in the room's doorway. "Oh, you!" she cried, stamping her slippered foot. "You started without me!"

"No, we didn't!" Cindy replied, but then shrugged. "Well, maybe we did, a little . . ."

"Are they gone?" Ki asked, as best he could; it was rather difficult for him to speak while Cindy was stroking him in such an endearing fashion.

"Well, yes and no," Sally replied, a merry glint in her

209

blue eyes. "I told the men that you weren't here—"

"Thank you!" Ki sighed in relief.

"But I also asked them to put guards at both the front and back doors, to protect us poor girls from the likes of you!"

"Now we've got you!" Cindy taunted gleefully.

"Why did you do that, Sally?" Ki demanded, and then moaned, despite himself, as one of the blondes tongued his ear.

"Because we don't want you to be leaving us," Sally explained. "Three months ago we five were on our way by train from San Francisco to Denver. We'd heard that there was a business opportunity for us in the Larimer district. A madam was selling her house. Anyway, Will Sayre's men stole *us* along with the mail, and, truth to tell, we weren't positively *against* coming along. If you've seen one red-light district, you've seen them all, and just us five controlling the lovemaking monopoly among all these men promised to be very lucrative." Sally smiled. "*And* very pleasurable, as well. After all, we'd heard the most *amazing* stories about the Ladykiller Gang . . ."

"Yeah," Cindy moped, her green eyes showing disappointment, "but stories were all that they turned out to be!"

"They do not pay you for your favors?" Ki asked.

"Oh sure, they pay us," Sally laughed. "They'd damned well better! We're the only females within two days' ride! If they don't pay us we stop being sweet, and if we stop being sweet, these outlaws are out of luck!"

"It's not the money," one of the blondes complained. "There's not one man in the entire gang that knows how to make a woman happy." The blonde was barely five feet tall, with a plump hourglass figure that strained the rose-colored silk of her gown in all the right places. She had beestung lips that looked delicious when she pouted.

"We've serviced these no-accounts for months," Sally told Ki. "Now we want you to service *us!* When we heard the men talking about how you whipped those blacksmiths,

210

we thought that maybe a real man had finally come to this godforsaken place."

"You're going to make love to every one of us!" Cindy declared. "If we're satisfied, we'll keep you safe from that nasty Rube Silva."

"And if we're not satisfied, we will complain!" the second brunette warned. She was a sloe-eyed, Mexican señorita, wrapped in an alluring combination of black silk and gray lace. "We will complain to Rube Silva!" she added with a tempestuous toss of her long, dark mane.

"Hold on," Ki interrupted.

"I *am* holding on!" Cindy chortled as she gave his marble-hard erection a playful tweak.

"I mean, why complain to Rube Silva?" Ki persisted, despite the distraction. "What about Will Sayre?"

"What about him?" Sally shrugged, a little more of her pink silk gown slipping past her shoulders in the process.

"Well, Sayre is the leader," Ki remarked. "And the gent who gave the Ladykillers their reputation between the sheets," he added as an afterthought.

"Maybe so, on both counts," Sally admitted. "But we've been here for three months and have never laid eyes on him."

Things were not adding up, Ki thought. Rube Silva had said that Sayre was on a job, but these women hadn't seen him in the three months that they'd been here. Granting that there were complicated robbery schemes that might take months to execute, why would Sayre arrange to have his daughter abducted at a time when he couldn't be present to greet and comfort her?

There was a lot to puzzle out, but Ki was realistic enough to know he was not going to figure any of it out right now— not when he was bare-assed and hard as a rock, with five beautiful, sex-starved women crawling all over him!

"Enough talk!" Sally decreed. "It's time for our handsome catch to start earning his keep. Everybody out!"

After the other four had left the room, Sally shut and

211

locked the door. Ki shrugged off his shirt and kicked off his jeans, then sat down on the edge of the bed. "I wonder if I could have something to eat before we start?"

"Oh, you'll get plenty to eat," Sally assured him. "And if you're good at it, I'll even cook you a meal."

She let the last of her robe slide to the floor. Underneath it she wore nothing but her high-heeled slippers. The soft lanternlight in the windowless room lent an amber luster to her pale skin. She had full, high breasts with pink rosettes that began to pucker as she played with her nipples. She stood slightly spread-legged, jutting out her sassy rump like a cat in heat.

"Come here, Sally," Ki called huskily. He held out his arms as she pranced over to him, performed a little hop and wiggle, and, with an expertise honed through long practice, firmly impaled herself upon his lap.

"Ahhh," Sally murmured, throwing back her head and shutting her eyes in bliss as she rode him, her pink bottom cheeks slapping rhythmically against the tops of Ki's thighs. "We'll keep you in this back bedroom—ohhh, yes, hold me that way!—And we'll each take turns..."

"Won't you ladies have business to attend to?" Ki asked. Meanwhile, Sally's perky nipples were bobbing just inches from his lips. Like the little boy locked overnight in the candy store, he just couldn't resist the opportunity to lick and suck to his heart's content.

"The men won't come to see us until tonight, if at all," Sally purred, grabbing Ki around the waist to give herself a better angle of leverage. "Rube will have them all too busy searching for you." She ground herself against him, arching her back as she began to climax. "Quick now! You started my fire and now you've got to put it out!"

Considering the constant state of sexual arousal that Ki had been suffering through since blundering into this man-hungry harem, he was more than willing to do as he was told. He fell back against the mattress, moaning in relief as Sally pumped him dry.

"Wheee! You're the first real man I've had in months!" she crowed, flopping down to rub her breasts against Ki's chest.

"I'm quite willing to repay all of you for keeping me hidden," Ki remarked modestly. "As long as you all understand that I have to have a certain amount of rest between—"

"You poor dear," Sally chuckled, tenderly stroking Ki's cheek. "You still don't get the picture, do you?"

There was a knock at the door. Ki heard Cindy impatiently demand, "Well? Is it my turn now?"

Chapter 17

Longarm and Jessie rode along a granite slope, following the trail that Teddy Rolling-Rock had put them on after last night's escape from the Ute renegades' camp. Ahead of them was the ghost town along the river that Teddy had mentioned.

"Sure is funny how anybody passing through this way has got to ride through that town," Longarm remarked.

"You think it's safe to ride through?" Jessie asked.

"We've got no choice if we want to find Sayre's hideout," Longarm replied.

"And Ki," Jessie agreed. "We've made up some of the time we've lost by riding through the night, but I don't think we can afford to try to find a way around the town. Anyway, there's hundreds of places along the trail where Sayre could have had us ambushed if he'd wanted; why would he pick that ghost town?"

"It's not an ambush that I'm worried about," Longarm muttered.

"What, then, Custis?"

Longarm smiled at her. "You'd make fun of me if I told you. Let's eat this apple one bite at a time. We'll ride through the town, see what we can see, and then double back and watch what goes on."

"What goes on?" Jessie asked, puzzled. "You think there's somebody living in that place?"

"Bet you a kiss there is," Longarm replied. "Come on!"

They rode hard through a stand of aspen, only slowing once they'd entered the town proper. There was just one

215

dusty street, with the river on one side, and the gutted remains of a few rickety buildings on the other.

"I'd say I've won our bet," Jessie began as they approached the end of the street. They were passing the town's ruined saloon. A weather-warped, sun-faded sign reading LIL'S hung lopsidedly over the broken batwing doors. The sign creaked endlessly as it swayed in the wind coming off the river.

"Looks like *I* win!" Longarm pointed as a rag-garbed, cowled figure darted like a rodent across their path.

"Stop, we won't hurt you!" Jessie called to the scurrying form, which hurried to the sanctuary of the busted-up saloon before pausing to scrutinize them. As it did, its hood fell away.

"Why, it's an old woman!" Longarm exclaimed, surprised.

Old isn't the half of it, Jessie thought. The crone looked ancient, with wispy white hair, and leathery skin. The worst of it was the drool running out of her slack-jawed, toothless mouth. It hung glistening from the hairs sprouting on her chin.

"I'd call her a witch, Jessie," Longarm said quietly.

"Custis! How cruel of you!" Jessie scolded.

The hag, meanwhile, her rheumy eyes upon them, let loose a high-pitched, cackling laugh that set goosebumps rising on Longarm's skin.

"Cruel but accurate," Jessie hedged thoughtfully, shivering as the old woman's coyote-like laughter reverberated throughout the ghost town.

The old crone backed into the saloon, vanishing like a wraith into the cobwebs and shadows of the derelict structure. The sound of her laughter faded until it was hard to tell when the old woman's cackling left off and the endless creaking of the saloon's sign began...

"Do you think we should go after her?" Jessie asked.

"Why?"

"Well, she could starve," Jessie said uncertainly. "Of course, she hasn't yet..."

"You'd never find her unless she wanted you to," Longarm said. "Come on. I won the first bet, and now I'll make you another—that we haven't seen the last of that old witch."

Longarm refused to answer any of Jessie's questions until they'd crested a tree-lined rise about a quarter-mile beyond the ghost town. "We'll stop here for a few minutes, Jessie. Follow me," he said, dismounting and walking back through the trees until they had a clear view of the town. "Keep your eye on the second story of the saloon," Longarm instructed, pointing to the distant building that seemed to waver in the midday heat.

"Well, I don't see anything," Jessie complained after a few minutes.

"Don't be so impatient," Longarm murmured, keeping his eyes trained on the saloon.

Jessie glanced up at the sun shining brightly in the cloudless sky. "Custis, it's after two o'clock. Maybe we'd better get a move on."

"There!" Longarm chuckled. "You see that?"

Jessie nodded as she watched the bursts of light glinting from the saloon's flat rooftop. "A heliograph?"

Longarm shrugged. "Or just a mirror. Either would do. I told you she was a witch! That old lady is signaling to somebody in those hills ahead of us. I've won the last two bets and now I'll make you a third—that it's Will Sayre's sentries receiving that message!"

"That's quite a ruse he's got going for himself," Jessie said. "It gives Sayre plenty of time to send out a welcoming party to greet uninvited guests." Her smile faded. "Do you suppose Ki ran into this sort of set-up?"

"It's likely, Jessie," Longarm muttered. "Rube Silva probably led him right smack into it!"

Jessie started to voice her fears, but she bit down on her lip, saying nothing to Longarm. *Poor Custis is going to have it hard enough when we find Ki,* she thought.

Longarm hadn't brought up the matter, but Jessie knew that he was still trying to come to terms with the fact that Ki had placed himself on the wrong side of the law when

217

he'd busted Rube Silva out of jail. The death of Inspector Broadwick had further complicated the issue; the inspector never would have run into the Ute renegades if he hadn't felt the need to pursue his escaped prisoner. Jessie wondered if Longarm considered Ki at least indirectly responsible for Broadwick's death . . .

Come what may, Jessie knew that she would stand by Ki if he was still alive, and she believed he was; the two of them were so close that she was convinced she would know it in her heart if her oldest and dearest friend had come to harm. She would stand by Ki, but she would not presume on her relationship with Longarm to ask him to bend the law on her friend's behalf.

Longarm and Ki were the two most important men in Jessie's life. She was determined to be woman enough to hang on to the both of them!

Jessie continued to watch the bursts of light coming from the saloon's rooftop. "She's certainly sending a lot of signals!"

"Well, she's got to make sure that Sayre's lookouts see them. She might keep it up for an hour." Longarm shrugged. "The sentries might not be watching. After all, months must go by with nobody blundering into Sayre's territory."

"Can you make out her message?" Jessie asked. "I know Morse code, and that's certainly not it."

"No, it's not Morse, or any code, as far as I can tell," Longarm replied. "I'd guess it'd be too much to ask that senile old biddy to memorize a code she might not get a chance to use more than three or four times a year. I reckon Sayre just drummed it into her head to signal—period— when anybody passes through the town."

"Custis, you were onto the ruse from the beginning!" Jessie marveled. "How did you know?"

"Well, I didn't know for certain," Longarm smiled. "But if a lawman lives long enough, he learns to trust to his instincts. Something just pure *smelled* funny about this set-up. I expected that we'd find somebody in that ghost town, but when it turned out to be an old woman, I knew that I was on the right track. There's no way somebody that old could survive in rough country like this unless somebody was grubstaking them."

Jessie nodded thoughtfully. "So some of Sayre's men will likely be coming down the trail to meet us?"

"Yep."

"But if we're right about that mirror-flashing being just a signal and not a message, they'll only know that *somebody* is coming. They won't know how many."

"Right again," Longarm said. "Are you thinking what I'm thinking?"

Jessie winked. "Let's set up an ambush of our own!"

Longarm was sunning himself on a flat-topped boulder at the foot of a craggy slope when the four riders came, two abreast, around a bend in the narrow trail. The surprised riders pulled their mounts up short, groping for their guns as Longarm grinned at them from his sun-baked resting place.

"I wouldn't slap leather," Longarm advised them, drawing his own .44 before they could argue the point.

The four riders exchanged uneasy glances. "Never mind him," the man in the lead said. "It's still four against one. There ain't nobody that can shoot *that* fast, if it comes down to shooting." The man stared at Longarm. "We were wondering where you were," he said with a smirk.

"Oh? You knew I was coming, did you?" Longarm asked.

"Sure we did!" the man boasted. "Nothing gets by us, mister. Did you know that you'd entered into Will Sayre's territory?"

"Fancy that," Longarm chuckled. "I thought they'd named this part of the country Utah."

"You're a smart one, eh?" the lead outlaw scowled. "We'll see how smart you are when Rube gets finished with you. What happened to your horse?"

"My horse!" Longarm snapped his fingers. "I knew I'd forgotten something."

"Yeah," the outlaw growled, spitting toward Longarm's

boots in disgust. "A smart one. All right, mister, get on your feet! You'll ride double with one of us, but first you'll hand over that gun."

"I don't think so," Longarm said pleasantly.

"You're coming with us!"

"Nope, actually you boys are staying here, as my prisoners."

"The hell with this," one of the other riders announced in bored tones. "Shoot the bastard and be done with it."

"I'll kill the first man who goes for his gun," Longarm snapped, all the pleasantness gone from his voice.

The lead outlaw nervously shifted in his saddle. The others were scanning the rocks. "Shit! Look!" one of the riders in the rear of the bunch swore. "To our left! A rifle's aimed at us!"

"Nobody move!" Jessie shouted down.

"Hell," the lead outlaw scoffed. "It's a woman. A damned woman! How good can she shoot?"

"A lot of dead men have wondered that," Longarm said.

"It's still four against two . . ." the lead rider said, licking his lips.

"But we've got our guns out and you all haven't," Longarm countered. "Don't be fools, boys. We've got you and you know it."

"You the law?" the lead outlaw asked.

"I am."

"Shit," the man muttered, shaking his head. "No matter what, we can't give up, mister. We're all wanted men. We'll take our chances on that little filly up there being all bark and no bite."

"Sorry to hear that," Longarm said softly.

There were a few seconds of silence then, when nothing could be heard but the creak of saddle-leather, the faraway cawing of a crow, and the harsh, shallow breathing of men who knew that the next short space of time might well be their last on earth.

"You might give us a chance," the lead outlaw suggested.

"No sense in us asking you to holster that .44 of yours, just to even odds, seeing as how your girlfriend up there has a Winchester trained on us?"

"Nope, no sense in you asking that, at all," Longarm said. "Now why don't you boys either shit or get off the pot! I'm getting sunburned, sitting here waiting on you."

The lead outlaw nodded, then smiled. "We tried our best to bluff you, mister, but I guess it didn't work." He twisted around, resting his right hand on his saddle's cantle. "The hell with it, boys, we'll give up—" he began, and then his right hand flew the short distance to the Colt riding high on his right hip!

"Nobody move!" Jessie shouted down to the four outlaws on the trail. They were about one hundred feet below her. She had her Winchester steadied on the nearest man in the rear of the bunch; Longarm had been adamant on that particular point.

"They can't come up this narrow trail more than two abreast," he'd said. "However many there are, you concentrate on the ones to the rear, and leave the ones up front to me, I don't want us both aiming at the same man while some other jasper gets a clear shot at me."

She kept her target aligned in her rifle's front and rear sights, trying like hell not to see the man's face. The rider kept sneaking frightened glances at her up the slope, kept glancing apprehensively up into the single, black, .44-caliber eye of her Winchester. He knew it was capable of spewing out his death at any second...

Never focus on the target, focus on your gunsights, Jessie reminded herself. It was sound advice for target-shooting, especially when your target was not composed of paper, but of flesh and blood...

She shifted her elbows on the rock she was crouched behind, ignoring the gnat buzzing her ear, and the rivulet of perspiration running from beneath her Stetson's sweatband, down the line of her jaw, to bead upon the varnished

221

wooden stock of her rifle. She held her breath throughout the tense exchange between Longarm and the lead outlaw, smiling faintly at the outlaw's gall in suggesting that Longarm holster his Colt. She sighed in relief when it looked as though the four badmen were going to surrender, after all—

But then the lead outlaw drew his gun, and shot at Longarm! Jessie heard the whine of the bullet as it ricocheted off the granite slab, and out of the corner of her eye she saw Longarm roll off the rock, his Colt firing fast, knocking the front two outlaws off their horses as if they were tin cans lined up on a fence.

And that outlaw she was sighting down upon was staring up at her again. She looked down along the blued barrel of her rifle, into the man's wild eyes, and found that she could not shoot—

But then the outlaw's revolver appeared in his hand, to begin its relentless rise towards her position—

Jessie squeezed the Winchester's trigger, felt its stock thud against her shoulder, and through the blue smoke puffing out of the Winchester's barrel, she saw the man's neck spurt blood an instant before he fell off his horse.

The fourth and last rider's mount reared in panic as the outlaw squeezed off shots at Jessie's position. She saw the flame winking out of the muzzle of his gun as one of his rounds struck close, sending granite chips flying to sting the back of her hand. She levered a cartridge into the Winchester's chamber and shot the man in the chest. He fell, but one of his boots remained wedged in its stirrup. His crazed horse trotted forward a few yards, dragging its rider's limp body along the rock-strewn trail, before Longarm managed to grab its reins, bringing it to a grudging halt.

Longarm climbed the rock slope to meet Jessie where they'd left their horses. He found her sitting on the ground with her back against the trunk of an aspen, her head slumped, her Winchester across her knees.

"What's the matter?" he asked, alarmed. "You weren't hit, were you?"

222

Jessie looked up at him and shook her head. Longarm saw that there were tears in her eyes.

"It was awful!" she blurted. "It was like ... oh, I don't know ... *like murder*. I've killed men before. I don't like to use a gun, but I'm not afraid to use one. Do you understand the difference?"

"I do," Longarm said quietly. "I understand very well."

"This business of sitting up in the rocks with a Winchester wasn't at all like that. It felt coldblooded!"

"Setting up an ambush is dirty business, no matter what side of the law you're on," Longarm agreed.

"Oh, I know that," Jessie said, her voice small.

"And we gave those men every opportunity to surrender. They fired the first shot," Longarm added.

"I know *that*, too ..."

"And you've got to look on the bright side, Jessie. We learned something just now. It's a good bet that Ki is still alive!"

Jessie started. "Custis, do you really think so? I mean, *I* believe he's alive, but I didn't say anything, because I was afraid you'd make fun of my 'woman's intuition.'"

"Here now, young lady," Longarm said mock-sternly. "It was intuition that warned me to watch for that old witch's signal back at the ghost town, right?"

"Right!" Jessie smiled shyly. "Why do you believe Ki is alive?"

"Well, those four didn't want to kill us as much as they wanted to take us prisoner, so—"

"So, if that's the Ladykillers' method, it's logical to assume that Ki was treated the same way!" Jessie interrupted excitedly.

"We can't be certain of it, Jessie," Longarm warned her, "but it's a reason to have hope."

"Hope," Jessie echoed, pursing her lips thoughtfully. "It's sure better to think about Ki being alive and well, than to think about that ambush we just pulled. Custis? What we just did, is that what war is like?"

Longarm thought back through the years to that misty

dawn at a place called Shiloh, when he was just a boy in a uniform, watching another boy in a different-colored uniform loom large in the sights of his rifle...

Jessie must have seen the answer to her question in his face. She nodded mournfully, saying, "Then I understand why it's men who fight the wars. We women never could!"

"I don't reckon that to be women's failing, as much as it's their strength," Longarm replied.

Jessie slowly got to her feet, setting down her Winchester. Her green eyes were as round as saucers, transfixing him. "We can't head into Will Sayre's outlaw town until dark, right?"

"Right."

She unbuckled her gunbelt, letting it fall to the ground, and began to undo the buttons of her blouse. "I don't want to think about killing anymore, Longarm. Make me not think about it."

Longarm was already moving to their horses, unhitching and hauling off their saddles, to get at the blankets underneath. He spread them beneath the aspen tree, thinking that Jessie had been right about the need to wait until dark.

Besides, he mused, *it'll do the horses some good to have the rest, just as it'll do their riders some good to have the loving...*

Jessie was just stepping out of her jeans. She set them down by the rest of her things and turned to face Longarm.

A soft breeze whipped the tendrils of her red-gold hair against her upturned face as she stood there before him, as vulnerable in her nudity as she was lovely. Longarm moved to embrace her, feeling himself harden in response to the silken feel of her in his arms. Her soft lips fluttered against his cheek like a butterfly's wings as his palms traced the fluid, sculpted lines of her back, and then the swelling rise of her round, taut bottom. Her buttocks twitched as his callused hands lightly cupped them.

He held her close, even a bit roughly, sensing that roughness was what she just now craved. Her eyes were closed, and she was emitting an unintelligible, birdlike cooing from

224

deep inside as she gently undulated against him. Then, abruptly, she pressed hard, flattening her breasts and making her nipples swell as she rubbed them against the rough tweed of his frock coat. She clamped her long, tawny, sculpted legs around his thigh and began to rub herself against his hip. She lifted up on tiptoes. Her musky scent swirled like smoke around him as she sawed the fiery fur between her legs against the front of his gunbelt.

Longarm looked down. There, glistening on the brass of his belt buckle, were the first sweet drops of her nectar...

He swept her up in his arms and carried her over to set her down beneath the tree. He quickly stripped off his own clothes, setting his Colt down beside her as he joined her on the blankets.

"Please, please, make me forget..." Jessie implored him, spreading her thighs, drawing him toward the golden, downy softness at her very center. "Oh, fill me, Longarm!"

Longarm did, knowing that what they both wanted now was not long, languid lovemaking, but fast, fierce tumbling in an animallike embrace.

"Yes, like that!" Jessie urged him breathlessly. "Harder! Harder!" she growled through clenched teeth as Longarm bucked and plunged within her, not letting up, not even when they'd rolled off the blankets and into the dust, rutting like wild things come together for a brief mating season. Jessie, kicking and crying, bawled her way through a fluid cascade of orgasms, her strong legs locking him in place as he came. His own climax was almost painful in its intensity, and when he threw back his head and roared, Jessie roared with him. In that instant, both thought that they'd experienced the other's sensations...

Both wondered how that could be, and both knew that they'd experienced something very rare. Perhaps this was how lovemaking had been between Adam and Eve, before she'd found that apple...

"Thank you, Custis," Jessie mumbled sleepily a few minutes later. They were back on their blankets, beneath the aspen tree. Jessie was nestled in his arms. "So much better

225

to make love than to fight," she murmured, and drifted off into sleep.

Longarm gently extricated himself from underneath her slumbering form. He smoked a cheroot down to its stub, content merely to watch her. Then, sighing in resignation, he silently dressed.

Jessie is right, he thought as he buckled on his Colt. *Lovemaking is finer than fighting* . . .

But fighting was what he did best. He was a lawman. It was time to get back on the job.

Chapter 18

Dusk was coming on. The slate-colored Utah sky was as dark as the finish on Jessie's Colt when she awoke. "Custis?" she called, yawning and stretching.

"Right here," he replied. He was seated cross-legged on the ground, smoking a cheroot and cleaning her Winchester and his Colt—by touch rather than by sight, Jessie guessed. The tip of his cheroot glowed red as he puffed on it in the twilight.

She sat up, running her fingers through her tangled mass of curls. "I must have been asleep for hours."

"You surely were."

"That's what happens when a woman's been well loved," she said. "I don't suppose you'd like to come on over here and see if you can put me to sleep till morning?"

"I don't suppose you'd like me to put you across my knee?"

"No, I wouldn't!" she laughed gaily, jumping to her feet, setting her pert breasts jiggling prettily. "This bottom has got too much sitting in the saddle to do to have something like *that* happen to it! And if spanking it is all you've got in mind, it had best get some clothes on, before it freezes to death!" She sighed. "I sure could do with a wash to freshen up."

"Now that's a wish I can grant," Longarm said. "Take a couple of those canteens around the other side of that tree, and you can do your freshening up in private."

"Can we really spare our water?" Jessie asked doubtfully.

"It ain't *our* water. Those canteens belonged to our four dead friends down below."

Jessie hesitated.

"Lady, you've got to let go of your sorrow over what happened!"

"Yes sir," Jessie replied meakly. "Toss me my saddle-bags?"

He did. She gathered them up, along with the canteens and her clothes, and vanished behind the tree. A few minutes later she returned, striding over to where he was seated. She looked fresh as a daisy, and twice as sweet. Even her long hair was freshly combed.

"I'm starving!" she exclaimed as she buckled on her Colt. "I suppose dried beef and biscuits will have to do, since we must be too close to Sayre's campsite to make a fire?"

"That's right," Longarm said as Jessie sat down and began to eat. "I did some exploring while you were asleep. The entrance to Sayre's canyon hideout is just a couple of miles down the trail. But it's no camp, it's a bona fide town!"

"And you ran into no other guards?" Jessie asked.

"Not a one. Either Will Sayre has gotten cocky in his old age, or else he's gotten senile."

"Maybe he's away," she offered as she munched at a biscuit.

"Huh?" Longarm cocked his head. "Now why would you think that?"

"Because I listened this afternoon while you were sassing those four riders. They said that you wouldn't act so smart when Rube got finished with you. They didn't say 'Will,' they said 'Rube.' I'm sure of it."

Longarm nodded. "You're right. Rube was the name they used." He grinned. "We're in luck! Will Sayre would never have been so sloppy, but thanks to Rube Silva, we're going to be able to waltz right in!"

"Waltzing in is one thing," Jessie said, "Waltzing *out* is something else! We're going to need more than luck. We're going to need a plan!"

"I've got one," Longarm said. "We'll take our own two horses and two of those outlaws' mounts, and hitch them up just outside the canyon entrance. They'll serve as our getaway horses. They'll be nice and fresh, which will be damned necessary, because when we come out of that canyon we're going to have to ride like hell!"

"A horse for each of us, and the other two for Ki and Dorsey." Jessie nodded. "So much for getting away, but how are we going to get in undetected?"

"I told you that I did some exploring. Well, I found a way up to a summit overlooking Sayre's town. The trouble is it'd make a mountain goat think twice, especially at night. If you were any less of an expert rider, I wouldn't let you try it, Jessie." He shrugged. "But I think it's manageable, if you're game to try."

"Of course I am."

"Good girl! We'll use the remaining pair of outlaws' mounts, and once we're up on the summit, we'll unsaddle them and turn them loose. I reckon they'll manage all right. We'll have to climb down a fairly steep rock face."

"In plain view?" Jessie worried.

"It'll be dark, remember? I'm not worried about being seen, I'm worried about you taking a fall."

She patted his knee. "Then you've got no worries at all. Ki taught me how to rock-climb years ago."

"All right!" Longarm commended her. "We'll leave most of our gear, including our rifles, with our own horses. Once we're in there, any shooting we're likely to do will be close-up work."

"Well, I now know how we're likely going in, and I know how we're supposed to get out! What I don't know is what we intend to do while we're there. And don't you *dare* tell me to eat the apple one bite at a time!"

"I wouldn't dream of it," Longarm laughed. "What we're going to do is create a diversion, and search out Ki and Dorsey Sayre in the confusion."

"What sort of diversion?" Jessie asked.

"Well, I've been thinking about how helpful that fire was to our escape back at the Utes' camp. The big old house guarding the canyon's entrance is built of stone, but the surrounding buildings are wooden. They should burn easily enough."

"I take it you're not going to try to arrest Rube Silva?"

He shook his head. "Nor Will Sayre, if he should be there. I figure either one or both of them will come right along on our heels to get Dorsey back. There will be plenty of opportunity to arrest them back at Nettle Grove. Assuming that we make it back!"

"And what about Ki?" Jessie blurted. "Damn..." She blushed. "I wasn't going to ask."

"But you did," Longarm replied evenly. "So I'll answer you. I intend to arrest him for participating in Rube Silva's jailbreak. A judge can sort everything out later." He paused. "Jessie? Do you understand that I've got to enforce the law impartially, no matter what?"

She nodded sincerely. "Of course, Custis. I wouldn't expect anything less of you."

"When we get back to Nettle Grove, I'll testify on Ki's behalf, of course," he muttered. "I mean, about how he wanted to rescue Dorsey and all. Ki's a friend of mine. I surely don't want him to go to jail."

Jessie moved close to put her arms around him. "Longarm?" she murmured.

"Yep?"

Jessie gazed at him in adoration. "Later will sort itself out eventually. We'll eat this apple one bite at a time..."

It was ten at night before Jessie and Longarm reached the canyon floor of the outlaw town. Their night ride up to the summit and the treacherous climb down the canyon's interior rock face had been long and arduous. Now, grateful to be back on solid, level ground at long last, they staggered to the boulders footing the cliff, and collapsed among the rocks in exhaustion.

Some fifty yards away, the outlaw town's outer ring of supply shacks was dark. It was only amid the town's central cluster of buildings, including the big stone house, that lanterns burned and windows were lit.

"It looks to be a real party," Jessie said, peering over the boulders at the town's boisterous activity. "The place is lit up like a Christmas tree," she added, confident that the musical crash of breaking glass and the whoops of drunken men would mask her quiet voice.

"Not much for those fellows to do between jobs but get drunk," Longarm puffed. He scowled. "How come you're not out of breath?"

"I don't smoke those nasty cheroots," she said sweetly. "You going to live?"

"Yes, thanks to you," he replied. "I thought I was a goner for sure when I lost my hold on the rock face about halfway down. Thanks for being so quick to grab my wrist."

"What are friends for?"

"You say that Ki taught you to climb like that?"

Jessie nodded. "The basic principle is to move so fast that you don't have time to fall," she chuckled.

"Well, whatever it is, it works," Longarm said. "And speaking of Ki," he went on, getting to his feet and slapping the dust from his clothing, "it's time to find him—and Dorsey. The sooner we're out of this nest of scorpions, the better I'll feel."

"Amen to that," Jessie said. "Where do we start the fire?"

"Stable seems the likely place," Longarm mused. "There's plenty of hay to burn, and these outlaws can't very well chase us until they round up their horses."

"And even when they do, their saddles and bridles will be all burnt up!" Jessie said. "Let's do it!"

They moved out, staying low, angling toward the stables. Longarm abruptly motioned Jessie to hang back, and then to crouch down behind some barrels about ten yards from the split-rail corral.

"What's wrong?" she whispered.

"Hard to tell, what with all the saddles and the like resting on the corral's top rails, but thought I saw movement. Yes! There!" Longarm hissed, pointing. "Leaning against the railing to the left of the watering trough—two men!"

"I see them now, bless your sharp eyes," Jessie breathed.

"What do we do now?"

"We can't risk shooting."

"Wouldn't anyway!" Jessie said stubbornly. "I've had my fill of ambushing for the time being."

"We'd best forget about the stables," Longarm told her. "We'll find something unguarded to set on fire."

"Hey, did you hear something?" one of the men by the corral muttered, nudging his companion. "Hey? Is that you, Mike?" the outlaw shouted toward Jessie and Longarm.

"Shit," Longarm grumbled. "There's no choice now. You stay here," he ordered.

"It's two of them against one—" Jessie began to argue.

"Mike?" the outlaw called, punctuating his query with the metallic sound of a Winchester being cocked. "Answer me, you dumb shit, or I'm going to start shooting!"

"Stay here!" Longarm hissed, and then rose up from behind the barrels, careful to keep his hands in plain view as he casually ambled toward the two leaning against the corral fence.

The two guards seemed to relax as they stared at Longarm's approaching shadowy form. "What the hell you doing here?" the man with the Winchester demanded, letting the barrel of his rifle dip down. "I might have shot you for that Chinaman! I told you to keep watch around back."

"Don't look like Mike—" Longarm heard the other man say, but he was now just a few paces away from the pair of them. The man's fist wavered indecisively above the grips of his holstered revolver. "Can't see my own damned hand in front of my face in this dark—"

Longarm kept his eye on the downward-pointing rifle as he closed on the two guards. "It ain't Mike!" he said as he stomped his foot down upon the Winchester's barrel. He let his foot slide down its length until the edge of his boot sole caught the weapon's front flange sight, driving the muzzle into the earth and jerking the rifle from the startled outlaw's grasp. At the same time, his right fist rose in a powerful uppercut that clipped the man's jaw, knocking off his hat and slamming him hard against the corral fence.

The other outlaw managed to draw his gun, but Longarm jarred it out of his grip by bringing the edge of his left hand down sharply on the man's wrist. The outlaw tried to connect with a right, which Longarm blocked, landing a right cross of his own that flattened the man's nose and crumpled him to the ground. Longarm glanced at the first outlaw, who seemed out on his feet, propped up by the corral fence, and figured that was that—

"Duck!" Jessie shouted.

Longarm instinctively threw himself to the ground. He heard the shot, glimpsed the orange flash, and saw the bullet chew off a piece of the corral railing where he'd just been standing. He was rising up and drawing his .44 when Jessie beat him to the shot. She fired twice, her rounds staggering the gunman and driving him away from the corner of the stable.

"He's not finished yet!" Longarm warned Jessie as the wounded outlaw snapped a shot in her direction. Longarm fired once, knocking the man down.

"You okay?" Longarm asked as he rejoined Jessie, who was still standing behind the barrels.

"I'm fine," she replied, thumbing fresh cartridges into her Colt. *"That* must have been Mike!"

Longarm turned toward the sound of shouts and footsteps rushing toward them from the center of the outlaw town. "And here comes his friends!"

"What do we do now?" Jessie asked. "Setting a diversionary fire seems a little foolish, considering."

"The hell with the fire!" Longarm yelled, grabbing Jessie and swerving sideways as shots peppered the barrel.

"You've got to pay more attention!" Longarm reprimanded her. "People are trying to kill us, you know!"

"Who saved you from good old Mike?" she demanded.

"This is no time to argue. Come on!"

As they sprinted around the far side of the stable, the pair fired a few rounds over their shoulders to slow down the pursuing mob.

"Slow up! We can hide in here!" Longarm said, pointing

out what seemed to be a blacksmith's lean-to attached to the stable's rear wall.

They crouched down behind the smith's anvil, trusting to the night, the impenetrable blackness of the lean-to's cluttered interior—and luck—to camouflage them. As they waited for the mob of pursuing outlaws to pass them by, Jessie saw something dart out from around the wooden platform on which the bellows rested.

"Oh, Custis!" she squealed. "I hate rats!"

A shrill, yapping bark began to fill the lean-to.

"It's a dog!" Longarm muttered distastefully. "A nasty little nuisance of a dog, and it'll give us away!" His eyes fell on a good-sized wooden bucket. He grabbed it and lunged toward the mutt, neatly trapping it beneath the over-turned bucket. He looked around, saw what appeared to be the handleless head of a sledgehammer, and set it on top of the bucket to weight it down.

The dog shut up. Seconds later the first of the outlaws searching for them ran past the lean-to.

"You didn't hurt the poor little thing, I hope?" Jessie asked.

"Of course not. I just gave him something to think about." Longarm grinned to himself. He could just hear the mutt's tiny little claws futilely scratching at the inside of the stout wooden bucket.

"Just remember to let him loose when we leave here!" Jessie admonished.

"Don't worry about the dog. He's no worse off than we are."

"We can't outrun them indefinitely," Jessie agreed. "And we sure can't outshoot them all."

"Don't worry, the shooting will let up when they realize they can't keep spraying lead without running the risk of shooting each other. And I don't aim to keep running away from them!" he declared firmly. "Once the ruckus around the stable settles, you and me are going to head straight for that big stone house! That's got to be where they've got Dorsey stashed. Once we nab her, I'll wager that the entire

234

gang will receive orders to hold their fire!"

"I wish Ki were with us," Jessie fretted. "Then, once we had Dorsey, we could get out of here!"

Longarm cocked his head, listening. "All right, I think it's safe for us to move."

"Custis! You forgot about the dog!" Jessie exclaimed as they left the lean-to.

Cursing, Longarm hurried back to release the mutt. It skittered out from beneath the bucket and ran off soundlessly, its tail between its legs. "Always had a way with dogs," he chuckled to himself, and set off after Jessie.

They'd left the stable area and were running past a rather large, windowless cottage with a high-topped, fenced-in backyard. "Now what in tarnation would that be?" Longarm wondered, slowing his pace.

"Look out!" Jessie shouted as a figure detached itself from the shadows cast by the front of the cottage and leveled what looked to be a shotgun.

Longarm fired at the outlaw a split second before the man's shotgun cut loose. He missed, but the outlaw didn't. Longarm winced in pain as he felt the buckshot chew up his left leg, knocking him flat, almost before he'd had time to hear the thunder and see the lightning spewing forth from the scattergun's twin barrels.

"Custis!" Jessie screamed.

"Run away! Run!" Longarm whispered hoarsely, because whispering was all he felt fit enough to do. Just before blacking out, he saw Jessie standing over him.

His last thoughts were of how beautiful she looked, and how defiant, as she prepared to shoot it out with the man who'd dropped him...

Ki was in bed, desperately feigning sleep in a last-ditch attempt to dissuade Sally's amorous advances, when he heard the first shots. They sounded as if they were coming from the stable area.

He sat up and tried to get out of bed in order to gather up his clothes. Sally moved her head from his lap.

"Whereyougoing?" the tireless brunette asked as best she could, with her mouth full . . .

"Something is going on out there, and besides, it *must* be dark by now," Ki insisted. "It's impossible to know what's going on in the world when one is inside this window-less pleasure palace!"

Sally turned his turgid member loose and tried to push him back down against the pillows. "Just a little while longer, please, Ki? Besides, those guards are still at the front and back doors, and they're toting shotguns!"

Ki gave her what he hoped would be construed as a platonic kiss. "Since the outlaws are not shooting at me, they may well be shooting at friends of mine who have come to look for me. I must find out."

The samurai dressed quickly. "Are the other girls . . . entertaining . . . at the moment?"

Sally shook her head. "Rube put us off-limits until his men found you. That's why we all hate to see you go. You've been *wonderful,*" she sighed.

Ki allowed himself a smile. "Coming from you, that is quite a compliment. Sally, you and the others were initially brought here more or less against your will. Do you wish to leave? If so, I'll do my best to see that you are escorted out of here."

Sally sat up in bed. Her lush, bare breasts hung heavy just above the sheets gathered around her marvelous hips. "You're sweet to ask, but I can speak for the others when I say that we'll stick here. When this party breaks up—and I think that you're going to help break it up real soon—us girls will move on. We know how to take care of ourselves."

"Then this is goodbye, Sally. Say goodbye to the others for me, will you?" The samurai paused at the bedroom's doorway. "You and the others saved my life before—"

Sally, her eyes wet, gave a jaunty little wave. "And you saved ours . . ." She grinned. "See you next time you hit the wrong side of the tracks."

Ki entered the dimly lit corridor that stretched the length of the cottage, from the kitchen to the empty front parlor.

236

The other girls had all drunk themselves to sleep. It had been a long day for them as well as for himself, he thought with considerable pride.

He decided to go out the back way. The yard's high fence would shield him from view during his initial struggle with the guard, and until he could get a sense of what was going on in the outlaw town.

He hesitated in the cottage's kitchen, and briefly debated taking one of the kitchen knives as a weapon. He decided against it. Rube Silva, or some of his smarter minions, might spot him with it, fathom out where he'd gotten it—and in whose beds he'd been hiding all of these hours—and retaliate against the girls.

The cottage's lack of windows had been a blessing before. Now the lack was a curse; Ki had no way of knowing just where the guard was, without opening the door and giving himself away. If what Sally had told him was true— if the guards were armed with scatterguns—it compounded his danger. Ki's *te* training had made him fast, but a double-barreled shotgun was a great equalizer in the hands of an adversary. If the guard outside had anything approaching quick reactions, Ki would be in a lot of trouble.

He pressed his left palm against the kitchen door and turned the knob with his right, carefully opening it a fraction of an inch at a time, to minimize as much as possible the potential danger of a squeaky hinge. He peeked out.

Luck was with him; the guard was just a few feet away from the samurai, with his back to the door. The scattergun was pointing downward, cradled in the crook of the outlaw's elbow.

Ki edged through the partially open door and moved silently toward the unsuspecting guard. The samurai whipped the outside edge of his right hand against the outlaw's neck, grabbing the shotgun with his left as the guard folded to the ground.

So far, so good, he thought as he broke open the double-barreled weapon to check its load. As much as the samurai disliked firearms, he decided to hold on to this one, at least until he could find a weapon more to his liking.

He turned toward the fence as he heard running footsteps approaching.

"Now what in tarnation would that be?" a male voice wondered aloud, somewhere on the other side of the high fence.

Ki's eyes widened in surprise as he realized that the voice was Longarm's!

"Look out!" cried another voice, a woman's voice—Jessie's!

Then there came the report of a large-caliber pistol, followed within a split second by the deep bass roar of a shotgun.

"Custis!" Jessie screamed, just as Ki, the scattergun in his hand, bounded over the fence.

"Run away! Run!" Longarm whispered hoarsely. He must have blacked out, but for only a second or two, because when he next opened his eyes, Jessie was still standing over him, her Colt spitting brilliant orange fire and hot lead at the man who'd shot him. Longarm saw the outlaw's shotgun tilt up toward the night sky as Jessie's rounds struck home. The outlaw fell back, and then Jessie was kneeling beside him, gently examining his wounded leg.

"You've got to pay more attention," she said softly, winking at him. "People are trying to kill us, you know."

"Ouch! Be careful!" Longarm griped. "And don't nag a dying man..."

"You big baby! You're not dying. It's not bad at all," Jessie comforted him. "A few pellets merely grazed you. Some are still embedded, but once we get them picked out, you'll be as good as new."

Longarm tried to stand, but the pain of the buckshot under his skin was too much. His leg buckled beneath him. "You get out of here," he grimaced. He stared at Jessie. "I said git!"

"I'm not leaving you!" she countered. "We got into this together, and we'll get out of it the same way."

"Listen to me!" Longarm cut her off urgently as the sound of the outlaws' thudding footsteps grew in their ears. "I'm caught, no matter what. If you remain free, you can rescue me later."

"It's a bit late to be giving Miss Starbuck advice," Rube Silva said, sauntering towards them from out of the darkness. He had his gun trained on him, as did the four outlaws backing him up. Two of them were carrying crackling torches. The glaring, flickering torchlight lent a garish nightmare quality to the scene.

"All right, you've got us," Jessie acknowledged gloomily, raising her hands.

"I agree," Silva smiled. "And I haven't forgotten how you pistol-whipped and hogtied me, Miss Starbuck. No," he repeated, his smile fading, "I haven't forgotten *that* at all..."

More of Silva's men were approaching, but he waved them away. "We've got this under control!" he called. "The rest of you fan out! Her Japanese partner might still be around!"

"Hear that?" Jessie murmured to Longarm. "We're not done yet."

"I wouldn't count on that!" Silva turned back to Jessie. "We'll get Ki, just as we got the two of you."

"This man is wounded. He needs medical attention!" Jessie demanded.

Silva threw back his head and laughed. "Where do you think you are, Miss Starbuck? Still in Nettle Grove?" Silva's hatchet-thin face, with its flattened nose and white scar, took on a gargoyle's grotesque hideousness as he leered down at his captives. "Well, you're not in Nettle Grove! This is *my* town!"

"Not Will Sayre's?" Longarm asked loudly.

Silva sputtered for a reply, but settled on a hard glare.

"If looks could kill," Longarm taunted the enraged outlaw, "you wouldn't need that Colt you're waving around."

"Shut up! You just shut up!" Silva snarled.

"Oh, you talk big," Longarm said, "but if somebody took

239

that gun out of your hand, I reckon you'd pee right where you stand, just like a scared mouse!"

Silva cocked his revolver and aimed it at Jessie's kneeling form. "You two aren't going to need a doctor. You're going to need an undertaker."

Longarm reached across his belt buckle for his holstered Colt. Silva saw the movement and swung his own gun in Longarm's direction. Longarm was fast enough to clear leather, but in his supine position on the ground, he couldn't bring his .44 to bear on Silva before the man booted it out of his grip.

"All right, whoever you are," Silva said, stepping across Longarm to straddle him. "If you're so impatient, you can go first—"

"No!" Longarm heard Jessie cry. He stared up into the wide black tunnel that was the muzzle of Silva's revolver, and waited for his death to come rolling out of it. When he heard the earsplitting double *boom!* it took him an instant to realize that what he'd heard was not a revolver firing.

"It's Ki!" Jessie cried out joyously, as Silva's two torch-bearers went down screaming in a deadly shower of buckshot.

Jessie was on her feet and grabbing sideways in an instant, executing a lightning draw. The two outlaws trying to track her never stood a chance against her sharpshooting. She squeezed off four rapid-fire rounds—two apiece—that left her pair of opponents dead, their corpses bleeding in the dust.

The action took place in seconds. It had all happened so fast that Rube Silva—still straddling Longarm—seemed momentarily unsure who to try to shoot first—Longarm, Jessie, or Ki, whose pantherlike form was just now hurtling toward the outlaw from the backyard fence of the nearby cottage.

Longarm took advantage of the outlaw's confusion to jackknife straight up from the waist, his left hand deflecting Silva's gun while his right, curled into a fist, landed a walloping punch to the only area of Silva's body within easy reach—his crotch!

Silva's mouth opened wide in a soundless scream. He dropped his gun as he clutched at his agonized privates, then he began to sob as he sank to his knees across Longarm's lap.

"Sorry about your balls, old son," Longarm said. "I purely didn't know you had none."

Chapter 19

Smiling, Ki walked over to where Longarm was sitting on the ground, flanked by Jessie and a moaning, pale-faced Rube Silva.

"I'm so glad to see you!" Jessie beamed. "But where have you been all this time?"

Ki glanced back at the windowless cottage. "You could say that I've been getting the lay of the land." He nodded to Longarm. "It's good to see you, my friend."

"Same here, old son," Longarm replied. "Incidentally, you're under arrest."

"Of course, for the jailbreak." Ki nodded docilely.

"Right, but for now, you're deputized—"

"Excuse me," Ki interrupted earnestly, "but how can I be under arrest and also a deputy? That would make me my own prisoner!"

"It's a tough job," Longarm agreed, "but if any man can handle it, it's you. Now bring over that scattergun. I can use it as a cane of sorts to get around."

"I will carry you," Ki offered, handing over the shotgun.

"Nope." Longarm bit down on his lip against the pain as he managed to rise to his feet. He eased the weight on his injured left leg by leaning on the shotgun. "I'll make it all right, Ki. You keep hold of Rube here."

"A pleasure," Ki grinned. He grabbed hold of Silva by the nape of his neck, shaking him the way a mother cat does a kitten. "You won't escape from me a second time," he said, hauling the sullen outlaw to his feet.

Jessie fetched Longarm's Colt and handed it back to him.

"What's our next step?" she asked as she reloaded her own gun.

"We get Dorsey and make our way out of here," Longarm said.

"You're not going anywhere!" Silva spat. "You'll die here! All of you! This is my town!"

"He has a point," Ki remarked, pointing toward the stone house. A sprawling mob, many of them carrying torches, was approaching. They halted about thirty feet from where their leader was being held captive. The outlaws' weapons glittered in the torchlight.

"It seems as if I've got the numbers," Silva smirked. "Now then, you tell Ki to turn me loose, and you hand over your guns."

"You've forgotten something, Rube," Jessie smiled, nudging him in the ribs with her Colt. "We've got *you!*"

"Right!" Longarm chuckled. "Rube, you're going to be our ticket out of here."

"Hey, you over there!" one of the outlaws in the mob's frontline shouted. "Turn him loose, and surrender!"

"Do it quick!" somebody else in the mob yelled. "Or we start shooting!"

"Ki, haul Rube around in front of us," Longarm instructed. "Okay, Rube," he continued. "It's up to you now. If they start shooting, you'll be the first to go."

"What do you want me to do?" Silva stammered, glancing apprehensively at the drawn guns of his own men.

"Order them to throw down their guns and surrender!" Jessie said.

"No, please!" Silva begged. "They'll never go along with that! They're all wanted men! They'd as soon see me dead as risk their own skins for me!"

"I can understand that," Longarm said dryly. "All right, Rube. I reckon we can't ask the world on your account. Just order them to stand back. We're going to march right into that stone house." He turned to Jessie and Ki. "I figure we'll get Dorsey and leave the canyon, taking Silva along with us. With Sayre himself away, I don't reckon any of that mob will care enough about either Dorsey or Rube to come after us."

"Sounds good to me," Jessie agreed.

Longarm glanced inquiringly at Ki.

"As both a prisoner and a deputy, do I get one vote or two?" the samurai asked.

"Just come along!" Jessie scolded him affectionately. "Okay, Rube!" she jammed her revolver into his side. "Tell them to make way, or else!"

"L-listen to m-me!" Silva called hoarsely. "M-make way for us! We're going to the house!"

The mob stood its ground. "Rube?" one of the outlaws shouted. "You know that once they're in the house, they can hold us off?"

"Never mind that!" Silva screamed. "Get out of the way!"

There came a low rumbling from the outlaw mob. "Can't do that, Rube!" one of the men in the front shouted.

Jessie cocked her Colt. "I'd start convincing them, Rube."

"Goddamn," Longarm chuckled ruefully. "It looks as if they think even less of you than I suspicioned . . ."

"Listen, all of you!" the panicked outlaw shouted. "You know that Will Sayre put me in charge before he left! You're to do as I say! Move aside!"

The mob's growl once again filled the night. "All right, boys, stand aside," one of the lead outlaws grudgingly ordered. "Come on through, Rube!"

The mob parted, men stepping to either side, until a long, torch-lined gauntlet to the house had been formed.

Longarm and Jessie locked eyes. "Let's go!" Longarm said, taking the lead.

Jessie prodded Silva with her Colt. "Get moving. Any funny stuff, and a pistol-whipping and hog-tying will be the *least* of what you get!"

"And when Jessie is done with you, you will have to deal with me!" Ki added, keeping a firm hold on Silva's shirt collar.

They kept their eyes straight ahead as they passed along the narrow corridor the mob had formed. The outlaws on either side were so close they could hear the men's breathing in the tense silence, could feel the heat of the torches some of the outlaws held.

"Didn't Moses manage a feat something like this?" Jessie murmured to Longarm.

"He did, but he had it easy. As I recall, he had God on his side."

"God had better be on our side as well," Jessie replied, "because we sure as hell could do with some reinforcements!"

Ahead of them the stone house beckoned. It seemed to take an eternity to reach it, but at last they did. Inside the main room, a fire burned in the slate hearth, and a lantern glowed on the oval table in the room's center.

"Ki! Get those shutters closed!" Longarm ordered. "Otherwise we'll be sitting ducks for a sniper." He moved the lantern and painfully hoisted himself up on the table. "I've got Silva covered," he said, drawing his .44.

Jessie holstered her Colt. "I'll go upstairs and get Dorsey," she said.

"Can you handle it alone?" Longarm asked.

"Sure!" Jessie shrugged. "Why not? We're her rescuers, remember? I can't understand why she hasn't already come downstairs. She must be petrified at all the shooting, poor thing." Jessie scowled at Silva. "Unless this one tied her up. If you did, I'll take it out of your hide, mister!"

"She ain't tied up," Silva mumbled.

"Rube wouldn't do such a thing to his bride-to-be, I imagine," Ki said, as he finished closing and latching the last of the room's shutters.

"His bride-to-be?" Longarm asked, startled. He glanced questioningly at Silva, who was standing with eyes downcast in the room's center. "What's it all about, Rube?"

"None of your business..." Silva moped.

"Clearly the courtship has been a rocky one." Ki moved to where his weapons were still piled on the bureau near the fireplace. He shrugged on his vest, checking its pockets to assure himself that everything was in its place. "I will

246

sterilize one of my *shuriken* blades in the fire, and then I will tend to the buckshot in your leg, Longarm."

"I'm sure that Dorsey will put an end to this nonsense about her marrying Rube Silva," Jessie muttered, heading for the stairs.

"How many rooms upstairs?" she heard Longarm ask the outlaw.

"Just one, like this room," Silva replied.

Jessie felt her way through the dark vestibule, groping until her hand hit the banister. She made her way up the unlit staircase to the dark second-floor hallway.

"Dorsey?" she called. "Have they kept you in the dark up here?" she wondered out loud. Carefully she shuffled along, keeping her outstretched hands in front of her as she felt along the hallway's wall. *If the layout is like the one downstairs,* Jessie thought, *the archway into the room should be right about here.*

She found it, but the room beyond was an impenetrable wall of blackness. *Shutters must be closed,* Jessie thought. *This is crazy; I can't see a thing.*

She was about to return downstairs for a lantern or candle when the sound of quick, muffled breathing seized her attention. "Dorsey? Are you all right?"

She took several steps into the pitch-dark room. "Dorsey? Answer me if you can, honey. It's okay—"

The crisp metallic click of a revolver's hammer being drawn back gave Jessie scant warning, but it was all the warning she needed for her quick reflexes to come into play. She threw herself to the floor as the pistol shot reverberated within the closed room. The revolver's muzzle flash illuminated the scene for only a split second, but that was time enough for Jessie to see Dorsey—the girl's lips drawn back into a snarl of hatred—grasping her revolver in both hands. She was aiming down at Jessie, to try for a second shot!

i was crouched in front of the fireplace, holding his *shuken* blade to the flames in order to sterilize it, when the und of gunfire coming from upstairs filled the house.

"What the hell?" Longarm blurted.

The samurai whirled, bolting across the room, into the vestibule, and up the staircase.

Rube Silva took advantage of the momentary confusion to try a getaway. He made a mad dash for the vestibule's front door, and the freedom beyond.

"Halt!" Longarm commanded, bringing up his Colt. "Halt, or I'll shoot!"

He had a clear, easy shot at Silva's back, but he didn't fire. "Aw, shit . . ." he sighed as the outlaw careened around the corner of the main room's doorway, and out of the house.

Jessie rolled sideways. Dorsey's second shot plowed a furrow in the floorboards where she'd just been. "Dammit, it's Jessie!" she yelled, but the click of Dorsey's gun hammer being drawn back a third time convinced her that Jessie Starbuck was exactly who Dorsey wanted to kill!

Jessie clambered forward on all fours. Dorsey's third shot put a hole in the ceiling as Jessie tackled her knees, knocking her backward to the floor. Jessie scuttled up the struggling woman's body, her hand frantically reaching for Dorsey's gun. She found it, and locked her fingers around the revolver, holding it away from both of them as she tried to talk some sense into the seemingly possessed female.

"Don't you understand?" Jessie winced as Dorsey's left fist pounded against her ribs. "It's Jessie! I've come to rescue you!"

"No!" Dorsey cried in rage. "I don't want to be rescued I want to kill you!" She tried to angle the gun at Jessie for another shot. "Owww!" she yelped as Jessie bent back her fingers, loosening her hold on the gun prior to batting it out of reach.

"Oh, damn you!" Dorsey seethed in frustration as the pistol skated across the floor. "I want to kill you!" she shrieked.

"Not today," Jessie said tightly. Her left hand located and cupped Dorsey's cheek. Her right, curled into a fist connected with a short jab to the edge of Dorsey's jaw, just

248

beneath her ear. Dorsey groaned, stiffened, and then relaxed into unconsciousness as Jessie carefully lowered her head to the floor. She was rising to her feet when Ki burst into the room. The match in his hand flared to life as he thumbed it alight.

The room was empty of furniture, except for a narrow bed along one wall. Jessie knelt on the floor next to the unconscious Dorsey, and Dorsey's gun lay some distance away.

"Who shot at you?" Ki asked.

"Who do you think?" Jessie replied, nodding toward Dorsey. "Makes a person wonder why we're going to all this trouble," she added ruefully, then said with a sigh, "Come on, let's get her downstairs."

Longarm was still on the oval table, and all alone, when Jessie trudged into the main room with Ki following her, carrying Dorsey.

"What happened to Rube?" Jessie asked, looking around.

"He made a break for it, and with this bum leg, I couldn't hardly chase him," Longarm grumbled.

Ki sat Dorsey down in a straight-backed chair. "I think I'd best tie her hands behind her," the samurai said regretfully, pulling a length of cord from one of his vest pockets.

"I guess you'd better," Jessie agreed. "She took a bunch of shots at me upstairs," she explained to Longarm. "Said that she didn't want to be rescued."

"Fancy that," Longarm said thoughtfully. "This is one apple that's getting wormier by the minute..."

"Speaking of shooting, why didn't you shoot Silva when he ran?" Jessie asked.

"Hell," Longarm said, his tanned face reddening, "I'm no backshooter, not even when it's the back of a rat like old Rube."

"I figured as much," Jessie chuckled, eyeing him affectionately.

"You in there! Open up one of them shutters!" It was Rube Silva, hailing them from the side of the house facing the canyon's interior. "Open up, I say! We got to parley!"

"You might as well, Ki," Longarm shrugged. "Won't hurt us to hear what he's got to say."

Ki opened a shutter, then helped Longarm limp over to the open window. Silva and his torch-bearing outlaw army were about twenty yards away, strung out in front of one of the bunkhouses.

"Go on and parley!" Longarm yelled. "We're listening!"

"You can't get away!" Silva began. "We got both sides of the house surrounded, and even if you did manage to fight your way out of the canyon, you'd not get far on foot! We found the four horses you had stashed outside the entrance!"

"So far you've just jabbered what we *can't* do. How about telling us what we *can* do?"

"You can surrender!" Silva yelled.

"Try again!" Longarm laughed.

"Then send out Dorsey!" Silva yelled. "You give her up, and we'll let you go!"

"Is that your final offer?" Longarm asked.

"It is!"

"Then here's ours. You don't get Dorsey. What you get is your freedom if you ride out of here. My name's Custis Long, and I'm a deputy U.S. marshal! That means that you jaspers aren't just feuding with Jessie Starbuck—and she and Ki alone could kick your mangy asses all the way to the Rio Grande! You're feuding with Jessie Starbuck and the law!"

"Some of us have heard of you, Longarm!" one of the outlaws blurted. Rube Silva snarled, "Shut up!"

"Listen to me," Longarm addressed the bunch of outlaws at large. "Will Sayre ain't here, and when Sayre ain't around, you all ain't the Ladykillers, you're just a bunch of no-account wanted men! If I were you, I'd git! Saddle up your horses and ride out of here! We didn't just stumble into this canyon! We *knew* where it was!"

"You did?" Ki quickly asked Jessie, who shook her head.

"Teddy Rolling-Rock told us how to get here," she began, quickly filling Ki in on their adventures along the way, including the Ute attack, and Inspector Broadwick's heroic last stand.

"There's a posse on our heels," Longarm continued shouting. "You men know that as long as we control this house, there's no way you can defend your town against a posse! When the law arrives, you'll be trapped like rats in this box canyon!"

"He's bluffing!" Rube Silva screamed. "There's no way they would have come in alone if there was any posse! They found us purely by luck, and now their luck's plumb run dry!"

"I don't know, Rube," one of the outlaws spoke up. "Maybe we oughta cut and run."

"No! You can't!" Silva shouted, turning to confront the outlaw mob. "It'd mean the end of the Ladykillers! Is that what you all want? How long could you survive without Will Sayre's organization, his protection? We've got to kill those intruders! If they get away, the location of our hideout will no longer be a secret, and a posse *will* come! You've got to back me, for Will Sayre's sake. And when he returns, he'll pay you all a bonus share to reward your loyalty!"

"All right! We're with you, Rube!" one of the outlaws yelled, bringing shouts of approval from the others.

Silva whirled, triumphant, to confront Longarm. "There's your answer. The time for talking is over. And your chance to surrender has passed by as well! You, Ki, and that Starbuck bitch are dead meat, no matter what!"

"Look there," Ki whispered to Jessie from his position next to the open window. "I see a rifleman peering over the peak of the bunkhouse roof. He intends to shoot at Longarm."

The samurai quickly fetched his bow and quiver from the bureau and left the room, to slip out the front door.

"Where'd he go?" Longarm asked.

"You'll see," Jessie said. She stood on her toes to watch the goings-on over Longarm's shoulder.

"You've got this choice!" Silva ranted. "Let Dorsey loose, and we'll kill you quick and merciful-like!"

"This fellow is all heart," Jessie murmured.

"Make us come in and get you, and we'll kill you so slow you'll *beg* to be finished off!"

"Rube, you're starting to rile me," Longarm countered. "You know that we can hold out forever in here..." His voice trailed off as movement up on the bunkhouse roof caught his attention. "There looks to be a sniper up there," he warned Jessie, edging her away from the window.

"Don't worry about it."

From outside, near the house, they heard the soft twang of a bowstring, and then the serpentlike hiss of an arrow soaring through the night. The outlaw on the bunkhouse roof reared up, a dark, writhing silhouette, his agonized thrashing outlined against the lighter night sky. The men down below scattered as the would-be sniper's rifle clattered down the pitched roof and fell to earth. The outlaw toppled soon after, an arrow piercing one side of his neck and protruding out the other.

"Shit! Did the *Chinaman* do that?" one of the outlaws muttered.

"Like I said," Longarm yelled to the jittery mob, "we've got the means to hold out. You boys had better recruit a few hundred more men if you want to take us!"

"You've got until midnight to make your decision!" Silva roared.

Longarm closed and latched the shutter as Ki reentered the house. "Make sure that door is locked," he told the samurai. "Then tend to my leg. It looks as if we've got ourselves a siege!"

Chapter 20

Ki moved Longarm upstairs to doctor the deputy's leg, bringing along the kerosene lantern. Jessie meanwhile found some candles on the fireplace mantel. She lit one, and after checking on Dorsey, who was still unconscious, she went into the kitchen to see what their supply situation was like.

The kitchen was small and windowless. There was a woodburning stove and a soapstone sink, but no hand pump for water. There were, however, plenty of tinned goods stacked on the shelves of a narrow, shallow floor-to-ceiling cupboard built into the wall. Tinned fruit would make a monotonous diet while they were here, but at least they would not die of thirst.

She heard footsteps coming down the staircase and re-entered the main room in time to see Longarm and Ki peering out through the various gunslits in the closed shutters. Longarm was limping slightly, but except for his tattered, bloodstained trouser leg, he looked none the worse for wear.

"You okay?" she asked.

Longarm smiled at her. "Sure. Ki got those pellets out of my hide, and he had a little tin of some smelly gunk in his vest pocket."

"A salve with healing properties," the samurai corrected him. "Smelly gunk, indeed!"

Longarm winked at Jessie. "I just love to get his goat. Anyway, we tore up some of Sayre's bed linen to make a bandage. I'll be fine."

"Ohhhh," Dorsey moaned, coming around.

Morosely, Jessie eyed her childhood friend. "She'll be wanting her hands untied."

"We'll see how she behaves," Longarm said. "Jessie, did you find any guns or ammunition around?"

"I've searched high and low, and I haven't found a thing like that. It's funny, too," she added. "I mean, if this stone house was to be a stronghold, you'd think that the gang would have stockpiled some arms in here."

"Speaking of which, how are you fixed for cartridges?" Longarm asked her.

"I've got a full load of six in my Colt, and four extra, counting the two in my derringer."

"Damn," Longarm cursed. "I've got six in the cylinder, and just the two in my derringer."

"What about Dorsey's gun? It should be lying on the floor upstairs."

"I checked it while Ki was doctoring me," Longarm replied. "The three shots she took at you turned out to be the only three she had."

"Custis, we can't hold this place for long with just eighteen rounds," Jessie worried. "Even with Ki's arrows," she added, nodding in appreciation to the samurai.

"I know it." Longarm looked around in frustration. "Dammit! We're missing something. I just *know* we are!"

"Oh, my jaw," Dorsey moaned. "Somebody, please . . ." Her brown eyes fluttered open. "Oh! Where am I?" She struggled to rise from the chair, and found that she couldn't. "Who tied me?"

There was more despair than anger in Dorsey's voice at that instant, Jessie thought. "Custis, I'm cutting her loose. She can't do any further harm."

"All right, Jessie," Longarm agreed reluctantly. "You'd do what you had a mind to anyway, no matter what I said."

"Ki," Jessie called as she began to unwind the cord from Dorsey's wrists. "Would you go into the kitchen and bring her back something to wet her whistle?"

"Good idea," Longarm said wryly. "She's got a lot of explaining to do!"

254

The samurai hurried into the candlelit kitchen and removed a tin of peaches from the cupboard.

The cupboard . . .

Ki stood in the dimly lit kitchen, the tin of peaches forgotten in his hand. There was something about that cupboard. He reached out, tentatively running his fingers along the surfaces of the wooden shelving.

"Ki!" Jessie shouted from the main room. "Hurry up with that drink!"

Dorsey was wide awake and glaring fiercely at Jessie when Ki returned to the room with a tin mug of strained fruit juice. He handed it to Dorsey, who gulped it greedily, and then, eyeing Ki, nodded a sullen thanks.

"I guess there never really was a kidnapping, was there, Dorsey?" Ki asked softly.

Dorsey brushed her ash-blonde tresses out of her eyes as she shook her head. "I eavesdropped on that last conversation Mama and Papa had two years ago in Cough Creek. I heard Papa ask if Mama and I could come back with him to live. I was heartbroken when Mama refused. As Papa left, I went to him and begged him to let *me* come along with him." She looked at Jessie. "I begged him then, just the way I'd begged him not to leave me when we were just little girls."

"I remember," Jessie said.

"Well, Papa thought I was too young back then, and I guess he thought I was still too young to go with him that night in Cough Creek. He told me to stay with Mama, that Mama needed me." Dorsey's brown eyes filled with tears. "I understood about that. Oh, I understand *need*, all right! I needed my father!" She took several deep breaths to regain her composure, and then continued, "A little while ago Jack Bean came to Nettle Grove to see me."

"Jack Bean!" Longarm interrupted. "Your papa sent a rough owlhoot like him to fetch you?"

"At first I was afraid of him, and the way he looked, with that bushy black-and-gray beard," Dorsey admitted. "But he told me that Papa couldn't come, that it was too dangerous for Will Sayre to visit me in town, but that Papa was lonesome for me here."

"When was that?" Jessie asked.

Dorsey thought back. "About three months ago."

"Strange," Ki mused. "Your father has not been here for at least three months, according to the . . . um, 'soiled doves' who live in that windowless cottage."

"Friends of yours?" Jessie asked, arching her eyebrow. "'Getting the lay of the land,' indeed!"

"You're trying to tell me that my papa hasn't been here for three months?" Dorsey scoffed. "That's impossible."

"No, I'm afraid Jack Bean lied to you," Ki said softly.

"Let's get back to Dorsey's story," Jessie cut in. "Was the kidnapping ruse Jack Bean's idea?" she asked.

Dorsey shook her head. "It was mine. I didn't want to hurt my mother. I figured that she'd be a marked woman when it got out that she was really Mrs. Will Sayre, and that her daughter had run off to join her husband in the outlaw life. Folks might get to ridiculing her—or worse, they might out-and-out shun her as unfit to be around decent folks."

"So you figured to take the onus off her by coming up with the bogus kidnapping?" Jessie asked.

"I figured that since everybody already blamed Will Sayre for every crime under the sun, why not let them blame him for stealing away his own daughter? I figured that folk would then have sympathy for my mama; they'd see her as the helpless victim she is, that she'd always been."

"No!" Ki exclaimed sternly. "Your mother battled both your family's misfortune and her own ill health to make life for the two of you. Remember how she struggled, turning her shotgun on Jack Bean and his accomplices this afternoon when we were together?"

Dorsey nodded and then turned away, unable to look in the eye.

"I understand now why Jack Bean and his men didn't draw their guns against your mother," Ki continued. "They had had no intention of actually kidnapping you. They we

256

merely trying to prepare your mother to believe in the false abduction when you finally ran off."

"She didn't know that it was all a set-up," Dorsey admitted, and began to cry.

"No, she thought it was real, all right," Ki said. "And so an old woman in a wheelchair took up a shotgun to drive away a band of ruthless outlaws." The samurai shook his head. "Your mother is no victim, Dorsey. You mother is a valiant warrior. It is you who are the helpless victim! All your life you have been victimized by your obsession with the past!"

"Please . . . just let me be . . ." Dorsey whimpered, sitting hunched over, the tears running down her pale cheeks.

"Ki, I think that's enough," Jessie began.

"No!" the samurai shouted. "It is not!"

"Whoa! Settle down, old son," Longarm soothed. "I've never seen you so mad!"

"I'm angry because I've broken my oath to Jessie, and broken the law helping Rube Silva escape from jail, and all because of you!" he shouted at Dorsey. "Jessie and Longarm have risked their lives by coming here to rescue you, and you repay them by trying to kill Jessie!"

"I never wanted any harm to come to Jessie!" Dorsey said. She turned to Jessie. "You've got to believe that!" she insisted vehemently. "That night when you blundered into Rube and the others in front of my mother's cottage, I screamed my head off trying to keep them from hurting you."

Jessie nodded. "I remember that. But what about just a little while ago?"

"I—I got mixed up, Jessie." Dorsey covered her face with her hands in shame. "I wasn't thinking clearly! Before, Rube had told me that you and the others would take me away from here before my papa could return. He said that my papa would then likely ride to Nettle Grove, ride to his own death at the hands of the law, to get me back. I couldn't let that happen, Jessie, don't you see?"

"What about your engagement to Rube?" Ki demanded.

"He told me that that was what my papa wanted," Dorsey whimpered. "Rube said there was a slim chance that Papa might not survive the dangerous robbery job he'd set out to do, and that if he didn't make it back, his last wish was for me to marry Rube."

"You would marry that animal Rube Silva on the strength of his word?" Ki taunted. "You are indeed a victim! You are hardly worth our efforts! I think we should give you back to Rube!"

Snarling, Dorsey leaped from her chair, her hands outstretched, fingers curved into claws. The samurai easily caught her by the wrists, so that she was helpless to do anything but listen as he berated her mercilessly. "You are worthless, Dorsey! You deserved the foul things that happened to you and your family!"

"I can't listen to this," Longarm growled, moving to rescue Dorsey from Ki's grasp, but Jessie stopped him, shaking her head. "Let them alone," she whispered.

"You are as worthless as your father!" Ki snarled directly into Dorsey's contorted, tear-streaked face. "He killed because he could not face the misfortunes of his life. You are also willing to kill—"

Dorsey twisted, trying to get away, as Ki's rebukes slammed into her like physical blows. "I never killed! I never would! Especially not Jessie! She's my friend; she always was!"

"So you tried to murder the best friend you ever had in the world!" Ki roared at her. "You are indeed wretched!"

"I didn't mean it, I told you!"

"Of course not! Blame it on the past!"

"I'm sorry I tried to hurt Jessie!"

"You are worthless!" Ki blasted her.

"I'm not!" Dorsey screamed back at the samurai. "I'm as good as anyone!"

Ki released his hold on her wrists. Exhausted, Dorsey sank to the floor, quaking as deep, wrenching sobs wracked her body.

"That is enough," the samurai said softly. "If you believe

you have worth, and take responsibility for your actions, you cannot be a victim." He bent, scooping her up as if she weighed nothing.

Dorsey threw her arms about his neck like a child. "I want to rest," she mumbled against his chest.

"I'll take you upstairs and you can sleep," Ki said.

"Stay with me?" she begged. "Hold me?"

"I will hold you."

"What the hell just happened?" Longarm wondered after Ki had carried Dorsey from the room.

"Couldn't say for sure," Jessie replied. "But what I think happened is that Dorsey just fought a battle against an enemy that makes Rube Silva and his men seem like small potatoes." She smiled. "And thanks to Ki, she won!"

Chapter 21

There were just a few minutes remaining until Rube Silva's midnight deadline when Ki came back downstairs. "She is sleeping," the samurai announced to Jessie and Longarm. "I'm sorry for subjecting both of you to that emotional outburst."

"Ki, what you said before about those women telling you that Will Sayre hasn't been around for months," Jessie said. "Do you think that's the truth?"

"I can think of no reason why they would lie about it," Ki shrugged.

"That means Jack Bean's first visit to Dorsey coincides with Sayre's dropping out of sight," Longarm mused.

"I think we have all come to the same conclusion," Ki remarked. "Rube Silva did Will Sayre in."

Jessie nodded. "And he's struggled to keep the Ladykiller Gang going, but with himself as its head."

"Right," Longarm agreed. "At some point he must have realized that he just wasn't the man that Will Sayre was. That's likely when he lit upon the idea of tricking Dorsey Sayre to come here. Rube probably figured that if he could manage to marry Will Sayre's daughter, he could use her to strengthen his hold on the men."

"Oh, I can just hear that silver-tongued rat now!" Jessie seethed. "'Look, boys! Poor old Will died on a job, but he gave me his daughter's hand in marriage as a symbol of his trust in me, and because he wanted you men to stick with me! Stick together.'" She uttered a short, mirthless laugh. "That little worm..."

261

"And Dorsey would likely have gone along with it," Ki muttered. "She felt weak, helpless, unloved. She might gladly have accepted the picture that Rube painted for her."

"How ironic!" Jessie marveled. "In Dorsey's view, all of this would have amounted to her just inheritance. She would be inheriting her father's empire—"

"Just as *you* inherited all that *your* father built," Ki added, smiling faintly.

"Well, Rube's scheme still might work," Longarm declared. "We're low on ammunition, and there's not a hope in hell of anybody riding to our rescue."

"We have this," Ki said, holding up his arrow quiver.

"You're a terror with that bow, all right," Longarm conceded. He was peering out through a gun-slit at the dark town. "But we're going to need more than arrows to stop this bunch."

"And I have more than arrows in this quiver," Ki replied. "The quiver is designed with a false bottom." He laid the quiver on the table and carefully twisted free what appeared to be a quart-sized leather cup from its bottom end. The samurai then removed four different-colored, egg-sized objects from the cup and lined them up on the table.

"These are called *nage teppo*," the samurai explained. "They are bombs. They have different purposes, but all explode upon impact, when their fragile shells shatter and the compounds within are exposed to the air. The red one creates smoke. The yellow one explodes in a flash of harmless but temporarily blinding light. The green will detonate with approximately the explosive force of one stick of dynamite."

"Approximately?" Longarm echoed, keeping a straight face.

Ki nodded earnestly. "More or less. The white is filled with a compound that erupts into flame. All the *nage teppo* can be thrown, but I have arrows that are specially designed to hold the bombs. The arrows will allow for a far more accurate delivery."

"Wooo-eee!" Longarm gleefully rubbed his palms together. "Those little fellers are sure going to wipe the smiles off the faces of Rube Silva and his bunch! Ki, why don't you head upstairs with those toys of yours and set up your firing position?" He paused. "Ki? Are you listening?"

The samurai had been turning his arrow quiver over in his hands, obviously lost in thought. "Oh, sorry, Longarm. I was just thinking about this quiver's false bottom, and . . ." His voice trailed off and he was silent for a moment before continuing, "I'll be in the kitchen. There's something about that cupboard . . ."

"No time for that now," Longarm muttered from his place at the shuttered window. "Here comes Rube and his bunch!"

As Longarm spoke, he saw muzzle-flashes wink out at him from the bunkhouse's rooftop. Several rounds spanged off the stone house's outer walls, while some slammed into the wooden shutters. Longarm breathed a sigh of relief when he saw that not even rifle rounds carried enough punch to penetrate the thick wood.

"What are they doing?" Jessie wondered as the three watched Silva and a number of his men push a pair of high-walled contraptions into position in front of the bunkhouse.

"Rube is very clever," Ki sighed in resignation. "He has dismantled a portion of the high fence that surrounded the bordello cottage, and has mounted the fence sections broadside on wheels."

"I get it," Longarm said. "They'll push those things along ahead of them, to absorb our gunfire, and when they're close enough, they'll set to work battering down the front door."

"And we don't have the bullets to stop them!" Jessie exclaimed.

"Take your little bombs upstairs and see what you can do, Ki," Longarm said. "We'll hold our fire as long as possible in order to conserve our ammo."

"Longarm!" Rube Silva called. "It's midnight! Your time's up! You see what I've done! I've outsmarted you! Admit it! Surrender! I promise to be merciful!"

"Why, that little shit!" Jessie blurted, and then blushed

as Longarm stared at her in surprise. "Pardon my language," she apologized demurely.

"Aren't you ready yet?" Longarm shouted over his shoulder at Ki, who was busy loading his multicolored grenades into his arrows.

"You know what?" Jessie mused languidly from her place at one of the gun-slits. "I think I could pick him off." She stared out at Silva, who was capering like an ape behind the movable barricades, exhorting his men to take their positions. "Yep, I think I could."

"Maybe, but at this range it's a tough shot with a handgun," Longarm cautioned. "Otherwise I would have tried it already. Let's wait for Ki to strut his stuff."

"Done!" Ki declared, loading up his quiver, grabbing his bow, and vaulting towards the stairs.

Dorsey was sitting huddled on the narrow bed when Ki entered the second-floor room. "Maybe I should go out there and try to talk some sense into those outlaws," she said. "Maybe I could convince them to turn you all loose."

Ki smiled. "It is a worthy thought, Dorsey, but Rube Silva would not allow it." He turned down the flame on the kerosene lantern to the merest flicker, then quietly unlatched one of the shutters. There was no need to open the window itself; the sporadic rifle fire coming from the bunkhouse roof across the way had already shattered the glass panes.

"I could try to talk some sense into Rube," Dorsey offered, flinching at the gunfire pouring toward the house from outside. "I could promise to..." She hesitated. "I could promise to marry him like he wants, if he lets you all go."

"Rube is past reasoning with, I'm afraid." Ki selected a white-tipped *nage teppo* arrow and nocked it into his bowstring. "He would agree to anything you asked, but he would kill us just the same, once we presented ourselves to him. For Rube, this is an all-or-nothing venture. He hungers to be the new Will Sayre."

"What do you mean?" Dorsey asked quickly. "The *new* Will Sayre? But my father is still alive."

Ki swallowed hard. "I'm sorry I said what I did. However, you ought to face the truth. Your father is likely dead, killed by Rube Silva."

"No!" Dorsey cried out. "He can't be!"

The gunfire from the bunkhouse increased. The rooftop snipers were attempting to lay down a barrage of covering fire for the outlaws moving forward behind the rolling fence barricades.

"For your sake, I hope I'm wrong about your father," Ki said. "But now I must return to business." He aimed his arrow out through the partially opened shutter.

"What do you intend to do with just an arrow?" Dorsey asked skeptically.

Ki pulled back his bowstring. "Make things hot for the boys on the bunkhouse," he murmured, and let his arrow fly.

The firebomb-tipped arrow gyrated over the heads of the men behind the approaching barricades, to strike the overhang of the bunkhouse's roof. The *nage teppo* exploded with a *whoosh!*, billowing upward in a burst of white flame that sent spurts of sizzling liquid fire in every direction. There were screams from the snipers as they hurled themselves off the blazing structure, plummeting through the dark night, trailing flames like miniature comets.

The two barricades, separated by about fifteen feet, had covered half the ground between the bunkhouse and the outlaws' objective. Ki quickly nocked his green-tipped *nage teppo* arrow and let it fly. It hit the right-hand barricade, exploding in an ear-shattering blast that sent shards of fencing, cartwheels, and bodies flying. It was only the fact that many of the outlaws were sheltered behind the remaining barricade—now indecisively stalled in the middle of no-man's land—that allowed them to survive the blast.

Ki heard Longarm calling to him from the foot of the stairs.

"The other side of the house, facing the canyon entrance!" Longarm shouted, straining to be heard over the crescendo of gunfire and the singsong whine of bullets ricocheting¹ off stone. "A bunch of them jaspers have blind-sided us! They're pounding on the shutters! They could break through!"

"I'll get right to it!" Ki yelled down sarcastically. "When I joined, I did not know that this would turn out to be a one-man army!"

"You're doing a great job, old son!" Longarm shouted. "Just do something about those bastards splintering the shut-ters!"

Grumbling to himself, Ki crossed to the side of the house where Longarm had said the outlaws were congregated. Dorsey watched him.

"Can I help?" she asked weakly.

"Why, yes, you can," Ki told her as he set down his bow and extracted his yellow *nage teppo* from its arrowhead holder. "Quietly open that shutter and slide open the win-dow. Then get out of my way." He smiled. "Oh, and close your eyes when you are done, and keep them closed until I tell you, all right?"

Dorsey nodded, and did as Ki had instructed. She quickly stepped aside, squeezing shut her eyes.

Ki stuck his head out the window and looked down. A half-dozen outlaws were busy slamming sledgehammers into the downstairs shutters.

"Yoo-hoo!" the samurai called. The outlaws stopped, craning their necks to gape up at him. Some went for their guns. As they did so, Ki threw down the *nage teppo*, angling his toss so that the yellow grenade cracked against the house's stone wall about a yard above the outlaws' upturned faces.

The samurai pulled in his head, closing his eyes. The insides of his eyelids flared red as the yellow bomb exploded in a burst of dazzling light as intense as the sun. The light was brilliant enough to blind a man momentarily during the day. At night its effect was devastating. When Ki next looked out the window, the six outlaws were rolling on the ground, mewling as they clawed at their eyes.

The blindness would wear off after ten minutes or so, but until that time had elapsed, the six men would remain out of action. Ki shut and latched the shutter, and picked up his bow. "Let's go downstairs," he told Dorsey.

"Nice work. That bunkhouse will burn to the ground," Longarm complimented the samurai when he and Dorsey entered the main room. "They've pulled back for the time being."

"We had to do some shooting to keep the men behind that remaining barricade back," Jessie said. "I've only got four rounds left."

"I've got five," Longarm said, checking his Colt. "And that includes my derringer, which I emptied a few minutes ago. Silva's still got maybe ten men scattered out there."

"And the six I just now immobilized will soon recover the use of their eyes," Ki frowned. "Seventeen against four is still terrible odds."

"Too bad we don't know where the secret door is," Dorsey moped.

"What door?" Jessie asked.

"I heard Rube mention to one of the others something about a hidden cache of guns and ammunition somewhere in the house," Dorsey said. "I have no idea where it could be."

"I do!" Ki laughed triumphantly. "The cupboard! The confounded kitchen cupboard!"

They all followed Ki into the candlelit kitchen, standing back as the samurai swept the tinned goods from the shallow shelving.

"I knew there was something odd about this cupboard," Ki muttered as he began prodding the various shelves and cross-braces of the structure. "In my homeland, the castles of warlords often have concealed trapdoors, rooms with false walls—like my quiver's false bottom—or concealed doorways behind spring-operated panels."

There was a muted clicking sound as Ki pressed one of the angle-irons supporting the cupboard. The entire unit swung away from the wall to reveal a doorway. Stone steps led down into a pool of darkness.

Longarm shook his head. "Well I'll be!"

"I am ashamed for not realizing what this was before now," Ki apologized. "But there have been so many distractions."

"It's like Ali Baba and the Forty Thieves!" Jessie blurted.

"Try 'Will Sayre and the Forty Thieves,'" Longarm grinned. He patted Ki's shoulder. "Thanks to this jasper, we managed the 'Open Sesame' part all right..."

Jessie grabbed a candle. "Come on!" she said excitedly. "Let's see what's down here." She led the way. "Be careful, these stone steps are slippery."

The stone staircase descended steeply to a low-ceilinged cellar that appeared to extend beneath the entire house. Jessie's candle illuminated only a very small part of the cellar, but what the four explorers could see greatly heartened them.

"Look here!" Longarm said. "Jessie! Bring that candle over!"

The four clustered around a floor rack that held a score of rifles sheathed in oil-soaked rags to protect their mechanisms from the cellar's dampness. Longarm unwrapped one, laughing in satisfaction as he examined the weapon.

"A Winchester! In perfect condition, as are all these others, I'd wager!"

"And here's a strongbox filled with cartridges for them!" Ki called out.

Suddenly they heard the scrape of a match, and glimpsed a flare of light coming from the far corner of the pitch-dark basement. Longarm and Jessie whirled as one, both drawing their handguns and standing ready.

All four of them stared.

The matchlight was enough for them to see that the far corner of the cellar was laid out like a room. There was a table and a chair and a narrow canvas cot. There were boxes of supplies and water. There was even a foul-smelling slop bucket.

There was also a wizened, white-haired, long-bearded old man, wearing low-topped shoes and soiled clothing that looked to be several sizes too large for him. The old man was holding his sputtering match to the wick of a kerosene lantern. The chain extending from the iron ring embedded in the cellar's stone floor to the manacle around the old man's ankle chimed musically as he fussed at the lantern, finally getting it going.

Dorsey had gone as white as a ghost. She kept moving her lips, but nothing came out. Finally, in a voice that sounded as if it should have belonged to the old man, she croaked out, "Papa...?"

"My god," Jessie murmured. "It's Will Sayre!"

Chapter 22

"D-Dorsey, is it really you?" Will Sayre simultaneously laughed and cried as he embraced his sobbing daughter. "Am I dreaming, or is it really you?"

"How long have you been down here?" Jessie asked him, looking around in horror at the sparse comforts within reach of the ankle-chained old man in the damp, dark cellar.

"Three months, damn Rube Silva's soul!" Will Sayre cursed savagely. "He and Jack Bean, damn that bearded bastard, cooked it up between them, they did! They were hungry to take control of the gang! They set up this miserable corner of the cellar, and then lured me down here. Next thing I knew, they had their guns on me, and had put that damned manacle around my ankle."

"Hold still," Ki instructed Sayre as he crouched down to work at the manacle's lock with the tip of one of his *shuriken*.

"Once a week they'd bring me down fresh water and food. At least they kept me well supplied with kerosene for the lantern," Sayre muttered, his arm around Dorsey. "I have to give them that! I would have gone mad down here in the dark."

"Done!" Ki smiled as the manacle fell away from Sayre's foot.

"Bless you, whoever you are, son." Sayre looked at Jessie and Longarm, his brown eyes blinking in confusion. "Whoever *all* of you are."

"My name's Long, Will. Custis Long. I'm a United States deputy marshal."

271

Sayre started to laugh. "I never thought I'd see the day
I'd be glad to have the law in my town, but I'm glad to see
you, Deputy Long!" Sayre turned back to Jessie. "And who
would you be, ma'am?" he asked, stepping away from his
daughter to execute a courtly bow, one made not the least
bit ungallant by his unkempt appearance. "I swear, you do
look familiar, but that could be a trick of an old man's mind.
I've had some godawful visions during my three months
down here all by my lonesome. I tell you, it was far worse
than my time in Fort Delaware."

"Yes, Will, I know all about that," Jessie said, her em
erald eyes sparkling.

"Now how would a young thing like you know that about
the likes of me?" he mused, and then his eyes narrowed.
"My Lord, could it be? Jessie?" he asked faintly.

"It's Jessie Starbuck, all right, Papa!" Dorsey laughed
joyously.

"I'll be danged!" Will Sayre said, astounded. "I knew
it! I saw some of your papa shining out at me from them
purty eyes of yours!" He frowned abruptly. "I heard you
papa got himself killed by some foreigners a while back.
I'm sorry, Jessie. He was a good man."

"Papa, you thought well of Alex Starbuck?" Dorsey asked
her father.

"'Course I did! Oh, sure, I was a mite hotheaded the
night that Alex and I had words, but deep down I alwa
knowed that he was my friend. Just like you and Jessie we
always friends, right, girl?"

Dorsey, her eyes shining, gazed at Jessie. "Yes, Pap
deep down we always were, I hope."

"You *know!*" Jessie declared, grinning.

"But what are you all doing here?" Sayre demande
"What's going on?" He scowled. "A soul can't hear a blas
thing in this cellar when that cupboard door is closed."

"Speaking of which, I'd best get back upstairs and ke
an eye on things," Longarm announced. "I've loaded u
couple of these Winchesters," he added, and then star

272

up the stone staircase with the rifles in hand.

"What's that lawman jawing about?" Sayre asked. "And where's he going with them long guns?"

"We'll tell you everything upstairs, Papa," Dorsey said. "Come on, let's get you into the fresh air!"

Sayre nodded and took several steps forward, but then his knees buckled. Ki moved quickly to catch him before he hit the floor.

"It's my ticker," Sayre groaned. "It wasn't all that sound before. Being locked down here all these months ain't helped it any."

Longarm was at the shutters when Jessie and the others came upstairs and entered the main room. "How you doing, Will?" Longarm asked.

"Hell of a lot better than you, son, if you think you're going to get out of here alive!"

"What?" Longarm asked, startled.

"We told him everything that's happened so far, Custis," Jessie said.

"Even the part about Rube trying to convince me that my papa wanted to marry him," Dorsey blurted.

"Longarm, Will Sayre has a plan to end this stalement," Ki said. "Perhaps you should sit down and discuss it with him. I'll keep watch at the window."

Longarm leaned the Winchester against the shutter and went over to the oval table where Will, Dorsey, and Jessie were all seated.

"All right, what's your plan?"

"First off, I don't want you to underestimate Silva, lawman. He's smart—smart enough to lay back with the men he's got left and starve you out. It might take a week, it might take two weeks, but Silva will stay at it with all the patience of a cat batting around a bird with a broken wing. When you're all too weak to use them Winchesters you found, he'll batter down that front door, waltz in here, and finish off any of you who ain't already dead." Will Sayre's

273

gnarled hands clenched with rage. "I owe that bastard for what he's done. I owe him for coming so close to actually marrying my daughter. Imagine! That snake thinking he was worthy of being my Dorsey's husband!"

"Calm down, Papa," Dorsey urged. "You're still weak."

"I'll calm down," Sayre said, a gleam coming into his brown eyes. "I'll calm down to make sure this lawman takes me seriously." He paused to stroke his long, white whiskers as he looked at Longarm. "'Cause right now I can see that he doesn't!"

"Now, Will, there's no call to get riled," Longarm began.

"I ain't riled. I just want you to know that you're dealing with the man who put together the Ladykiller Gang. The man who kept it together down through the years. It took a strong man to do it. I was strong then, and I'm strong now."

Longarm shrugged. "I've got no call to think otherwise, Mr. Sayre."

The old man nodded. "Jessie told me what put you on my trail. That mail car robbery had nothing to do with me. It was all Rube Silva's doing, but folks will blame it on me if I don't do something drastic to change their minds. That's half of the reason why I want to do what I'm about to tell you." Sayre glanced adoringly at his daughter. "Here's the other half. In my life I've killed five men who deserved to die. But I was also partly responsible for the killing of a man who didn't deserve it. For that one mistake I've paid! I've lived my entire life on the run, missing my family." Sayre slapped his palm down upon the table. "Now, if I can right that mistake by calling off those dogs outside, I aim to do it, lawman—"

"Call me Longarm."

"Longarm," Sayre said with a grim smile, "I want to square off with Rube Silva!"

Longarm thought it through. "You've been locked up for months, and unless I miss my guess, you had yourself some trouble mounting those stairs."

Sayre grinned. "You got good ears, son."

"We'd best have good *everything* in our line of work, Mr. Sayre," Longarm smiled back. "Rube Silva's good too. Not as good as *us*, in our prime, of course. But then, you *ain't* in your prime, Will. Do you think you're fast enough to take him?"

"Longarm, I think I've got to try. Win or lose, the rest of the boys seeing me go against Rube might be enough for them to give up this nasty game." He winked at Longarm. "Anyway, I got my little girl here with me. I'd like to show her that her old man ain't the cutthroat desperado some folks have made him out to be."

"I don't know, Will," Longarm hedged.

"Come on, son!" Sayre coaxed. Beneath his white beard and pale complexion he suddenly seemed hale and hearty. "If I win, you'll all be free to go, and I'll come along with you as your prisoner."

"Papa!" Dorsey blurted. "No, Papa!"

"Hush, girl!" Sayre told her. "I'm too old and tired to go on running. Longarm, if I fail—well, Will Sayre lived his life as a legend. He might as well die as one!"

Longarm smiled. "You got a handgun?"

"Well, now, deputy," Sayre drawled. "I was fixing to ask for the use of yours."

"It'd be an honor for me, Mr. Sayre," Longarm replied. He stood up and unstrapped his Colt. "Cross-draw rig," he warned, sliding the holstered weapon across the table.

"I favored that set-up myself," Sayre nodded, sliding the Colt out of its holster. "Hmmm, .44 double-action, cut down to a five-inch barrel, with the front sight filed off. Is it loaded?"

"Five in, with the hammer resting on an empty chamber," Longarm said.

Sayre laughed. "Didn't have to ask, I reckon. I knowed the kind of man I was dealing with as soon as I saw you!"

"That's why I lent you my gun," Longarm replied.

Sayre, smiling, stood up and strapped on the Colt. "I

275

used to take a larger belt, but I reckon I lost me some weight in that damned cellar." He sighed. "Let's go on out and get it done, Longarm."

"Papa, please be careful!" Dorsey begged him as he headed for the door.

Sayre chucked her underneath the chin. "Hell, girl," he said tenderly. "I ain't *never* been careful in my entire life! What's the point of starting now!" He turned to Longarm and the others. "On second thought, it'd be best if you all stayed in the house. You'll be safer here. And none of you can help me in what I got to do."

Longarm waited until Sayre had left the house, then he turned to Jessie and said, "I'll cover this window with one of the Winchesters. Stay close by with your Colt. Ki, you get upstairs with your bow. There's no telling what might happen if Will's ploy fails. We've got to be prepared for an all-out attack."

They stood at their posts and watched as Will Sayre left the house, to confront Rube Silva and what remained of the Ladykiller Gang. It was sometime in the wee hours of the morning, and still as dark as pitch, but there was plenty of light, as flames from the charred, skeletal remains of the bunkhouse continued to lick fitfully at the predawn sky.

Rube Silva and his men were clustered around their makeshift barricade when one of the outlaws spotted Sayre. "Holy smokes," the man gasped in surprise. "It's Will!"

"Will Sayre?"

"Where?"

"It is, it's Will himself!"

"Listen to me, all of you!" Sayre called out, his deep voice rolling like thunder against the stone walls of the canyon. "Rube lied to you all! He had me locked up, Rube did! But now I'm free, and I aim to make him pay with his life for what he did to me!"

"That's right, I did lock him up!" Rube Silva cut in, his voice a high, staccato counterpoint to Sayre's. "I *chained* him up, like an old yard dog!" he laughed giddily.

"It sounds as if Rube's been drinking," Longarm confide

to Jessie inside the house. "That could be to Will's—and our—advantage."

Jessie nodded, then glanced around. "Where's Dorsey?"

Longarm shrugged. "Must be upstairs with Ki."

"I was able to chain Will up because he's old and weak!" Rube Silva continued. "I'm young and strong! From now on *I'm* running this gang!"

"No you ain't, Rube," Will Sayre said calmly. "You ain't going to get the chance. I say the Ladykillers is finished." He paused. "I'm saying that *you're* finished."

"You calling me out, old man?" Silva chuckled, nervously fingering the scar that ran down his cheek. "Will, you don't want to be calling *me* out."

"I just did, runt," Sayre replied. He drew back his scarecrow rag of a coat to reveal Longarm's cross-draw rig cinched tight across his gaunt belly. "I aim to shoot you, coming *or* going. The choice is yours."

Silva sauntered around from behind the barricade to square off with Sayre. Less than twenty feet separated the two men, as the flames from the bunkhouse etched shadows across their grim, determined faces.

"Age before beauty, old man," Silva scoffed. "Make your move."

"Custis..." Jessie breathed. Longarm, peering out through the partially opened shutter, squeezed her hand.

"And after I'm through with *you,* old man," Silva taunted, "I'm gonna start on your daughter—"

The two adversaries' movements were so fast that it was impossible to say who slapped leather first—impossible to separate the single, sustained explosion of their guns...

But it was Will Sayre whose knees suddenly sagged, his revolver falling to earth; it was Will who crumpled to lie curled and still at Rube Silva's feet.

"Oh God," Jessie swore, blinking back her tears.

"Get ready, Jessie!" Longarm muttered. "Anything can happen now!"

"Custis, where's that second Winchester?" Jessie asked.

"Rube!" Dorsey cried out, careening around the side of

277

the house, the Winchester in her hands. "Rube!"

Silva was spinning to fire at her when Dorsey's rifle spat flame. Rube staggered back, his battered features in agony as he clutched at his left side. He was struggling to bring his gun to bear on her when Dorsey fired again, knocking the outlaw to his knees.

"My name's Dorsey Sayre!" she howled to the awestruck outlaws watching. "I'm finishing what my father started!"

She levered another round into her Winchester. Rube Silva's gun was inexorably rising toward her when Dorsey aimed carefully and shot him square between the eyes. Rube flopped back to lie still, his bloodied, sightless orbs staring up at the first faint glimmerings of a dawn that he would never know.

Longarm kicked open the shutters and shouldered his Winchester. "Any man moves to hurt her, I'll kill him!" From above came the sound of a pair of second-story shutters being opened. Longarm didn't have to see it to know that Ki's bow was trained on the outlaws.

A man stepped around from behind the barricade. His gun was holstered, and his hands were reaching for the sky.

"Longarm! It's Rufus Cane! You remember me?"

"I do, Rufus, but the last I recall, I had you locked away in Nebraska for cattle thieving."

"You recall right, deputy, but I busted out," Rufus Cane grinned. "That's neither here nor there, Longarm. That offer you made us, the one about us leaving you be and riding out of here unmolested—does it still hold?"

"I reckon it does, Rufus, if you'll leave us horses to ride out when we've a mind to."

"That's square with us, Longarm. We didn't know 'bout poor old Will being chained up. He was a good man. One of the best. The world won't see his like again, nor the likes of the Ladykillers." He shrugged, lowering his hands. "You can come out of there if you've a mind to. This old valley has seen more killing tonight than it's ever seen. The killing is over and done!"

The remaining outlaws wandered off, the dawn's breeze

scattering them. Jessie, followed by Longarm and Ki, threw open the stone house's oak door and rushed out to where Dorsey was kneeling by her dying father.

"Papa, Papa," Dorsey was sobbing.

"Here now, girl." Will Sayre grinned up at her. "I had nothing to look forward to but a jail cell, anyhow." He glanced up at Longarm. "Right, deputy?"

"Likely, Will," Longarm nodded. "There are a lot of warrants out on you."

"*Were* a lot," Sayre chuckled, and then winced as the bullet in his chest bit deeper. "You'll be able to clear up a whole load of paperwork in just a few seconds' time, lawman."

"Reckon so, Will," Longarm said, "but I'll have you know that I'd rather it went the other way."

"Thank you, Longarm," Sayre whispered. "I guess you lawmen ain't such a bad lot, after all." His eyes closed. "Jessie?" he called faintly.

"Here, Will."

"Jessie, I'd take it kindly if you'd watch out for my daughter. If you're as good a friend to her as your daddy was to me, she'll be a lucky girl."

"We're friends to the end, Will," Jessie swore.

"Oh, Papa, I love you so!" Dorsey cried.

"You do? Oh, that's good to hear, child," Sayre mumbled, reaching blindly to pat his daughter's cheek. "Then I guess that old Will Sayre ain't had such a bad life after all..." he managed, right before he died.

Chapter 23

The sun rose strangely that day, staining the morning sky as blood-red as guns and fire had stained the previous night. By midmorning the sun was a pale, white circle in a gray sky flecked with the spread wings of constantly circling buzzards.

The buzzards were waiting for the last of the living to quit the canyon and give it over totally to the dead.

The last of the outlaws who had once belonged to the Ladykillers Gang had ridden out at dawn's first crimson light, taking with them the five 'soiled doves' who sheltered Ki in his time of need. Now Will Sayre's outlaw town was a ghost town, soon to be populated by nothing but ghosts.

Longarm was seeing to their horses when Jessie strolled over to him. "Dorsey and Ki almost ready to ride?" he asked.

"Almost." She put her arms around Longarm's waist. "I just wanted to tell you again how much I appreciate what you told Ki last night, about not pressing charges against him."

"Hell," Longarm scoffed, "I never figured on pressing those fool jailbreak charges, anyhow. I'm interested in seeing to it that justice is done, and in this case it *has* been. Rube Silva is dead, partly thanks to Ki. Will Sayre is dead, as well; that should make poor old Lloyd Broadwick's superiors at the Post Office happy. As to Lloyd's death, we can't rightly blame Ki for that." He smiled at Jessie. "Remember the lesson that Ki taught Dorsey last night, that a soul has got to be responsible for his own actions? It was Lloyd who got himself killed, just as it was Lloyd who made himself a hero."

"Just like Will Sayre," Jessie said thoughtfully.

"Reckon so. Of course, Ki will have to answer to Hank Stills when we get back to Nettle Grove. It was *his* jail that got busted. But I don't see Hank being too tough on our friend." Longarm shook his head as Ki and Dorsey approached. "I'm more worried about that young woman," he muttered.

"Don't be," Jessie replied. "I heard in town that she'd had a number of eligible ranchers trying to woo her. Now that she's buried the past, she'll make a fine life for herself. And she's got me to look after her. I'm a good friend to have!"

Longarm winked. "Don't I know it."

"And don't I intend to make sure you *remember* it as soon as we can check into my room at the Nettle Grove Hotel!"

"There's just one thing you got wrong, Jessie," Longarm said, his smile fading. "Poor Dorsey's still got some of her past left to bury." His eyes moved to the dismal, canvas-shrouded corpse cinched across a pack mount.

Dorsey, just then coming up to them, must have overheard Longarm's last remark. "I know that it's a heap of trouble for you to help me bring my papa back to Nettle Grove..."

"No trouble for us, girl," Longarm said kindly. "But it is more heartache for you."

"I just want my papa buried near my mama and me. He's been away so long, it's time he came home." She smiled. "And home is Nettle Grove."

"Home it is," Jessie said. "Let's ride."

"Before we leave, I just want to thank you all," Dorsey blurted. She reached out for Ki's hand and gave it a squeeze. "Thanks for everything," she added, gazing at him.

Ki smiled at her. "What are friends for?"

Watch for

LONGARM AND THE COWBOY'S REVENGE

seventy-ninth novel in the bold
LONGARM
series from Jove

and

LONE STAR AND THE BUFFALO HUNTERS

thirty-fifth novel in the exciting
LONE STAR
series from Jove

both coming in July!